D0610166

The Last Goodbye

CAROLINE FINNERTY

EAST AYRSHIRE LEISURE TRUST	
507748	
Bertrams	19/06/2014
GEN	£6.99

This novel is entirely a work of fiction. The names,
characters and incidents portrayed in it are the work of the
author's imagination. Any resemblance to actual persons,
living or dead, events or localities is entirely coincidental.

Published 2014
by Ward River Press
123 Grange Hill, Baldoyle
Dublin 13, Ireland
www.wardriverpress.com

© Caroline Finnerty 2013

Copyright for typesetting, layout, design, ebook
© Poolbeg Press Ltd

The moral right of the author has been asserted.

1

A catalogue record for this book is available from the British Library.

ISBN 978-1-84223-618-5

All rights reserved. No part of this publication may be reproduced or
transmitted in any form or by any means, electronic or mechanical, including
photography, recording, or any information storage or retrieval system,
without permission in writing from the publisher. The book is sold subject to
the condition that it shall not, by way of trade or otherwise, be lent, resold or
otherwise circulated without the publisher's prior consent in any form of
binding or cover other than that in which it is published and without a
similar condition, including this condition, being imposed on the subsequent
purchaser.

Printed by CPI Group (UK) Ltd
Author cover photo Peter Evers of Penry Photography

www.wardriverpress.com

For Mam, who still holds my hand in hers.

A mother is she who can take the place of all others but whose place no one else can take.
Cardinal Mermillod

Kate

2012

Chapter 1

I had always thought that she was selfish for doing what she did. I knew that was harsh but I felt if she had done things differently, then everything could have been very different. I often wondered, if she had known the outcome, the way that it would all play out, would she still have made the same decision? It was on my mind a lot at the time, the questions spinning around and around inside my head, especially when I was left alone with my idle thoughts. I suppose with everything going on, it was only natural. There was just no escaping it, though, no matter how much I tried.

The Tube jerked to a stop and the doors slid apart. No one was getting off, yet more people managed to squash on. It never ceased to amaze me how, just when you thought it was impossibly packed, there was always room for one more person. The crowd moved back to make way for the new people, causing the crotch of the man standing in front of me to move even closer towards my face. The rhythmic motion of the carriages snaking along through the tunnels made me feel sleepy. I closed my eyes and listened to the voice broadcast the stops as I did every morning. Finally it was Green Park and I stood up, feeling light-headed as I did. The man sitting beside me had his paperback folded back on itself and was smiling to himself as he read. A grubby bookmark with a furry monkey's head rested on his knees. It was at odds with his pinstripe suit and leather briefcase – like he had robbed it from his child in a hurry. I grabbed onto the pole to steady myself. Disgustingly, it was still sticky with sweat from the last person. I squeezed through the small gaps between bodies until I got to the doors. Some people hopped off to let me out before getting back on again.

I stepped onto the platform and made my way to the escalator. A wall of warm air hit me full force in the face as I walked and I thought I might be sick. Beads of sweat broke out all across my forehead and I could feel my mouth beginning to water. *No way, not here.* I ascended on the escalator from deep down in the bowels of the city, gliding past posters advertising films, books and shampoos that claimed to reduce split ends by 52%.

When I finally emerged into the fresh morning air, I breathed it deep into my lungs and felt better instantly as my body started to cool down again. The low sunlight was glinting off the shop windows on the street and burning a golden trail on the footpath in front of me. The gallery was only a five-minute walk from the Tube station. The London traffic inched forward on the road beside me, the roofs of the black cabs sticking out amongst the mêlée of cars like hard-shelled beetles. I knew some people hated this city – they hated its relentless pace, how it sucked you in and then when it was finished with you, after you'd given it your all, when you were broken, when you were spent, it just chewed you up and spat you back out again – but I loved everything about it. I felt alive here – the endless possibilities of things to do, the centuries of history fronting every pavement. The streets were always full – you never felt alone here.

Soon I was at the gallery. I pushed the door open. Nat was already in.

"Morning."

"Hi, darling," she replied.

I walked over and lifted the strap of my yellow satchel over my head before putting it onto the white contemporary Formica desk. Our reception desk was the only piece of furniture in the gallery, which was all stark white walls, with black-and-white photos inside black frames, and honey-oak floors.

"Want a coffee – I've just boiled the kettle?" Nat asked.

"Nah – better not."

I turned on the computer and waited for it to boot itself up while she went into the kitchen and came back out a minute later with a mug of instant coffee clasped between her hands. I had brought the mug back for her from Majorca a few years back. It was one of those tacky ones with the caption *Someone I Know Went to Majorca and All They Brought Me Back Was This Mug*.

Nat and I practically ran the Jensen Photography Gallery ourselves. We displayed the work of several high-profile photographers – they paid us a small rent for the space and a commission for any work we sold. The owner, a lady called Tabitha Jensen, spent most of her time living *la dolce vita* in her villa in Tuscany. She only came to check up on us a handful of times a year. We emailed her a weekly report with sales figures and a summary of what was happening in the gallery and she was happy with that.

"What's wrong?" Nat said as she combed her fingers through her thick auburn hair before tying it up loosely with a bobbin so that the front of it stuck up bumpily like waves on a choppy sea.

"Nothing."

"C'mon, I know you too well."

"It's Ben," I sighed. "He's like a dog with a bone."

"Is he still harping on at you about going back to Ireland?"

She said 'Ireland' in the way that all English people said it. I have always liked the way their accent made it sound – like it was a place that you might *actually* want to go to.

She perched herself on the end of the desk with her two hands wrapped around her chipped mug.

"Uh-huh. He just won't let it go." It had been eight years since I was home last – I hadn't been back since my younger brother Patrick's wedding. And I wouldn't have even gone to that except that I might as well have severed whatever thin ties

5

with my family that were left if I hadn't. I had got a flight to Dublin that morning and flew straight back home to London first thing the following morning, less than twenty-four hours later.

"He's never even met them, has he?"

"Nope."

"Well, maybe now would be a good time – you can't stay away forever."

"You sound just like Ben . . ."

"Well, he just wants to meet them – find out more about where you come from –"

"I've told him all he needs to know – why does he need to meet them?"

"Come on, Kate – stop being unreasonable."

"He knows what happened – I'm not keeping anything a secret from him."

"He's not asking for that much – he just wants to meet your family!"

"He reckons I have 'unresolved issues'." I sighed wearily at the phrase Ben was so fond of quoting at me.

"Well, you do!" She laughed, showing her teeth. She had good teeth, straight for the main part and just slightly overlapping on the bottom. Most people would probably get them straightened but I thought they suited her better like that.

I started to laugh then too.

Nat had known me a long time, even longer than Ben had. We'd met when I first moved to London at seventeen years of age. I had finished my Leaving Cert and then the very next day I packed my rucksack and took the boat to Holyhead. I would have gone sooner but Dad wouldn't let me leave school without having my Leaving Cert. As soon as the ferry had pulled out from Dun Laoghaire Harbour, I'd felt nothing but relief. Not even a twinge of sadness or regret. From Holyhead I took a very long and slow bus down to London because I couldn't afford the train fare. We travelled through Welsh tunnels carved out of rock, chocolate-box villages and acres and acres of tumbledown country estates.

For the first few nights after arriving in London, I had stayed in a hostel full of American backpackers and students who were all inter-railing around Europe. They would be comatose in the bunk beds every morning after only getting into them only a few hours previously, while I got up early to look for a job. I would try and make myself look somewhat presentable, peering in the hostel's dimly lit, six-inch-square bathroom mirror, before heading out onto the streets to start my hunt. I had a very limited amount of money to tide me over so I needed to get work quickly before the cash I had saved from my part-time job in the local supermarket at home ran out. I didn't have a clue about what kind of job I wanted to do – I was just so glad to be away from home that I would have taken anything. I dropped into a few of the large department stores on spec but they weren't currently hiring. So after a few days of not getting anywhere, I decided my best bet would be to register with a recruitment agency.

As I was walking down the street to the address I'd been given, I walked past a gallery with a beautiful taupe-and-green striped awning outside. I noticed a handwritten sign in the bay window, which read *Now Hiring*. Deciding that I had nothing to lose, I pushed back the door. It had one of those old-fashioned bells that gave a *'trrrrrrring'* when the door was opened.

A tall, thin girl stood up from behind the counter. She looked to be about the same age as myself. She had the kind of build that women described as 'striking' often have. Her height was further emphasised by her hair, which was backcombed several inches off the top of her head. She was wearing a black scoop-necked bodysuit tucked into a tight stonewashed denim skirt, which laced like a corset up the back. Her make-up was dramatic, with heavy kohl accentuating her cool blue eyes with their vivid flecks of green. My eyes travelled down her body and landed on a pair of scuffed Doc Martens. Her style was way beyond anything I had ever seen at home – suddenly I felt self-conscious in my baggy jeans and frumpy sweatshirt. My hair didn't have a style – it was just dead straight and hung down at both sides of my face like a pair of curtains framing a stage. I

7

had only ever seen people dressed like her on TV. If I had worn those clothes in our village, let alone the hair, I would have been the talk of the town. I had felt intimidated by her. I wanted to turn around and run back out the door again.

She looked at me expectantly, waiting for me to speak.

"I'm here about the job?" I said timidly.

"You Irish?" Her accent was pure London. I had only been there for a few days at that stage but already my ear was starting to distinguish the different accents. She looked at me quizzically with her head tilted to the side as she tried to assess me.

"Yeah."

"The owner's not here at the minute – hang on and I'll give her a call . . ."

"Okay." I stood there, idly glancing around the gallery while I listened to her talk on the phone.

"Yeah, yeah, yeah, okay. Got it. Byyyye." She hung up the phone and turned back to me. "She says it's fine with her, once I'm happy with you. The name's Nat – what's yours?"

"Kate," I said.

"Well, Kate, looks like you've got yourself a job."

"What? Don't you want me to do an interview or something?" I had only been enquiring and it felt like the job had just been thrust upon me. And even though I was desperate for work, I wasn't sure I wanted to work with her. I didn't even know what kind of work I would be doing.

"Nah, no need!" She waved her hand.

"Okay, well . . . I suppose I should say thank you."

"Do you smoke?"

"No," I said, feeling instantly like a Goody Two-Shoes. "I gave up a few months back – because I couldn't afford them," I added so she knew I wasn't completely square.

"No worries – here, can you hold the fort while I run round to the shop and get some fags?"

"Em . . . okay," I said, looking around at the high gallery walls, wondering what I had let myself in for.

"Listen, Kate, there's no need to look so scared – I'm not

going to bite you, love." Then her face broke into a big grin and I started to relax.

I knew then that we were going to get along just fine together.

It was such an eye-opener for an Irish girl from Ballyrobin coming to London. It was so depressing at home – both in my house and in the country in general. All I seem to remember when I think back on those years is grey. Grey weather. Grey classrooms. Grey people. There was a whole generation of people who left Ireland for London in the eighties and I was a decade late. Just as I was leaving, the economy was starting to pick up. People were buying new cars and they weren't ashamed of it. There were jobs to be had now and for the first time in decades expats were starting to return home to work. But I went in the opposite direction. My dad couldn't understand why I wanted to emigrate at a time when things were finally starting to go Ireland's way. In the eighties he had spent a lot of time worrying if his kids would have to leave the country like almost all young people had to at that time. So when it looked like things were on the up, he was relieved. For the first time since the eighties there were jobs to be had and not just in Dublin. But it wasn't about the work – it was never about the work. I know Ireland is a different place now of course – I can see it's changed whenever I meet other Irish people or watch the news. But London was like the place that I belonged in as soon as I arrived. Within days of coming over here, I had felt more at home than I had in my seventeen years in Ireland. The anonymity was a revelation. People wore what they wanted to wear. People didn't whisper wherever you walked – they didn't talk in scandalised tones because the Gardaí had brought you home last night because they caught you necking back some snakebite up in the playground.

Nat turned out to be the best friend that I could have asked for. When she heard I was staying in a hostel to save money, she invited me to sleep on her mum's sofa until I found somewhere to live. She introduced me to all her friends so they quickly became my circle too. After a week in her mum's house, I found a poky two-roomed flat in Clapham. Although there was only one bedroom, Nat decided to move in with me. We shared a room with two single beds and not much space for anything else. The paint was peeling off the walls and there were black mildew spots in the corners of the ceiling. The seventies' furniture looked as though it was taken from the landlord's family home and he was just looking for somewhere to get rid of it. There was too much of it to be functional. A huge sideboard was squashed into the hallway so that you had to turn sideways to walk past it and, even though it was only a one-bedroomed flat, the long rectangular table in the kitchen could sit eight people around it comfortably.

Yes, the flat was tiny, but we had so much fun there. I could go out when I wanted to and come home at whatever hour I chose. There was no one banging on my door calling me for Mass on a Sunday morning. We would go home from work in the gallery and then we would usually head straight out to a party or a club or have friends over to ours. We were out almost every night of the week. For the first time in my life I had freedom. I didn't have the weight of home dragging me down. Leaving was without doubt the best decision I ever made.

London was where I belonged now.

Chapter 2

At six o'clock we turned out the lights in the gallery to head home. We said bye to one another and Nat put her bag into the basket on the front of her bike and cycled off while I walked in the other direction to the Tube. It was a warm summer's evening and people spilled out of the pubs and onto the streets, keen to make the most of the evening sun. I weaved my way around where they stood on the path, beer bottles in one hand and taking long drags on cigarettes with the other. Their laughter carried on the summer air. Joggers overtook me on the pavement before cutting into the park.

I arrived in the door to the smell of curry. Even though I had bought the ingredients for it myself the day before, now the smell of the coconut milk just made me want to hurl. I stopped at the door into the kitchen, where Ben's broad back was towards me as he stood in front of the cooker. He was angling the chopping board and tossing green peppers into the frying pan. Our kitchen was so poky: a few small grey-painted presses, a sink, washing machine, cooker, fridge and a small table and chairs was it. We had a few pots of herbs growing on the windowsill – they were Ben's babies, not mine.

"*Euuuggggh!*"

11

He turned around and smiled at me from where he was stirring the pan.

"Don't tell me – the smell is making you sick?"

I pinched my nose and nodded my head. He left the pan and came over and wrapped me in a hug. This was without doubt my favourite part of the day – when I would come in wrecked from work and Ben would put his strong arms around me and all my worries and stresses would just fade away.

Ben was a primary school teacher so he was always the first one home. I was spoiled rotten because he usually had dinner ready and waiting for me when I got in every evening. He loved his job. I knew most of the children in his class by name myself, just from listening to him talking about them.

"How's Baby Pip doing?" he asked, nuzzling at my neck.

"I think I started to feel kicks today – it's so faint though, it's hard to know."

We called her Pip because when I had first found out that I was pregnant the book said that at five weeks she was the size of a pip, and somehow it had stuck even though we both thought that it was a bit cheesy.

He placed his hand on my tummy. "I can't feel anything."

"Well, *duh* – the movements are only tiny at this stage plus she –"

"Or he," Ben interjected.

"Or he – isn't moving at the moment. It's a girl anyway."

"How do you know?" He started to laugh.

"I just do."

"Please can we find out the sex at our next scan?"

"No! I told you already, I don't want to find out – but I know I'm right."

He held me at arm's length and stared at my tummy.

"You're getting a bump."

"Yeah, I know – I haven't got long left in these trousers. I had to open the top button this afternoon when I was sitting down behind the desk."

"Well, I'd say that looked good! Although you could pretend

it's some new form of artistic expression. So did you think any more about going home for a weekend?"

"Not now, Ben!" I pulled away from him. "I'm exhausted. I think I'm going to go and have a soak in the bath."

Later that evening, as I lay in bed reading on my own, I could hear Ben laughing away on his own at the TV in the living room. The sounds were muffled as they travelled through the walls to our bedroom. We lived in part of what was all originally one house but in the eighties the owners had decided to convert their upstairs bedrooms into an apartment and rent it out. It was a red-bricked terraced Victorian house. We had two bedrooms, a galley-kitchen, a living room and a small bathroom. The rent was typical of London – big money, small place. We were saving up to buy our own place but then I had found out that I was pregnant so we decided to put our plans on hold for a while until after Baby Pip arrived.

There must have been something particularly funny on the TV because Ben was howling with laughter.

Ben was definitely the smiley one in our relationship. He was always in good form – he had what you might describe as a 'sunny disposition'. It wasn't that I was a grumpy person but I just wasn't constantly in good form like he was – nothing ever seemed to get him down or to send him into a rage like me. Everyone loved him as soon as they met him – he was just one of those people. And he always knew how to pull me out of a mood. I was fascinated whenever we were out together, watching how everyone automatically migrated towards him. I would hover somewhere on the periphery, staring, taking it all in. Ben saw the good in everyone whereas I was a lot more cynical. I tried not to be but I couldn't help it. I think that was why he wouldn't let the whole trip to Ireland go – he wanted to make everyone happy just like him and he thought that a trip home would do that for me too. It was like the baby had put a deadline on it – he wanted it resolved before Pip came along. But it was never going to be that simple: twenty years of anger and hurt can't be just reset with a quick visit home. I knew he meant well though.

I put my book down and placed my two hands flat on my bare, swollen stomach. I could definitely feel Pip moving. I knew I wasn't just imagining it. It was such a surreal feeling to think that there was actually a baby in there, growing away, doing its thing, doing everything that it needed to do and knowing when to do it. The pregnancy was going well – except for the nausea, which still wasn't showing any signs of abating even though I was nearly at the halfway mark. I had been assured by all in the know that once I entered the second trimester the morning sickness would go and I'd get a new burst of energy but they were all liars because I still felt like shit.

The whole thing was making me think a lot though. I wasn't prepared for that side of it – it had brought a lot of old memories back to the surface. And Ben wasn't helping by constantly banging on about it. I had known this was what would happen and that was why it had taken me a while to come round to the idea of having a baby with him. Ben had been broody for a long time – he was the one who would stop a mother on the footpath to coo over her infant whereas I just saw sticky hands and a runny nose. While I had always wanted children, it was more a case of 'one day' so it came as a bit of a shock when I found out that I was pregnant. But when I had seen the two pink lines on the test stick, I'd got really excited – the time was right, Ben loved me and I loved him.

Ben came up to bed soon after and spooned me from behind. He pushed up my pyjama top to put his two hands on the skin of my stomach and Baby Pip started up again just like she knew that her daddy was there. I turned over to face him and smiled.

"She knows you're here."

"Really?"

"Yeah, she's started kicking again."

"When will I be able to feel them?"

"Not for a few more weeks according to the books."

He propped his head up on his elbow. "So when are we going to Ireland?"

"Will you just leave it out, Ben?" I said testily.

"Come on, Kate! When are you going to tell your dad?"

"Soon."

"You're nearly five months pregnant – your family don't even know. You need to tell them – I've never even met them for Christ's sake!"

"I will tell them."

"When?"

"I'll ring Dad."

"You can't keep on carrying this baggage with you. It's not good for you or the baby."

"Will you stop going on about it?"

"You can't keep running away from it."

"I'm not running away from anything!"

"Oh Kate – you're infuriating!"

"Please, can we leave it for tonight? I feel like crap – I'm exhausted."

"All right, all right, but you need to face up to your demons sooner or later." He sighed.

Blah, blah, blah. I turned away so my back was towards him and he did the same on the other side.

Chapter 3

Ben and I had met at the zoo of all places. I'd had a day off so I'd gone for a stroll around Regent's Park. When I got there I decided to go into the zoo because it had been a while since I'd been in. I'd been watching the meerkats and I was just turning around to go on to the next enclosure when I saw a small boy standing in the middle of the path on his own, crying. He was wearing a navy raincoat, jeans tucked inside wellington boots and he had a small backpack on his back. I guessed he was probably about five or six. He was obviously lost. I looked around to see if his parents were anywhere nearby but there was no-one near us that looked like they had lost a child.

I can still remember getting lost in a department store at Christmas time when I was small. I had been playing with my brothers Patrick and Seán, hiding under rails of clothes, but when I came out again my family had all gone. Even though we were only separated for a few minutes, I'll never forget that fear. It had felt like hours. It was as though my world had ended and I was going to be the resident orphan of Dunnes Stores. Of course I was too young to realise that a lost child is not the same as a lost glove and that Mam and Dad were in an equally right state looking for me too.

I bent down to the boy and asked him his name. Through

snotty tears he told me he was called James. I reached down and held his hand and he had clung on tight. We walked over to a nearby security guard but no-one had reported a missing child. At that stage they probably hadn't even realised he was missing. The guard escorted us to the coffee shop. While he put a call out over the radio to the other guards, I rooted in my purse for change and bought James a gingerbread man with eyes and a smile made from icing and three Smarties down the front for buttons. He wiped his nose on his sleeve and quickly began to open the cellophane wrapper on the gingerbread man.

Suddenly a man came blustering through the door.

"Oh thank God!" He rushed over and bent down to the little boy. "Where did you go to?"

"I just wanted to see the meerkats' house."

"I told you already, you can't keep wandering off like that, James," he scolded him gently. He turned to me then. "Thank you, thank you, so much!"

"Don't mention it. I was at the meerkats and I turned around and just saw him there on his own, crying."

I had to admit that James' dad was very good-looking. He was tall and muscular and, judging by the tan on his face and hands, I guessed that he loved the outdoors. He was dressed casually in a pair of Converse trainers, jeans and hoody, with a backpack slung over his back.

I supposed he must have got an awful fright.

"We were doing so well," he said. "We'd managed to round up the twenty-four of them every time but he must have slipped away between the meerkats and the next enclosure. It was only when we did our head count just there that we realised that we'd lost him."

"You have twenty-four children?" I said, shocked.

"Not me!" he grinned. "We're on a school tour – the other teacher is waiting with the rest of the class."

"Oh, I see . . . of course." I laughed, feeling a bit stupid then. "Well, it must be hard keeping track of that many."

"You can't take your eyes off them for a second! We're lucky you were right there."

"Don't mention it."

James was happily munching on his gingerbread man – he had devoured both his legs and his right arm. His distress of the last few minutes seemed to be forgotten.

The man and I looked at each other for a fraction too long.

"Well . . . I'd better go," I said quickly.

"What's your name?" he asked me then.

"It's Kate."

"Kate – I'm Ben." He stuck his hand out to shake mine. "It's nice to meet you."

His handshake was strong around mine. I liked that in a man – there was nothing worse than a watery handshake. By this stage the gingerbread man was decapitated.

"Okay, well, thanks again, Kate."

I watched him walk off with James – the two of them threw their heads back then and started laughing at something. There was definitely something attractive about a man who was good with kids, I thought.

I decided to grab a take-away coffee while I was there and continue on my way around the zoo. I walked along the path admiring the elegance of the giraffes as they stretched their long necks to reach up to the higher branches. I watched them as they munched on mouthfuls of leaves. Their fawn-coloured markings were like a beautiful mosaic covering their skin. It was just starting to drizzle and as I was taking my umbrella out of my bag I heard a little voice behind me interrupting my thoughts.

"Hi, Kate."

I turned around to find James standing there, looking up at me. He had his hood pulled up over his head. He was beyond cute with his chubby cheeks.

"Hiya, James." I looked over and saw Ben, a woman and the rest of the class a short distance away.

"Did you know that giraffes and humans have the same number of bones in their neck?"

"No, I didn't know that," I said, laughing.

"Do you know how many bones –"

Ben rushed up beside him then. "James, I told you, you can't keep on running off on us like that." He sounded exasperated. "Hi again, Kate."

"He's a real handful."

"You don't know the half of it!"

"Mr Chamberlain likes you!" James blurted out.

"Sorry?" I wondered if I had heard him right.

"James!" Ben said, looking mortified.

"You do! You said she was a very nice lady!" he protested, his eyes wide with innocence.

"Yeah, but . . ."

"And pretty – you said she was very pretty too." He went on.

Ben looked at him in horror. Redness crept up along his face.

I have to say I felt sorry for him. "Hey, don't worry – you know what kids are like." I laughed nervously. I wanted the ground to swallow me whole. Or James preferably. Either one of us would be fine.

We both stood there awkwardly for a few moments. James was pulling out of Ben's hand. I could see the other teacher and the rest of the class looking over, wondering what was going on.

"Look, I'd better –"

"God, Kate, this whole thing is well . . . so embarrassing . . . I don't usually do this, believe me . . . but, well . . . would you like to go for dinner with me?"

James was staring up at me expectantly, waiting for my answer.

"Sure, I'd like that."

Ben pulled out a sheet of paper from his rucksack and scribbled down my number. And that was it. He called me the next day and we arranged to go for dinner and we've been together ever since, all thanks to little James, who probably is not so little any more.

Chapter 4

As soon as I woke the next morning, I reached up onto my locker and felt blindly until my hand came upon my packet of crackers. I had kept a packet on the top of my locker for the last few months now. Eating one before I got out of bed usually helped to settle my stomach and keep the nausea at bay for a little while. When I opened my eyes, I saw that Ben was sitting on the edge of the bed, pulling off his trainers. He stood up again and pulled his sweaty T-shirt off over his head and tossed it onto the floor. Being the health freak he is, he went out for a run most mornings before school while I clung on to my duvet for dear life and put my alarm on snooze for another half an hour.

"Morning. Did you sleep okay?"

"Well, no, thanks to you!"

"Look, I'm sorry about last night." He stood in front of me, his muscular body toned and tanned. "I just want you to be happy." He sat down again on the bed beside me.

"I am happy. And I'd be even happier if you left me alone about going back home."

"C'mere." He linked his fingers with mine. His naked body was still damp with sweat. He pulled me closer and started to kiss me.

I was still as attracted to him as ever.

"We can't – I'm going to be late," I said, pulling back.

"Nat will cover for you for five minutes." He was kissing my neck, tracing his warm lips against my skin. He knew I could never say no to him.

"Five minutes! Is that all I'm getting?" I put my arms around his neck and pulled his face towards mine.

"Sorry I'm late," I apologised to Nat who was hunched over the iMac computer, her eyes fixed on the screen. She had a mug of coffee clasped between her hands.

"No worries – you feeling okay?" She turned around to me.

"Yeah, I'm good." I tried to keep the smile off my face but Nat saw it.

"What's got into you?"

"Nothing."

"Okay, weirdo – the kettle's boiled anyway. Sam Wolfson rang to say he'll be a little late – there's a problem with his train."

Sam Wolfson was a new photographer who was interested in displaying some of his work with us. He was coming in to talk us through his portfolio and we were going to show him around the gallery. An hour later and a blustering Sam came rushing through the doors, apologising for being late and bemoaning line closures. I was taken aback by his age – he looked no more than twenty. I brought him up to the mezzanine to show him the space that we had earmarked for him before bringing him back downstairs where he talked us through his work. His pictures were stark. Urban decay was his thing. I thumbed through his photographs, which mainly featured buildings that had lost their former glory. There were historical houses with cracked plaster walls, neglected factories with crumbling concrete and broken-glass-littered floors, decaying warehouses with peeling steel girders and acres of empty racking. They weren't pretty but they were real and we had seen a lot more

21

demand for this kind of work lately. Although he was young, it was evident that he was very talented and we knew he would be a good fit with the gallery. We went through the figures with him and we were just agreeing the terms when the bell tinkled and a delivery man came through the door with a huge bouquet of blush-coloured roses. There must have been at least fifty of them. I stood up to take them from him. Ben is so sweet, I thought. A smile crept onto my face again as I thought about that morning.

"Nat Anderson?" the man asked, looking from me to her.

"For me?" Nat was shocked. "Thank you!" She beamed as she got up off her stool and took the flowers from him.

I sat back down again, feeling embarrassed for being so presumptuous.

"Wow, Nat, they're gorgeous!" I said.

Sam nodded in agreement. "Someone likes you!"

Nat took the card out from its envelope and read it. I peered over her shoulder. There was just one word written on it, followed by three bold exclamation marks: '*Amazing!!!*'

Nat started to blush and quickly put the card back inside the envelope.

"They're from him then?" I said.

"Yep!"

I could tell that Nat was thrilled. She went into the kitchen to find a vase to put them in.

After we had firmed things up with Sam, we all shook hands and said goodbye to him.

"Things are going well then?" I said.

"*Sooo* well. Couldn't be any better!" she sang. "I know – why don't we go for something to eat – the four of us – so you and Ben can get to know him better?"

"Sure . . ." I cringed inwardly. Ben was going to kill me.

"Have you anything on this Thursday?"

"Mmh . . . no . . . I'll have to check with Ben though."

"Great – I'll arrange it with Will. How about Ransan's?"

"Yeah . . . why not. The food's always good there." Ben was

going to kill me doubly now. It was a posh eatery close to Holland Park and pricewise it was way out of our league.

I had arranged to meet Ben in the park for lunch that day. We sat on the navy tartan rug that he had brought and unwrapped the paper from around the sandwiches we had picked up in the deli. Mine was an egg salad, his was chicken with pesto. It was a glorious May day and the sun was warm against my skin. I bided my time before I broke it to him about Thursday.

"What? But you know what I think of him, Kate!"

"I know – I'm sorry. I couldn't get out of it."

He groaned. "The whole thing is a mess."

"I know, I know, but it's Nat – so even though I'm not happy about the situation, she's my best friend and I have to support her."

"Well, I don't agree with it – he's married, he has kids for fuck sake! I don't want to be part of it all."

Ben never swore.

"I know, it's terrible, and I don't know what Nat sees in him – I really don't know why she feels he is so worth all the hassle – but it's her choice at the end of the day."

"It will all end in tears."

"Probably."

I lay back on the rug with my head resting on Ben's lap and closed my eyes for a few minutes. The hum of the bees rang loud in my ears. They sounded like horseracing pundits commentating on a race. The sun was warm on my face – the forecast said it was to hit thirty degrees this week. We never had weather like this back home even though Ireland and the UK weren't that far apart geographically but I suppose London is more southerly.

I must have dozed because suddenly Ben was shaking me and telling me that it was time to get back to work. I groaned – I never seemed to get enough sleep those days. I could sleep for a week and it still wouldn't be enough. We folded the rug up and put it back in the basket and then Ben walked me back to the gallery and kissed me goodbye before continuing on to his twenty-two six-year-olds.

Chapter 5

As I got changed for dinner on Thursday evening I nearly had a mini-meltdown when I realised that there was no way that my trousers were going to zip up. I had tried lying back on the bed and sucking in my tummy but they were not going to close. Luckily I had bought maternity trousers the weekend before. I had gone into a hot and stuffy changing room in Oxford Street where I thought that I might faint from the combination of the lack of air-conditioning and my persistent nausea. I had to stand in a queue to wait on a cubicle with two other women ahead of me, all faring the same as we tried to fan ourselves with our hands. The worst part was that there were two men sitting on chairs looking up at us pityingly while they waited on their partners who were trying on clothes.

I took the trousers out from my wardrobe and looked at their corded elasticated panels on the sides. They were dowdy and in a style that I normally wouldn't go near – high on the waist and flared at the ends. The woman in the shop had assured me that the flares would help to balance out my shape, especially when my bump got bigger, but I wasn't so sure. Well, we will be seeing a lot more of each other over the coming months, I sighed as I ripped off the tags and sat on the edge of the bed to pull them up. But the feeling of comfort when I put them on was amazing.

I should have worn them weeks ago, instead of trying to squeeze into my normal jeans. I put on my black platform boots and a flowy black top with gold beading along the bottom. Looking at my appearance in the mirror I felt frumpy. My roots needed touching up too but I'd have to wait until payday. Highlights were an expensive habit.

"Not too shabby, Kate!" Ben said as he looked me up and down when I came into our living rom. "You look lovely."

"Yeah – a lovely whale."

"Come off it, Kate – you're pregnant. Seriously, you look amazing – in fact, I don't think you've ever looked better." He came over and put his arms around me. "Do we really have to go to this thing?"

"Yes!" I said firmly. "Look, it's just dinner and I can make the excuse that I'm tired so we won't have to stay late."

"Right," he sighed. "Do I look okay?"

He was wearing a pink striped shirt under a grey V-necked pullover, jeans and tan leather brogues.

"Gorgeous."

"I really wish we didn't have to go there tonight."

"I know," I sighed. "But we do, so come on."

We got off the Tube at Kensington and walked towards Ransan's. The one thing that could be said for the place was that they knew how to charge. I had been there once before: at a Christmas dinner that Tabitha had organised for all the photographers represented in the gallery. It was favoured by rich executives, who knew that you were always guaranteed a top-notch dish. More importantly for Will, it was also discreet. Its dim lighting and subtle staff meant no-one made any comment if you happened to dine with your mistress for lunch and your wife later that same evening. The seating was laid out in such a way that it always felt like private dining and you knew that no-one at the table beside you was eavesdropping on your conversation. It was not the kind of place that Ben and I could afford to go to usually but I knew the evening was important to Nat.

"Come on," I said and steered him into the restaurant.

The rosewood-panelled entrance hall led into an interior decorated in warm red tones. The maître d' greeted us and showed us over to the table. The maroon wallpaper, red-velvet upholstery and subdued lighting created a rich atmosphere. A huge display of wine bottles stacked on their sides took up one entire wall. I knew from reading the wine list the last time we were here that some of the bottles went up to over two thousand pounds in price. There was a good crowd in and the room was filled with lively chatter as we walked through the tables.

"Kate, Ben!" Nat stood up from the table and hugged me. She looked great as usual, wearing grey cigarette-leg pants and a nude silk knee-length tunic over them. She had layers of beads around her neck and she was wearing impossibly high heels, which put her easily over six foot. Her glossy auburn hair was pulled back into a simple bun, showing off her angular face.

Will stood up to greet us. He leant over and kissed me on the cheek. "Kate – it's great to see you again. You look brilliant – pregnancy suits you!" He was dressed in a blazer and open-necked shirt, revealing some dark chest hair at the top. He had a faint shadow of stubble on his jaw and his hair was carefully styled up with gel. Together they made a striking couple.

Ben and Will shook hands awkwardly. If Ben didn't like Will, the feeling was mutual. I always got the impression that Ben was just a little too strait-laced for Will. Will was a man's man, a complete alpha male. He worked long hours in the City and he lived by the motto 'Work hard, play hard'.

We took our seats opposite them and the waitress passed out menus. She handed the wine list to Will.

"Love the jeans, Kate!" Nat said as she opened her leather-bound menu.

"Shut up, you! Clothing manufacturers must think that pregnant women lose all sense of style as soon as they get pregnant. We'll see how well you'll do when it's your turn."

"Well, you'll be waiting!" She laughed that deep throaty laugh of hers. Men loved Nat's laugh.

We read through our menus.

"It's so hard to decide what to choose!" Nat moaned. "I'm torn between the venison and the beef."

"Well, why don't you go for the venison and I'll get the beef so then you can try both?" Will suggested.

"You don't mind?"

"Of course I don't – anything to keep my lady happy."

They exchanged a smile.

When we were done, we closed the menus shut again and placed them onto the table in front of us.

"Your hair really suits you like that, Nat," I said.

"See, I told you!" Will said, turning towards her. "It shows off her beautiful face, doesn't it?"

I nodded in agreement.

Nat blushed. "I couldn't decide whether to put it up or down coming out tonight."

"Well, either way, you always look good." He pulled her in towards him and kissed her tenderly on the forehead.

Ben and I need not have been there. I tried not to let my shock show at how attentive and affectionate he was being towards her. He was all over her. I had only met him casually a couple of times before so I had never really observed them properly together.

"So now for the all-important bit," Will said, opening up the wine list. "What are we having, guys?"

"The Châteauneuf-du-Pape is good – remember, we had it the last time we were here, Kate?" Ben said.

"Yeah, it was," I said. "Pity I can't drink it tonight though."

"What about the Barolo – everyone happy with that?" Will asked, not even listening to Ben's suggestion.

The waitress came back over and placed a basket of bread on our table.

"This one here is squid-ink bread." She pointed towards a black-coloured one. "This dark-brown one is Guinness bread and this here is Spanish tomato bread. I hope you enjoy them."

"Looks good," Nat said.

"Are you ready to order yet or would you like me to leave you to make up your minds for a little bit longer?"

"I think we're all ready," Will said, looking around at us.

"Yep, I'm good to go – I'm starved," Ben said.

Nat and I nodded in agreement. We ordered our food and Will ordered the Barolo.

"Good choice." The waitress nodded in approval, which seemed to make Will happy.

We sat in silence for a while and I watched Ben as he idly dipped his finger into the wax that had dripped from the candle and let it cool before picking it off again.

Will broke the ice. "So, Kate, you're almost halfway there now, Nat tells me. What hospital are you going to?"

"St Mary's."

He picked up a slice of the squid-ink bread from the basket and pulled it apart. "Very good. That's quite close to you guys, isn't it?"

"Yeah, hopefully we'll have plenty of time though on the big day."

"I hope you've got the fastest route worked out, Ben? Believe me, if that baby arrives in a hurry you'll be glad you did."

"It's on my to-do list – I think every man fantasises about having the excuse of an emergency dash to hospital with his labouring wife to drive like a Formula One driver through the streets."

"Eh, darling, I hate to ruin your childhood dream but we won't be having any Formula One antics when I'm in labour, thank you very much!" I said.

We all laughed.

"I hope you're looking after yourself, Kate, and putting your feet up because it's the last time you'll be able to do it for a while. It's a tough station being pregnant – us men wouldn't last a week. Isn't that right, Ben?"

Ben nodded. "Props to the ladies there." He picked up his glass and took a sip.

We all started to relax a bit and chatted easily until the waitress came back over and set four shot glasses down in front of us.

"Compliments of the chef. Tomato and peach gazpacho."

We picked up the accompanying spoons and sampled the appetiser.

"Mmmh, this is good!" I said.

"It is, Kate, isn't it?" Will said. "Very refreshing."

He was the kind of guy who when he was talking to you his eyes were on you and you only. I had to admit that I could see his charm. He used your name and always appeared interested in what you were saying. It was all 'Yes, Kate', 'Is that right, Kate?' or 'Good point, Kate'.

"Well, I'm sure everyone you meet is full of advice, Kate," he said now, "but the sleep deprivation is torture. Get a night nanny – it's the only way."

"I think we should be able to manage," I said. "I'm sure the sleepless nights are tough but we can take turns."

"You eager first-timers are all the same!"

"But surely that's all part of it," I protested. "You can't just take the good bits and let someone else do all the hard work for you. Where's the fun in that?"

He threw his head back and started laughing then. "Well, don't ring me when you're walking the floors at three in the morning with a screaming baby in your arms."

"Don't worry – I won't." I knew my tone was testy but he had annoyed me.

"Right then, who's having the roast partridge with chanterelles and pear?" The awkward moment was broken by our waitress who was back with the starters.

"That'll be me." Ben nodded at the girl, glad of the interruption.

As Nat and I chatted, I could hear Will talking to Ben.

"So how's school, Ben? What class are you teaching now?"

"Year two."

"*Aaaaarggh*, how do you do it, mate – listening to a bunch of screaming six-year-olds all day?"

Although he never dared say it, I knew that Will viewed teaching as a woman's job and couldn't understand why a man would choose to do a job working with children.

"It's not that bad," Ben said.

"Listen, I have one six-year-old at home and it's more than enough." He took another gulp of wine, then clicked his fingers at a passing waitress and pointed to the bottle on the table, which was running low. Everything about Will, all his mannerisms and actions, were fast. "But I suppose the holidays help. Imagine that, Nat," he turned to elbow her, "imagine having six weeks off in the summer on full pay? It's some life." He lifted his glass again.

I reached for Ben's hand under the table and gave it a squeeze.

Will picked up the wine bottle and filled his glass with what was left. I wasn't drinking and Ben and Nat still had half-full glasses. I continued my conversation with Nat but from the corner of my eye I saw Will lean in conspiratorially to Ben.

"Listen, mate, enjoy your last few months of freedom while you can. Don't get me wrong, I love my three boys to death, but sometimes I miss that freedom of being able to do whatever it is you want to do, y'know?" He sounded melancholy as he raised his glass to his lips and gulped back the red wine. "Once kids come along, your life will never be the same again . . ."

I could see Ben biting his tongue. The cheek of him to blatantly talk about his family like that – yet sit here with Nat and not even bat an eyelid.

After our starters were eaten, and having drunk a good bit more wine, Will pushed his chair back from the table and relaxed back on the seat. He slung his right arm around Nat's shoulders and was running his other hand up and down along her thigh.

"How's work at the gallery, girls?" he asked.

"Well, we have a new photographer coming on board next week," I said.

"Yeah, so Nat was saying – Sam Wolfman, isn't it?"

"Wolfson," Nat cut in.

"Sorry – *Wolfson* – I do listen, darling, I swear." He laughed and Nat smiled indulgently at him.

"We're very excited," I said. "His work is very different to what we usually display in the gallery so fingers crossed now it does well."

"Well, it better or Tabitha will be coming after us!" Nat laughed.

I watched the hand inch a bit higher. Will turned in towards Nat and then was kissing the nape of her neck gently like they were the only ones in the room.

Ben and I ate our mains of Cornish turbot and jowl of pork as quickly as we could without making it obvious that we were rushing and we both claimed to be too full for dessert even though the portions in Ransan's were minute.

"But you always have dessert, Kate – it's your favourite part of the meal!" Nat protested. "Well, you have to at least stay for a coffee."

"Of course we will." I looked at my watch. It was only ten o'clock. Ben and I had coffee, while Nat and Will both had Tanqueray cocktails.

When we were finished Ben signalled the waitress over and asked for the bill. She came back moments later and handed it to him. I balked when I saw the final total over his shoulder. The wine alone was £118 a pop. We couldn't afford this.

"I'll get this, guys," Will said, taking the bill from Ben's hand.

Ben pulled it back again and after a brief stalemate said, "No, no, we'll pay for our share."

I groaned internally. Will could well afford to foot the bill and I knew Ben was just being proud. We left the money for our half and said goodbye to them. I told Nat that I'd see her in the morning.

"I might be a little late," she said, winking at me as she turned to smile at Will.

"I can't believe we just spent the equivalent of over a week's rent for the pleasure of eating out with that twat!" Ben said on the Tube home. "We're supposed to be saving money."

"I know," I yawned. "I could have had my roots done all year for the price of dinner tonight." I was exhausted and rested my head on his lap. I had a hard time trying to stay awake. I was rocked by the motion of the carriage. At least it was quiet at that time of the evening. "His poor wife!" I said.

"I wonder if she knows that her husband is having an affair? Or maybe she turns a blind eye to it so long as the money is coming in and she's living the Chelsea dream?"

"Who knows? But I'm so surprised at Nat. Yes, he's good-looking and charming but he's a complete alpha male. I don't know how you kept so calm when he was dissing your job!"

"Because he's a fool – it doesn't matter what he says."

"Yeah, you're right. I'm going to try and talk to her again about it tomorrow – see if I can get her to see sense."

Back at home we fell into bed. Ben wrapped me in his arms from behind and I fell asleep instantly.

Chapter 6

The next day I watched from inside the bay window of the gallery as Will's Aston Martin pulled up on the path outside. Ben always called it his "midlife-crisis car". Nat breezed through the door seconds later with a big smile on her face.

"Good night then?" I asked.

"The best!" she said dreamily.

She was still wearing the grey trousers and tunic from the night before. There was a trace of black eyeliner smudged beneath her eyes. Her hair was scraped back into a loose bun, not neat like the one she wore last night. She must have forgotten her hairbrush.

"Last night was good fun, wasn't it?" she said. "The food was great!"

"Yeah – they always get it right there, but it's bloody expensive."

"I know – I hope it was okay for you guys?" She seemed concerned.

I brushed her off. "Don't worry about it."

She took off her silk scarf and plonked her bag on the desk in front of her. She went into the kitchen and made herself a black coffee. She came back out, clasping the mug between her hands.

"So what did you think of him?" she said, sitting onto her chair.

"Yeah, he's charming. He seems to really like you."

"Well, I'm glad you guys got to know each other a bit better."

"So where did you stay last night?" I asked. She obviously hadn't been home.

"Oh, he left his car in town last night and we didn't want to waste time getting a minicab back to my place so we checked into a suite in Claridge's."

I raised my eyebrows.

"Oh my God, Kate, it was the most amazing place I have ever stayed in! I bumped into Cate Blanchett in the corridor this morning. I mean literally bumped into her – I was so embarrassed."

I vaguely remembered seeing something on TV the day before that Cate was in town to promote her new film.

Will rang Nat a while later and I was subjected to listening to the two of them talk about how amazing the night was. The conversation seemed to be about how good the sex had been. It started to irk me so I stood up and took my laptop upstairs to get a head start on the weekly sales report for Tabitha. Was it the glamorous lifestyle and the money – or did she genuinely like him? It was as if I didn't know her any more. She wasn't the same Nat that I knew. She was a good-looking girl with a lot going for her, so why was she ready to waste herself at Will's beck and call? Yes, he seemed to like her but it could only end in tears – there could never be a happy outcome.

When Nat finally finished the phone call, I heard her come upstairs to me.

"Sorry – was I talking too loud?"

"No, I just thought I'd make a start on the sales figures," I lied.

I decided to seize the moment and tackle her about Will.

"Look, Nat, tell me if it's none of my business – but what are you doing? Where is this going?"

"Where is what going?"

"You and Will."

"Oh . . . well . . ."

"What worries me is that he makes no effort to even hide the fact that he's married with kids! It's like he thinks it's perfectly legit to go around having affairs –"

"Affair," she corrected.

"Come on, Nat – I doubt you're the first and you certainly won't be the last either."

"Well, cheers, Kate!"

"But what about his wife and children – surely you must feel bad for them?"

"Of course I do – it's horrible! But it's complicated. I absolutely hate myself every time I think about them. But he and his wife lead separate lives."

"Oh come on, Nat – that's what they all say – don't be so naïve."

"No, really they do – separate bedrooms – the lot. I know he'll stay with her for the sake of their children – he has always been upfront with me about that. But it doesn't mean that he has to miss out on another chance of finding happiness. Sometimes love just finds us and no matter what your head tells you is right or wrong, your heart will win out at the end of the day."

Nat was a hopeless romantic. It made me want to slap her stupid sometimes.

"But you deserve more than just a piece of a man! You're getting some other woman's sloppy seconds!"

"It's not like that."

"Oh yeah?"

"Yeah. When we're together, it's well . . . *amaaazing*." The smile from earlier on crept back onto her face. "Look, Kate, when you love someone you have to make sacrifices sometimes."

"Well, I'm sorry, but no matter how good the sex is I wouldn't put up with sharing a man."

"I know *you* wouldn't, Kate. But that's because you don't have to – you've got Ben. Do you have any idea of how hard it is to meet a man without any form of baggage today?" Her tone was defensive.

"No, I suppose I don't." I had met Ben when I was twenty-seven. I never had to endure the carnage that Nat told me was the London dating scene past the age of thirty.

"Well, please don't lecture me then." She turned on her heel and walked back down the stairs, then turned around again. "Oh, and Kate?"

"Yeah?"

"It's *not* just about the sex!"

Chapter 7

Things were tense between Nat and me over the next few days. Although we were talking to each other, I could tell that she was annoyed with me, but we had an exhibition coming up soon so we both knew we had to leave our differences aside and get on with the organisation for it. We needed to brainstorm for ideas so I suggested that we treat ourselves to cakes in the bakery down the street. We sat down inside the bay window and ordered – well, I did – Nat was trying to be good – she was on a healthy eating buzz although Lord knows she didn't need to lose any weight.

"Here, give me a bite of that." She finally gave in to temptation and dug her fork into my sticky toffee pudding. A river of toffee sauce came oozing out. It ran down the side before pooling thickly onto the white plate in front of me. "It doesn't count when it's on someone else's plate."

"Right," I said, opening my notepad and flipping it over onto a clean sheet. I wrote the words 'To Do' at the top of the page and underlined them twice. I loved lists. There was no better feeling in this world than crossing things off a to-do list. Sometimes I even wrote down tasks that I had already done just so that I could put a line through them. I knew it was silly.

Nat had come up with the exhibition title of *Silence*. She had a good eye so she always curated our exhibitions while I organised the admin end of things such as the invites and the food and wine. She had always had an interest in photography herself. She was forever clicking away with her SLR whenever we were out somewhere.

"Your photos belong on these walls too, you know," I would say to her whenever she showed me some of them.

But she would shake her head in disagreement. "Not yet."

She had been saying this for years. I wasn't sure what she was waiting for. Maybe confidence that might never come?

I made a note that I needed to order more vinyl to put the names of the artists in the gallery window because we were nearly out of it. I also had to get booklets printed with a small biography for each artist and a price list for their work. I needed to draft up the press release and update the website, plus I needed to find someone to launch the exhibition for us. There was a lot of behind-the-scenes work that went into the exhibitions. The bigger galleries around town would use a PR person to do the majority of that work but we weren't in that league so it was up to just me. We had only four exhibitions a year but most of our sales for the year took place on these four evenings so they were important for the bottom line. My notebook was littered with scribbled reminders. I had underlined some with thick blue lines so that I wouldn't forget them – other tasks were linked together by arrows. There was so much to be done and my head was spinning just thinking about it all. I sat back, closed the notepad and let out a heavy sigh.

"Any plans for the weekend?" I asked Nat.

"Well, Will will be with his family for most of it but he's promised me that we'll do something on Saturday night," Nat said through another mouthful of cake.

"I see." Things had been awkward between us since our argument last week, so I bit my tongue and didn't say what I really wanted to say – that she was putting up with second best, gratefully snatching whatever crumbs of his time he was able to throw her way. She deserved more. So much more. But, at thirty-three years old, she was a big girl now.

"Are you doing anything?" she asked.

"We're heading down to Ben's parents in Surrey. His sister Laura is coming home for the night so we said we'd go down too." Laura was Ben's older sister and had followed the family tradition of law and was now a barrister working up in Manchester.

"Nice. Well, I hope you have your Barbour jacket packed."

"Yeah, and my Hunter wellies too." I laughed. She always made a comment like this whenever I mentioned Ben's parents. But, in fairness, although they were lovely people – well, his mum was anyway – they were very posh.

On Saturday morning we set off in Ben's Volkswagen Golf along the A3 for the Surrey countryside. Ben insisted on having a car even though it spent most of the time parked up on the street below our flat. Because we lived in central London, we took public transport everywhere but Ben liked the freedom of being able to get out of the city whenever the mood took us.

It was a warm summer's day and the radio was playing softly in the background. We had the windows down to let some air in but not enough to blow us out of it completely.

"So when are we going to Ireland?" he said to me as we drove along.

I groaned. "Soon." God, he was persistent.

We passed over a railway bridge and, at exactly the same time, a train passed beneath us, our journeys intersecting briefly before we headed off in our respective directions.

"Come on, Kate – the weeks are flying along now."

"Will you just leave it, please?"

We travelled along the rest of the winding country road in silence. The road weaved through neatly trimmed hedgerows and bright yellow fields of rapeseed. When we met another car we would have to pull into a gateway to let it pass.

Finally we turned into the gravelled lane of Elderberry Farm, the house that Ben was raised in. We drove the length of it before pulling up in front of the imposing house, where Ben's Golf was dwarfed by his parents' bottle-green Land Rover Discovery.

The beauty of the house never failed to take my breath away. The first time I had come here with Ben, I had been awestruck by the seventeenth-century house with its yellowing sandstone walls, clay roof tiles and majestic portico. It was the kind of house that had usually nowadays been taken over by the National Trust or turned into a wedding venue because the owners couldn't afford the up-keep. Ben had never let on that he came from such a wealthy background. The house was the seat of the Chamberlain family and had been in his family for generations.

"Ben, you said it was a farmhouse – not a big fuck-off mansion!" I had said in a panic. "Are you royalty or something? Why didn't you tell me you grew up in a mansion?"

"You never asked."

"Oh yeah, I forgot that that was normal first-date get-to-know-you talk: 'So did you grow up in a mansion or not?' I'm just waiting on Prince Charles to wave out the window at me!"

He started to laugh then. "Come on, Kate – I think that's a slight overreaction."

"But when you said 'Elderberry Farm'– I assumed as in 'farmhouse'." All the farmhouses at home were either cottages or bog-standard three-bed bungalows like the one that I had grown up in.

He shrugged his shoulders. "What difference does it make?"

"Well, you could at least have warned me," I had said sulkily. I'd already been feeling nervous about meeting Ben's parents for the first time and this had just ratcheted everything up ten notches.

Now, as we climbed out, their two spaniels Admiral and Max came running from the back of the house. They started barking until they realised that it was Ben and then they both rushed at him, clambering over one another, competing for his attention.

"Easy, boys!" Ben said to them and then jumped up and down, causing them to get even more excited.

"I thought I heard a car." Ben's mum, Edwina, came from the back of the house to greet us. She was dressed in her usual uniform of navy wax jacket, cords and wellingtons. She had a wicker flower-basket brimming with stems of freshly cut lavender in one hand and her secateurs in the other. She placed them down on the ground and then took off her gardening gloves and stuffed them into her pockets.

"Hi, Mum!" Ben threw his arms around her neck and they hugged.

Then she came over and gave me a kiss on the cheek.

"Look at you – you are positively blooming!" she said in her plummy accent. She was what Nat would describe as a 'jolly hockey sticks' kind of woman.

"Eh, less of the blooming, please!" I said, laughing.

"Oh, I'm sorry, Kate – I don't mean to insult you. I do remember what it's like being pregnant! Come on inside, I'll put the kettle on. I have some freshly made scones." She poked Ben playfully in the ribs. She knew he always devoured her homemade scones. "Laura's not here yet but she's on her way."

We walked inside, with Ben linking her arm. I could tell she was excited at having her son return to the nest even if it was just for one night.

We went around to the rear of the house and in through the back door. They never used the front door these days. We followed Edwina down through the dark, cool passageways and into the kitchen. Old wooden beams crossed the ceiling above the aged brick walls. I sat down at the circular table covered with a blue checked oilcloth. The kettle whistled on the Aga and the smell of fresh baking filled the air. Edwina fussed around, serving us tea in china cups and scones with real butter melting on top. Originally this used to be the servants' kitchen but now the family used it for themselves. They still had a housekeeper and a cook that came for a few hours every day but otherwise the days of a having full complement of servants was long gone.

"I don't know where your dad has got to," she said apologetically. "I think he's down in the study reading over a brief. You know what he's like . . . I'll go and call him."

Ben's father, Geoff, was a barrister.

"It's good to be home," Ben said, sitting back into the chair when she went in search of his dad. The two spaniels lay at his feet on the flagstones, their tails wagging rhythmically as he rubbed them with his foot in turn.

Edwina came back into the room a minute later. "He'll be up in a minute."

"Admiral is getting on. Come here, old boy!" Ben said. The dog obediently got up from his lying position on the floor and rubbed his back alongside Ben's thigh.

"Well, he is almost fourteen," said his mother. "His joints are quite stiff in the mornings but he has a new lease of life seeing you today."

"These scones are great, Edwina," I said.

"Well, eat your fill, dear – you are eating for two after all! Now then, you two, have you got a photo to show me of my first grandchild?"

I took my treasured black-and-white scan picture of Baby Pip out from my bag and handed it to her. You could see the large head, bones of the spine and its two legs curled up. She (or he) was sucking her (or his) thumb in the grainy image.

"Well, isn't that just amazing!"

I saw tears brimming in her eyes.

"Of course they didn't have things like this in my day. Isn't technology just marvellous?"

"It is indeed, Mum."

"Now if you need anything when the time comes, anything at all, do not be afraid to ask. I would be delighted to help out – you know that."

"We know, Mum, thanks."

"I've told all the ladies in the Women's Institute – I'm so looking forward to this stage of my life. We all love our children but it goes by so quickly and it is hard work, no matter what people say, so you never really get to enjoy it properly – but I've heard so many friends say that grandchildren give you a new lease of life. I can't wait!"

Ben smiled indulgently at her.

"How's school going, dear?"

"Good, Mum, they're keeping me on my toes."

"Oh, I bet they are! And Kate – how's work in the gallery?"

"Well, we've just taken on a new photographer and we've already had a lot of interest in him so we're pretty excited about that."

Just then the broad figure of Ben's father filled the doorway. He stood there, clearing his throat loudly. He stood at a towering six foot five inches tall. Ben was tall at six foot three but he hadn't quite reached his dad's stature.

"I believe congratulations are in order!" he boomed, coming over and shaking both our hands.

Pouring himself a cup of tea, he sat down alongside us at the table. He had been away the last time we had come to tell them the news.

I noticed Ben sit up a bit straighter.

"Thanks, Dad."

I could hear nervousness in his voice. His father always had this effect on him. He always turned into a schoolboy around him when he was so confident and self-assured in every other area of his life. Ben's dad couldn't accept that Ben had dropped out of law at Cambridge and had then chosen to be a teacher. He believed law was in their blood – three generations of Chamberlain men had studied law and Ben would have been the fourth – but he broke the line and it seemed that his dad couldn't forgive him for that.

"So how have you been keeping, Kate? Good, I hope?"

"Very well, thank you." He wasn't the kind of man who would be entertained with tales of morning sickness and expanding waistlines. Because Ben was nervous around him, it made me nervous too.

"Jolly good. I dare say it will be hard though, raising children

44

on a teacher's wage." He exhaled loudly through his nose and took a bite into the scone that Edwina had buttered for him. He chewed loudly.

I breathed in deeply. There it was: the first dig of the day. He just couldn't help himself – the words tumbled effortlessly out of his mouth. He was like a boxer waiting on the right opportunity to throw a punch. It always went like this – Geoff would spend the whole time making snide and cutting remarks about his son's choice of career.

"Well, I'm sure they'll manage, Geoff," Edwina said, in a tone which warned him that that was enough. She turned to us. "Why don't you two take Admiral and Max for a walk – they need to run off some of the excitement at having you home and I'm sure you'd both like to stretch your legs after the drive down?"

Eager to escape the atmosphere in the kitchen, we did as we were told, chose some wellies from the endless pairs lined up at the pantry door and set out across the sloping fields. The dogs ran on ahead of us. We held hands as we walked along, stepping through the long grass. It felt so good to breathe in the fresh country air – it was definitely different from the air in London, heavy with its fumes and pollutants. You could feel its goodness as it filled your lungs.

I knew Ben was brooding. His footsteps were just that little bit too heavy as he trampled on the grass underneath.

"Are you okay?"

"Yeah – I'm used to it by now."

"It still doesn't excuse it. I don't know why he can't just be happy for you – you love your job and you would have hated every day of being a lawyer. It's just not you."

"He's a lost cause."

"Well, for a supposedly intelligent man, he's a bit stupid. Some people get so entrenched in their beliefs that they overlook the important things in life. It's very sad actually."

"Well, I'll never be like that to Baby Pip – no matter what he wants to do –"

"Or she," I reminded him playfully, as he was so fond of doing to me.

"Or she – once she or he is happy, then I'm happy."

I put my arms around his neck. "You're going to be a great father."

"I hope so," he said seriously. "It's a big job being responsible for a little person, doing your best to mould them into a well-rounded adult . . ."

"You think about things too much."

"Well, it's a big thing raising a child. I just hope we get it right, that's all."

"Jeez, Ben . . . will you stop freaking me out!"

Laura was seated in the kitchen when we got back to the house.

"Congratulations, little brother!" she said, jumping up and throwing her arms around Ben's neck as soon as we came in the door. "And of course you too, Kate – let's face it, it's you who's doing most of the hard work!" She gave me a kiss on the cheek and hugged me warmly. We had told her our news on the phone but this was the first time we'd seen her face to face since we'd found out I was pregnant.

"Eh, I've had my part to play in it too, you know!" Ben said, grinning at her.

At thirty-seven, she was two years older than Ben and she never let him forget it. Laura was tall too – their whole family was tall. She must have been at least five foot eleven in her bare feet and she never shied away from heels. I liked that about her – she had a take-me-as-I-am attitude and she wasn't hung up or insecure about how she looked – unlike other people who would fret over their tummy or the size of their nose, Laura seemed to be blissfully unaware. She was genuinely happy in her own skin.

"I can't believe I've been outlapped by my younger brother!" She plonked herself back down on to the chair. Ben and I sat down across from her while Edwina placed a pot of tea and more scones on the table before joining us. I was glad Geoff was nowhere to be seen. The atmosphere was always heavier when he was in the room.

"So how is my favourite spinster-in-the-making doing then?"

"Shut up, Ben – and I'll have you know that that title no longer fits – I'm seeing someone actually."

"Oh yeah?" Ben and Edwina both looked incredulous.

In the whole time that I had been with Ben, I had never known Laura to have a boyfriend. Her last boyfriend had been a fellow barrister and a complete pratt by all accounts. Ben had never liked him. Although he was in the legal profession, he had felt the law was for other people, not him. He had been arrested for drink driving but had managed to get it hushed over because of who he was, so was never prosecuted. But the real straw that broke the camel's back came when Laura had found out that he had a bit of thing for using prostitutes on the side. She had seen his car one night pulled into a lay-by on a road near their home, so, thinking that he must have broken down, she pulled up beside it. She got out of her car and went over to his and when she looked in the window, she saw her boyfriend with his trousers around his ankles and his head thrown back in pleasure as the woman crouched down over him. She had banged on the window then. "He actually had the audacity to look irritated because I had disturbed him – and it wasn't as if he wasn't getting it at home!" she would say to anyone she told the story to.

"So who's the new guy then?" Edwina asked.

"His name is Tim Templeton."

"What kind of a name is that? He sounds like a character out of *Noddy*," Ben said. "Are you sure he really exists and isn't a fabrication of your overactive imagination?"

"I'll have you know he is a living and breathing, sound-minded human being and we love each other very much."

"Who in their right mind would call their child Tim Templeton?" Ben said, laughing.

She fired a cushion at him.

"Hey, stop it, you two!" Edwina scolded.

"So what does this Tim Templeton fellow do?" Ben was trying to keep a straight face on when he said his name.

"He's a musician actually – he plays the cello in the Philharmonic Orchestra."

"And does he know that he is dating someone who is completely tone deaf?"

"I'm not that bad, Ben."

"Oh yes, you are."

"Mum – tell him!"

"Well, let's just say you were the only child that was asked *not* to sing during the school concert."

"Mum!"

"It's true, Laura – the other children complained that they found it off-putting." Edwina started to laugh heartily at the memory.

"Well, I must say – I have a jolly lovely family!" Laura said in mock indignation.

We chatted easily for a while until it was time to go and change for dinner. Ben's family were very traditional in many respects – everyone still changed for dinner and reconvened back in the drawing room for an aperitif before going into the formal dining room to eat. The first time I had come to meet them, I had panicked because I hadn't brought any clothes to change into. The only other clothes that I had brought with me were jeans and jumper for the next day. But if she had noticed, his mother had never said anything to me, which I was grateful for.

I got changed into a forest-green jersey dress, another one of my new maternity-wear collection. That was another thing that I had noticed: all of the maternity clothes in the shops were made from jersey fabric. I mean everything. I looked at myself in the mirror. I had recently had my blonde hair chopped into a bob and I still got a fright whenever I saw my reflection. I needed something to brighten up the outfit so I wrapped a burnt-orange patterned silk scarf around my neck. We were just about to leave the room when I decided to grab a cardigan to put on over the dress because, once you left the kitchen, which had the Aga to keep it cosy, the house was bloody freezing. Even at the height of summer.

We went into the drawing room where Ben's parents were seated on the Chesterfield sofa. Candles filled the room with a soft glow as the light illuminated the dark age-spots on the mirror. Laura was seated on a wing-backed armchair. Edwina hopped up when we entered the room and offered us an aperitif of Dubonnet. I abstained but Ben took one of the crystal glasses from her and we sat down on the four-legged sofa across from them. I hated this sofa – it was perched up high on four castors and was so deep that when I sat back into it properly a short-arse like me felt like a child whose feet were dangling over the edge.

We chatted for a while and then went through to the parquet-floored dining room and took our seats at the polished mahogany table. It could comfortably seat twenty people and Ben told me stories of fabulous dinner parties his parents used to throw when he was a child. These days Edwina was lucky to have five people around her table. The walls were papered in Chinese hand-painted wallpaper, which Ben's parents went to great lengths to preserve. Gilded paintings of Ben's forebears stared down sternly on us all.

"I wonder what they would think of your career choice?" I muttered to him. "They're probably turning in their graves right now."

He gave me a dig in the ribs.

"*Ouch!* Watch the baby!" I said in mock anger.

After we had eaten our goat's cheese starter, Ben's mum served up a goose and roast potatoes dripping in its fat.

"Bloody hell, Edwina – there's only five of us!" said Geoff. "We'll be eating the leftovers of that bird for weeks to come yet."

"Nonsense, Geoffrey – you know I like to cook a special meal whenever the children return. I had Rob kill it for me yesterday."

Rob was the farmhand who had been working with the family for over fifty years now.

"How is he doing?" Ben asked as he helped himself to some peas. He served me some before passing the dish to Laura. "We used to have such fun with him – hey, Laura, remember that time we took the tractor out but we didn't know how to stop it and he had to run after it and jump on?" Ben turned to her and laughed.

"I never knew that!" Edwina said in shock. "My Lord, you could have both been killed!"

"Eh, that's why we didn't tell you," Ben said.

"Any sign of him retiring?" Laura asked.

"Not yet, thank goodness," Edwina said. "I dare say it will be a sad day when he finally does."

"He's irreplaceable." Ben nodded in agreement.

"No one is irreplaceable," Geoff cut in.

"Well, dear, I would argue that Rob comes pretty damn close to it," Edwina said tersely.

We all looked at our plates and ate the rest of the food without much talk.

After pudding, the rest of them sipped dessert wine but I stuck with the water. I never could stomach dessert wine, pregnant or not.

"So how's school, Ben?" Geoff asked but the words seemed to stick in his throat as they came out.

"Great – I have Year Two, so we're just starting the basics of addition and subtraction."

"Hmmh."

"Ben is really good at his job, you know." I don't know what possessed me to say this. Suddenly all eyes were on me. "He received the school's Teacher of the Year Award last year and he's being put forward for the head of the Maths Department, aren't you, Ben?"

"Fantastic!" Edwina said.

Ben glared at me. Nobody spoke for what felt like an eternity.

"Well, isn't that wonderful? So not only do you have a woman's job but you also let your girlfriend do the talking for you, Ben." Geoff slammed his wineglass down hard onto the table so that the crystal was left ringing.

I felt stupid then. I had just made everything worse. Much worse.

"Dad!" Laura said.

"There is no need to be so rude," Edwina said sharply to her husband. "I get to have my children home only a handful of times a year and then you have to ruin it for everyone!"

"I'm just stating the obvious."

"I will not let you speak to my son like that!"

"Although you would never think it, he is my son as well actually," Geoff continued coolly and he took a sip from his wine.

"Well, then act like it!" she said, her voice steely, before she pushed back her chair and walked out of the room.

Ben and I averted our eyes. I just wanted the ground to swallow me whole. What had I just started? We both sat there rooted to our chairs, neither of us knowing whether we should go after his mother or just stay where we were.

"Well, I hope you're happy now, Dad!" Laura said, standing up, her eyes blazing. She turned and went out after Edwina.

Geoff got up then and walked out of the room, leaving us on our own.

"Well, that was fun." Ben let out a heavy sigh. He took his linen napkin off his knee and tossed it onto the table. Its corner landed in the gravy boat and I watched as the white linen soaked up the brown liquid.

I stood up and took it out again. "I'm sorry, Ben – I know I shouldn't rise to him but it just came out. I get so annoyed with how he belittles you all the time. I just wanted him to know that you are a success – you may not work in law but you are good at what you do." I reached out for his hand.

"I know you meant well but there is no reasoning with that man."

"I'm so sorry."

"It's not your fault."

"Maybe you should go after your mum. She looked upset." I

rubbed my temples. "I think I'll head up to bed." I could feel a tension headache coming on. The evening had left me exhausted.

I climbed the dark staircase and headed to our bedroom. The room we were staying in was at the front of the house. I drew the drapes that hung on either side of two huge windows overlooking the driveway. The room was furnished with all the original dark mahogany furniture. A tall standing mirror stood over in front of one of the windows beside a lacquered screen. The bed was covered with a pelmet and a roll-top bureau sat in the corner beside the fireplace. All the rooms had open fireplaces although the family never used the ones in the bedrooms any more. The floorboards were covered with Persian rugs that were almost threadbare they were so old.

I got changed quickly because the room was so cold and hurriedly climbed under the covers. I was glad to find that Edwina had put a hot-water bottle in the bed earlier to warm the sheets.

I read my book until the door opened a while later. Ben came in and closed it softly behind him.

"Well, how is she?" I said, putting my bookmark between the pages and closing the book shut.

"She's okay – a bit upset though."

"Of course she is. Did he apologise to her?"

"Dad – apologise? Some chance!" He sat on the edge of the bed and took off his boots.

"Well, I'm sorry, I know he's your dad but he really is an ignorant man."

He climbed into bed beside me and put his cold feet beside mine on top of the hot-water bottle and started moving it over to his side.

"Oi! Get lost!" But I let him take it anyway. "I feel really terrible about it all."

"Why? You did nothing wrong."

"I know but I should have just kept my mouth shut. I feel bad for your mum – she enjoys your visits so much but then this happens."

"I don't let him get to me any more – it used to. It used to really upset me when he would say things like that but now I know I'll never get his approval no matter what I do, so there's no point even trying."

"You don't need his approval."

"I know," he sighed.

"Here – it's my turn," I said, using my foot to bring the hot-water bottle back over to my side. "Well, I think now you'll be taking a leaf out of my book."

"How do you mean?"

"Well, after tonight I wouldn't blame you if you wanted to avoid going home for a while. I can give you some tips!" I said, laughing.

The following morning I could tell that Edwina was putting on a brave face as she served us up breakfast. She was trying to force cheer into her voice. Laura was chatting about her flat-mate, telling us some anecdote about how she came home steaming drunk and tried to get into bed with her.

None of us mentioned what had happened the night before as we tucked into our Eggs Benedict. Ben was noticeably quieter.

Laura set off for home after breakfast and Ben went out to put our cases in the car, so it was just myself and Edwina alone in the kitchen. After a minute she placed her knife and fork down on her plate and turned to me.

"Is he all right?"

"He's okay. I think he's used to it by now."

She let out a long sigh. "I'm at my wits' end with him."

"Who? Ben?"

"No – Geoffrey."

Edwina never confided in me about her husband and I wasn't sure what to say.

"We had a blazing row after you two went to bed last night – there is just no getting through to him."

"I see."

"You know, he's going to be a grandfather soon and I think it's time to just let bygones be bygones, but he is resolutely stubborn."

"But why can't he just be happy for Ben? Ben loves his job. He is happy. I wish Geoff would just accept it."

"So do I," she said wearily. "So do I. But it's not just about his job – it's been going on for years. I can remember one time very clearly – Ben must have been only about eight or nine and he came home from school and said quite innocently to Geoff that his friend Richard's dad was a solicitor, just like he was. Geoff started to roar at him. 'I'll have you know I am not a solicitor, you stupid boy!' he spat. 'I am a *barrister* – there is a world of difference!' I'll never forget it – the look of fear and confusion on poor Ben's face. He didn't understand what he had said wrong. He was too young to understand his faux pas. I told Geoffrey to calm down, that it was a silly mistake, and that Ben was only a child. But Ben had got such a fright that he started crying which added fuel to his father's rage. Then Geoffrey shouted at him to 'stop being such a mummy's boy'." Her hands fluttered to her neck and she fingered the chain around it. "That was the start of it, Kate. From that point on they always seemed to be rubbing each other up the wrong way although Geoff should have had more sense. Ben was only a child."

"Ben never told me any of this."

"I'm not surprised. I'm sure they aren't his favourite memories of his childhood. Then there was rugby – as you know, Geoffrey is big into his rugby and he had always assumed that when he had a son he would follow in his footsteps and play schools rugby and beyond. But Ben never had an interest in the game. It wasn't that he didn't like sport because he competed in athletics and he liked rowing in school but just didn't enjoy rugby. Geoff just couldn't accept it – he would force Ben to tog out at the side of the pitch for under-eights training and poor Ben would wait all game and only be brought on for the last five minutes. Then, when he'd go on to the pitch, he'd get trampled on and Geoffrey would shout at him the whole time – '*Tackle him, Ben! Take him down, Ben!'* But it wasn't in Ben's nature to be rough – he'd rather let people hurt him than hurt somebody else. Then in the car on the way home Geoff would spend the whole journey telling him what a disappointment he was. Ben only told me about it all recently – obviously, if I had known back then, there was no way I would have let Geoff get away with doing that to him."

I was stunned. Ben had never told me any of this. It probably hurt too much. I couldn't believe what a bully Geoff actually was. My heart broke for Ben. Maybe that was why he was so patient with the children in his class – because he knew how horrible it was to be shouted at as a child.

Ben came back into the kitchen. "Right then, we're all packed up – time to hit the road."

"Yes, of course," said Edwina. "You don't want to leave it too late, or you might hit traffic with everyone making their way back up to town again for work tomorrow." She stood up from the table and brushed down her skirt.

She walked us out to the car and we hugged goodbye and set off for home. Geoff didn't surface to see us off. He stayed down in whatever room he was içnoring us from. I knew that even after we were gone the tension between Ben's parents would probably linger on. Poor Edwina! She didn't deserve any of this. It must be awful to be caught between the man you love and your children, especially when he was such an obstreperous oaf.

Chapter 8

The next morning I watched Nat through the window as she chained her bike up on the railing outside, even though there was a sign affixed to the front of it saying '*No Cycles Please*'. She would keep watch periodically in case a warden came around to remove it.

"So how did you get on in Surrey?" She pronounced 'Surrey' grandly as 'Sorrrey'.

"Yeah, we had a nice time. It was good to see his mum and Laura but his dad didn't disappoint as his usual arsehole self."

"That man sounds like a complete dick."

I had told Nat countless stories about him before.

"To put it mildly – I can think of other words," I said. "How was your weekend?"

"Really good, Kate – we went out with friends for drinks on Saturday night."

I hated the way she used the word 'friends'. To be honest it made my skin crawl. All of Will's friends had mistresses on the side. Nat had told me this before and I knew this was who she was referring to. I had been horrified when she first told me. She had made it sound like it was just another hobby to these men – the way Ben goes running or another person might enjoy knitting. They would all go out together just like any normal group of friends, except they weren't – the one thing that they had in common was that all the men had wives and children tucked up in bed at home. Some of them even holidayed together – Nat had told me about two couples that had just come back from ten days in Langkawi. They had lived it up in a five-star all-inclusive resort and told their wives that they were in Asia 'on business'. I thought the whole thing was seedy and horrible and couldn't understand why Nat would want to be involved in a circle built on lies like that. I knew that she and Will were seeing a lot more of each other these days, at least several times a week, but she thought that they were different to those other couples. To her, those women were a bit on the side whereas what she and Will had was different, more special somehow. But I bet the other mistresses thought the same about her.

Sunlight started to creep across the honey-oak flooring and up along the white walls as the day went on. It was quiet. We had a few time-wasters who liked to browse around the gallery but had no intention of buying anything. You could spot them a mile off – they were usually the same old faces that lived in the leafy streets surrounding the gallery and had nothing better to do with their lives. Then they would question us to the nth degree about the photographer and his subject matter and who his muses were, like they were going to buy, but they just never bit the bullet.

My phone rang then and I rooted around in the bottom of my bag and managed to get it on the last ring. I saw Edwina's number flash up.

"Hi, Edwina, is everything okay?" Even though I got on very well with my mother-in-law, she usually rang Ben if she needed to talk to us.

"Yes, of course, dear. I know you're probably in work now but I just wanted to say that I'm sorry we never got to finish our conversation yesterday but I didn't want Ben to know that we were talking about him."

"Don't worry, I won't say a word."

"Oh, thank you. It's just that I think Ben is a bit embarrassed

by it all, although Lord knows Geoffrey is the one who should be embarrassed! I also just wanted to, well . . . apologise for his behaviour."

"You don't need to apologise –"

"Well, one of us does and hell will freeze over before it's Geoff. I love having you and Ben to visit – I just wish it didn't have to turn out like that every time." She sighed heavily.

"Me too."

"You will come again, though, won't you? You won't let Geoffrey put you off?"

"Of course we will."

"Oh good." The relief in her voice was obvious. "It's just with your baby on the way, well, I don't want to be cut off from the child's life because of Geoffrey."

"Don't worry, Edwina – we want you to be a big part of this baby's life."

Chapter 9

The weekend after, Ben and I decided to have brunch in Café Les Cloches down the street. It was a warm sunny day and we strolled along, Ben's arm slung around my shoulders. We liked to do it now and again – it was our treat to ourselves on a lazy Saturday morning after a busy week in work. Anton, the owner, was from Lyon in France and had moved over to be with his English girlfriend Flora and they had set the café up together. Its pretty periwinkle-blue timber shop-front stood out on the otherwise residential street. Café Les Cloches was a treasure. It was tiny with seating for a mere twenty people inside but Anton had recently put some more seats on the pavement out the front to accommodate his ever-growing number of customers. Those of us in the know kept Les Cloches a secret for fear we'd never get a seat there if the rest of London found out about it. It was a busy little spot and had a reputation for its breakfasts. You needed to get there early at the weekends because it was full of people like Ben and me lounging over a long breakfast and reading the newspapers. I'm sure Anton was driven demented because the table turnover was so slow but that was why it was so popular. Sometimes you'd have to queue to get a table but we were lucky to see a couple getting up to leave just as we arrived, so we were able to get their seats outside in the sunshine. We sat down at the Parisian-style table and chairs, as people stopped on the street to read the chalkboard menu listing the daily specials. For once I was actually looking forward to the food and didn't feel queasy at all. Maybe my nausea was finally starting to go. Our Polish waitress had taken our order and I had decided on the Full English while Ben had gone for waffles with fresh berries. He had asked her to leave off the whipped cream.

After we had eaten our breakfast, we ordered coffees – decaf for me, a macchiato for Ben. I always felt a bit pretentious ordering specialty coffees – I could imagine Dad's voice saying, *'It was far from macchiatos you were raised!'* And it was – coffee was unheard of in our house when I was growing up – coffee was for other people. Tea was what we drank and if you came to our house you were only offered tea – there was no choice in the matter.

Ben had the newspaper stretched wide between his toned arms and I was flicking through the magazines, which were my favourite part. We had been at a gig in the Old Vic Tunnels the night before and my ears were still ringing from the sound that had bounced around inside the old barrel vaults.

"See, you can get flights to Dublin for only £9 plus taxes each way," Ben said as he read aloud from the paper.

I knew he was waiting for me to say something so I pretended that I couldn't hear him and continued to read a review of some play in the Culture section. He just wouldn't quit.

"*Oh shit!*" Nat said that evening as she rushed back into her kitchen. A cloud of grey smoke rushed out to meet us. She had invited Ben and me over for dinner that evening. She was really pushing the whole 'get-to-know-Will' thing – I had to resist the urge to tell her that we had already got to know him, and we still thought he was a dick. I knew Ben was dreading it as much as I was.

She was in a flurry as she slid her hands into a pair of oven gloves and removed the offending dish from the oven. She stood fanning the smoke with the gloves.

"I'm so bad at timings – this is the first and last time that I will be having a dinner party."

Her hair was parted in the centre and plaited elegantly in two French plaits, which were gathered up loosely on the back of her head. She was wearing black peg-leg trousers and a long-sleeved silk blouse with delicate pearls sewn along the neckline.

"Need a hand?"

"Brill – Kate, could you stir that sauce for me, please? Oh and Ben, would you mind opening this bottle of red? I could do with a glass."

"Sure." He took the bottle off the worktop and started rooting in a drawer for a corkscrew. He uncorked it and poured them both a generous glass.

Nat sat on a stool and took a sip. "I needed that, I'm parched."

"Where's Will?" I asked.

"Well, I'm not sure – he should be here soon though." She glanced up at the clock.

Suddenly she bolted up from the stool.

"Crap! I forgot to put on the potatoes!" she wailed. "Fuckedy fuck!"

We made ourselves useful while Nat busied herself peeling potatoes. I could see the worry lines knitted between her eyebrows. I knew she was wondering where Will was. It was nearly eight thirty and I was starting to wonder if he was going to show. I suppose that was one of the hazards of dating a married man – you never really knew if he would be able to make it to events you had planned together – his wife might blow him out of it at the last minute, asking questions about where he was going, or his kid might get sick. You probably could never fully relax.

At eight forty-five, Nat had to take the meat out of the oven.

"Damn it!" she said. The pork belly that she had been slowly cooking was now nicely charred on top.

"Don't worry," I said. "We can just cut that bit off."

"I'll just try and ring him again . . ."

Ben and I pretended to be deep in conversation while Nat phoned Will.

"There's no answer . . . I hope nothing has happened . . ." She bit down on her bottom lip nervously.

"Don't worry – I'm sure he's on his way." I rubbed her arm. She had gone to a lot of trouble for this evening – I hoped he wasn't going to let her down. The table was set and the tea-light candles that she had scattered around the room flickered softly. Florence & The Machine was playing in the background.

Nat topped Ben's and her glasses up again. The bottle was nearly gone now. I felt desperate for her. I wanted to go and give her a big hug. Plus I was starving and Pip was thrashing around inside me, complaining about the delay to her dinner.

"Do you think we should eat?" I finally asked when it was close to nine. I thought I was going to collapse if I didn't eat soon.

"Yeah, I suppose we'd better – no point in letting it all go to waste." She sighed.

Ben uncorked the bottle we had brought over with us and handed a glass to Nat.

Although she hadn't said it, I had seen Nat phoning Will twice more but he hadn't answered.

"Are you –" I was interrupted by the buzzer.

Nat rushed over to it and pressed the button to sound the intercom.

"I'm so sorry, Nat!" Will was panting on the other end.

She buzzed him up and went out into the hallway to let him in.

"I'm so sorry!" I could hear him saying to her over and over again breathlessly.

They came in the door then.

"Sorry, guys – I hope you weren't hungry?" he said. "It was Noah's birthday party today and of course some of the parents didn't get the brief that the party was over at six and we couldn't get rid of them. Cue fourteen overtired, screaming four-year-olds and, even worse, their hyperactive parents getting excited at the sniff of free wine and the chance to compare every mundane milestone in their kids' lives! I'm so sorry." He turned to look at Nat forlornly. He gently brushed a piece of hair out of her eyes. A look passed between them. Ben and myself might as well not have been in the room.

I wondered what lies he had told his wife to get here. *'Sorry, darling, I promised to meet some of the lads for a few drinks'*? Or maybe, *'Sorry, darling, I've got to entertain some clients who are in London for the weekend'*? I don't think *'Sorry, darling, I'm going to meet my mistress and her friends for a quick bite to eat'* would have washed somehow.

"Well, don't worry, you're just in time. We haven't started yet. Here –" She handed him a glass of wine before hurrying into the kitchen to put the pork belly back in the oven to warm it up again. She started plating up the now cold starter of fried halloumi with cherry tomatoes. We all sat down around the circular table.

"God, this is good," I said through a mouthful. "You can nearly taste the sunshine from those tomatoes. Where did you get them?"

"In the market up the road."

"Did you see the footie today, Ben?" Will asked. He was necking back the wine – he'd only been here for five minutes and already his glass was empty.

"No, I didn't get to see it – myself and Kate were out looking at buggies."

After breakfast we had decided to tackle the minefield that was buggy-shopping. Ben had done a lot of research into the different types of buggies – manoeuvrability, ease of folding and tyre specs – but I, being a bit more shallow, just cared about what looked best. We had gone to a nursery store to road-test a few before we made up our minds.

An awkward silence lapsed between the two men.

"So how did the meeting go yesterday?" Nat turned to Will.

"It was a fucking nightmare. The whole thing is a mess – it ended up being complete carnage and old Smithy was shown the door."

"No way!"

"But I told them that was what was going to happen – our customers don't want to deal with a computer interface no matter how 'real time' it is. These are people that are investing a lot of money with us and they want to get a real person on the other end of the phone to answer their questions, no matter what time of the bloody day or night it is."

Nat was nodding in agreement.

"We've spent millions on installing this system and no one wants to use it now!" Will went on. "The whole thing is a damp squid. I said it all along but Smithy was too far up the board's arse for anyone to notice. It's such a complete waste of money."

"It's 'damp squib' actually," Ben said.

"What?" Will looked at him irritably as if he was a fly on his arm that he couldn't manage to swat.

"The phrase – it's '*damp squib*' not 'squid'."

"Whoa there, teacher boy!" Will raised his hand to Ben. "Relax, would you, mate – you seriously need to get out more." He put the glass to his lips and drank more than half of it back in one gulp.

We all sat in awkward silence until Nat pushed back her chair and got up to serve up the main course. I got up to help her.

Soon we were busy eating the overcooked pork belly.

"This is great, Nat," Will said.

"Are you sure it's okay? I won't be offended if you can't eat it."

"Once you cut away the burnt bits it's great," I said.

It was after midnight by the time we finished the lemon meringue pie that she had made for dessert.

"That was amazing, Nat – I'm stuffed," Ben said.

"You did really well – you're not just a pretty face. Sorry

again for being late, sweetheart." Will put his hand over hers on the table and gave it a squeeze.

When Nat got up from the table and started clearing plates, Will stood up to help her.

"Can we do anything? I feel bad looking at you two cleaning up," I said, standing up.

"Sit down, Kate – you're our guests for heaven's sake!" Will said.

Nat cleared the leftovers into the bin and then passed the plates to him to stack beside the sink. There was something about them working together, doing the most banal of chores. Even I had to admit that there was a certain tenderness between them.

To look at them there, they were like any ordinary couple that had invited friends around for a bite to eat and were now doing the clearing-up. I found myself wondering if Will helped out like that at home. I seriously doubted it – I'm sure, with his money, he had cleaning staff to take care of things like that.

When they had finished the dishes, Nat made Irish coffees for everyone, while I just had a regular coffee. I needed it – the meal had made me sleepy. I was trying hard to stifle my yawns. They sat back down at the table again and Will topped up everyone's glass with more wine. He sat back and draped his arm over Nat's shoulders.

I watched them, relaxed in each other's company, as we chatted. The lamplight glinted off Nat's hair so you could see its reddish tones. They were a good-looking couple – they matched each other in the beauty stakes. His six-foot-two height complemented Nat's five-foot-ten. When you were out with them, eyes naturally followed them. They attracted attention wherever they went.

"Would anyone like the last slice of pie?" Nat asked.

"Maybe Kate would like it – she's eating for two after all?" Will suggested.

"God no, I'm grand."

"I love the way you still say 'I'm grand' after fifteen years living here," Ben teased.

"What part of Ireland are you from?" Will asked.

"Mayo, in the west."

"Do you go home much?"

I squirmed on my chair. "Now and again."

I could see Ben looking at me open-mouthed. I shot him a look.

"My mum was Irish," Will said.

"Oh yeah?"

"Yeah, she was from this tiny little village called Inistioge in County Kilkenny."

"Oh, gorgeous spot."

"Yeah. We went over there once on holidays when I was thirteen and, coming from a council estate in Slough to a farm in rural Kilkenny, I thought we'd arrived in the most backward place on Earth. The first day we arrived I witnessed a man sticking his hand up inside a cow's you-know-what to artificially inseminate her!" He laughed.

"*Euggghhh!*" Nat said.

"But it wasn't all bad. I did have my first kiss there . . ."

"Oh yeah?" Nat said sitting up.

"Yeah, her name was Cathy. A fiery little thing she was – jet-black hair and cool blue eyes. She took no shit, did Cathy. She was a real eye-opener. I thought we'd do a long-distance relationship – y'know, wait by the payphone at five o'clock on a Tuesday because she said she'd ring, or write letters to each other – but my cousin rang me a few weeks later and told me she had met another boy from the town and it was 'Bye-bye, Will'."

"Ah, my poor Will!" Nat laughed as she tousled his hair.

They were so touchy feely. They couldn't keep their hands off one another.

"Yeah, I was heartbroken, I really was. Absolutely gutted. There's nothing quite like your first love," he said wistfully.

"Do you think there's only one person for everyone?" Nat asked.

"Hardly," I said.

"Do you know what, Nat?" Will said. "I think there might be. I mean, I think that you can love a lot of people but there's an ultimate one out there for all of us." He smiled at her and there was a look exchanged between them. "But one wrong decision can change how things work out for the rest of your life . . ." He sounded sad.

"But if that's the case what happens if 'the one' is living in a yurt in Outer Mongolia?" I said.

"Well, then you just have to hope that destiny intervenes and brings you together," said Will.

"But what happens if 'the one' is already dead?" I said.

"I never thought of that," Nat said. "God, that's very sad, isn't it? To think of someone spending their whole life looking for 'the one' and not knowing that they're never going to find them!"

"Nah. I'm pretty sure there are lots of 'ones' out there for us," I said.

"Thanks a lot, Kate!" Ben said, feigning indignation.

"Oh, you know what I mean . . ."

"You are such a cynic, Kate Flynn!" Nat said.

"No, I'm not, I'm just realistic. We can't all be hopeless romantics like you." I smiled at Nat who was looking very comfy cuddling up to Will.

Everybody was well on, Ben included, but I had hit the wall of tiredness. I couldn't help myself from yawning. I tried swallowing them back but I couldn't stop – it was like my body was trying to search out the last of the oxygen in the room. Finally I couldn't fight them any longer.

"Sorry, guys, I'm falling asleep – I'm such a lightweight."

"Well, you're also nearly six months pregnant," Ben said.

"Yeah, maybe we should start making tracks." I yawned again.

"Really? Ah, that's a pity!" Nat said.

They both saw us out to the door. Will had his two arms around Nat's waist from behind and was lightly kissing her hair.

"Well, thank you for coming," she said.

"No, thank *you* – we had a great time," I responded.

They closed the door behind us and Ben turned to me and said, "Asshole."

Chapter 10

On Monday morning I had a meeting with Charlie, the graphic designer we used whenever we needed to get artwork designed for our exhibitions. I wanted to talk to him about the booklets and the postcards. He was waiting for me outside the door of the gallery.

"Sorry, Charlie," I said, rushing up and opening the door to let him in. Usually Nat was there first but she wasn't in yet.

"No worries, I was a few minutes early," he said.

He took a seat while I got myself organised. A few minutes later Nat came in.

"Morning!" she said breezily. "Oh hi, Charlie. How are you?"

"I'm good, thank you, Nat."

She was wearing a burgundy dress with a repeating cat pattern, knitted mustard tights and brown suede ankle boots. Her hair was tied up loosely on top of her head.

While Charlie set up his laptop, I went down to the kitchen and made a pot of coffee.

First Nat talked him through the theme of *Silence* and what photos we would be displaying. Charlie flipped open his notepad to take notes. Then I talked him through the practicalities, the number of artists displaying work, the style of booklet we wanted, the colours and fonts. Rather than use a standard template, we liked to have it newly designed for each exhibition to keep it all looking fresh.

After Charlie had gone, I started work on the press release while Nat made some calls to a few of the photographers to discuss some more of the details.

"Thanks again for Saturday night, Nat. We really enjoyed ourselves.' That pork was amazing." I wasn't lying – we had enjoyed ourselves even with Will's arrogance. Although I still didn't approve of her relationship with him, I was tolerating it for her sake.

"Yeah, it was fun."

"Did Will stay long afterwards?"

"No, he was up with the lark."

"But how does his wife not hear him come in?"

"They're in separate rooms – you know that! She doesn't know what time he gets in at – once he's there when she gets up in the morning, she doesn't notice. I hate when he has to leave me though, to go back to his family. It's getting harder every time. Just for once I wish we could just wake up together in the morning without him running home at some godforsaken hour in the middle of the night."

"It goes with the territory, I suppose."

"I know, Kate, I'm just saying, that's all."

I knew it sounded bitchy and I felt contrite then. We were only just getting back on track again after our last argument about Will. I knew that I needed to leave my judgmental side out of it but I couldn't just stand back and watch her get hurt. I could see that she was falling deeper and deeper for him. And the truth was that after watching them together the night before, I couldn't blame her. He was so attentive towards her, it was easy to see why she had fallen for him. It was obvious that he idolised her and he was affectionate, kind and considerate. The only problem was that he was also married.

"But you don't have to put up with half a relationship, Nat."

"It's not 'half a relationship' – it may not fit into a

stereotypical box but that doesn't make what we have together any different from other couples."

"Come on, Nat, you just said yourself you're getting fed up of sharing him with his family. It's only normal to want more."

"Well, he can't leave his wife because of the kids and, as someone who grew up in a broken home, I have to say that I respect that."

"Well, at least he's not filling you full of lies."

"He's not like that, Kate. We get on so well. He always says that if only we had met at another time, things could have been so different."

I'm sure he was full of lots of romantic nonsense when it suited him. Nat was a sucker for things like that.

"So you're happy to settle for being the other woman then?"

"For the moment, yeah. I'm happy to just be with him and whatever comes with that I'm willing to accept. It's part and parcel of loving someone, for better or for worse."

I didn't say it but they were the same vows that he once would have made to his wife.

Chapter 11

The following Saturday evening Ben had arranged to meet the boys for drinks – it was his mate Thom's stag party so it was going to be a wild one. I had persuaded Nat to call over and we were going to order a take-out. I heard the buzzer just after seven. I buzzed her in but, when I opened the door, I saw she wasn't alone. Another woman was standing beside her.

"Hi, Kate – this is Gill."

"Hi, I hope you don't mind me crashing on your evening like this?" Gill smiled weakly at me.

"No, not at all, come in."

We all went inside and Nat and Gill sat onto the sofa while I rooted in the drawers for the take-out menu.

"You don't mind if we have a glass, do you, love?" Nat asked me, holding up a bottle of Pinot Noir.

"No, not at all – we can't all abstain." I would have given my right arm for a glass of the red stuff. I knew I could have a small one if I really wanted to but then I'd just want more so it was better to have none at all. "I'm going to drink a small river though when this baby is born."

"Bet you won't," said Gill.

"Eh, why not?"

"Women who are pregnant always say that but then when

72

their little bundles arrive they are usually too in love to miss drink any more."

"Hmmh, well, we'll see." I put two wineglasses and a corkscrew down on to the coffee table.

The others read the menu and then I ordered the food.

"Any word from Pete?" Nat said, turning to Gill while we were waiting on our food to arrive.

"No." She sighed heavily.

"Who's Pete? Your boyfriend?"

She nodded.

"Gill was let down at the last minute, weren't you, darling?" Nat said.

"Yeah, he has to baby-sit his kids – his wife had to go to visit someone in hospital at the last minute."

Ah, it was one of *those* 'friends', one of Nat's mistress friends. I had been wondering why I had never met her before. Gill was attractive, mid-thirties, well kept, trim figure – probably from not having had children yet, brown glossy hair, nice tan – probably from using sun beds. It was easy to see why a middle-aged married man going through a midlife crisis would be attracted to her.

"Well, you don't *'baby-sit'* your own kids," I said.

Nat shot me a look. "Oh, you know what she means, Kate," she said wearily.

"I'm just saying . . ."

Gill looked a bit scared of me so I said no more about it after that.

The food arrived and we all tucked in. I was dying to ask her why she put up with the limitations of being in a relationship with a married man but I knew Nat would probably kill me. Just like Nat she seemed ordinary – there was no obvious childhood traumas or apparent lack of self-worth – but I didn't understand why two beautiful women would sell themselves so short.

The girls called a cab after eleven and I headed up to bed myself but I was woken up after four by Ben's loud snoring. He always snored when he had been drinking. He had himself wrapped up in the duvet and I only had an inch to cover me. I yanked it back out of his arms and turned over again.

The next morning I opened the window to let the smell of stale air out of the room. I left Ben to sleep it off and went out and started cleaning up the flat. We were rapidly outgrowing it – there just wasn't enough room for all our stuff. I was a regular in IKEA, snapping up all their latest storage gadgets but I now needed somewhere to store all the storage. What was it going to be like when Pip arrived? Everyone knew that babies came with contraptions and all sorts of bulky equipment.

Ben finally roused from his slumber after eleven. I was sitting with my feet up on the sofa flicking through a magazine.

"It's awake! How was last night?" I said, putting the magazine down.

"Good, I feel rough," he croaked. He sat down at the kitchen table. "Have we any painkillers?"

"Yeah, hang on a sec." I got up and rooted around the presses and popped out two tablets for him with a glass of water. I sat down at the table beside him.

"Thanks. It must have been a dirty glass."

"And nothing to do with the ten pints you sculled back of course."

"Leave me alone, I'm dying."

"Rate it on the scale."

When we had first moved into the flat we had thrown a house-warming party involving Mediterranean quantities of red wine. We had been horribly hungover for days afterwards. It was full on – the shakes and reactions slower than the last hour of work on a Friday evening. We felt dire for three days straight. That party was our gold-standard scale for hangovers ever since – we now rated all of our hangovers against it.

"Eight point five."

"Wow, that *is* bad. My poor Ben!" I said, stroking his head.

"*Ouch*, that hurts!"

I laughed.

"It's not funny, Kate!"

"Oh, I don't miss hangovers. That's definitely one of the pluses to this pregnancy business."

I made him a cup of strong coffee and then threw sausages, rashers and eggs into the frying pan to make a big fry-up breakfast. Normally Ben was so health-conscious that he wouldn't touch a fried breakfast but today he was glad of the greasy salty food to feed his hangover.

"So how about we do some baby-shopping today then – cross a few more things off the list?"

"No, Kate, pleeeeease, not today! Any day but today!" he pleaded.

"Don't worry, love, I'm only winding you up. I'm not that cruel."

That afternoon, I persuaded Ben to take a water-taxi down the Thames to Greenwich. There was a gastro-pub there that we both loved and I had been dreaming about their sausages all morning from before I had even got out of bed. The sausages I had cooked for breakfast hadn't killed my craving. The weather was hazy as if the clouds were just too lazy to fully move off and let the sun come through. We walked up past the Cutty Sark and along the pretty streets until we reached it. We went inside the dark interior and sat down on a comfy couch in the corner. I almost salivated over the menu even though I already knew what I was having before I even went in the door. We ordered a battered cod with mushy peas for Ben, bangers and mash for me, and Ben also asked for a bottle of beer. The pub was full of thirty-somethings like us, catching up with friends over a hearty lunch. Finally our food arrived and we both tucked in. A couple came in with their dog who lay down obediently at their feet.

"So have you thought any more about going back to Ireland?" Ben said for what seemed like the hundredth time over the last few weeks as he cut into his cod.

I could feel my tummy wind itself ever tighter into a knot whenever he mentioned it.

"Can you just leave it, please, Ben?"

"Kate, you have to face up to it – you can't run away from it forever. When was the last time you even rang your dad?"

"A few months ago."

"No, it wasn't! It was Christmas Day, that's when!"

"Really?" Even I was surprised. I thought back over the last few months. He was right. It was now June – I hadn't rung home in over six months. I'd had a missed call from Dad a few months back but I had forgotten to ring him back. I felt a pang of guilt then. Dad was getting on – he had retired from the farm and my brother Patrick had taken it on. I knew he was disappointed when I hadn't gone home for his sixtieth the year before. The rest of them were all there of course.

I pushed away my plate of half-eaten bangers and mash. My appetite was gone now.

"Are you not eating that?"

"I'm not hungry."

"But you've been banging on about the bangers here all day!" He shrugged, then pulled the plate over towards him and started taking my uneaten food and piling it all onto his own plate.

We went home soon after and Ben went out for a run. Unlike me, his conscience always got the better of him whenever he pigged out. I was feeling sleepy so decided to climb into bed for a quick snooze. I seemed to be spending my whole life catching up on precious sleep these days.

I had just got comfy when the buzzer went a few minutes later. I groaned, assuming it was Ben after forgetting his keys. I got out of bed and went down to the kitchen and pressed the intercom.

When I heard Nat's voice, I knew there was something wrong. She didn't just drop in, she always called first.

"What's wrong? Has something happened?" I said as I let her in.

Her whole body was shaking as she plonked herself down on the sofa.

"Have you got any alcohol?"

"Em, I only have wine . . . or hang on a minute . . ." I checked the press above the cooker. "Vodka?"

"Vodka."

I poured a generous measure into a glass, mixed it with some orange juice from the fridge and handed it to her. She took a big sip and exhaled loudly.

"Are you going to tell me what's happened?"

"I saw him with his family earlier in Hampstead Heath."

"Who? Will?"

She nodded. "I was cycling along and there they were, having a picnic."

"Well, you did know he was married," I said, trying not to sound too harsh.

"Yeah, but it was different actually *seeing* them in real life. The three boys were running around on the grass in front of them – I recognised them from photos on his phone that he had shown me before. Oh, it was horrible – it only really hit me there how young they actually are, I mean Jacob has only just turned one!"

"Did he see you?"

"No, he didn't. I thought I was going to fall off the bike in front of them though – my whole body just went weak but I got out of there as fast as I could."

"I'm sorry, Nat."

"Just seeing them like that – it was such a shock, y'know?"

I nodded but I didn't know. I wasn't the one having an affair with a married man.

"I've been thinking about it the whole way over here. Who am I kidding? He's married, he has children. I can't do this to his family any more. It's very different hearing about these people because then they aren't real to you – you've never met them and you can distance yourself from them. If they enter your head you can block them out again but seeing them there like that with him playing happy families – well, it made it all very real."

"Well, what are you going to do?"

"I can't do it to them any more – to the three boys especially." She took a deep breath. "I've made up my mind to end it."

"Really?" I was shocked by her decision.

"Yeah, Kate, I can't do this. I love him but it's not right. I don't want to be a home-wrecker."

"I think that might be for the best, Nat," I said softly.

"Oh God, I'm dreading it. It's going to be awful – the thought of not being with him is tearing me apart but I think it's the right thing to do – before anyone else gets hurt. I can't do it to his kids . . ."

I was trying to leave my feelings out of it but secretly I was relieved. "You're doing the right thing."

"I'm going to call him tonight and tell him."

"Will you be okay? Do you want me to come over?"

"No, I think I just want to be by myself if that's okay? It's something that I need to do on my own."

"Okay, but you have to promise to ring me straight after and let me know how it goes."

Nat rang me that evening as she had promised.

"So how did he take it?"

"Not good. He was very upset. It was awful." Her voice was quivering.

"I'm sorry, Nat. Maybe he just doesn't like not being in control."

"No, that's not it, Kate – he was genuinely gutted. He begged me to change my mind. It's just so hard." Her voice broke and she began to cry. "Why does he have to be married? Why, Kate? You were right all along – you said it would all end in tears and it has – mine."

"Well, I don't want to be right if that makes you feel any better. Look, are you sure you don't want me to come over? You sound like you could use a tissue-holder?"

"No, I just want to be on my own right now."

"I hate hearing you upset like this."

"It just hurts, that's all – knowing that both our hearts are breaking but we still can't be together."

That night in bed, I was lying back against Ben's bare chest. He was reading his book and I was rubbing hand cream into the backs of my hands.

"I hope she's okay?" I said again. "Maybe I should have just gone over there to check if she's okay?" I sat up and turned towards him.

"But she said that she wanted to be on her own, Kate – you have to respect that."

"Yeah, you're right," I sighed, sinking back down on my pillow. "This is going to be so hard on her though – she really fell for him."

"Well, you're just going to have to be there for her and help her through it."

"I know. I have to say, though, I'm very relieved – I was getting really worried about the whole situation."

"Yeah, it's hard on her having to go through this but it's for the best – it could have got very messy if his wife found out."

"Yeah, you're right." I sighed and lay back against his chest and he hooked his arm around me as he continued to read his book. "Ben?"

"Yeah?"

"I'm very lucky to have you – I don't think I tell you enough."

He put the book down and looked at me. He wasn't used to such bursts of emotion from me. "Are you feeling okay?"

I laughed and gave him a kiss on the lips.

Chapter 12

The next morning, I pressed snooze on my alarm clock before I eventually dragged myself out of bed. I got into the shower and then dressed. I texted Nat to see how she was and to tell her not to bother coming in if she wasn't up to it, I could hold the fort. When I was finished I blow-dried my hair and checked to see if she had replied but there was no message back from her, which made me anxious. She was normally quick to text back.

With a slice of toast in my hand, I kissed Ben goodbye and hurried to the Tube station. I held my Oyster Card up to the reader at the turnstile but the barrier didn't open and then I remembered that I hadn't topped it up. The man behind me sighed loudly so that I, and the whole Tube station, knew he wasn't impressed with me. I felt the knots tighten in my shoulders as I moved out of his way and went over to the machine. Finally, when I had money on my card, I made my way to the platform and stood there shoulder to shoulder with every other weary commuter, all wishing that we were still in bed.

I came up from the Tube and, as I walked under the archway of the Ritz, I checked my watch. It was already five past nine. I hurried on half running, half walking, until I reached Jensen's. I put the key in the door and went inside. I turned off the alarm, took the strap of my bag from around my neck and let it slide down my arm until it landed with a thump on the desk. I switched on the computer and while I waited for it to load up I went and made myself a cup of ginger tea. I came back out front and sat down and started filing away invoices.

A few minutes later I saw Nat's head passing the window before breezing through the door. She literally had a spring in her step. I placed the folder I had just picked up back down on the desk in shock. As she got closer I could see that she was actually beaming. This was a very different woman to the one that I had spoken to last night. This was not a woman who had just broken up with the man she loved.

"Eh, Nat, but did you win the lotto or something between last night and this morning?"

"It's even better. You'll never guess what?"

"Go on." I said nervously, picking up my tea. I was dying to know what had brought about this transformation.

"Well, a couple of hours after I got off the phone to you last night, Will showed up on my doorstep. He's left her." Her voice was triumphant.

"*What?*" I accidently banged the mug on to the desk with the shock.

"Yeah, I know! Can you imagine how shocked I was?"

"Wow!" I was stunned. "But I thought you said he would never leave his wife and kids?"

"That's what I thought but I guess when it came down to it he just didn't want to be without me." Her face broke into a big grin.

"So he's moving in with you then?"

"Uh huh – for the time being anyway – and we might look at getting somewhere else when things settle down a bit."

"Jesus."

She grinned widely as she took off her furry gilet and hung it over the back of the chair.

"Are you sure this is what he wants? I mean, it's a big step leaving his wife and children."

"I know, Kate, but I never once asked him to leave them. This was entirely his decision. Of course he's a bit hurt and lost but this is what he wants so I'm going to help him through it."

"And how's his wife doing?" All I could think about was this poor woman who was probably falling apart right now behind the four walls of some big posh house in Chelsea.

"Well, Will said she was devastated . . ." She trailed off.

"I bet she is."

"Look, it's difficult for everyone involved but hopefully things will settle down soon for the boys' sake."

"Well, it's going to be tough – I hope you know that?"

"Kate, please, I know things are going to get worse before they get better but isn't it better for the boys to have parents who are happy instead of making each other miserable?"

"That's not for me to say."

"Oh Kate, just for once can you not at least try to be happy for me?" she said wearily before storming off into the kitchen.

I had to admit that this really had shocked me. This was the last thing I'd expected. I was obviously happy for Nat that he loved her enough to choose her over his family but, on the other hand, there was a family out there that had just been ripped apart because of her and it was hard to jump up and down to celebrate about it.

The rest of the morning went by with Nat and me barely speaking to each other. When I was going up to the deli at lunchtime, I offered to buy her a sandwich but she said she would pick something up later. So I went and bought my sandwich and took it to the park to eat it.

We didn't really say much to each other for the rest of the afternoon. I heard her and Will on the phone making arrangements for him to get keys cut so I got stuck into tidying up the press release that I had drafted before sending it out. I needed to check with Nat to confirm if one of the photographers who had been a bit indecisive about coming on board had made up his mind yet.

"Has Darryl Jones come back to you yet?" I said when she was finished on the phone.

"Nope." Her eyes were fixated on the brochure in front of her.

"He's not interested then?"

"Nope."

"So he's definitely not going to do it?" I asked.

"That's what I said, didn't I?"

"All right! I was just checking."

It was uncharacteristic of her to be snappy with me and I didn't like it. She was my best friend but lately we just seemed to be constantly at each other's throats and it was all because of Will. I was glad that I had to leave early anyway that day because I had a check-up in the hospital.

"Okay, well, I'm off so I'll see you tomorrow then," I said, picking up my satchel and slinging it around my neck.

"Bye." She didn't even bother to look up at me.

I met Ben outside the hospital and we walked to the antenatal clinic together. We sat down on the plastic seats in the waiting room and waited to be called. When I told him what had happened, he couldn't believe it either.

"What?" He was as stunned as I was. "He left his wife and kids for Nat?"

"Yep."

"So that's it now? They're shacked up together in Nat's place?"

I nodded.

"Well, I hope Nat knows what she's letting herself in for! The whole thing could get really messy if things get bitter. He'll be dragged through the courts, custody battles, the lot!"

"I know, that's what I'm afraid of – you know what Nat is like – she's so soft, she'd never be able for anything like that."

"Well, you can bet your house on it that his wife is going to take him to the cleaners and screw him for every last penny."

"If we had a house," I sighed wearily. "I can't say I blame her though."

All was going well with Baby Pip – she was growing away and doing everything she was supposed to do. It really was amazing every time to see her. I could never get bored of watching her. I could see her practising her swallowing. Her arm was over her eyes.

"I think your baby is a little camera-shy today," our sonographer said.

Ben was leaning forward, studying the screen intently.

"Stop trying to peek at the sex!" I said.

He sat back on the chair again. "I can't help it. It's killing me not knowing!"

Chapter 13

"C'mon, we'd better make a start at hanging some of these photos." I sighed wearily. The exhibition was taking place the following day and we liked to have the photos up the day before so we could spend the day itself doing all the last-minutes bits and pieces. I was sitting on the top step of the gallery while Nat was standing on the stepladder.

"To the left a bit," I directed.

"There?"

"A little bit more. Stop."

"There?"

"Hmmh, just a tiny bit to the right . . . hang on, stand back for a sec."

She climbed down from the ladder and we both stared at the photo on the wall.

"Looks good to me," she said.

She picked up another one and dragged the ladder across the floor to do the same thing again.

"Look, Nat, I'm sorry about the other day – of course I am happy for you but it's just a messy situation." It had been two weeks since Will had left his wife for Nat. We'd had another argument about it a few days before and we still weren't really on speaking terms. We communicated where necessary about things for the exhibition or when an email came in from Tabitha asking about something but that was the extent of it. I just wanted everything to be normal between us again. I hated this constant battling between us. Even when we were speaking, all it took was one stray remark to get Nat's back up and unravel the whole thing again.

"No offence, Kate, but no matter how 'messy' you think it is, it really doesn't impact on you, now does it?"

"Well, no . . . I guess not." I paused. "Please, Nat, can we just forget about it? I hate fighting with you."

"Sure – it's all forgotten about."

But I knew by her tone that it wasn't.

I set about sticking the vinyl of the artists' names in the window while Nat was doing something up on the mezzanine. When she came back down the stairs, I offered to get her a coffee from the deli, my treat. I wanted to get myself a scone anyway. I was so hungry all the time these days. I would bring little tubs full of fruit and nuts or carrot sticks with houmous to work with me but inevitably I would have eaten them all by ten o'clock and I would be still hungry, so I'd have to run down to the deli for a scone to keep me going until lunchtime.

"Nearly there now," the woman in the deli said to me as usual. She had been saying this to me since my bump became noticeable.

"Yeah, I'll be glad when it's all over . . ." As usual I forced a smile on my face. We had this same conversation every day. She said to me, "Nearly there now" and I usually replied with a variation on my standard response as above but, unlike me, she never seemed to find our daily exchange awkward or embarrassing whereas I was cringing at its predictability. In fact I think she enjoyed the repetition, maybe she was the kind of person that hated surprises. Maybe she liked to know exactly what was coming next in life, even in her conversations. The machine started hissing and splurting as she busied herself frothing milk. When she was finished, I chose a red velvet cupcake too because I knew they were Nat's favourite. I paid for the lot and she handed me the coffee for Nat with my brown-paper bag and paper napkin. And I knew we would do the same thing all over again tomorrow . . .

When I got back to Jensen's I handed Nat the coffee and cupcake.

"What's this for?"

"It's my way of trying to say sorry."

She smiled then. "Thanks, Kate."

I started spreading butter and then jam thickly onto my scone.

"I wish I was pregnant so I could eat all around me with no guilt." She sighed as she watched me.

"There are matchsticks bigger than you! You're tiny – I'm really starting to think you have body dysmorphia!" Nat always thought she was much bigger than she actually was. "Anyway eating for two is a myth, you know. You only actually need an extra three hundred calories a day when you're pregnant."

"What? But that's not even a Yorkie bar!" She was horrified.

"I know."

"But that's not fair – I've been looking forward for years to making a complete pig of myself when I'm pregnant!"

"Yep – it's cruel all right."

"Christ on a bike, I'd go so far as to say it's right up there with finding out about Santa!" She was tucking into her cupcake.

I decided to broach the subject. "So how's it all going?"

She knew I was referring to her and Will.

"Great."

"Has he seen his kids since?"

"He's picking them up tomorrow afternoon."

"I see. He must miss them a lot."

"He does – that's the hardest part. I know it's going to be a difficult transition, especially for the kids, not having their dad living with them any more, but I just hope that she makes it as painless as possible for everyone involved."

I didn't say anything else. I was afraid we'd end up arguing again.

She left a little before six that evening because she wanted to run to the market to pick up ginger before it closed. She told me that they were having friends over for dinner so I told her to go on and that I would close up on my own.

When I got home that evening Ben was fuming. I could feel the tension in the air as soon as I opened the door. He was moving noisily around the kitchen, opening the cupboard doors and banging them shut again. He didn't even hear me come in. He had been in good form when I said goodbye to him that morning.

"Who rained on your parade?" I asked, going to the fridge and pouring myself a glass of juice.

He swung around when he heard my voice.

"Sorry, love, I'm just having a bad day. How are you doing?"

"Want to talk about what's bothering you?"

"It's just this kid – remember the one I was telling you about that was falling behind the rest of the class even though usually he was right up there on top?"

"Elliott, right?"

"Yeah, well, you know how I had called his parents into a meeting today?"

"Uh-huh."

"Except his parents didn't even bother their arses coming – they sent the au pair along instead!"

"No way!" I was shocked that there were parents out there who would actually do that.

"At first I thought it must have been Elliott's older sister but then she introduced herself as Annika, the family's Swedish au pair! She must have been about seventeen and she really didn't seem too interested in my concerns. I felt like such a fool. I mean, if they're not concerned enough to turn up to a school meeting, well, then, why should I be?"

"Yeah, you should just let it go," I said absently as I scanned through the post that Ben had left on the counter.

"But I can't just leave it, you see? That's the problem – it's bugging the hell out of me. There's something going on at home, I just know there is. I mean, to look at him he's perfect – he's always very well turned out and he has the best of everything, but there is something troubling him."

"You don't think he's being bullied, do you?"

"Well, that was my first thought, but I'm with the class the whole time and I've been keeping an extra close eye on him in the school yard, but he seems to be fine with his friends."

"So what can you do now?"

"Well, I can either give it another shot and ring the parents again or else I'll have to refer it on to the principal."

"Are you *that* worried about him? Are you sure you aren't overreacting? I don't know much about kids but don't they go through, y'know, *phases* and things like that? He might catch up again in a few weeks."

But he shook his head. "There's something more to this, I'm telling you."

"Hey, don't let it stress you out." I put the letters down and reached out to rub his arm.

"I try not to but it makes me so mad. It's funny – this kid never wants for anything financially – he has the best of everything, yet he doesn't get the one thing that he needs which is his parents' time!"

"You really do care for those kids – they're very lucky to have you as their teacher."

His face flushed from my compliment.

Chapter 14

We spent the next day sorting out the final bits and pieces for the exhibition. We had the champagne chilling in the fridge and the glasses all washed and ready to go. I had managed to get the renowned photographer Kimy Flowers to launch it for us. He was always a supporter of Jensen's anyway so he was happy to do it for us.

I pointed to a photo. "We need to straighten that one up a little more."

Nat, who was closest to it, walked over and tilted it to the right slightly. "Okay now?"

I stood back and looked at it critically. "A bit more."

"There?"

"Yeah . . . go on . . . that's better. So how did his visit home go?"

Nat had been a bundle of nerves all day yesterday worrying about it – she was hoping it would go okay for everyone's sake. I think she was still so surprised by Will leaving his wife for her that she was really afraid of something going wrong.

"Yeah, it went okay – as well as can be expected, I suppose. He picked the boys up and they went and played football in the park, they got something to eat afterwards and then he dropped them home again. He didn't go into the house though – he stayed in the car."

"Were the boys okay?"

"They were super-excited when they saw him waiting for them outside but they got upset when he was dropping them back home and they realised that he wasn't going to be coming inside with them. They kept telling him that their mummy wanted to see him and asking why wouldn't he come in . . ."

"Oh God, the poor little things!"

"I know, it's so hard on them. Sometimes I just feel awful for being such a home-wrecker . . ."

I said nothing. It was true after all.

"Will didn't sleep at all last night. He tossed and turned all night long. It's really tough on him right now."

"Ouch!" I said.

"What's wrong?" Nat asked concernedly.

"Just Pip kicking the life out of me." I placed my hand on my bump and tried to move the offending leg out of the way.

She smiled. "You're very lucky, Kate, you know."

"What – for getting kicked alive by my baby?"

"Well, it must feel very special to know there's another life growing inside you."

"Yeah, it is, I suppose. So have you and Will, y'know . . . ever talked about babies?"

"No." She shook her head. "I guess it was never really on the agenda for discussion before – but now that we're a proper couple . . . well, who knows? I really hope so, Kate."

I knew that she wanted kids – she was more excited than me when she found out that I was pregnant – but I wondered if Will was done with that stage now. He had already done the family thing – he had just decided that it wasn't for him.

I had to eat humble pie and admit that things seemed to be going from strength to strength between them since Will had moved in with her. Although she didn't talk to me about him much – it was still a touchy subject – they seemed to be very loved-up. She said she knew that he was finding the adjustment hard but it was so good waking up every morning, knowing that he would be still in her bed. They were keeping a low profile in case they bumped into friends of his wife – they didn't want to rub her face in it. I would overhear them on the phone during the day, chatting about what they were going to have for dinner that evening – or he would ask if she would mind picking up his dry-cleaning. She would go to the market during her lunch-break and stock up on fresh ingredients to make dinner – there was no Uncle Ben's for her and Will. I think Nat was enjoying being able to care for him properly. They had already slotted into the cosiness of domestic life. I think they were also enjoying nesting in for the first time like every other couple does when they move in together. They would spend weekends lazing around her place – probably in bed, I thought to myself. She no longer had to grab snatched moments where he could sneak away – or plan their dates around his wife's schedule. She had a proper boyfriend now and she was enjoying not having to share him for once. Nat was a positive person anyway but it was like she was permanently walking on a rainbow. Nothing could get her down. I knew that he must care for her or he wouldn't have left his wife but I was still finding it difficult to accept that he was Nat's partner now. I knew I had to put my feelings aside if I wanted to keep Nat as a friend but I still couldn't forget the murky origins of their relationship.

I was exhausted when I finally put my key in the door that evening. Ben was sitting watching some cookery show on TV. He turned to greet me when I came in.

"So how'd it go?"

"It went really well. Kimy attracted a big crowd, like I knew he would and the gallery was full to the brim. We sold quite a bit of stock, which the artists were happy about. Tabitha should be impressed when I send off the report at the end of the week. I'm glad it's all over though, I can tell you – it takes weeks to plan it and then it's all over in less than a few hours."

"Well done! Do you want something to eat?"

"No, myself and Nat had something before the exhibition started." I plonked down on to the sofa beside him. "Did you get through to Elliott's parents?"

"Yeah, I decided to phone the house this time so that they couldn't avoid me. His mother answered but she was really noncommittal when I asked her if she wouldn't mind dropping by in person. She actually said that she would drop in 'at some stage' when she was doing the school run over the next few weeks!"

"What is wrong with the woman?"

"Well, I said that if she didn't make it a priority I would have no choice but to refer it higher up the line, so I think I managed to get through to her and she said she'd call in when she picks him up from school tomorrow."

"Well, hopefully you'll get to the bottom of it then."

I knew that whatever was going on with Elliott was bugging the life out of him. He really did go above and beyond for the kids in his class.

Just then my mobile rang. When I picked it up to see who it was, I saw Dad's number on the caller display. I let it ring out without answering.

"Who's that?" Ben asked.

"Oh, it's just one of those market-research companies – they rang earlier wanting me to take part in a phone survey but I was busy – I recognise the number from before."

"Well, they really pick great times to contact people," Ben grumbled.

We both turned back and focused on the TV.

Chapter 15

I could tell by her eyes that Nat was hungover when I saw her come through the door. She was pale and her eyes were glassy. She told me that she and Will had stayed up late over a few bottles of wine after she had gone home after the exhibition. They were still all wrapped up in one another, it seemed. I offered to go down to the deli to get her a proper coffee – I knew that the instant stuff wouldn't cut it for her this morning.

The day flew past with people coming in for a browse. We had a well-dressed American tourist come in who seemed interested in a group of Sam Wolfson's photos of Battersea power station with its iconic four towers reaching up to the grey sky, bleak black-and-white photos showing the landmark in a grim and pitiful manner. I walked over and enthusiastically talked him through Sam's choice of lighting, angles and perspective.

"See, it's taken from Chelsea Bridge. The photographer is Sam Wolfson – you may have heard of him? One of his pieces sold at our exhibition last night for over £3,000 – he's very up and coming. We're lucky that he started out here at Jensen's and his work seems to be in demand. The galleries are falling over themselves to display his work at the moment. It's likely to be a good investment piece in years to come."

I couldn't believe it when he said he would take all three. I secured them in bubble wrap and then wrapped them in brown parcel-paper and tied them up with string for him to take away. He thanked us profusely and went off on his way, delighted with his purchases.

"Hi, love," I said as soon as I came in the door that evening.

Ben was sitting on the sofa – I looked around and saw that he hadn't even started to make dinner. "What's wrong?"

"Sit down, Kate. I need to talk to you about something."

I did as I was told and sat on to the sofa beside him. "What is it? You're starting to worry me now."

"Well, you know that I had that meeting with Elliott's mum after school today?"

"Sorry, I forgot that was today. How did it go?" My brain was gone to pot these days – it was like my body was too busy looking after Pip to put the energy into something as insignificant as actually being able to remember things.

"Well, I was correcting exercise books and I didn't hear her come in until I saw a manicured hand with a bloody huge emerald stone stuck under my nose. She introduced herself as Thea Boucher." He looked at me and paused.

"So?"

"Well, I told her to take a seat but she said she'd rather stand because she was in a bit of a hurry. So then I stood up because it felt as though she was talking down to me. Anyway I told her that I was concerned about Elliott because he had been falling behind the rest of the class, though he was usually one of the top performers. 'I know,' she said. 'That's why I sent my au pair to meet you. I don't understand why you need to see the both of us though.' So I lost my patience then and told her that I didn't need to see 'both of them' – I needed to see *her*, as Elliot's mother. Of course she took offence at my tone then, so I explained as patiently as I could that Elliot was making no effort – that, in fact, he had regressed. That he also had no interest in learning new songs and joining in like he usually did."

"And?"

"Well, she said, 'He's a bright boy, maybe he needs more stimulation' as if it was all my fault!"

"The cheek of her!"

"Anyway, I said that I agreed with her, that he was a bright kid but I didn't think that that was the problem. So I asked her if there was anything going on at home? And as soon as I said that, her straight face lost its composure and I knew that I was on the money. And that was it – the poor woman broke into a million pieces in front of me. She sat down on the chair and the tears flowed. I didn't know what to do – it wasn't like I could exactly put my arms around her!"

"So what did you do?" I asked.

"I offered her a tissue from the box on my desk. 'I'm sorry,' she kept saying as she dabbed at her eyes. She said that was why she'd sent Annika her au pair to meet me – because she knew she herself would never be able to keep her emotions in check. So I asked her again what was going on and that's when she said she recently discovered her husband was having an affair."

Immediately an alarm bell went off in my head. It all sounded too familiar.

"Oh my God, Elliott is Will's son, isn't he?" I said.

Ben nodded. "When I thought about it, I remembered Will mentioning that he had a six-year-old son, that night we were in Ransan's."

I nodded. "So what did you do then?"

"Well, obviously I had to try and compose myself and act professionally. So I asked her if her husband was still in the family home, even though I already knew the answer to the question. But this is the worst bit: she shook her head and said, no, that she had thrown him out three weeks ago!"

"But Nat said that he left her!"

"I know," Ben said, nodding.

"But Nat wouldn't lie to me!"

"Well, someone is telling lies," Ben said. "And I bet that it's Will . . ."

"So you think his wife threw him out and then he told Nat he had left her?" I was fuming.

"Well, I wouldn't put it past him and he would have needed somewhere to stay . . ."

"The bastard!" My blood was boiling. I'd known the whole thing about him leaving his wife for Nat was too good to be true. "Oh God, poor Nat, she's going to be devastated."

"So anyway, I said to her that that made sense because it was around the same time that I had first started noticing problems with Elliott. She got very upset then, saying, 'God, I can't believe this has affected the kids – I've been trying to keep it all together. I've been putting on a brave face and I thought the kids were doing okay but clearly not. I'm not good at anything – I thought I was a good mother but clearly I'm not even good at that. God, I can't believe I'm telling you all of this – I'm so sorry, Mr Chamberlain – you must think I'm frightful!' So I told her not to be so hard on herself, that she was obviously going through a difficult patch in her marriage and that it's hard to keep it all together when you're falling to pieces yourself. 'That's exactly how I feel,' she said. 'My heart is breaking because of what my husband has done, and then also because my boys are asking me when their daddy is coming home and I just feel as though I'm being pulled apart at the seams.'"

"Oh my God, this is just awful!"

"It gets worse . . ."

"Go on . . ."

"Well, then I asked her if there was any hope that her marriage could be salvaged."

"You did not?"

"I had to, Kate –"

"What did she say?" I felt sick in the pit of my stomach, waiting to hear what he was going to say.

"She said that she hoped so, that she doesn't want to raise the boys on her own and that they're clearly suffering. She still loves him but she knows that he never really loved her in the same way and that it was probably her own fault because she had always hoped that he might one day grow to love her, especially after the children arrived. Basically she wants to fight for her marriage even though she knows that it's going to be hard to trust him again, but that the boys have to come first."

"Oh no!"

Ben nodded his head.

"So she's going to take him back?"

"Well, that's the impression I got. And it sounded as though it was her decision – like Will will do whatever she tells him to do!"

My heart broke for this woman but it also broke for Nat because this wasn't good news for her.

"I felt so guilty watching her break down in front of me when all the time I've been complicit in her husband's affair."

"You didn't know though."

"It's such a mess – are you going to tell Nat?"

"I don't know what to do, Ben – she's my best friend but this will break her heart. I can't believe the bastard told her that he had left his wife for her!"

"What is he playing at?"

"Oh God, I really don't want to be the one to have to tell her, Ben. This is going to kill her . . ."

"I know, Kate, but you don't really have many options, do you?"

I stood up off the sofa, pulled my hands down over my face and exhaled loudly. "Shit!"

Chapter 16

I didn't sleep that night, worrying about telling Nat and how I was going to break it to her. I took my time walking down the sandstone pavement towards the gallery the next morning, trying to delay the inevitable. I saw her outside, chaining up her bike.

"Morning!" she sang brightly as I got closer to her.

"Hi, there."

We went inside and busied ourselves with our usual morning routine. My stomach flipped every time I thought about the conversation that I needed to have with her. After several false attempts, eventually I took a deep breath and came out with it.

"What school do Will's children go to?" I tried to sound casual but even I could hear the nervousness in my own voice.

"Oh God, Kate . . . I'm not sure of the name of it . . . what do you want to know that for?" She used her baby finger to pull a strand of hair away from in front of her eye.

"Well, what are his kids' names?"

"Why do you want to know, Kate?"

"I think one of them might be in Ben's class."

"Oh! Well, Elliott is the only one in school – the other two are in nursery."

"Sit down, Nat."

"Why – Kate, you're freaking me out -"

"Will didn't leave his wife – she threw him out."

"What are you saying?"

"Ben is Elliott's teacher. He had a meeting with his mum yesterday, Will's wife – Thea – is that her name?"

"Yes, but –"

"He was concerned because Elliott was falling behind and he knew something was up so he called Thea in to meet him and she broke down in front of him and told him that she had thrown her husband out recently because she discovered he had been having an affair."

Nat looked as though I had kicked her full force in the stomach. Her face blanched. "But how do you know she wasn't lying?"

"Why would she lie to Ben – what reason would she have? She didn't know that he knew you and Will!"

"Will wouldn't lie to me."

"Well, someone is telling lies here . . . look, there's more."

"What?"

"Well, she said she's going to take him back – she sees the children are suffering and she wants to try and save her marriage for their sakes."

"Well, then, why was he still in my place this morning, Kate? You've got this all wrong!" She looked at me despairingly like she was rapidly losing patience with our friendship.

"Well, it only happened yesterday so perhaps they haven't spoken about it yet."

"Kate, how can you be so vindictive? You don't even know for sure."

"But, c'mon, Nat, you have to admit it's a bit too much of a coincidence!"

"I know you never approved of Will but this is a step too far even for you, Kate! Will wouldn't do that."

"But why would his wife lie to Ben?"

"Well, I'll call him now then, shall I?" Angrily she lifted the phone and punched out Will's number.

I looked away while she waited on him to pick up.

Eventually she left a voice message. "Hi, it's me – look, can you call me when you get a second, please?"

We didn't say much after that. I went upstairs and took Sam's photos off the wall – we were moving him into the window downstairs as we were getting such a good reaction to him.

We didn't really speak for the rest of the day. The tension was heavy in the air between us. I knew she was pissed off and I was starting to doubt myself. What if Ben and I had got this all wrong? Nat might never forgive me for it. I hoped I hadn't just thrown away our friendship.

I saw her pick up the phone later. I presumed she was trying him again. I could see that she looked uneasy.

"Look, Nat, do you want me to go home with you – y'know, just in case?" I said when we were finishing up to go home.

"Oh I don't think so, Kate!" she said, grabbing her bag off the desk.

I picked mine up too and put it over my shoulder. We locked up wordlessly and Nat unchained her bike and cycled off without even a goodbye.

Nat

2012

Chapter 17

I pounded the pedals on my bike the whole way home. All I could think of was fucking Kate and her stupid theories. Why couldn't she just be happy for me for once? She always had to stick her nose in. And why the fuck was Will not picking up? We were supposed to be going out tonight but I hadn't heard from him all day.

I breathed the city air deep into my lungs and powered on. I stopped at a red light, before taking off again when it changed. I went to go straight but the car beside me was turning left and he had to jam on. I stopped the bike just in time. He sat on his horn. Instantly I felt my temper rise.

"Watch where you're going!" I roared at him. I could see him shouting back at me through the glass. I gave him the finger and got back up on my bike.

I reached my flat and opened the door. Will's car was already outside. Well, thank goodness for that, I thought. I wheeled my bike into the hall and climbed the stairs.

When I opened the door and saw the suitcases, the same ones that he had used to move in just three weeks earlier, I knew. The expression on his face said the rest.

"What's going on, Will?"

"I'm sorry, Nat – I'm so, so sorry." There were tears in his eyes. "I have to go home."

"No – Will – no – please don't do this!" I begged.

"She wants me back – I have to go."

"But why?"

"I have to – she rang me today to talk. The kids have taken the break-up badly and she wants me to come home."

"But you left her for me – you can't just change your mind three weeks later!"

"I didn't."

"Didn't what?"

"I didn't leave her . . ." He let out a heavy sigh. "She threw me out."

So Kate was right. "But, but . . . you said, you said that you left her?"

"No, I didn't, Nat, I never said that I'd left her."

"But . . ." None of this was making any sense to me.

"She overheard us talking on the night you rang to finish with me. She confronted me then. After talking to you I was a broken man and I didn't bother trying to deny it. So I came clean. I told her everything and she threw me out. And then when I turned up here with my suitcases, well . . . you just assumed that I had left her and I didn't have the heart to tell you . . . I'm sorry, Nat, I should have been upfront with you."

"So you came running to me then – oh, good old Nat will take me in, was that it?"

He shook his head and came over and put his arms around me. I pushed him away.

"No – it wasn't like that. I wanted to be with you."

"*Wanted?*"

"Want – I still want to be with you. The last three weeks, waking up beside you every morning, have been the best of my life – but I have to go."

"So that's all I was then? A roof over your head – a stopgap while your wife made her mind up about what the future held for her marriage?"

"No, Nat – that's not it at all. That was never it. I love you, you know I do."

"But you lied – you let me think that you had left her to be with me!"

"Because I knew you'd think I didn't choose to be with you otherwise."

"*Well, you didn't!*" I was screaming now. I could hear my own voice shrill with emotion and it didn't sound like me at all.

"But it's you that I want to be with – you know that if things were different –"

"I never asked you to leave your wife! I was happy with the way things were. You didn't have to lie to me, Will!"

"I know, Nat – if you only knew how shit I feel right now."

"I had accepted that you would never leave your kids, so then, when you landed on my doorstep telling me that your marriage was over, I thought it was a dream come true – something I had never dared hope might happen! You've sent me up to the top of the world so I felt I was flying above the clouds and then brought me back down again, without the parachute!"

He said nothing.

"I just can't believe you would do that to me. I thought what we had was special," I said in disbelief.

"It was – is. Look, you have to believe me: if I had my time again, I would be with you and only you."

"There you go again, why do you keep saying that? Look, it's not too late, Will. You don't have to go. Just stay here – with me. I know it will be tough for a while but you'll ride it out – you're strong." I walked over and brushed his cheek with my finger. There was a faint trace of stubble. I ran my finger over the scar in his eyebrow from when he fell against the kitchen table as a child. I knew every inch of his face – what his face felt like under my fingertips. What he tasted like. How he breathed. Everything.

"But can't you see? It's just not that straightforward. We have three children together and she doesn't want them to grow up in a broken home. Elliott's teacher called her in for a meeting yesterday because he's falling behind. It's affecting them."

"I know."

"How do you know?"

"Ben, Kate's husband, is Elliott's teacher."

"Ben is Mr Chamberlain?" he asked incredulously.

I nodded.

"But when did you find this out?"

"Only today," I sighed. "Ben was telling Kate about his meeting with a pupil's mum yesterday and they put two and two together and realised that the pupil's mum was also your wife."

"I see." He ran his hands down over his face. "Fucking hell, what are the chances of that in a city of over eight million people!"

"Please don't go, Will."

"She calls the shots. It could never be any other way – it's not my decision!"

"Of course it's your decision."

"I have to go, Nat – whatever she wants I have to do it."

"No, you don't, Will. No, you don't! You're a grown man so why can't you stand up to her?"

"She has me over a barrel – she hasn't told her father about what happened yet but, if she does, I can guarantee that he'll squeeze me out of the firm."

"But even if you go back to her, she still could tell her dad and what's to say he won't push you out then?"

"He wouldn't do that, because it would injure her and the children. In any case, she won't tell him – I know her – she's too proud. And everything – our whole lives – is built around my job. If I go home we'll go back to our charade of happy families and no one will ever know about this."

"So that's what it all comes down to – the prestige of your job means more than what you have with me – is that it?" I spat at him.

"It's not that simple, Nat – you know that. It's not just the job – we have three children together too."

"But you can't, Will, you can't do this to me!" I was trying hard to digest what he was telling me. I started to cry then. I think it was starting to hit me. "Why did you marry her?" Tears of frustration and desperation spilled down my face because things were spinning so far out of my control. This was not in my hands.

"You know why. I had no choice."

"Yes, you had – we all have choices in life but you wanted the glory of being at the top."

"Yeah, you're right, I did."

"But you don't have to keep on living by one wrong choice."

"Yes, I do," he said wearily. "My whole life is built around Thea – she's my wife, the mother of my children, the daughter of my boss, the friend of my friends' wives."

"But money isn't everything. You would walk into another job tomorrow. Surely love means more than a job?" I knew I was pleading, begging even.

"It's not just a job, Nat – I have worked hard my entire life to prove myself and to get to where I am today – I have three children who I can afford to put through the best public schools and top universities, who can go on skiing holidays to Klosters in the winter, Sandy Lane in Barbados in the summer and to the south of France at half-term. They do after-school activities that I have never even heard of. They will grow up and marry people like them, who grew up with the same privileges that they had. I can give them all of that. They can have everything that I never had growing up. Love can't put food on the table or provide the upbringing for my family that I never had, but money can."

His words pierced through me. I slapped him across the face then. It just happened – I didn't know I was going to do it. We both recoiled from the shock. I had never hit anybody in my life before.

"I suppose I probably deserve that," he said as he put a hand up gingerly to touch his face.

The palm of my hand stung as the blood rushed to the surface of my skin from the force of the slap, so it must have hurt him.

"So that's it then, it all comes down to money," I said, my voice bitter.

"Please, Nat, I don't want things to end like this."

He reached for my hand. I could feel the roughness of his skin as I pulled away from his touch.

"I think you should leave now," I said coolly.

I held open the door for him. He walked out the door with his cases. He stood there and looked at me.

"I'm sorry." And then he turned and walked down the stairs.

I knew this would be how it ended – deep down I had always known it.

After he had gone, I closed the door and dissolved into a heap on the floor. I raged and I threw things around my living room. Bell X1's 'Eve' was playing on the radio in the background. I had never listened to the words properly before but they seemed so apt now. Then I had to run to the bathroom to be sick. I sat on the cool white tiles of my bathroom floor, with my back resting against the shower door. I cried breathless tears that just kept on coming.

I don't know how long I stayed like that because when I woke up I was still slumped on the floor and it was bright outside. My neck was stiff and sore from the angle that my head had been hanging at. I stood up, using the shower to lever me, and walked over to the sink and splashed water on my face. I stood staring at myself in the mirror, water dripping off my face. I looked terrible. My mascara had run down my cheeks leaving kohl trails, like something painted by a child on a white page with watery paints. My whole body literally ached for him. I had given him my heart and he had trampled on it.

On autopilot, I took off my clothes and got into the shower. I just stood there, letting the water drain down around me, unable to squirt shower gel onto my loofah or raise my arms to shampoo my hair. This was what happened when you opened yourself up to someone, I thought – you paid the price.

Chapter 18

I honestly never set out to have an affair. In fact, I would even go so far as to say that I always thought that women who had affairs with married men were somehow weak and needy and even a bit dysfunctional. But I now know that we don't choose who we fall in love with. My usual types were musicians, artists, that sort. The scraggly hair, unkempt clothing, that whole skinny-tortured-artist look did it for me. They were usually distant sorts and usually had their problems. But Will was the very opposite of all of that. He was loving and attentive – when I was with him no one else mattered. He wore suits tailored in Savile Row, white-collared dress shirts with cufflinks, silk ties and shiny Oxford shoes – in fact, he was the furthest removed thing from a tortured artist. He was a partner in a leading City investment bank. But he did have something in common with those other men, a roughness around the edges. He had a ruddiness in his cheeks and lines in his face that no amount of money could eradicate.

He grew up on a council estate in Slough – his dad was a plumber and his mum a cleaner. He went to the local co-ed school. He got the job in the bank through a stroke of luck. He had been selling cars as a seventeen-year-old when a banker came in to buy a car from him. The man had been so impressed by Will's bolshiness that he had offered him a job as a junior trader. Will moved to London and had started on the floor alongside people with college degrees, but he had quickly learned the ropes. His aggressive nature stood to him and he wasn't afraid to put in the hours. He was promoted to senior trader soon after, then to floor manager, and he continued to work his way up until he was made partner. It was where he had met his wife Thea. She was the daughter of the company's founder and head of the board but he hadn't known this when they first met. He told me that it was clear that she liked him from early on, so he had asked her out. They had started seeing each other casually for a while but it was obvious that she wanted more from their relationship whereas he wasn't looking for anything serious. It was at the same time that Will had made up his mind to finish with her that she had dropped the bombshell of who her father was. He hadn't had the balls to end it then. Will knew already that he didn't quite fit in with the usual fuddy-duddy Eton-educated types that populated the top ranks of the company and he was afraid that if he crossed her, he could kiss goodbye to any chance he had of gaining access to the higher echelons that he so desperately craved. So their relationship had coasted along and he tried his best to make it work. He had wooed her with romantic gestures like punting along the River Cam and lunchtime picnics on the Heath. He had even surprised her with a once-in-a-lifetime holiday to the Galapagos Islands. Weekends were spent visiting her friends or licking arse on the golf course with her parents. He had asked her father for her hand in marriage soon after and then he had proposed. He told me that their wedding had been a lavish affair – there were more people from the firm there than from his own family but it suited him that way. Their honeymoon had cost more per night than most people in London spent on rent in an entire month. Two weeks after they came back from honeymoon, Thea had found out she was pregnant and then her father had finally made him a partner. That was the way it was.

We met when his firm had hired the gallery for a party to thank their clients. We did it the odd time, rented the gallery out as a venue – usually it was to friends of Tabitha's or to some of our regular customers that enquired about using it. It provided some further income and also we sometimes sold photos during private events, so it was good for marketing as well. I was liaising with Will's personal assistant to organise the details like the catering and the wine. I had been left open-mouthed at the wine bill – each bottle cost upwards of two hundred pounds but it seemed as though money was no obstacle for this company. After the guests had gone home, Will had come down to thank us. I had been struck by his tall broad stature and the twinkle in his eyes. I guessed that he was close to fortyish. He had a little paunch around the waist but other than that he was in good shape. He had given Kate and me a leftover case of wine to share – we had debated as to whether or not to sell it on eBay but then Kate had said, "Fuck it – when are we ever going to get the chance to try wine like this again!" and we uncorked a bottle, then another and another.

He had called me personally the next day to thank me for my help. The party was very successful and their clients had been impressed. He used the gallery a few more times after that for other events and I came to know him. Then, by chance, I met him in a wine bar one night and we got chatting and ended up spending the whole night together just talking. Properly talking. I had never felt so at ease with anyone before.

He told me from the start that he was married – he never hid it from me – but the chemistry between us was obvious and we both knew it was the start of something special. There was an intensity between us that I had never experienced before. We could spend hours just staring at each other, with neither one of us needing to speak. It soon became a regular thing and, yes, the sex was great – some of the best I had ever had – but there were also tender moments when I would lie against his bare chest with its sparse hairs that shot up randomly and we would just talk until the sun came up. It wasn't the money or the glamorous lifestyle that attracted me – I can honestly say that none of that mattered to me.

The only way I could describe the aftermath of Will leaving was that I existed day to day. I went to work, I came home. I could still smell his aftershave on the sheets – it took me ages to finally give in and wash them. I went out with friends or over to Kate and Ben's place to hang out. Kate had tried talking to me about it but it just hurt too much and I would change the subject. Anyway she had enough going on with being pregnant and everything. And, if I'm honest, I wasn't sure that she really got it. I think Kate thinks that I have commitment issues. She always says that I choose men that are wrong for me. I reckon she thinks that I chose Will purposely because he was married but that's just silly. She sees it as quite black and white, that I was just another mistress being cast aside as soon as the wife found out and in many ways I was, but I knew I meant more to him than that. I could almost see Kate trying to leave her judgment-hat off and just listen to me but she really thought I'd been saved more heartache in the long run. I knew she and Ben felt sorry for Thea and I did too – I felt sorry for everyone involved in the whole sorry mess – there were no winners. Kate kept telling me that I would meet someone else but I wasn't looking for a replacement – I didn't want to be with just anyone. I wasn't sad because I was on my own, I was sad because I had lost him. She didn't see that. I just wanted Will, not anybody else, just him. You can't substitute one love for another.

I saw him two weeks later, just by chance, in a café. I was ordering a coffee to go and there he was sitting in the corner. I had to look twice. My heart had started racing and I could feel myself starting to sweat. He didn't see me though – he was too engrossed in writing a message on his Blackberry. I was glad because it allowed me to stare at him for a few moments. I longed with every part of me to go up to him and for him to take me in his arms and hold me against his chest so I could hear his heart and whatever other rumblings went on beneath his skin. I desperately wanted to touch his familiar face. He was so near – I reckon there were about five metres between us. I knew I could just walk over there and in a few strides he could be back in my life again. It was that close. My heart said it was fate and that I should take my chances and go over to him. I longed to be back in his life even if I could only just have a small part of it but, instead, I had taken my coffee and left the shop quickly. I forgot to get my sugar.

If anyone had asked me if I would do it all again, knowing the way it was going to end, then I would have said 'Yes, in a heartbeat'. The few months that he was in my life were worth the pain, rather than saving myself the heartache and never having met him at all. He had changed me. He was the first man I had ever truly opened myself up to. I now knew what true love really was and for that I was thankful.

Kate

2012

Chapter 19

Nat didn't show for work the day after I told her about Will so I knew something had happened. I tried ringing her but she didn't answer. I decided to write a 'closed for lunch' sign by hand and stick it inside the door and make my way over to her place. When I arrived I pressed the buzzer but there was no answer so I pressed it again. When there was still no answer I took out my phone and rang her. I looked to the upstairs window and there was a light on so I sat on the buzzer again.

"Look, Nat, I know you're home – just let me in."

Soon after I heard the latch release and I pushed the door and went upstairs.

She looked frightful. She didn't need to say anything. I knew that he was gone. I went over and threw my arms around her and she sobbed into my shoulder.

It broke my heart to see Nat so upset over the next few weeks. I was trying really hard to be understanding and to be there for her but I never seemed to be able to do or say the right thing. I would invite her over to ours for something to eat and she and Ben would share a bottle of wine while I stuck with my sparkling water – with a slice of lime if I was feeling really wild. But it was like Nat had changed as a person on the day that he had left her. It was just a slight change and, if you didn't know her too well, you wouldn't notice it, but there was a change in her nonetheless. She didn't have that same enthusiasm and energy for things any more. It was like she was just going through the motions of life. I knew she found it hard to open up to me about it all. I would ask her how she was doing and she would brush me off, saying she was fine, or she would try to change the subject. But something had shifted between us when she had broken up with Will. It was unsaid of course but we both knew it was there all the same. I think it was partly because Ben had actually met Thea. There was just a little bit of awkwardness between them although neither would admit it. I knew Ben was very sympathetic towards Thea and of course my sympathies were with Nat, but I also felt awful for poor Thea. Ben had said there had been a dramatic improvement in Elliott in the days following his meeting with Thea and he could only assume it was because his dad had come home again.

Nat had met Gill, the woman who was seeing a friend of Will's, for lunch. She heard that he was trying really, really hard to make a go of his marriage but that he had been devastated when his relationship with Nat ended. I was glad to hear that he was making a go of it though, at least for his kids' sake. If anything good was to come out of it, it was that.

A few days later I came in from work and I sat down to dinner with Ben. He had made a lamb tagine for us, which I practically inhaled I was so hungry. My appetite had come back full swing over the last couple of weeks and I was making up for all the food that I hadn't eaten at the start.

We started cleaning up after dinner. Ben was cleaning down the worktops while I did the dishes and let them air-dry even though I knew it was a pet peeve of Ben's. I sat down again at the little table which we had bought in IKEA because its sides could be folded down. We thought we'd do it after dinner every evening to give us some space but after the first few days we got lazy and never bothered doing it any more.

"I have something for you." He turned away from the cooker where he was busy scrubbing off a tomato stain. He took two pieces of paper off the worktop in the kitchen and handed them to me.

"What's this?" I asked, unfolding them.

"Tickets."

"For where?"

"Dublin."

I looked up at him.

"How dare you!" I said angrily.

"Look, Kate, if I don't make you go, you never will."

"When are they for?"

"This weekend."

"This weekend! But I probably won't be able to fly."

"I've already checked – the airline will let you fly up to thirty-five weeks and you'll be just gone thirty-one – but you will need to get a cert from your doctor. It's only short-haul anyway."

Typically Ben was Mr Organised. I checked the tickets. We were flying out on a Friday morning and returning on a Sunday. Two whole days.

"Well, I might not be able to get the time off work." I knew it was lame.

"Come on, Kate – since when have you ever had a problem getting time off? And it's only the Friday that you need! You know Nat will cover for you for one day, like you do for her when she goes away."

"You shouldn't have done this. You think a trip home will fix everything – well, it won't!" Even just thinking about it made my stomach lurch. My heart was beating wildly in my chest. "You can't interfere in my life."

"Kate, it isn't just your life now – we're having a baby together, remember?" He looked hurt.

"Yeah, well, I don't know why you're so obsessed with raking over the past!"

"Go on – ring your dad now and tell him you're coming home."

"I can't now!" I spluttered. "It's too late, it's nearly nine o'clock – he'll think there's something wrong if I ring at this hour of the night!"

"Well, then, ring him first thing in the morning, okay?"

"Okay."

"Promise?"

"I promise."

Chapter 20

The next day in work I was trying to concentrate on the words on the screen in front of me but I was finding it difficult. My mind kept wandering. The thought of ringing Dad and then what I was going to say to him kept interrupting my concentration. It was one of those things where it was actually embarrassing how long I had put off ringing him and now it was very hard to pick up the phone.

At lunchtime Nat went to the deli up the street to get our usual order of sandwiches. While she was gone and I had the gallery to myself, I took a deep breath and dialled Dad's number. It rang and rang and I was secretly relieved at the reprieve when he didn't answer. I was just about to hang up when I heard his voice on the other end.

"Hello – 065873."

He still insisted on repeating the old number back whenever he answered the phone. That was the number when we were kids – there was a six in front of it nowadays. His voice sounded croakier than the last time. Older.

"Hi, Dad – it's me."

"Kate? Is that you, Kate?"

I knew he was happy to hear from me and then the guilt wound itself ever tighter.

"How are you, Dad?"

"Well, I'm grand now, Kate – all the better for hearing from you. How are you getting on over there?"

"Great, thanks, Dad."

"And how's Ben keeping?"

"He's good. How are Patrick and Seán?"

"Ah sure, not a bother on the pair of them! Patrick is kept going on the farm and Seán is working all hours in Acton's. He always was good at the sums, that fella."

Acton's was an accountancy practice in the town. It was a third-generation family business and was now run by George Acton, the original founder's grandson.

"Well, I hope they're paying him well." The Acton family was always known around the town for being tight with their money.

Dad laughed. "And Aoife is good too . . ."

"Oh right . . . yeah."

There was an awkward pause.

"Look, Dad, the reason I was ringing is because, well . . . Ben and I are going to come home on a visit – this Friday actually."

"Well, that's great news, Kate – I'm looking forward to finally meeting him."

"We have some news for you as well."

"Oh yeah?"

"I'll tell you when we get there – no point doing it over the phone."

"Well, I can pick you up in the airport."

"There's no need, Dad – we can get the bus or hire a car."

"I haven't seen you in so long, Kate – there's no way I'm letting you get the bus."

After I had given him our flight details we said our goodbyes and hung up. Nat came back then and handed me my sandwich. But, even though I had been dying for mine, I found I couldn't stomach it.

"What's wrong, darling? Did I get the wrong sandwich?" Nat said, noticing my expression. "I asked for the usual – I'll go mad if they've made a mess of it!" She took the sandwich back off me quickly and took it apart to check that it contained the ham, cheese and tomato that she had ordered.

"It's nothing – it's just my stupid hormones, is all." I felt tears prick my eyes and wiped them quickly with the backs of my hands.

"Well, bloody hell, that's some mood-swing! When I left you five minutes ago you were fine!"

"I just rang my dad."

"Ah, I see. And?"

"Well, Ben bought tickets for us both to fly home on Friday. I rang Dad to tell him."

"I'd say he'll be delighted to see you," she said gently.

"Yeah, he sounded happy all right. And he's really looking forward to meeting Ben." My stomach knotted just thinking about it.

The bell tinkled just then as a rain-soaked tourist came into the gallery.

"Look, you'll be fine." Nat took my hand and clasped it in between her own. "You'll have to face up to it eventually, especially now that you've a baby on the way. You're doing the right thing, Kate."

"I hope you're right," I sighed wearily. I wrapped the sandwich back up in the greaseproof paper and put it in the fridge. Maybe I would want it later.

Chapter 21

It was the night before our trip home and Mr Organised was taking down his suitcase and folding clothes neatly before putting them into it. I had spent the last few days in an anxious mess because of the impending trip. I was snappy with him because he had put me into this situation.

"I'm really looking forward to meeting your family," he said.

"Look, Ben, just don't get too excited, okay?" I found myself saying this a lot lately. He was like a child waiting on Santa and I was trying to rein in his enthusiasm.

At my hospital appointment the day before we were just going out the door when Ben stopped dead in the hallway. Two midwives who were walking down the corridor towards us had to separate and walk around him.

"We forgot the letter," he had said. "You might not get on the flight without it."

"It'll be fine, come on," I said, grabbing his arm to go.

"No, Kate, I'm not taking any chances."

"Right," I sighed and went back in and requested the 'fit to fly' letter from the doctor.

I was absolutely dreading the trip. I had palpitations just thinking about it all. I had tried explaining it to Ben but he just didn't get it. He was going around with his big cheery head on him, thinking that I would go home and play happy families with them all and everything would be forgotten about. Well, he was very wrong.

"What do you think I should pack?" he asked me.

"Rain gear."

"What?"

"It always rains at home."

"Don't you think you're exaggerating ever so slightly?"

"Well, when you're getting pissed on don't blame me."

"Okay but, besides rain gear, do you reckon I'll need to pack a shirt and some proper trousers? Will we be going out over there, do you think?"

I nearly choked with laughter except this situation wasn't funny.

"I'll take that as a no then, will I?" he said impatiently as he hung the shirt he had taken off the hanger back up in the wardrobe. "Aren't you going to pack, Kate? We've an early start in the morning and we don't want to miss our flight."

"Heaven forbid," I muttered under my breath. "Sure all I have to do is just grab my raincoat on the way out the door."

"Seriously, Kate, I'm not going to be late tomorrow – so if you're not packed then, tough – you'll be wearing my clothes all weekend."

"All right," I said sulkily, swinging my legs over the side of the bed.

I opened my drawers and took out a few things. I stuffed them into my hold-all before zipping it shut, all while Ben was busy neatly rolling a pair of boxer shorts together and stuffing them inside a shoe.

"There, happy now?" I said.

On the train to the airport the next morning my heart was beating in my chest and the palms of my hands were sweaty just thinking about what lay ahead. Ben seemed oblivious to how I was feeling and chatted away to me even though I wasn't talking back. He actually seemed to be excited. Well, he was going to be seriously disappointed. Here we go, I thought. I took a deep breath and climbed the steep stairs and walked across the tarmac until we were inside the terminal.

"Can you see our check-in desk?" I asked impatiently.

My case rattled as the wheels bumped over the gaps in the tiles as I pulled it along the concourse.

Ben checked the ticket and then looked up at the board. "It's desk number seventeen."

We walked over and got in the queue.

"I'm really looking forward to meeting them all," he said for what felt like the zillionth time since he had bought the tickets.

I gritted my teeth. After we had checked in, Ben bought a paper in WHS and I tried reading the magazine that came inside it but I couldn't concentrate on it. I would start reading the first paragraph and then realise that my mind had wandered and I would have to reread it. Finally our flight was ready for boarding and I stood up and got into the queue.

We boarded and of course ours were the seats at the very back of the plane so we had to wait while every other person put their case up in the overhead bins and then realised they'd forgotten their sucky sweets or something equally useless and had to go back out into the aisle and reach up to take their bag down again. Why they couldn't just stand in until everyone else had boarded and then go out into the aisle to take down their bags was beyond me.

When we finally took our seats I buried my head in my book but it didn't stop Ben from chatting away incessantly throughout the whole flight. A rosy-cheeked baby in the seat in front of me was playing peek-a-boo with me. She would throw her toy over the seat and I would pick it up and give it to her and she would do it over and over again, never getting fed up of the repetition until it was time for the parents to put her seatbelt on. I couldn't believe that in less than three months' time Baby Pip would be here with us, all going well. I thought about Pip and tried to imagine us with a baby doing the same thing but I couldn't no matter how much I tried. The turbulence, due to high winds, did nothing for my mood.

"See, I told you this was a bad idea," I said, turning to Ben as the plane lurched once again.

"It's only a bit of turbulence, Kate."

It wasn't long before I could see Dublin Bay in the distance. I looked down through the small window as we swooped in over it. A patchwork of velvety green fields was knitted together with seams of dark-green evergreen trees. The wispy clouds were perfectly suspended as if hanging from invisible strings between us and the ground below. The stewardess went along picking up any rubbish and checking to make sure seat belts were closed and tray tables were up.

"This is amazing." Ben peered out the window over my shoulder. "Where is that?"

"Howth Head." It looked lusciously green from up above. I had forgotten what a magnificent sight it was.

"I can't believe I never made you bring me back here before now." There he was again, all excited, like we were on a mini-break ready to explore a new country, not a country that held nothing but bad memories for me. The plane descended. The landing gear dropped down and soon after we came to a juddering halt on the runway.

"*Tá fáilte libh go léir go dtí mBaile Átha Cliath . . .*" The familiar Aer Lingus greeting welcomed us to Dublin.

In the terminal we headed for passport control. It felt so strange to my ear now, hearing the soft Irish lilt all around me. We had brought our cases as carry-on luggage so we didn't need to go near the cattle mart that was baggage reclaim.

As we walked out through the doors that would lead us into the arrivals hall my stomach somersaulted. If I had been nervous before, it was nothing compared to how I was feeling now. All I saw were a sea of faces as I tried to find Dad's. I had looked from left to right and back again when finally I saw him step forward.

"Kate, Kate, over here!"

"Dad!" I said, forcing myself to sound happy.

Caroline Finnerty

He looked smaller now than I had remembered and his hair, instead of being salt-and-pepper-coloured, was now entirely grey. He was wearing glasses now too – he didn't have them the last time. He was still dressed the same as always – a beige anorak covered a pullover with a shirt underneath and brown slacks.

"Kate – how are you, my love?" He wrapped me into a big hug before pulling back and holding me in his arms, taking me in.

I could smell the farm off him. Even when I had lived there it was hard to ever really get the smell off your skin. I felt self-conscious and wriggled a little so he dropped his arms. I felt bad then.

"Dad – this is Ben. Ben – this is my dad."

"Pleased to meet you." Ben pumped Dad's hand enthusiastically.

"Kate, are you . . . expecting?" Dad asked.

"Yep."

"Well, I'm shocked! Congratulations! So this was the news you wanted to tell me! Isn't that fantastic? When are you due?"

"September."

"Lovely time of year for a baby to be born – it won't be too hot or too cold."

"We're very excited," Ben said, taking hold of my hand, but I pulled it away from him.

"Right then, let's go," I said.

"Oh yes, this way – follow me," Dad said.

Outside, we walked along, ducking our heads in the rain.

"I'm sorry for the weather – it's desperate," Dad said. "We had a few days of sun in May and it's been raining since.

"Well, shame on you for not having the sun out for us."

But he didn't get my sarcasm and I just sounded mean and bitchy.

I let Ben sit in the front of Dad's Nissan Micra because of his height. I took the back seat and we set off for Mayo.

"So Kate tells me you're a teacher, Ben?"

130

"I am indeed."

"Great job, teaching! Sure with the paid holidays and a pension you couldn't go wrong."

Our parents were poles apart. I think Dad was more impressed by the fact that Ben was a teacher than if he had been the CEO of a Fortune 500 company. In my dad's eyes, nothing compared to the security of having a state-protected job. I suppose he had seen Ireland in far worse times than I had, but they were back again by all accounts – you only had to lift a newspaper or watch the news to hear tales of Ireland's woes.

"Are your parents teachers too, Ben?"

"No, my parents are both barristers actually. Well, Mum was – until myself and my sister arrived on the scene."

"Barristers no less – well, isn't that something? It's always good to have a few legal eagles in the family, eh, Kate?"

"It sure is."

I couldn't believe there was a motorway practically the whole way home. The last time I was home there was a bit of motorway then the road would go into a single carriageway before coming back to a dual carriageway again. It would chop and change depending on which County Council had had the funds to upgrade their road network. But now it all had been completely transformed. The motorways were all joined together and, instead of getting caught in Friday-afternoon traffic in villages along the way, we cut the journey time in half almost.

As we drove into Ballyrobin village I couldn't believe how much the place had changed since I was last home. Huge warehouses greeted us on the approach road as well as a red-blue-and-white-box Tesco. There were sprawling new housing estates everywhere.

"Wasn't that where the paint factory used to be?" I asked, pointing out the window to what was now a half-finished housing estate. The walls were up but there were no roofs and the gate was padlocked. There were huge puddles all along the roadway. It was a depressing sight.

"It was but McCarthy sold out to a developer at the height of all the madness and six months later the whole thing crashed. It's a ghost estate now – the place is littered with them! This country is gone to the dogs, I tell you – we'll all have to get off the sinking ship. The last man out may turn out the lights!"

I had seen this kind of thing on the news whenever there was a piece about Ireland but seeing it in reality in the village where I grew up really brought it home to me.

I wasn't sure if Ballyrobin could be even called a village any more. It was no longer the same sleepy place that I had known as a child. Finally we turned onto the familiar road where I grew up. All the bungalows on this road were the same, our own house included – the front door was on the left-hand side and there were three windows to the right of it. I think their design came from a book of plans that did the rounds in the seventies. When Seán was born Dad had built on a flat-roof extension at the back of the house. That was the only thing that distinguished our house from our neighbours.

As we turned into my childhood home, I almost felt sick. Unlike the rest of the place, here it was like time had stood still. Nothing had changed. We drove past the small lawn to the front where there used to be flowerbeds full of pansies and dahlias in the summertime but I didn't think they flowered any more.

"There you are now," Dad said as he turned off the engine, the wipers coming to an abrupt stop.

We followed him in the back door and into the kitchen.

"Sit down there at the table and I'll put the kettle on. I'm sure you're parched after the journey."

He made a pot of tea and put it on the table with three mugs. Coffee wasn't an option so I had warned Ben not to bother asking. Dad laid down a plate of buttered brown bread in front of us.

"It's lovely to finally see where Kate comes from," Ben said as if I wasn't in the room.

"Well, it's great to have you here – we don't get to see her often enough – but I know you're busy over there, love. Patrick and his gang will be over soon and Seán will be down to see you this evening. You haven't met little Daniel and Mia."

He was referring to my niece and nephew, Patrick's children. I felt an acute wave of guilt wash over me.

"Yeah, I'm really looking forward to that. What age are they again?"

I could see Ben looking at me in disbelief.

"Well, Daniel was six last month and Mia is three."

"Wow, time flies." I could feel myself reddening under Ben's glare.

All the same ornaments and figurines were on display in the glass cabinet. There was a china doll, with pale skin, rosy cheeks and a lacy petticoat, that I had been mad about as a girl. I used to beg to be allowed to play with it.

After we had finished our tea I got up from the table. "We should bring our bags down to the room." As we walked down the hall to the bedroom, I noticed the navy carpet with its green flecks had been replaced by laminate wood flooring. I glanced briefly at the old family photos that still hung on the wall. I remembered when one large family photo had been taken. We had all been marched to a photography studio in Ballyrobin, dressed up in our Sunday best. Our clothes and hairstyles looked so old-fashioned now. With my blonde pudding-bowl-style haircut I could easily have passed for a boy except for the corduroy dress with the embroidered trim that I was wearing. Ben had a right laugh when he saw it.

"So you're a natural blonde then!"

It was the first time he had ever seen a childhood photo of me.

"I told you I was."

"But I can't understand why you need to fork out a hundred quid every few weeks getting highlights then?"

"And that's because you're a man."

"What do you mean?"

"You wouldn't understand."

I held my breath as I pushed back the bedroom door. The same cream floral wallpaper was still on the walls. It was all a bit dusty and the air was musty even though Dad had opened the window to air the room before we came. All my old books with yellowed pages – from Enid Blyton to Judy Blume and right up to Stephen King – were still on the shelves. My rosettes from my horse-riding days still hung on the wall. But the bed was a double one instead of my old single.

A poster of Jared Leto hung down by one corner.

"What is it about that guy? My sister Laura was mad about him as well." Ben picked up the corner and tried resticking it with the Blu-Tack that was the still on the wall but it just kept on folding back down on itself so he eventually gave up.

"I was obsessed with him as a teenager – I was convinced we would have been so suited if only I could have met him in real life."

"People say I look like him, y'know?"

"Yeah, Ben, about as much as I resemble Angelina Jolie."

"Harsh." He shook his head.

The rain hopped off the flat-roof extension where my bedroom was in staccato beats.

"I never knew you could play the violin?" He was pointing to my Grade Two exam certificate that hung on the wall.

"I can't. Well, not now anyway. I hated practising so I didn't keep it going."

He continued poking and examining stuff as he went around the room.

"Here, what's this?" he said as he grabbed something off the bookshelves.

I recognised it straight away.

"Here, give it to me, Ben!"

"No way." He held it over my head and started flicking through the pages as I tried to reach up and take it back off him. This was where his height came in handy for him.

"Ben, give it to me *now*!"

And he knew by my tone that I meant it. He handed the diary to me.

I looked at the orange cover, practically covered with inky

blue doodles. I sat on the bed and opened it up. I read the date on top of the page: *2nd September 1994*. I did a quick mental calculation. I would have been fifteen. As I read through the entry it all came rushing back to me. Suddenly I felt like I was back there again in that exact moment, sitting under that mountain of hurt. I could remember exactly how I had felt when I had written it. I may have escaped it all in London but all it took was something small like this and I was right back there again. Tears brimmed in my eyes.

"I'm sorry, Kate – I thought it was just a silly teenage diary. If I had known I never would have picked it up like that."

"God, this is ridiculous – I can't believe the effect all this still has on me." I wiped my eyes with the backs of my hands.

He came up beside me and draped his arm across my shoulders. "Sorry, Kate, I didn't realise. C'mon, please don't cry, this isn't good for you or the baby."

"Well then, you should never have made me come back here."

Chapter 22

Later that evening Patrick and his wife Luisa called over. Luisa was Brazilian and had moved to Ireland to work in a local factory over ten years ago. She had met Patrick in a bar and the two of them had teamed up and got married. I hadn't seen them since their wedding day and that had been my first time to meet Luisa.

Patrick looked older now. Even though I was a little over a year older than him, he looked years older than me. He had flecks of grey in his hair near the temples. His skin was more lined too, from working the farm in all weather I supposed.

I went to give him a kiss on the cheek but he went for the other side and we awkwardly bumped heads.

"And Luisa – good to see you again!" I gave her a hug.

Her black curly hair was longer now and her figure was a bit curvier but I supposed kids do that to you. I would know soon enough.

I introduced them to Ben and everyone shook hands politely.

"And this must be Daniel and Mia!" I bent down to the children. They were beautiful exotic creatures – I'm sure their Brazilian darkness meant that they stood out from the usual pale-faced children around these parts.

"Say hi to your Auntie Kate."

But the children remained rooted to the spot. Daniel stared at me open-mouthed and Mia started to hide behind her mother's skirt, pulling it over her head as an embarrassed Luisa tried to yank it back down again.

"Hi, guys, I brought you presents."

I gave Daniel a Ben 10 watch, which seemed to do the trick – it was hard to know – but Mia didn't mask her true feelings when I gave her a *Dora the Explorer* torch.

"I no like Dora," she said, her huge brown eyes looking up at me.

"Don't be silly, Mia!" said Patrick. "Say thank you to your Auntie Kate."

I could see he was embarrassed.

"No!" she said defiantly.

"She's grand – don't worry about it," I said. "I probably should have asked you what she is into first before I bought anything."

There was a pause.

"Why don't you all sit down," Dad said.

"So I see you two are having a baby then?" Patrick said.

"We sure are." I placed my hands on my rapidly growing bump.

"When are you due?" Luisa asked me in an accent that now had a tinge of Mayo in it.

"September."

"Nice time of the year to have a baby."

"Yeah, not too hot or too cold," I said, repeating what Dad had said earlier on because it was all that I could think of to say. "How's the farm going, Patrick?"

"Grand – we'll be starting the harvesting next week if we get a dry spell at all." He paused. "How long are ye home for?"

"We're heading back Sunday morning – Ben has school on Monday."

"You're a teacher, aren't you, Ben?"

"Yes – I teach Year Two."

"I wouldn't know what that is."

"Oh sorry, of course – six-year-olds, like himself there." Ben gestured at Daniel.

"You talk funny!" Daniel piped up.

Ben started to laugh.

"Daniel!" Patrick chastised him. "You have a bit of the accent yourself, Kate."

"Do I?"

"Well, I suppose fifteen years will do that to you," Patrick said.

"Wow! Am I gone that long?" Even though I knew that I was.

He said nothing. He didn't need to. The words hung there in the air between us.

"Who's for tea?" Dad said, breaking the silence.

He placed the teapot down on the table with the mugs that he had looped through the fingers of his other hand.

He poured the tea and we all added our own milk and sugar.

Soon after, Seán stopped by on his way home from work.

"Hiya, Kate!" He stuck his smiling head around the back door.

"Seán!" I stood up and walked over to hug him. I was four years older than him but he was still my baby brother.

Was I imagining it or did I catch Patrick rolling his eyes?

"And this must be Ben?" He walked over and shook hands with him. "And what's the story with this?" He pointed to my bump.

"It's a baby – duh!"

He laughed. "Well, fair play to you! Congratulations."

"I hear you're working in Acton's?"

"Yeah, for my sins, but it's grand."

"Are they still as stingy as ever?"

"Worse. They're tighter than a camel's arse in a sandstorm, the miserable gits. Ah, sure it's handy for the time being – but I'll give myself a couple of more years and then see where I end up. Who knows, I might even head to London!"

"Well, you're very welcome any time, you know that."

"So what are yeer plans for the weekend?"

"I'm not sure really, to be honest."

"Well, I'm meeting a few of the lads in Doyle's later – will you and Ben join us?"

Doyle's was the main pub in the square in Ballyrobin. There were three pubs in the village – one was a tiny old-man pub and the other had a reputation as a rough spot, so Doyle's was the place where everyone went.

I was just about to make an excuse when Ben interrupted me, "That'd be great thanks, Seán."

I could feel butterflies in my tummy instantly – God only knew what old faces I would bump into there.

"How about you, Patrick – fancy a few drinks?" said Seán.

"I won't, Seán – I've an early start in the morning."

"Dad?"

"I might go for one so – it's not every day that Kate comes home to visit us."

After dinner, we got changed and walked down to the pub. I took a deep breath as Seán pushed open the door and we followed in behind him. We got a seat in the corner. Seán asked us what we wanted to drink and went up to the bar to order the round. I watched as he chatted easily with a man sitting up on a stool at the bar. He was such a friendly type of guy – everyone loved him. He had been like that as a child too.

"Pity Patrick couldn't join us," Dad said.

"Yeah," I said but really I was glad because I couldn't handle any more of his disapproving looks, laced with guilt trips. I picked up a beer-mat and started fiddling with it idly.

The pub started to fill up a while later. I recognised a few faces of people from around the village.

As the others drank their drinks I stuck with the sparkling water. Seán entertained us with stories about Mr Acton and we were actually having a bit of a laugh. I could tell that Ben was enjoying himself anyway.

Whatever way Baby Pip was lying, she seemed to be sitting on my bladder constantly these days. Seán laughed at me as I moved past him on the seat to go to the toilet again.

I had just come out of the cubicle and was washing my hands when the girl at the basin beside me looked across at me.

"Kate – Kate Flynn, is that you?"

I turned to look at her – she was vaguely familiar.

"Yeah, hi." I desperately tried to remember her name.

"Jane – Jane Dwyer. We were in school together."

"Oh yeah, it's great to see you again, Jane." I tried to pretend that I remembered her but I knew she wasn't fooled.

"I haven't seen you round these parts in a while?"

"No, I'm living in London now – I'm just home for the weekend."

"Very nice! What are you up to over there?"

"I'm working in a photography gallery. And you?"

"I'm in the bank – it's grand – close to home so it only takes me five minutes to get to work."

"That's handy."

Her clothes aged her – even though she was only my age she could easily have passed for a forty-year-old. I suppose Ballyrobin was hardly Fashion Central.

"And you've a baby on the way." She nodded at my bump as she turned to use the hand-towel. She jerked the roll down and dried her hands on it.

"Yeah."

"Your first?"

"Yeah. How about you, do you have any yourself?"

"I've three actually. Gary is four, Luke is three and Danielle one."

"Well, you've been busy."

"Tell me about it. So when are you due?"

"September."

"Nice time of year to have a baby –"

"Not too hot or too cold," I said impatiently.

"Yeah . . ."

I could see her looking at me, as if trying to figure me out. There was an awkward silence between us.

"Well, nice seeing you again, Kate and I hope all goes well in September." She turned quickly and walked out of the bathroom.

Chapter 23

"What's the story with the shower?" Ben shouted out from the bathroom the next morning.

"Oh, I should have remembered! I'll have to turn on the immersion for you. But it'll take some time."

Dad still hadn't progressed to an electric shower. I went and flicked the immersion switch.

Ben came back into the room. "Your family are great, Kate. I'm so glad to have finally met them."

I said nothing and continued typing the text message that I was sending to Nat to see how she was doing.

The water still wasn't very hot when Ben finally went to shower and he used up most of it – when it was my turn it changed from lukewarm to cold intermittently so I had to keep jumping back out and then I would stand under it again when it warmed up a bit. When I was finished I climbed back out over the bathtub – the shower head was rigged up over the bath – and wrapped myself in a towel which was rough from years of being washed with no fabric softener.

As I went back down the hall to the bedroom, I could smell the fry that Dad was cooking for breakfast. Ben was lying back on the bed with a towel wrapped around his waist, reading the newspaper he had brought over on the plane with him the day before.

"C'mon, Ben – get dressed. I'm going to show you a real breakfast." There was nothing like the sausages and black pudding from home. They were probably the only things that I actually did miss.

We got dressed and went along to the kitchen.

"Morning," I said to Dad.

"Good morning. Did ye sleep well? That bed is a bit springy."

"Well, I slept great," Ben said.

"Me too – apart from Ben snoring."

"Was I? Sorry, love."

"You're always the same after a few pints."

I devoured the breakfast that Dad put on the plate in front of me: rashers, sausages, egg, black and white pudding, and fried potatoes. When Dad saw me getting stuck into it he put a few more sausages into the pan for me.

I buttered a slice of soda bread generously, put a slice of pudding on top and ate it. "*Mmmh*."

"I got them in Reilly's specially for you."

Reilly's was the butcher in the village.

"These are great – I can see now why you always moan about the sausages in the UK!" Ben said, laughing.

When he was finished cooking, Dad sat down beside us at the table.

"What are you two at today then?" he asked.

"I don't know – we might take in the sights around Ballyrobin," I said, laughing.

"Well, I thought you might like to go and visit Granny and Aoife today?" Dad said seriously.

I groaned inwardly. I didn't dare to do it out loud. I had thought that I could avoid this one.

"Great idea," Ben said enthusiastically.

"Well, I –"

"What?" Ben cut across me.

"Well, I thought maybe we might head off for the day. Y'know – I could show you around the West?"

"You can't come home after eight years and not visit your grandmother, Kate!"

"Right, okay." I knew I was fighting a losing battle. "We'll go . . ."

After lunch, Dad drove us to Granny's house down the road. I was more nervous about this visit than anything else. Dad pushed back the tiny wrought-iron gate and we followed him around towards the back of the cottage. He stopped to pull up a few weeds that had grown up through the cracks on the path. He pushed open the door and I followed him into the kitchen.

Granny was dozing in her chair by the range. She had sat in that chair ever since I could remember. The smell of turf filled the air. I noticed the worn lino had small burn marks from where the sparks had jumped out on to the floor.

"Look who's come to see you, Josephine," Dad said softly.

"Hi, Gran."

"I didn't hear ye come in!" she said as she woke with a start.

"Sorry! We didn't mean to scare you," I said. I knew by her that she was embarrassed to be caught sleeping.

"How are ye?" she said, using her stick to lever herself up out of the chair. She didn't have a stick the last time I'd seen her.

I rushed over and held onto her elbow to help her up.

"It's great to see you, Granny." I gave her a big hug.

She held my face between both her palms and kissed me on the forehead. Once again the guilt caught up with me. The woman was nearly ninety. The soft mushy skin on her face smelt warm and comforting.

"And are you with child?"

"I am, Granny."

"Oh, that's great news. Great news altogether." If she was put out by Ben and me not being married she didn't show it. She fished around in the pocket of her dress, took out a relic of Padre Pio and started to bless my bump with it. "That'll keep you safe."

I turned to Ben. "Granny, this is Ben."

"You're welcome to Ballyrobin, Ben," she said, shaking his hand vigorously.

"Is Aoife not home from college yet?" Dad asked.

"She's on her way – she rang me before she left – she had an exam today, y'know, Kate. God love her, that course of hers is very hard."

"She's well able for it, Josephine," Dad said.

"Oh, don't I know it, but my fingers are nearly down to the bone from saying the rosary for her. She wasn't nervous at all going off this morning – I was worse." She started to laugh.

The back door opened then and a tall girl dressed casually in a hoody, blue skinny jeans and fake Ugg boots came in. Her white-blonde hair was parted in the centre and it went down dead straight past her shoulders. You could see that it was her natural hair colour. It made her look very innocent and childlike still. She was beautiful in a Timotei-ad sort of way. She had enviably clear skin, no freckles or blemishes. It was like staring back at my reflection. Only then did I realise it was Aoife. The last time I saw her she had been eleven.

"Ah, Aoife, you're back!" Dad said.

The surprise at seeing me there was written all over her face.

"Kate," she said but I knew she wasn't happy to see me.

"Hi," I said nervously.

"This is Ben," Gran said then because I seemed to have lost the power of speech.

Ben stepped forward and shook her hand.

"Nice to meet you, Ben." Her voice was so soft that it was barely audible.

"How did you get on, love?" Gran asked.

"It went well, I think, Gran. I got stuck on a small part but other than that everything that I had studied came up."

"Well, thank God for that – you see, all those rosaries worked after all!" she said triumphantly.

Aoife smiled indulgently at her.

"I'm sure you did great – she has brains to burn, doesn't she,

145

Josephine?" Dad said.

"Ah, she does, Noel."

Redness crept upwards on Aoife's cheeks.

"Did you have your lunch yet, Gran?" Aoife asked.

"I did, thanks, love. Do you want me to make something for you?"

"No, I'm grand – a few of us got a sandwich in the canteen afterwards."

"Ah good."

"I'll make a pot of tea then."

"Good girl, Aoife," Gran said.

When Aoife had made the tea, we all sat down around the table. The Sacred Heart lamp glowed red on the wall above us.

"So, Aoife, what are you up to at the moment?" Ben said.

I shot him a look.

"Well, I'm in university in Galway – I'm studying architecture. I live up there during the week and then I come back home here at the weekends."

"She takes great care of me," Gran said. She put her hand over Aoife's on the table and patted it. "I'd be lost without her."

Aoife blushed and looked down at the cup of tea in her hands.

"Well, you couldn't have picked a worse thing to study!" I said. "You'll probably have to join the dole queue when you graduate."

I could see Dad and Ben glaring at me but I didn't care. "I'm just saying that every architect I know is unemployed at the moment."

But instead of standing up for herself, Aoife just said nothing.

"Well, Aoife will land on her feet, I just know she will. Won't you, love?" Gran said.

Aoife smiled back at her.

I felt a small twinge of jealousy.

"So when is your baby due, Kate?" Aoife asked timidly.

"September."

"That'll fly in."

"Hardly! It's already starting to drag."

I noticed that her eyebrows, even though they were fair, could do with a plucking. She could also have done with tinting them. They were more like two sheens across her forehead.

"So how come we didn't see you in Doyle's last night?" Ben asked Aoife, obviously trying to change the conversation.

"I'm not a big drinker actually," she said quietly.

We drank the rest of our tea without saying much. Granny asked me about my job and we talked about the weather until Dad said that we had better make tracks.

The whole way home in the car I had to listen to Ben singing Aoife's praises.

"She's lovely, isn't she?" Ben, in the front seat, said to Dad.

What was he doing? What had got into him?

"Ah, she is – she's a gentle soul all right," Dad said.

I was pretty sure that that was a dig meant for me.

"There are not many young people who would have the patience to take care of an old person like she does," said Ben.

"She's hardly Mother fuckin' Teresa!" I snapped from the backseat.

"That's enough, Kate!" Ben said sharply.

"Well, she's not!"

He turned around and glared at me.

No one said anything for the rest of the journey.

When we got home I could tell by the way that Ben was huffing and puffing that he was pissed off with me. He didn't wait for me to get out of the car and he walked straight into the house ahead of me. Ben rarely got annoyed with me but today it just got my back up even more. This was nothing to do with him!

He stormed down to the bedroom and I marched down after him. Who did he think he was? How dare he just come home for one weekend and think that he knew it all!

I walked into the room behind him and slammed the door shut.

Caroline Finnerty

He swung around to face me. His eyes were on fire with anger.

"What has got into you, Kate?"

"How dare you – it's none of your business!"

"Yes, it is actually – when I'm there watching my girlfriend being so rude to the point that I'm embarrassed by her behaviour then, well, yes, I think it is my business!"

"You don't have a clue. You can't just breeze in here for one weekend and think that you know it all and everyone will be all happy families again!"

"No, but you could at least try. That was the whole point of the trip – to try to build some bridges with your family – but I think you have just burnt whatever chance was left of that!"

"Oh, shut up, Ben, you don't know anything! I never wanted to come home in the first place – in case you don't remember, this was all your idea!"

"I've never seen such a vicious side to you before and I'm not sure I like it very much. I was cringing the whole time, Kate – poor Aoife wouldn't hurt a fly and you just went through her for a shortcut!"

"That's it! We're going home. I'm not going to listen to this shit from the man who is *supposed* to be my partner and *supposed to be supporting me*!" I was screaming now and I knew that Dad could probably hear me up in the kitchen.

I took my phone out of my bag and googled the number for the airline. It took ages for the browser to load – the network in Ballyrobin wasn't the fastest. Finally the webpage loaded and I dialled the number. A woman answered in a polite sing-songy voice. I asked if they had any seats going to London – anything at all? I would even fly to Luton? She apologised that she had only one seat left. All the flights were booked up because of some bloody rugby match. I briefly thought of taking it and leaving Ben to follow me home the next day but I knew that wouldn't go down well at all so I declined.

"You're your own worst enemy, you know that?" Ben said when I got off the phone.

"Well, I'm sorry, Ben. I don't know what you thought was

148

going to happen this weekend but if you think that a two-day trip home is going to fix twenty years of hurt, well, then you're even stupider than I thought." And with that I walked out of the room.

I could hear Ben shouting after me. "That's it, Kate – you just keep on running – run away like you always do!"

I kept on walking past Dad who was sitting at the kitchen table and went straight out the back door.

Chapter 24

I walked along by hedgerows growing rampant with hemlock after the wet clammy weather. Anger put a pace in my steps as I powered along. Drivers greeted me with the one-fingered country salute as their cars passed me.

The weather was drizzly but I hadn't brought a jacket with me in my hurry out of the house so I was getting wet. I wasn't exactly sure where I was going to go but all I knew was that I wanted to be as far away from Ben and my family as possible. I wish we had never come home – the whole trip had been a disaster from start to finish. I knew we never should have come back but Ben had insisted and I had caved in.

I felt Baby Pip stretching out inside me. She could probably sense the stress and it wasn't good for her but she could blame her daddy for that one, I thought bitterly. I passed the ghost estate we had seen on the way in – it was in an even sorrier state now when I had a chance to look at it properly. Half-finished houses were thrown up all over the site like a Lego set a child had got bored with. All the windows and doors were boarded up. Litter gathered up on the wind and blew around in swirls. The whole place looked eerie. It reminded me of some futuristic film where the inhabitants had been wiped out by a natural disaster.

I had reached the village of Ballyrobin before I knew it. The town square was buzzing with Saturday trade and there was a queue out the door of Reilly's butchers. I thought about going to Doyle's for a drink and then I remembered that I was pregnant so I couldn't even indulge in that. A glass of red wine would have been heavenly right then.

The old stone church stood looming at the top of the town. God, I hated that place – it gave me the shivers just looking at it. I crossed over the bridge that divided the town in two and watched the wind skimming across the top of the water, making it look syrupy.

I decided to go into a coffee shop. I pushed open the door and it was a relief to be in out of the wind and rain. My hair was damp from the drizzle and clung to my face in strands. The place was tiny but it was cosy. There was any amount of tantalising cakes and buns on display behind the counter. I ordered a coffee and a slice of carrot cake.

"Would you like cream with that?"

"Yeah, go on."

I waited while the lady heated the cake and plopped a large dollop of cream on the side. I paid and took a seat by the window and watched the world go by. The hurtful words from the fight with Ben were sloshing and swirling around inside my head. I watched as a man came in soon after. He looked very familiar. Was it Aidan? I watched the man as he ordered a coffee and a muffin. Nah, it couldn't be, could it? He balanced a mug of tea in one hand and a plate in the other, with a newspaper tucked under his left arm. Then he turned around and made his way to a nearby table. It was definitely him – there was no mistaking those grey eyes. My heart started pounding against my ribcage. He was dressed in jeans and a green polo-neck T-shirt with a jacket over it.

Just then he spotted me too.

"Kate, is that you? What are you doing back here?" He walked over and put his mug and plate down on my table. He leant over and gave me a huge hug. He still smelt the same and suddenly it was like I was transported back to being a teenager again.

"Here, sit down," I said.

"It's so good to see you, what has you back in these parts?"

"I'm just home for the weekend – visiting the family."

"Well, you haven't changed a bit!"

"Please don't say that – I hope I've left the lank hair and spotty skin behind me, thank you very much," I laughed.

He sat down at the table.

"So how've you been doing?" I asked.

"I'm good – now." He laughed but there was a serious edge to his voice.

"I'm sorry."

"You just went!"

"You knew I was going to go."

"Yeah, but I didn't think you'd actually go through with it."

"I couldn't stay in Ballyrobin any longer – you know that."

"Well, you could have at least kept in touch . . ."

"I figured it would be easier for both of us if I didn't," I said quietly.

He let out a heavy sigh. "So what have you been doing since then?"

"Well, I'm working in a photography gallery – it was the first job I got when I first moved over and I'm still there now."

"Wow, fair play to you!"

"And my partner Ben and I are expecting a baby in September."

He glanced at my stomach, which was hidden by the table, as if to confirm. "I see. Well . . . congratulations."

"Thanks. How about you?"

"Well, I married Catherine Byrne last year – do you remember her? She was the year below us in school?"

"Tall girl, curly brown hair?"

"Yep, that's her. No babies yet but we're working on it. I'm a solicitor in a practice in Galway – I commute up and down every day."

The Last Goodbye

"You're a solicitor?" I almost laughed. Aidan had been wild as a teenager. The pair of us had. I couldn't imagine him in such a straight job.

He started to laugh then too. "Don't sound so surprised! It took me a while but I finally managed to get my life together after you left."

There it was again – the guilt – I knew I should never have come back here. No matter which way I turned someone else had some more in store for me.

"It's funny how things work out," was all I could think of to say.

"I called over to your house, you know – that day – and your dad had just found your letter saying you were leaving. The poor man was as stunned as I was. Why didn't you tell him you were going?"

"But if I had told you or Dad, you would have tried to talk me out of it."

"I thought what we had was special – I thought I would have been enough to make you stay."

I could see the hurt in his eyes.

"Look, you were better off without me – I just brought trouble. Look at what you've done with your life since I left!"

"Come on, Kate – I was devastated. I waited around for months for you to make contact, thinking that you would change your mind and come back home, but I should have known." He paused and looked at me seriously. "You can be very stubborn when you want to be."

"No, I'm not."

"Kate, seriously, you are the most stubborn person that I've ever met."

"Well, then you mustn't have met many people!" I knew it was childish.

"Here, remember the time we sprayed graffiti on the church wall and then had to listen to Father Ball in Mass the following week pronouncing how God knew who had done it and that they would be sure to rot in hell?"

I burst out laughing. "Stop! I was sure Granny knew that it was me."

"Well, maybe the '*K loves A*' gave it away?" he laughed. "Or what about the time we smoked that spliff right before Irish Paper II and then I got sick all over the exam hall. I failed Irish because of it! I had to repeat the Leaving the following year."

"Well, I don't even know what I got in mine because I never even bothered to ask Dad when my results came – but I'm sure that I wasn't far behind you."

"Y'know, we were good together you and I," he said wistfully.

"We were young."

"Maybe – but we still knew what love was. Do you ever think about . . . y'know . . . what might have been?"

"Hmmh . . ." I said. "Look, there's no point dwelling on the past because it won't change where we are today. I'm sorry for running off like that – I really am. I didn't want to hurt you but at the time I thought it was the right thing to do."

"I just wasn't enough for you."

"Please don't say that, Aidan."

"Well, it's the truth."

Silence filled the air, heavy between us. Suddenly I became aware of a woman at a nearby table who had her eyes fixed upon us. I felt very self-conscious under her gaze.

"It's so good to see you again, Kate." Aidan reached across the table for my hand.

"You too." I smiled.

We looked into each other's eyes for a moment, the grey eyes that I used to know so well. But I had moved on – we both had. We weren't seventeen any more. I pulled my hand back again quickly.

"I think I should go . . ."

I pushed my chair back so that it screeched loudly off the tiles and hurried out of the place.

Chapter 25

I found myself back out in the rain again and, if I had been feeling upset before going into the café, bumping into Aidan had made it twice as bad. I walked back up the street past Fidelma's Drapery. She still lined the window with orange film to stop the sunlight fading the clothes on display. I doubted she did much business these days but as a child we bought all our clothes there. Every child in Ballyrobin was dressed in clothes from Fidelma's and then at Christmas time as a treat we would get a new outfit from Dunnes Stores.

I wished I had never come back to this place – everywhere I looked and everywhere I turned there was another bad memory waiting for me. Why had I let Ben talk me around?

It was starting to get dark so I decided it was probably best to go home – I knew Dad and Ben were probably worried about me.

I pushed back the kitchen door and went inside. Ben and Dad were sitting at the table with their backs to me.

"Oh, thank God!" Dad said, swinging around to face me when he heard my footsteps.

Ben stayed as he was. I could sense the tension without even having to look at him.

"Kate, you had us worried sick – the weather is desperate out there and you pregnant and all. Are you okay, love?"

"I'm grand, Dad."

"Why didn't you answer your phone?"

"Oh sorry, I think I left it behind in the room."

"Well, why don't you go and have a warm bath and get out of those damp clothes – you'll catch your death in them. The immersion is on."

I went down to the bathroom as instructed, not because I wanted to but because I didn't want to see Ben. I hated it when he was angry with me. Turning on the taps, the water thundered into the bathtub. I found a bottle of own-brand bubble bath on the shelf and I poured some in. As I lay back into the warm water I instantly felt myself start to relax. I put my ears under the surface and let them fill with water, enjoying the peace of being submerged and being able to shut out the world. The top of my bump peeked out of the water like a small island and I watched as Baby Pip kicked away. I could see her movements from the outside now. It was comforting to watch her. I washed my hair and then stayed there until the water was gone so cold that I was starting to shiver. I climbed out and towelled my shrivelled-up skin and went back down to the bedroom and put on my pyjamas. I sat on the side of the bed and dried off my hair with the hairdryer.

Ben came in soon after. I waited for him to say something but it didn't come. It drove me up the wall when he ignored me. He started to pack his clothes back into the case. As usual, Ben liked to be organised and pack the night before whereas I would be stuffing things in my case in the car on the way to the airport.

"Well, I'm fine – thanks for asking."

"I didn't."

"Look, Ben, I know why you are annoyed with me but I told you that coming back here wasn't a good idea."

"Listen to yourself, Kate – it's all about you as usual. I've spent the last two hours chatting to your dad who was worried out of his mind about you and God knows you don't deserve his worry."

Just then there was a knock on the door.

Ben answered it. Dad stuck his head around the pine doorframe.

"I thought you would like some dinner, love – Ben and I have already eaten but I kept a plate for you?"

"Thanks, Dad. I'll be along in a minute."

He closed the door softly again.

"That man is a saint to put up with you!" said Ben.

"How dare you!" I said as I walked out of the room. "You don't know anything!"

Dad made no reference to the afternoon's events as I ate the dinner of mashed potatoes, pork chops and carrots.

"So what time is the flight tomorrow?" he asked, setting down a mug of tea beside me.

"Around eleven."

"Well, we'd want to be on the road for seven, just in case. You never know what the traffic up in Dublin will be like."

"Thanks, Dad." I couldn't wait until I was sitting on that flight and getting the hell out of this place again.

"Well, it's been good to have you home, Kate."

I looked up at him, wondering if he was taking the mickey out of me but his face was serious.

"I just bring trouble, Dad."

"Will you stop saying that? This is your home, we are your family and we would love to see more of you – and Ben. He's a grand fella, Kate."

"Hmmh." I wasn't so sure, given that we were not on speaking terms.

"He is, Kate – we had a good chat while you were gone earlier. He's mad about you, you know."

"Well, he certainly isn't acting like it," I muttered.

"He'll calm down – he just wants the best for you."

I said nothing.

"Seán called over earlier to see you again before you left."

"Oh really? That's a pity. I would have liked to have seen him before we head off."

"Well, you'll just have come home again soon – bring the baby back home to Ballyrobin to see us all."

"Maybe."

I wasn't promising anything.

We all sat and watched Saturday night TV but by nine I was exhausted after the day and I said that I was going to bed. Ben stayed up a bit longer with Dad and I felt him getting into the bed beside me a while later. I waited for him to put his arms around me like he always did whenever he got into bed after me but he just rolled over so we were facing away from each other.

I stayed awake for a while thinking over everything – what a disaster the whole trip had been from the moment we had arrived – and now Ben and I weren't even talking. The sooner we both got home and away from here the better. It couldn't come quick enough.

Chapter 26

The next morning the sun had finally decided to come out – it was like an omen. We drove most of the journey to the airport in silence. I think we were all exhausted from the strain of the weekend. It was a relief to be a step closer to being home. Ben still wasn't talking to me – he had said a polite few words over breakfast but I knew it was for Dad's sake rather than my own. Once we got home though I knew we could sort it out. That was the problem with this place. It brought nothing but trouble for everyone.

At the airport, we pulled into the set-down bay and Dad pulled the boot lever and got out of the car to help us take out our luggage.

"Well, it's been lovely to meet you," Dad said, shaking Ben's hand firmly. "And we'd love you to come over again soon."

"I'd like that. I've really enjoyed meeting all of you. And be sure to tell Granny and Aoife and the rest of them that we said goodbye."

I cringed as he pretended they were all best friends now – he had just met them once!

"I will, of course."

"Don't leave it so long the next time!"

"Well, safe journey home, Dad." I hugged him close.

"Before you go, I want to give you this –" He took an envelope from the inside pocket of his jacket and handed it to me.

"What's this?" I said, going to open it.

"Don't open it now." He put his hand over mine on top of the envelope. "Better to wait until you get home."

"But –"

"Look, I've debated for years whether to give this to you or not, but maybe now is the right time. I hope it might . . . well . . . help you to make sense of it all."

I clutched the faded envelope in my hands and watched Dad get back into the car. We waved goodbye to each other and suddenly I could feel tears in my eyes. I wiped them quickly away before anyone could see them. Wordlessly Ben and I went inside the airport terminal.

High winds and heavy rains delayed our flight by a few hours – the sunshine from the west had yet to make it across to the east of the country. Winds howled and rain hit the runway in diagonal sheets, making takeoff and landing unsafe. There was now a backlog of flights waiting to leave Dublin. We went for lunch while we were waiting. Ben read the newspaper at the table while I sat people-watching. I couldn't recall a time when Ben had stayed mad at me for this long. Finally, the winds died down and we got word that our flight was ready to board.

I took the envelope back out of my bag after I had taken my seat on the plane. I was so curious to know what was inside it but I had a heavy feeling that it was something big. I knew by Dad's manner and the way that he had told me to wait until I was at home before opening it, that I should listen to him. Whatever it was, it was important.

Back in Heathrow, Ben hailed a taxi. I was secretly glad we didn't have to criss-cross London on the train and Tube to get home.

When we arrived at the flat, he left the bags in the hallway and went straight into the kitchen. I followed straight behind him. Pulling back the fridge door, he took out a beer.

"You're going to have to talk to me sometime, you know?" I said, blocking his path from our galley kitchen back to the sofa.

"Leave it, Kate."

"You've no right getting mad with me – it was your idea to go to Ireland in the first place."

"You're so arrogant, do you know that? Your family are all lovely people – I don't know what I was expecting, to be honest, after everything you've told me about them over the years – but it certainly wasn't to come away not liking my own girlfriend!"

His words stung me to the core. I stood to the side and let him pass. He walked by me, turned on the TV and sat on the sofa with his back to me. I took the envelope that Dad had given me out of my bag and went to our bedroom.

I kicked off my shoes, sat back against the cushions on the bed and studied the outside of the envelope once again. It had a worn look and I guessed that it was originally white but had faded over time. I turned it over and saw that the flap was open. I felt along where the gum should be but the stickiness was long gone as if someone had opened it many times before. I was afraid of what I might find inside. There was something about Dad's behaviour that made me hesitate.

I didn't have to open it. Best to let sleeping dogs lie and all that. I briefly thought about throwing it in the bin – I didn't want any more upset in my life, especially if it was something to do with my family. I'd had enough of that over the weekend and even now I was still putting up with the repercussions of it – I had never known Ben to stay in a huff with me for so long. I knew I could just throw it in the bin now and be none the wiser but I also knew that Dad wouldn't have given it to me unless it was important. So I took a deep breath and pulled the letter out of the envelope. The paper was neatly folded in half. I opened it up and, as soon as I saw the leaning handwriting, I knew who it was from.

Eva

1992

Chapter 27

We both watched as the test turned positive. *Sweet Mother of Divine Jesus, Mary, and all the saints in heaven what was I going to do?*

I had just spent the last half an hour convincing Doctor O'Brien that there was no way, no way whatsoever that I could be pregnant. I had sat down opposite him and listed off my symptoms. He had asked me to do a pregnancy test "just as a precaution" but I had laughed and told him there was no way that I was pregnant and not to bother wasting his time.

"It's a tummy bug, I'm telling you," I had said.

Because I'd had it for over a week now Noel had talked me into getting it checked out. Never in a million years did I think that I could be pregnant. After three of them. I thought I would have known the symptoms. We were done – our youngest, Seán, was ten years old now, for God's sake!

"I'm sorry, Doctor, but is there any way – any way at all that these things . . . well, you know . . . can get it wrong sometimes?" I waved my hand at the test, which rested on the desk in front of him.

"I'm afraid not, Eva. There are no false positives."

I looked at all his medical certs hanging on the white wall behind him, willing him to be wrong. I had been coming to

Doctor O'Brien since just after I got married, when I was pregnant with Kate. I had trusted him with my life, especially when Patrick decided to arrive in a hurry and I didn't have time to get to the hospital – if it wasn't for Doctor O'Brien, I don't know what might have happened. I always brought my children to him now as well. He was a man of few words. It was like words cost him money so he chose them carefully and saved whatever was unnecessary. He would often fix his eyes on you, entertaining a long silence as he mulled things over in his head. Sometimes you would wonder if he was even listening but then he would come out with a diagnosis or treatment and you knew he was on the ball once again.

"What am I going to do?"

"Well, there's not a lot you can do, Eva – there is a baby growing away inside you there whether you like it or not!"

"But I'm almost forty!"

"Yes, it's obviously a riskier business at this age – the odds of complications go up immeasurably. Down Syndrome, Edwards Syndrome –"

"Jesus, will you stop! I'm barely getting my head around it without worrying about what might come with it!"

"Obviously this has come as a shock to you, Eva, but go home and talk to Noel – you'll work through it."

"I'm not so sure," I mumbled as I rooted around in my handbag to get my purse.

"I'll see you back here for your check-ups."

I paid him the money and with that I found myself back outside the door again.

I walked out of the surgery and onto the street in a daze. How had it happened? I was racking my head, trying to think. I thought we had been very careful since we'd had Seán but obviously we were not careful enough. We had purposely had the three of them close in age so that they would all grow up together – 'steps of the stairs' people called them. As I walked along I wondered how on earth I was going to break the news to Noel. I felt like a schoolgirl that had gone and got herself into trouble, except that it was my own husband that I was afraid of telling instead of my parents. I was tempted to buy a packet of cigarettes but I had given them up years ago so I knew having one would just make me sick and dizzy. And then there was Mam, what would she think of me having a baby at my age? I walked down the street, locked inside my own thoughts. I passed miserable Mr Acton the accountant putting the canary-yellow steering-wheel lock on his Mercedes even though it was parked right outside the door of his office, the fool! He wouldn't spend Christmas, that fella!

I nearly tripped over a dog on a lead as I walked. The owner glared at me.

"Sorry," I mumbled.

I didn't recognise him at all – he was probably a blow-in.

My mind flipped back to Noel then. Things were tight enough already – he was constantly stressed about money. We didn't earn enough off the farm to raise three children on, especially with Kate in secondary school now and Patrick due to follow her soon. He picked up whatever odd jobs were going around the town – turkey-plucking at Christmas time or getting a few days here and there in the meatpacker's whenever they were a man short. He had even let out a field last year to another farmer because at least it would be a bit of a steady income for us. It had killed him to break up the small bit of a farm that had been passed down from his own father but he didn't have much choice.

"Well, how did you get on?" Noel asked as soon as I came in the back door, a gust of wind rushing in behind me.

With force, I shut it closed.

He was sitting at the table, his two hands on either side of the newspaper.

"What? Oh yeah, grand." I couldn't tell him yet.

"What does he reckon it is?"

"Oh, it's some sort of tummy bug."

"Well, did he give you anything for it?"

"Yeah, just a few tablets," I lied.

"Did you get the bread?"

"What?"

"Bread – we're nearly all out – you said you'd pick it up while you were down there?"

"Oh God, sorry, I forgot it."

"Not to worry – I'll drive down later. You're looking very pale – will I put on the kettle?"

"Yeah, thanks, love," I sighed, sitting down beside him at the table.

"Are you sure you're feeling all right?"

"Yeah, not a bother." I forced a smile on my face. Jesus, if he only knew!

Noel headed back out to the fields a while later and I still stayed rooted to my chair. I looked around at the pine kitchen that Noel had made himself. He was good with his hands – give him a piece of wood and you never knew what he would turn it into.

Kate came in from school soon after. The boys would be late today because they had football training after school on a Wednesday. I watched as she arched her back and slid her arms out of the straps of her schoolbag so that the heavy bag plunged on to the kitchen lino.

"How was school, love?"

"Grand."

She opened up the fridge and stared into it.

"Did you get much homework?"

"Yeah."

"Did you get the results of your French test back?"

"Yeah."

"How did you get on?"

"I got a B."

"Well done."

She glared at me. "There's nothing to eat, Mam."

"Yes, there is – there's ham and cheese in there – why don't you make yourself a sandwich?"

"I don't want a sandwich."

"Well, what do you want then?" I sighed wearily.

"Pasta."

"There's some in the press."

She put a saucepan of water on the hob to boil. What would Kate say when I told her? I was nearly more scared of telling Kate than Noel – she'd have a conniption. She'd probably be mortified that her parents were still having sex.

"Can I go to Bergin's on Friday?"

"No way!"

"Why not, Mam? Everyone else is going!"

"I said no – I'm not going over this again. I've heard all sorts of things go on in that place and you're too young – you're only thirteen."

"Yeah – but it's an *underage* disco." She said it in a tone that implied I was stupid.

"Kate, I'm not getting in to another argument about it. *No* means *no*!"

"For fuck sake, you're such an auld one!"

"Don't use that language in this house."

"What 'fuck' or 'auld one'?" she said as she stormed out of the kitchen, slamming every door she encountered on her way to her bedroom.

Dear God, whoever thinks the terrible twos are bad should wait until they reach the teenage years. Kate had only just entered hers and I desperately wished we could go back to her toddler years again. My lovely daughter had turned into a complete anti-Christ in the last few months.

I walked over to the cooker and turned off the ring. I doubted she'd be back to eat her pasta now.

Patrick and Seán came in together soon after. Both came over and gave me a kiss on the cheek before going to check out the fridge in the same manner as their older sister had. I got up and made them a sandwich each and they ate them before heading down to their room to start their homework. The boys were much more straightforward than Kate – there were no dramas, no fuss – they just did what you told them to do.

Later on at the dinner table Kate breezed in, with no door

slamming or shouting. She seemed to have forgotten her earlier strop. I knew that she must want something.

I was passing the bowl of spuds around when she came out with it.

"Can I get a new pair of jeans?"

"You just got a pair in Dunnes a few weeks ago."

"Exactly!" She sighed. "They're from Dunnes – I want a pair of Levi's."

"Don't we all? You know we can't afford them, Kate."

"Dad, tell her!" she said, turning to Noel.

She always did this, tried to play me off against her father whenever she wasn't getting her own way with me.

"Well, how much are these Levi's you're talking about?"

"Don't listen to her, Noel – you could buy three pairs of jeans in Dunnes for the price of them." She was always asking for clothes that she knew well we couldn't afford. I was sure all her friends were wearing them and it was hard for a teenager not to be keeping up but we just didn't have the money. Especially now.

"You always go and ruin everything!" She turned to me, her eyes blazing. She pushed back her chair and hopped up from the table, clattering her cutlery off the plate.

"There she goes again!" Patrick said, rolling his eyes.

I had to stifle a laugh.

"Can I have an ice cream, Mam?" Seán asked me.

"Go on." I was too tired to fight with him.

He jumped up and went over to the freezer.

"Here, give me one and all." I might as well, I reasoned – I was going to be getting fat anyway.

Chapter 28

"I don't want to watch the *Late Late*!"

"Well, don't watch it then."

"Well, it's kinda hard not to, given that we only have one TV." Kate was forever complaining that her friends had TVs in their bedrooms, kitchens, sitting rooms, loos, garden sheds and God knows wherever else they could put them.

"I bet they're all there now having fun."

She was referring to the underage disco in Bergin's that I wouldn't let her go to. I pretended that I couldn't hear her.

"Everyone. As in the whole class. Except me."

"Will you give it over, Kate?" Noel said at last.

He was normally so mild-mannered that when he did get cross with her, she knew not to push it any further.

We all sat in silence then, watching Gaybo interviewing some singer that I had never heard of.

"Mam, can I go and meet Aidan tomorrow?"

"Well, what homework have you got?"

"Just an essay for Irish."

"Right, well, you can meet him after you've done that."

Aidan was Kate's boyfriend. They had been together for a couple of months now, which was serious enough at that age. He seemed like a nice enough fella and Noel knew his dad too which helped.

I let out another large yawn.

"You're tired, love," Noel said.

"Yeah, I think I'll hit the hay."

"But it's only half nine," Patrick said, more out of fear that he would be sent to bed too rather than concern for me.

Seán was already in bed. He had fallen asleep on the sofa and Noel had lifted him into his bed.

"Yeah, well, it's been a long day," I said. "You can stay up for another half an hour and then off to bed with you – do you hear me, Patrick?"

He nodded.

"Night, everyone."

As I lay in bed I wondered how on earth was I going to break it to Noel? We already had our hands full. And going back to the start again – all the night feeds, sleep deprivation, sterilising bottles, puréeing food and running around after a toddler – the thought of doing all that again was wearisome. And it didn't help that I kept doing the maths on all the different stages – the latest one to shock me was that I would be nearly sixty when the child would be eighteen!

The next morning I had to jump out of bed and run to the bathroom to be sick. I was trying to keep quiet so that I wouldn't wake the kids.

"Are you okay, Eva?" I turned my head from the toilet bowl and saw him standing in the doorway.

"Sorry, love, I didn't mean to wake you."

"I thought you said that O'Brien gave you something for it?"

"What? Oh yeah. Look, Noel, I have something to tell you."

"What is it?"

"Best put the kettle on."

We went quietly down to the kitchen. It was the only quiet time of the day before the three would be up, their noise running and reverberating throughout the house.

"Sit down there and I'll make the tea."

"What is it, Eva? You're worrying me now . . ."

My hand fidgeted with the seam on my dressing gown,

unravelling a loose thread. I pulled at it but it just unwound even more, so I let the thread fall away from between my fingers.

"Wait."

I quickly made the tea and came back with two mugs and put them down on the table.

"There you are now."

"Well?"

"Noel . . . when I went to Doctor O'Brien yesterday . . ."

"What is it, Eva – what's wrong?"

"I'm pregnant, Noel!" I blurted out.

"What?" He moved his chair back from the table with a screech.

"I know."

"But how?"

I shrugged my shoulders. "I guess we weren't as careful as we thought."

"Jesus, Eva!"

"Well, I hardly did it all by myself, now did I!"

"But what are we going to do?"

"What can we do?"

"But starting all over again – just as they're growing up a bit – things were beginning to get a bit easier. And the money – sure we can barely afford the three that we have!"

"I know, Noel – I know." I held my head in my hands.

He came over and put his arm around my shoulders.

"How far along are you?"

"I'm not sure – Doctor O'Brien said I should go to the hospital for a scan to confirm."

"Dear God – I just can't believe it. Sure I wouldn't know what to do with a little baby any more."

"Can you imagine what Kate will say?"

Noel started to laugh then.

"What? It's hardly funny!"

"I'm just thinking of how she's going to react – you can expect World War Three."

I smiled. "We'll be the talk of the town. People will think

we're at it like rabbits." I started to laugh then too.

"That'll be the least of our worries," he said.

"I'm nearly forty, Noel – when the child is Seán's age I'll be heading towards fifty – when it's getting married I'll probably be in my seventies." I groaned. "And, you know, at my age the risks of everything . . . go up."

"What do you mean?"

"Well, Down Syndrome and things like that."

"Right. I see . . . look, whatever happens we'll get through it, Eva." He took my hand in his. "Granted it's not ideal but I suppose everything happens for a reason. We'll get used to the idea."

"When will we tell the children? I bags not telling Kate!"

"Ah there's no rush – let's get our own heads around it first and we can tell them in a few weeks."

Chapter 29

I was exhausted as the weeks went on. Kate with her ever-increasing demands had me worn out. Patrick and Seán, although easy in comparison to Kate, still required minding and God only knew what would happen when you threw a newborn baby into the mix! I had been tired with the others but never this bad – I suppose it was my age. This was going to be a tough nine months – there was no doubt about it. I had started thinking of all the stuff that we would need. We had nothing – we would be starting from scratch again. Baby equipment, the steriliser, cot and clothes – I had given them all away. Even the toys that the kids had when they were small – I had tidied them up last year and given them to the St Vincent de Paul.

I had told Mam about the pregnancy after I had told Noel. I had to – I knew she would see through me if I tried to keep it a secret – and even she was shocked.

"I thought ye were done!" she'd said.

"So did I . . ."

"Well, the Lord works in mysterious ways – he has given you this child for a reason."

"Hmmh . . . maybe you're right."

"I am."

"How will we manage though, Mam? Financially things are

so tight at the moment and I'm already exhausted, I don't know how I'll cope at all."

"Don't worry, love, you'll be grand, you'll make things stretch. You'll get through it."

"I hope so, Mam."

"And sure I can give you a hand too."

After talking it through with Mam I started to think that maybe it wasn't the end of the world after all.

Over the next few weeks I slowly came to accept it. I now started to feel guilty whenever I had negative thoughts. I had been so excited about my three other pregnancies and it wasn't fair to this little baby to be brought into a world where I wasn't excited about it as well.

Noel had come round to the idea too.

He arrived in the door with a small crib one evening.

"Where did you get that from?"

"I made it myself." Redness crept up along his cheeks. "That's what I've been doing in the shed for the last few weeks."

He had been spending a lot of time in the shed but I'd thought he just needed some space to try to get his head around everything.

I went over and ran my fingers over the smoothness of the bars he had carved in the mahogany wood. The two ends were curved so the baby could be rocked. He had always been very good with his hands. He wasn't a trained carpenter but he could have been. His finish was always perfect. Tears came to my eyes.

"It's beautiful, Noel."

"Ah, sure, it will get us through the first few months anyway." He was embarrassed by my praise. He never could take a compliment.

"Come here."

He placed the crib down on the floor and we hugged.

"We'll be fine, Eva, don't you worry." He smoothed back my hair and kissed my forehead. "The more I've been thinking about it, the more I've got used to the idea. It'll be nice to have a little one running around the house again. It all went by so fast with the others, so it will be nice to get another chance at it – we might even appreciate it more this time."

"And the sleepless nights too?" I pulled back in his arms.

"Ah sure, what odds? It'll keep us young."

"That's one way of looking at it, I suppose. Maybe today would be a good time to tell the others?"

"Yeah, why not." He sighed. "They'll be on to us soon enough if we don't."

We decided to test the water with Patrick and Seán before we tackled Kate.

"You're just putting it off," Noel had said.

"No, I'm not – we can't hide it forever but no point in starting World War Three before we have to."

"Good point."

When Patrick and Seán came in from school, I knew we would have an hour before Kate arrived because she normally hung out with Aidan for a while before she came home.

"No time like the present," I said, catching Noel's eye.

We went down to the sitting room where they had turned on the TV.

I took a deep breath. "Boys, Dad and I would like to talk to you for a few minutes – we have something we need to tell you."

Noel walked over and switched off the TV.

"Hey, Dad, I was watching that!" Seán said.

"What is it?" Patrick asked.

"Your mother and I – well, we're having another baby."

"Is that it?" Seán asked, obviously wondering what all the fuss was about.

"Really, Mam?" Patrick said, looking at me. "You don't have a bump."

"Well, that's because it's still quite early on. The bump doesn't come until the baby gets a bit bigger."

"Well, that's going to be weird," he said. "Having a little baby in the house."

"Tell me about it!" I said.

"Can we watch TV now, please?" Seán asked.

"Yeah, of course," I said. "So you're okay with it then?"

"Yeah, I suppose so," Patrick said.

We left them at it and went back down to the kitchen.

"Well, that was easy," I said to Noel.

"Yeah, it went much better than I thought."

"Maybe Kate won't take it so badly after all, what do you reckon?"

"Yeah, maybe we're making a bigger deal of this than it actually is."

Of course we spoke too soon. We waited until the boys were in bed before telling Kate. We were all seated in the sitting room having a cup of tea with a packet of custard creams.

"We have some news for you, Kate," Noel said.

"What – you're finally letting me go to Bergin's?" She looked up at us, her eyes wide with excitement.

"Eh, no . . . something we need to talk about."

"Well, it better not be 'the talk' again – let's save us *all* the embarrassment of doing that again!"

I almost started to laugh. Oh the irony – maybe we should have paid more attention ourselves when we had been teaching her the facts of life.

"Look, Kate, we're going to have . . ." I said.

"Have what?"

"A baby."

"A baby?"

No screaming, no hysteria. We were doing well, I thought.

"Who is?" She looked from me to Noel and then back to me again.

"Myself and your mother, of course!" said Noel.

"No way! You can't do this to me!"

"To you? It's me that's pregnant –"

"You can't, Mam – I'll be the laughing stock of the school. Please say you're only joking!" She looked at us desperately. "Oh my God, you're actually serious, aren't you?"

We both nodded.

"Jesus Fucking Christ, how can you two be so stupid?"

"Watch your language, Kate!" Noel said. "Look, it's come as a shock to us as well but these things happen."

"No, they don't – at your age, Mam? What are you two even doing still having sex?" She looked at us in disgust and it felt like Noel and I were the school kids and she was the adult.

"Now, Kate – calm down," Noel said. "I know it's not easy on you to hear this – it's taken myself and your mother a while to get our heads around it as well but it's happening so you're just going to have to accept it."

"Oh my God, I can't believe you're doing this to me. Oh my God. *Oh my God!*"

"Kate, what other choice do we have?" I said. "I know it's a shock but you'll get used to it."

"No, I won't!" she screamed. "Never!"

"C'mon, Kate, please just calm down," Noel said.

"Well, thanks very much, because you've just ruined my life!"

"Kate, it's hardly going to ruin your life – stop being melodramatic!" I said.

"You disgust me!" she spat, before storming down to her bedroom.

The vibrations of the slamming door reverberated around the house.

"That went well then," I said.

"She'll come round."

Although it hadn't gone great, it was a relief to finally have it out in the open.

"I'm not so sure," I said. "You know what Kate is like – she can hold a grudge for months. It's a pity it isn't a subject in school because she'd excel at it."

"She's a teenager – the world revolves around her. She'll stew for a while but, wait and see, when the baby is born she'll be a great help, I bet."

"I wouldn't count on it." Then I laughed. "I can't believe she really thinks we don't have sex any more!"

"No one wants to think of their parents having sex."

"If only she knew." I dipped my biscuit into the tea and gave Noel a wink.

Chapter 30

Doctor O'Brien had arranged a dating scan for me in the hospital. I hadn't really had scans with the others – well, I'd had one with Seán towards the end but that was only because they thought he was measuring quite big. Nowadays it seemed I would be scanned quite regularly. Things had moved on.

I left Noel at home on the farm on the day – I didn't know how long I was going to be and it was a busy time of the year for him with the lambing.

I took the car and set off for the hospital. I was nervous and excited at the same time. I was looking forward to knowing when the baby was due for a start – it was a bit odd being pregnant and not knowing what stage you were at. My tummy was starting to push forward so I wondered if I was further along than I thought?

I went to the desk to check in and then took a seat. I sat with my file until a nurse called me into a small room to check over my medical history. I told her my age and she asked me about my previous pregnancies and deliveries.

"So I'd say this came as a surprise then?"

"It sure did."

"Well, don't be worrying – you've been through it all before – it hasn't changed that much since the last time." She smiled kindly and I felt at ease then. She handed me a sample jar and showed me a toilet where I could give a urine sample.

"I thought by this stage you'd have some high-fallutin' way of doing this, instead of dealing with the dipsticks still?"

"Nope – see, I told you, nothing has changed that much. I bet it's all coming back to you now."

She checked my urine. "That all looks good, Eva. Now I just want to take some bloods to be tested in the lab."

I pulled up my sleeve and waited for her to put a strap above my elbow. I pumped my fist like she told me to do and waited to feel the needle. I always felt the wait was worse than the pinch of the needle itself.

"There, all done now. If you can take a seat outside there and wait for your name to be called?"

I sat down again on the hard-backed plastic chair. I felt ancient as I looked around at the other women in the waiting room. All around me were young women in their prime, at the right age for having children, not auld ones like me. I felt out of place. I sat with my arms folded, resting on top of my handbag. Even my bag looked old-fashioned and dowdy compared to the stylish leather bags that the girls seated all around me had. Most of them had their partners with them too – when I was pregnant before, partners never came to the check-ups. Noel hadn't even been at Kate or Patrick's births but he had been at Seán's. Things were just beginning to change around that time and men were just starting to go into the delivery room.

I felt like everyone was staring at me, wondering what I was doing there. I knew I was probably just being paranoid.

Finally my name was called and my dowdy bag and I went into the tiny cubicle where the scanning apparatus was.

"Eva Flynn?" the man said, checking my file. He flicked through it and stopped to read the referral from Doctor O'Brien. He had a long angular face and his glasses were perched at the end of his nose. "Right then, so you're here for a dating scan, is that correct?"

"Yes."

"My name is John. I'm a radiographer here. Okay so, if you could climb up on to the bed there, please."

I lay back on the couch and pulled up my top and even though I was sure he saw it every day, I felt embarrassed by my flabby tummy and the remnants of faded silvery stretch marks from the other three in front of this young guy.

He squirted some cool gel onto my tummy and then ran the probe over it.

He was quiet for a while before he started to speak. He zoomed in on various bits.

"Here is the little heart beating away – the four chambers all look good." He moved onto another part. "Yes, brain looks fine. Judging from the measurements here I would estimate that you are nearly twelve weeks along, Eva."

"Twelve weeks! I got a few bonus weeks in there – that's great!" I hadn't expected to be so far along.

Then he zoomed out again and moved to the baby's limbs. He held the probe on one part and tilted his head to the side as if deep in concentration.

"Is everything okay?" I asked.

He had been quiet for too long. Dear God, I hoped he hadn't found something – the risks I had been warned about flashed through my mind. Down Syndrome, Edwards Syndrome and I can't remember how many other syndromes Doctor O'Brien had warned me about. Or what if it was twins? We'd never cope with that!

He seemed to be measuring something on the screen. He would drag the probe across and take a measurement and do the same back on the other side.

"Have you been experiencing any extra pain or discomfort lately?"

"Well, I'm pregnant, so yeah – look, do you mind telling me what's wrong?"

"It looks like you may have an adnexal mass on your right ovary. Now it might be nothing but we need to keep an eye on it."

"An ad-what?"

"It's a growth that arises from the uterus or Fallopian tube."

"Oh, is that all?" I let out a sigh of relief. "I thought you were going to tell me there was something wrong with the baby!"

"Hmmh."

"So what does that mean in normal English?"

"Well, it's hard to say just yet without a biopsy. Usually these things are benign cysts but I would like to get a second opinion. These machines aren't the best. I'm going to refer you on to my colleague Gareth O'Keeffe for a more detailed examination. Now, I'm sure it's nothing to worry about but it's best to get these things checked."

"But otherwise all looks good?" I said.

"Yes, the baby seems fine."

I went back out again and made arrangements to see Gareth O'Keeffe.

Then I decided to treat myself to a cup of tea and a sticky bun in the hospital coffee shop. I smiled at the black-and-white scan photo that the doctor had given me. It still didn't look like a baby yet, more like a jellybean, but I was excited. I tried to make out his scrawly handwriting in my chart but I couldn't make head or tail of it. I was annoyed with myself for not asking more questions. But there was no point in tormenting myself, wondering what it all meant. The appointment he had set up for me was the following week so at least things would be clearer soon enough.

When I went home and told Noel he just asked more questions.

"But what do you reckon it is?"

"I told you I don't know, Noel."

"But is it serious?"

"For the last time, I don't know – we'll just have to wait until my appointment next week."

"But the baby is fine?"

"Aren't I just after telling you that?" I snapped.

Noel had decided to come with me for the appointment with Doctor O'Keeffe the following week. He drove this time so I was able to sit back as we set off for the hospital. I had been thinking about it all week but then I had to remind myself that the radiographer had said it was probably nothing to worry about.

Doctor O'Keeffe came and met us in the waiting room. We followed him into his rooms.

My heart was beating as I climbed up on the examination couch. Noel took a seat near my head. I watched him twisting his gold wedding band round and round his finger. He did this sometimes when he was anxious. We both stayed quiet while the doctor did the scan, waiting for him to tell us what was going on.

Finally he spoke.

"It would appear that you have a large ovarian cyst, Eva. I'm measuring it to be approximately eight centimetres in diameter."

"Eight centimetres! Sure that's nearly the size of a sliotar!" Noel said.

"Now these things are usually harmless but we need to keep an eye on it."

"But you don't think it's anything serious, do you?" Noel asked.

"It's hard to say – I would like to see you back here in a couple of weeks so we can monitor it."

I was deflated when we went back outside. Doctor O'Brien had warned me about the possible complications of being pregnant at my age but never did I think it would be something like this that I would be dealing with. Whatever about my initial shock at discovering that I was pregnant, I had surprised myself by growing to like the idea of another chance of holding a little baby again. My mood had been lifted over the last few weeks as I went about my mundane jobs of doing the laundry, making dinners, cajoling the kids to do their homework. It had given me something to look forward to. And then this had happened.

Chapter 31

A couple of weeks later we were driving around the hospital car park looking for a space. We drove up and down the rows and then we would see someone pull out of one we just passed and another car would rush in and take the vacated space. The rain hit the windscreen hard and the wipers swished it away. *Eh-eeek, eh-eeek, eh-eeek.* One of them was squeaking like nails on a blackboard and every so often it would irritate Noel and he would turn them off but he would have to turn it on again a few seconds later to fend off the rain.

"I'll drop you up to the door – no point in both of us getting wet," he said.

I was going back to meet with Doctor O'Keeffe for the follow-up scan.

A short while later Doctor O'Keeffe was staring hard at the screen in concentration and we were staring at him.

"It looks complex and the borders are poorly delineated. Due to its size I would be very surprised if it resolved spontaneously. Now these things are usually benign but equally it may be malignant –"

"Malignant?" I said.

"Yes, as in cancerous. Now the rates of malignancy in ovarian masses during pregnancy are less than one per cent so it's only a tiny chance – but we have to err on the side of caution. In a non-pregnant patient we would usually perform surgery to remove the cyst and take a tissue biopsy to rule out malignancy. However, as I'm sure you can guess, abdominal surgery during pregnancy is associated with its own complications such as spontaneous miscarriage, rupture of membranes, preterm birth, infection, thrombosis . . . There are also the effects of anaesthesia on the foetus and the mother to consider."

"I see." I was stunned. All I could focus on was the ink stain from the pen that was sitting upside down inside his pocket.

"There is a lot of debate about whether surgical intervention is warranted in all pregnant patients that present with large cysts – in some cases close monitoring throughout the pregnancy and subsequent postpartum surgery can achieve good outcomes for both mother and baby. But in your case, Eva, due to its size and complexity, I would recommend surgery sooner rather than later."

"Are you saying that I have cancer?"

"No, not at all, but I would like to do a biopsy to know what we're dealing with here."

"But you just told me all the things that can go wrong after surgery."

"We need to weigh up the risks, Eva. Ultimately it is a decision that you and your husband need to make – whether you choose to have surgery or if you wish to continue without surgery. But, obviously, if it is cancer that we're dealing with here and we're not treating it, then . . ." he paused to choose his words, "there are other risks to think about . . ."

He didn't need to spell it out to me.

"And this surgery that you're talking about – what would it involve?" Noel asked.

"Well, Eva would be put under general anaesthetic and then a laparotomy would be carried out whereby we would do an incision through the abdomen to surgically remove as much of the cyst as we can. As I said it might be nothing to worry about –"

"But what about the baby?"

"We would, of course, take every care to protect the baby but, as I mentioned, there are risks that you need to be aware of. I'm sorry, Eva – situations like this are awful for everyone involved. I see so few cases like this but when I do it presents an awful dilemma for the parents. I want you and your husband to go home and talk about it – we can put you in touch with a counsellor if you wish to talk it through with someone. I'll give you a call in a couple of days to see how you're doing."

Noel and I drove home in silence, lost in our own thoughts. We didn't even turn on the radio. I tried to remain positive. When I thought of the stats they were in my favour. "Less than one per cent of adnexal masses during pregnancy are malignant," was what Doctor O'Keeffe had said and hadn't he also said that some of them resolve themselves spontaneously? I kept on telling myself this, so why then did I not feel reassured? It was like I was waiting, tempting fate, for something bad to happen. Just as I was starting to get excited about this little miracle growing away inside me, I knew something bad was going to happen. I could feel it in my bones. You know that feeling when everything in your life is going too well and it starts to make you uneasy and you just know something lies in wait around the corner for you? It's like someone is saying: 'Look at her getting all smug – let's just throw this at her and we'll see how smug she is then!' Well, that's how I felt.

We went into the house and Noel put the kettle on. It was an automatic reaction – we always did it when we came in from somewhere.

I sat down at the table. When he put the cup of tea down in front of me I didn't reach for it.

"Are you okay?"

I said nothing.

"Look, doctors these days are very advanced – they're much more skilful – he'll whip it out and you'll be as right as rain again in no time. You'll see." Noel was trying hard to be positive.

"But I can't."

"Can't what?"

"I can't have surgery, Noel."

"Why not? You heard what Doctor O'Keeffe said?"

"It's too risky, Noel – I couldn't live with myself if anything . . . were to . . . go wrong."

"But what about the other risks?"

"What of them?"

"Well, what if it is cancer? What if something were to happen . . . to you?"

"Sure, I'll be grand – tough as old boots, me! It would take a lot more than that to get rid of me!"

"Can you please just be serious for once?"

"I am being serious!"

"He advised you to have the surgery."

"He also said it might be nothing and I'm not prepared to take a chance. You heard what he said – less than one per cent of masses are malignant. I don't know about you but that to me seems like the odds are in my favour."

"Well, maybe . . ."

"Look, he's just being a typical doctor and covering his own arse – they have do that – but I'll be grand."

"Maybe you're right," he said uncertainly. "Well, we'll see what he says at your next appointment."

But I didn't feel as confident as my words.

Chapter 32

Noel and I didn't speak about it at all after that. I knew that I was probably doing a bit of sticking my head in the sand but I just couldn't face up to it. We never even mentioned it to the children.

Kate was still acting like the devil's child. I would catch her staring stonily across the kitchen at me, her eyes narrowed into piercing slits. Where had my blonde-haired angel gone? She was spending more and more time out with Aidan and her friends. Ordinarily I would have been pretty strict about her hanging around the town but under the circumstances I let it go. What is it they say: pick your battles? She was still on at me about going to Bergin's and I had finally caved – I didn't have the energy to fight her any more on it. The condition was that Noel would drop her down and pick her up – I knew she wasn't happy with that end of the bargain but she knew better than to push me on that one in case I changed my mind altogether.

At my next appointment, when Doctor O'Keeffe said that the mass had grown again in size and that he wasn't happy with the shape or complexity of it at all, I wasn't surprised. Noel reached out for my hand and squeezed it and I could feel the nervousness in his. I felt numb and removed from it all whereas poor Noel seemed to be very upset. I somehow found myself comforting him.

"What are our options?" Noel asked.

"I would strongly advise you to proceed with surgery, both to attempt to remove as much of the mass as possible and also to do a biopsy so we know exactly what we're dealing with here. Then we can decide on the best course of treatment."

"I don't want to do anything that may harm this baby." I put my hands protectively across my growing abdomen.

"You are out of the first trimester now. I think there is a good chance for a successful pregnancy, Eva."

"But you said there are risks too."

"Yes, of course, there are – with any kind of surgery during pregnancy – especially with the location of the surgery in this situation."

"Well, then, I can't do it."

"Eva – the risks to you may far outweigh the risk to the baby if we don't proceed with surgery."

"But you don't know that – you said yourself that less than one per cent of masses during pregnancy are malignant – you don't even know if it is cancerous. I'm sorry but it's just too big of a risk to take for a less than one-per-cent chance when it might actually be nothing at all."

"Will you stop being so stubborn?" Noel was looking at me, his eyes burning with upset. "Listen to the man – he is recommending that you have the surgery – why won't you be reasonable?"

"I am listening – that's why I am going to take my chances."

"Are there any other options?" Noel turned back to Doctor O'Keeffe.

"Well, without knowing if it is indeed malignant, then I'm afraid not. We can sometimes do a blood test to measure tumour markers but it isn't accurate for pregnant women as the levels of the antigen are usually elevated in pregnancy anyway. Look, ultimately it is your decision, I can only advise and then I have to respect whatever you decide on. I empathise with you both because it is a truly awful decision for any expectant mother to have to make."

I nodded. The whole thing felt like an out-of-the-body experience.

"We'll be keeping a close eye on you to see how it's growing. If you do change your mind, please ring me anytime and I can schedule surgery immediately."

"Thank you, Doctor O'Keeffe." Noel shook his hand gratefully.

My handshake was a bit more lacklustre.

"What is wrong with you?" Noel blazed as soon as we got back into the car. "You have three children at home you need to think about and yet you're putting a small risk to this unborn baby ahead of all of them! That's not fair, Eva. You need to think about this – about what you're doing here!"

"I am thinking about it – all I do is think about it! Do you think I can escape it for a minute? But I can feel the baby kicking away in there now and I can't do it, I just can't. The fate of the baby is in my hands."

"Well, you're selfish. Your other children need you just as much as that baby – if not more!"

"Please don't call it 'that baby'," I said wearily.

"Well, that's how I feel – suddenly it has taken priority over everyone else in our family!"

"Noel, please stop, I'm just trying to do my best by everyone."

"Everyone? The baby isn't even born yet, you don't know if it's a boy or a girl, you know nothing about that baby but you do know that you have three beautiful children – and a husband – who love you more than anything else in the world and yet you are choosing the baby before all of us!"

I was exasperated. "I'm not choosing anyone over anybody else – I'm trying to be fair. I'm trying to weigh up the risks that Doctor O'Keeffe spoke about and, when I do that, then I can't take the risk of surgery. It seems unwarranted."

"You're infuriating, do you know that?"

I said nothing.

"Come on, Eva, you don't need me to spell it out to you – he thinks that you have cancer."

"But he doesn't know for sure."

"He has seen enough of these things to know what he's dealing with here."

"Look, Noel, call me what you want but it's not going to change my mind. Now please, I'm asking you to support my decision."

We drove home the rest of the way in silence. I could see by the way his whole body was tensed up that he was furious with me. His shoulders were raised up around his neck and his hands were clamped around the steering wheel as he drove. It took a lot to get Noel mad – he was usually very easygoing – but when he did, he could brood for days.

He slammed the door of the car shut and stormed into the kitchen ahead of me. I followed in behind him and went straight for the kettle – I needed it after that.

Seán came in from school singing "We Will Rock You", oblivious to the tension between his parents. Freddie Mercury had died the previous November and Seán had since discovered his music. At the time it had been played on every radio and TV station and Seán was now obsessed with Queen. He kept on singing away to himself as he went about pulling apart the fridge and making himself a sandwich.

"Will you ever give it over, Seán!" I snapped.

"What?" He was in his own world. "Oh, sorry, Mam."

Out of the corner of my eye, I could see Noel glaring at me.

"You're all right, love, maybe just pick another song," I said contritely.

Mam called down to the house later on. I knew she was anxious to know how I had got on in the hospital again. Noel had headed out to the fields. He usually came in for his tea around five but there was no sign of him today. Patrick was down in his room doing his homework. There was no sign of Kate either, although that wasn't unusual and today I was glad of it – it gave me a chance to talk to Mam without fear of being overheard.

"It wasn't good news, I'm afraid, Mam." I served her up a

192

plate of buns and a cup of tea. "It's grown bigger again."

"Lord above! And I was praying round the clock for you – I even asked Father Ball to pray for you during Mass yesterday."

My mother was a devout Catholic – there was nothing that couldn't be cured by prayer – even potential cancer, it seemed.

"What did he say to you – the doctor?"

"Well, he wants me to have surgery to remove it but it's risky for the baby and I don't want to take the chance."

"And what does Noel say?"

"Stop – we're arguing over it. He wants me to have the surgery but imagine if I had the operation and something happened to the baby and then it turned out that the growth was nothing after all?"

"It's a hard decision, Eva – I don't envy you."

"What would you do, Mam, if you were in my shoes?"

"God, I don't know, Eva, it's a tough one." She sighed heavily. "I mean Noel is right – you have three beautiful children to think of as well –"

"But the risks are so small when you think of the stats Doctor O'Keeffe mentioned."

"I suppose so . . ." She wouldn't meet my eyes.

"You don't think I'm doing the right thing, do you?"

"Ah Eva, I can't say . . . sure none of us can know how we'd react in your situation until we were going through it ourselves."

"I can feel the baby kicking now, Mam. I couldn't live with myself if anything were to happen to it."

"And what if it were to happen to you?"

"Stop, Mam. Look, you'll just have to pray a bit more for me. I'll be right as rain, I know I will."

"Well, you can't knock that spirit." She took a sip from her mug. "I'll get a Mass said for you in Knock. Have you told the kids yet?"

I shook my head. "Not yet. I'm trying to work out how best to tell them. And I need Noel and me to be on the same page first or God knows what way they'll react –"

The back door opened then.

"Oh hiya, Gran!" Kate said, coming into the kitchen in her navy tartan school kilt and woollen blazer. I noticed she had the waistband folded up on itself so that the skirt was a couple of inches shorter than it should be. She was wearing make-up too – a bit of foundation that was too dark for her and mascara on her lashes. She chatted away to her grandmother, all sweetness and light. You would never think that she was the same girl who screamed and roared and backchatted at me constantly. She adored her gran – they had a great relationship and Mam thought she was an angel. She never saw the side to Kate that I saw here at home. No, that was reserved for me alone.

"How are you, love? Did you have a good day in school?"

"I did thanks, Gran. What are you two talking about? You look very serious."

Kate hadn't mentioned the baby since. Not to me or to her dad or even Mam. It was as if it didn't exist for her.

"Ah, this and that," said Mam. "Boring stuff that would be of no interest to you."

"Do you want a cup of tea, Kate?"

"Yeah, I will, thanks, Mam."

I was amazed how she could switch on and switch off her personality as she felt like it.

My mother would go home now and then the Devil Kate would return as soon as the door was closed behind her.

Chapter 33

Three days later and Noel still wasn't talking to me. That left Patrick and Seán as the only members of the family who deemed me worthy enough to talk to. Noel would exchange a few words as necessary if there was something about one of the children but that was the extent of our communication. I knew he was still seething. I was constantly asking myself if I had made the right decision but then when I thought of the little baby inside me I knew that I had. Noel didn't see the baby as a person yet but for me it was very real. I could feel it moving and turning – it was already a little person to me – we just hadn't met yet.

Kate on the other hand just gave me filthy looks as if I was the scum on the soles of her shoes. I knew we needed to talk so one day I went down to her in her bedroom. I knocked on the door but she couldn't hear me over the music being played on her stereo so I just walked straight in. She was sitting cross-legged on her bed, her head bowed deep in concentration as she used permanent marker to graffiti her schoolbag. The room was like a shrine to Nirvana and posters of a strung-out Kurt Cobain took over every spare inch of the walls. She didn't hear me come in so I walked over and lowered the volume. Her head shot up.

"What do you think you're doing?" she snapped at me.

"I thought you'd like to go into Galway at the weekend – just the two of us?"

"Why would I want to do that?"

"Well, I thought we might do a bit of shopping, get you a few new clothes?" I sat down on the edge of the bed.

"All right."

I knew she would never be one to turn down the opportunity of getting new clothes. Although God knows we couldn't afford it.

It had been so long since we had done anything together. The thing was that I missed her – Kate and I used to be so close. She followed me everywhere as a little girl. She would stand beside me at the bathroom mirror when I was putting on my mascara and I would have to let her put some on too – or she would traipse around the house in my 'hee-highls' as she called them, with my beads draped around her neck so that they were almost trailing on the floor and I was afraid of my life that she was going to trip up on them. She was my shadow and I loved having a little girl who wanted to try on my make-up and clothes. It was only when she had gone to secondary school that the mood swings had started and I became the enemy. I was hurt and upset at first but when I talked to friends they assured me it was just a phase – that all teenage girls go through it with their mothers but they come out again the other side of it. I also hoped, if we had a good day, then she might become more accepting of the baby. I still hadn't told her about the other thing.

The following Saturday we set off for Galway. We had a great morning, just the two of us. I ended up spending far more than I had planned. She saw a long peasant skirt that she liked so I got that for her, then there were a pair of runners she wanted and black nail varnish too. I knew I was probably buying her affection but I didn't care. We went for lunch in a fast-food place just off Shop Street that Kate chose. We both had fries and burgers and Kate ordered a milkshake.

"You've got a bump now." It was the first reference she had made to the baby since we had told her that I was pregnant.

"I do – it's big enough, isn't it?" People in town were starting to notice that I was pregnant even though I was wearing loose clothes. At Mass the week before I observed people's eyes being drawn to my bump as they wondered was I or wasn't I. The look of shock on their faces was amusing – they were almost as bad as Kate.

"Uh-huh." She nodded. "You look massive." She sucked up her strawberry milkshake noisily through the straw. Oh to be a skinny thirteen-year-old! I just had to look at a milkshake to feel the weight going on.

"Well, cheers, Kate!"

She smiled at me, her beautiful smile that reminded me of when she was a little girl.

"I'm nearly halfway there now," I said.

"I can't believe there's going to actually be a newborn baby in the house."

"Me neither."

"I suppose it'll be okay."

"Yeah?" This was a breakthrough.

"I've told Aidan and all my friends and they actually thought it was kinda cool – not the fact that you and Dad are still having sex, that's just gross, but that I'm going to have a new baby brother or sister."

"I see. Well, I think we'll all enjoy having a new lease of life around the house. This baby will be very lucky to have an older sister and two brothers all doting on it."

"But there's no way I'm bringing the baby out in case people think it's mine. And I'm definitely not going to be baby-sitting for you – I have my own social life to think about, y'know."

"Don't worry, no one is asking you to baby-sit just yet!" I laughed.

"What's wrong with Dad? He's been in a bad mood for ages now."

I didn't think she'd even noticed the tension between us. I decided while things were going well it might be best to come clean about what was going on.

"Look, Kate, during one of my scans – the doctor . . . well, he found a growth."

"What kind of growth?"

"Well, it's hard to say without doing a biopsy but that would be a risk for the baby so I'm not going to do it and your dad is just a bit annoyed about it, that's all."

"What's his problem?"

"Ah, you know what he's like."

"Sure, can't you just check it out after the baby is born?"

"Exactly!"

I didn't want to worry her with the risks – best to keep it simple.

When we came out of the burger bar we strolled arm in arm over the cobbles. It was so good to have my daughter back – it was times like these that lifted me to the top of the world and my heart would swell with love for her. I knew that in a couple of days she'd be back to being a raging hormonal teenager but every now and then I got to see a piece of the daughter I knew and loved so well and I was making the most of it.

I was tired, my legs felt like they had been poured full of lead and, although I wasn't usually one for napping during the day, I felt I could lie down and sleep for a week – but I didn't want the day to end just yet because days like this were such a rarity. I wanted to savour every minute of it. It was such a weight off my mind having Kate back on side again. Now it just left Noel – one down, one to go. I decided I was going to talk it out with him after the kids had gone to bed that night. I couldn't bear the atmosphere around the house any more especially seeing as the kids had picked up on it. We both needed to act like grown-ups. And the stress wasn't good for the baby.

"Hey, Mam!" she said as she stopped on the street in front of an A-frame board on the path.

"What?" I said warily as I read the sign: *Bodyart: tattoos, piercings on the spot.*

"Can I get my nose pierced?"

"No way!"

Things might have been going well between us but I wasn't a complete walkover.

"I knew you wouldn't let me." She started to laugh. "Maybe a tattoo?"

"Keep on walking." I steered her by the shoulders past the shop.

On the way home in the car I stole a sideways glance at her while we were stopped at traffic lights and was hit with a huge pang of guilt. I really hoped I had made the right decision in not having the surgery like Doctor O'Keeffe had advised. I wouldn't admit it to Noel but the odd time the doubts would get to me and I would wonder if he was right. Was I putting this baby inside me before our other children? Kate chatted away and she didn't seem to notice I was thinking. She opened up to me about Aidan and how much she really liked him. I just concentrated on driving and let her talk. When I got home, I couldn't keep my eyes open. I said to Kate that I was going in to bed for a lie-down for half an hour. I didn't have the energy to remove my clothes so I got in under the duvet fully clothed.

When I woke and saw the daylight giving the room that early morning glow, I knew I had slept all night. And I couldn't believe that I was still wearing my jeans and T-shirt. Noel was asleep in a mound under the duvet beside me. I raised myself on one arm to look at the alarm clock over on Noel's side of the bed. It was 6 a.m.. Jesus Christ, I had slept twelve hours straight! I lay there for a while thinking about everything, wishing Noel would be my support. We never fought. We were just one of those couples. People often said to me that we were both too easygoing to fight and I knew what they meant. But then, when he was mad with me, in this case madder than I had ever seen him before, it worried the life out of me.

I shook his left shoulder that was raised.

"What, what's wrong?" he said sleepily, pulling the sheet up over his shoulder.

"We need to talk."

He rubbed his eyes and looked at his alarm clock.

"It's seven minutes past six – go back to sleep." It was nearly time for him to get up and he was trying to make the most of the few minutes that he had left in bed.

"I can't, Noel, it's driving me mad. I don't like it when we fight."

"And you think I do?" He sighed as he propped himself up against the headboard.

"No, I know you don't – that's why I want to sort this out before it goes on any longer."

"Have you made your mind up?"

"I can't have the surgery, Noel – I just can't do it. No matter how many times I think about it I just can't do it." I could feel the baby kicking. I pulled up my T-shirt then, showing him my bump.

"Look, Noel – just look." As if performing on cue the baby kicked, visible from the outside. "I can't do anything that would jeopardise it."

He let out a long and frustrated sigh and looked up at the ceiling.

"Okay."

"What?"

"Okay – I'll support you. If this is what you want, I'll support you."

"Really, Noel – no more mention of surgery?"

"That's it – that's the end of it. If this is what you want, then I'll go along with it but I just pray to God that it will all be okay."

"Of course it will – sure you won't get rid of me that easily."

"I don't want to get rid of you." He put his arm under me and pulled me in tight so that my head was resting against his shoulder.

"I love you, Eva."

"And I love you. I told Kate about everything yesterday."

"Oh yeah?"

"Yeah, it was like there was a tiny chink in her armour and I got to see my real daughter for a while. We had a great day together. Just like old times. She has come to terms with the baby – her friends all think it's cool, so that helps."

"Does she know that it might be cancer?"

"Well, I didn't want to completely scare the life out of her so I just said it was a 'growth'."

"I see – well, it's probably for the best. We should probably tell the boys later on too."

When we told the boys, Patrick just shrugged his shoulders and Seán asked if we were done so he could go outside and play football. Again, we hadn't used the 'C'-word. I had debated it in my head whether we should just be upfront with them but, since I didn't even know myself that it was cancer we were dealing with here, there was no point in going down that road.

Chapter 34

A few weeks later I was due back at the hospital for my next appointment. I think they were hoping I would have changed my mind about the surgery but the more life I could feel growing inside of me, the more I knew that there was no way I would change my mind.

As feared, the scan showed that the mass had enlarged once again. I could see it myself on the screen. I saw on Doctor O'Keeffe's face that he was worried about it. He stared intensely at the screen, deep in concentration, as he did his measurements. Thankfully he didn't mention surgery to me this time, which I was grateful for. We had made up our minds and I didn't want to open it all up for debate again.

Although Noel had agreed to accept my decision, I knew it didn't sit well with him. Our truce was fragile and all it would take would be for Doctor O'Keeffe to make another recommendation and the wound would be opened all over again. The good news was that the baby was doing well, they were very happy with its growth and movements and the mass seemed to be having no effect on him or her whatsoever. This brightened my mood considerably and I knew that I had made the right choice.

I didn't mention it to them but I was starting to feel a lot of pain in my abdomen – pain that I knew wasn't coming from the baby. I presumed it was from both the baby and the tumour putting pressure on my organs. But I was afraid that if I said anything it would just strengthen the argument for surgery.

The pain got worse over the next few weeks and I was trying to manage as best I could but, when I woke up one Saturday morning and couldn't even get out of bed, Noel called an ambulance. I could see the look of pure fear and terror on the kids' faces but I wasn't able to talk to them. The pain had gripped me while I was being put onto a stretcher and wheeled into the back of the ambulance. Noel held my hand the whole way to the hospital. By the time we got there, the pain had eased off again but even I was frightened by how forceful it had been.

Doctor O'Keeffe was waiting for me as soon as we came through the doors.

"Don't tell me they called you in on your day off?" I said.

"Never mind that – there's no such thing as having as a day off in this profession. How are you doing?"

"I'll survive."

I couldn't help but notice a worried look on his face.

He carried out another scan.

"It's as I suspected, Eva. The mass has enlarged and now, with the pressure of your growing uterus, it is putting pressure on the other internal organs and causing torsion. Without surgery it will continue to get progressively more painful."

"I've come this far, doctor, I'm just heading into the third trimester, I'm on the home stretch, I can't do it now."

"I had a feeling you might say that."

I smiled at him. "We're getting to know each other very well."

"What I would suggest, Eva, is that we look at delivering the baby early by Caesarean section and try to debulk as much of the mass as possible at the same time."

"How early?"

"Well, you're coming up to twenty-seven weeks now and the pain is just going to get worse. I'd like to keep you in hospital from now on, I'm afraid – there is a risk of placental abruption if the mass continues to get bigger. I am quite keen to get a biopsy of this mass and if the results show that it is cancer, I would be eager to start treatment sooner rather than later. I think thirty-two weeks would be a good time – there is usually a good outcome for babies delivered at this stage in a pregnancy with very few complications – obviously there will be a stay in the special care unit but usually after a few weeks, once they have put on weight, the babies are able to go home."

"I see."

"We can give steroid shots for the baby's lungs to help the foetus to achieve lung maturity."

"Eva, you have to do it," said Noel. "I let you make the decision on putting off surgery but, now that Doctor O'Keeffe is saying there is a good chance for the baby, then we need to go with what he is recommending. You have a responsibility to the other three as well."

"Okay. All right." I was past fighting at that stage.

The next few weeks were tough. I was on a ward with five other women being treated for complications of pregnancy. One was a diabetic, two more had high blood pressure and another woman was being monitored for premature leaking of waters. It was grand to have their company during the long days. There was a TV at the end of the ward but most of the time I was too exhausted to get out of bed to watch it. The pain was awful but there wasn't much I could take because I was pregnant. It felt as though my organs were being squeezed and twisted inside out. Noel would bring the kids in to see me but I didn't like them seeing me like this. I could see their worried faces, Kate's especially. I tried to put on a brave face for them but some days I just didn't have the energy. Mam would come in and sit with me, her fingers knotted around her rosary beads, moving them swiftly through her fingers, but no matter how much she prayed it didn't ease up the pain. It didn't help that it was a warm summer – one of the hottest in years. I could see the colour on Noel's face from working the land when he would come in to visit me in the evenings. Kate had a sprinkling of freckles across her cheeks and along the bridge of her nose – it reminded me of when she was a little girl. She looked so healthy and beautiful. When I told her that, she had a fit of course – telling me they were the ugliest things and how she had spent hours putting on loads of make-up to cover them up and then I had to go and point them out straight away. I could never say the right thing as far as Kate was concerned.

One day when Noel had taken the boys to the coffee shop to get a sandwich and Kate and I were alone she asked me out straight.

"How serious is it, Mam?"

"I'm not sure, love. They won't know until they deliver the baby and then they can operate."

"But why can't they do that now? I can see you squirming in the bed in pain – it's horrible!"

"I'm sorry, love – in a few more weeks, once the baby has developed a little bit more and is a bit stronger."

"I wish this baby had never happened."

"Kate!"

"I do, Mam – it's caused nothing but trouble – look at everything you're going through for it!"

"Well, it's hardly the baby's fault, now is it, Kate?"

"I guess not."

"Look, once the baby is born, they can do the surgery and then I'll be right as rain again."

I knew Noel was finding it tough at home. The kids were on their summer holidays from school so he was trying to occupy them, keep Kate out of trouble, as well as staying on top of the farm. Mam was helping out too. She would call over and do the washing and make dinner in the evenings. Noel was saying that Kate was out with Aidan from the time she got up in the mornings until last thing at night and he didn't like it. She didn't even bother coming home for her dinner any more. He wasn't sure what way to deal with it. Noel never was good at the discipline. That was my job – that was the way we worked. He was also reluctant to come down too hard on her with everything going on. I told him not to worry, that it was just her way of coping. Things would all get back to normal after I came home. It was coming up to Kate's fourteenth birthday so I told Noel to get her a pair of the Levi's that she so desperately wanted. He balked when I told him the price of them.

"We can't afford them!" he said.

"Ah Noel, go on, she's going through a tough time of it at the moment – she could do with a little cheering up."

I felt so guilty for the kids, being wheeled in to see me and sit around a boring hospital when I'm sure they just wanted to be out playing with their friends in the sunshine. The boys would sit on the plastic chairs until boredom set in and they would start nudging and poking at each other before it would escalate and Noel would tell them to stop because the other patients on the ward were resting. He would give them money and they would run out to the hospital shop and stock up on sweets and other things full of neon colourings and e-numbers and bars so chewy that I was worried their teeth would come out stuck in the mess.

My appetite had decreased so that even minute amounts of food left me feeling full. Doctor O'Keeffe said it was because the cyst was compressing my stomach – any other time this would have been great news but now it just meant that I was worried about the baby. He assured me the baby was getting what it needed from me and would be just fine. He was more worried about me.

"I'm fed up of this place, Noel," I said for the umpteenth time. "I just want to go home."

"Well, you're nearly there now."

"How are the kids?"

"Great."

"Did you get those jeans for Kate?"

"I did – they cost enough though."

"I can't wait to see her face when we give them to her. Will you do it in here? I'd hate to miss it."

"Of course we will, love – we're hardly going to do it without you."

"Is she still out till all hours with Aidan?"

"Yep – he's a grand fella and all but I don't see them from one end of the day to the next and God knows what they're getting up to. I think she's smoking, Eva."

"Oh yeah?" I was lying back on the pillow with my eyes closed. My head was pounding like someone was thrashing a lump hammer between my brain and skull. It was so warm in the ward and the window at the end of the room could only be opened back an inch.

"Well, I could definitely smell something the other day and then a packet of Benson & Hedges fell out of her pocket during the week."

I opened my eyes and sat forward. A pain shot through my abdomen as I did so. I grimaced for a moment.

"Benson & Hedges? I thought she'd have better taste in cigarettes – bloody awful things they are!"

I had smoked briefly for a time in my twenties, before the kids were born, when it was a cool thing to do and people didn't know about the damage it did to your health.

"Can you just be serious for a minute, Eva?"

"Sorry, Noel – I'll talk to her the next time she's in. This is tough on her. First of all her mother is pregnant at forty years of age, then she ends up in hospital, possibly with cancer. I know she acts like she doesn't need me but teenage girls need their mothers more than ever to help them through the difficult years. Don't I remember it well myself?"

"Well, I just hope they're not having sex – we don't need any more unplanned pregnancies in this family."

"She'd have more sense," I said and we both laughed then.

Chapter 35

My life became more or less confined to my hospital bed. The nurses would help me out for a short walk down the corridor every day but other than that I was on the flat of my back staring at the mint-green walls of St Brigid's ward. My legs were sore and swollen and I was short of breath even though I wasn't doing anything. They were all the normal symptoms of pregnancy but magnified because of the growing mass.

Visiting hours were between six and eight in the evening so usually Noel marched the kids in to see me. Mam sometimes would come as well.

Kate's birthday came and went. Mam had baked a chocolate cake and we lit some candles and sang Happy Birthday to her. She was thrilled when she opened her present – she couldn't quite believe that she finally had a pair of the jeans that she so desperately craved. She had gone into the bathroom on the ward and changed into them straight away. I smiled at Noel and we both knew they had been worth every penny, just to see the happiness on her face.

"All by yourself today?" I said to Noel when he came in one evening.

208

"The boys were out playing – I couldn't get them in. And Kate, well, Kate –"

"What's wrong?"

"Ah, you've enough on your plate."

"Tell me."

"Well, Sergeant Trevor brought her home in the back of the squad car last night."

"Why, what did she do?" I tried to sit up straighter but my whole abdomen felt as though it was being pulled apart so I lay back down again.

"Herself and Aidan were found sculling back a flagon of cider in the church car-park."

"Ah for feck sake – she's only fourteen! She's too young for that carry-on."

"Tell me about it! And you should have seen the fanny pelmet she was wearing when she arrived home – she had gone out wearing her jeans! It was so short that she'd have every dog in the village sniffing after her and I told her as much!"

"I'd say that went down well."

"Ah you know yourself, lots of screaming and shouting and door-slamming, but she knew by me that she had gone a step too far this time."

Even I could see that Noel had been very snappy of late. Normally it took a lot to push his buttons but the littlest things would send him over the edge or off on a rant these days.

"I gave her a good talking-to this morning. That's why she wouldn't come in to see you – she's afraid of what you'll say."

"Well, she can't avoid me forever. God, this is a nightmare . . ."

"What is?"

"This whole thing – me being confined to hospital while the kids run wild and things fall apart at home – and I can't even do anything about it!"

"You're nearly there now and then we'll get you back home again."

"Yeah. It's dragging though – all day only allowed out of my bed to walk up the corridor to the shower and even that is such an effort. I'm sick to death of looking at these four walls. I'm so fed up."

We were interrupted by June, the nurse looking after me. She brought a wheelchair up to the side of the bed for me.

"Ah my wheels – what exciting place are you taking me to now?" I asked. It was bad when the highlight of my day was when June came along with my wheelchair.

"You've a date with Doctor O'Keeffe," she said brightly. "We won't be long."

"Do you want me to come too?" Noel asked.

"No, you go down and get yourself a cup of tea in the coffee shop."

"Well, how did you get on?" Noel asked when I got back.

It wasn't good news.

"It's been two weeks now that the baby hasn't put on any weight. They're saying something about the growth being restricted now by the mass – what did he call it – throw me over my chart for a minute, Noel."

He took my chart from the holder at the end of the bed where June had put it. I flicked it open and tried to read Doctor O'Keeffe's handwriting.

"Yeah, here it is – 'intrauterine growth restriction'. Although he didn't say it, I reckon he's thinking of delivering this baby pretty soon."

"Well, you're almost thirty-one weeks now . . . look, we just have to put our trust in him – he's the doctor, he knows what he's doing. You've given it your best shot."

"But it's so early!"

"I know but they can do wonderful things for babies born early these days – it's not like it used to be – things have advanced so much."

"I hope I've done the right thing."

"How do you mean?"

"Well, not getting the surgery. I never thought about this side of it – it's restricting the baby so that's not good either."

"Look, they're keeping a close eye on you, they won't let anything happen."

"I just want to hold him or her in my arms – that's all I want."

"You will, Eva, you're doing great. You're nearly there now, love."

"I know – I just wish I could fast-forward a few weeks and have the whole lot over me."

"Just hang on in there now, it'll all be okay and we'll have you and the baby back home again in no time."

"You look wrecked, Noel. Are you all right?"

"I'm okay." He was sitting forward, his elbows resting on the side of the bed, massaging his temples with his fingers.

"I know it's tough on you, keeping it all afloat at home."

"I'm grand. I'll be glad when it's all over though."

"Me too." The whole ordeal was taking its toll on both of us.

After Noel had gone home, I read my book for a while but I couldn't concentrate so I closed it again and put it back up on top of the locker. Today was one of the days where I was having doubts about my decision, although I would never admit it to anyone. I knew by the whispering and mannerisms of the team looking after me that they were worried about me. I had overheard their conversations with Noel – out in the corridor because they didn't want me to hear. But by now I was too far gone to change my mind. In for a penny, in for a pound. I would just have to ride it out. When I looked at Kate, full of her teenage angst and anger, or the innocence of the two boys, I would feel so guilty. Was Noel right? Had I put this baby before the needs of my other children? And God love them, they didn't realise how serious it all was. In their heads this was something related to the baby and once the baby was born, all would be well again. I desperately hoped that they were right. My three children needed me. In my mind the risks had seemed small but now it appeared that I might be on the wrong side of the statistic that I was so fond of quoting to Noel.

Chapter 36

Doctor O'Keeffe came round on his visit the next morning. He pulled over a chair to my bedside and sat down on it. He never sat down – he always did his morning rounds standing up. Noel wasn't in yet. He usually didn't make an appearance until visiting time in the evenings, after he had the farm sorted out.

"Eva, with your consent we would like to deliver the baby this week. As you know from the scan your baby's growth is being restricted by the mass so I don't think there is any benefit to be gained by leaving him or her in there any longer."

"When?"

"Ideally tomorrow."

"*Tomorrow?*"

"Yes. You are coming up to thirty-one weeks and usually babies born at this stage do very well. You have already had a steroid shot to help mature the baby's lungs. Now, obviously, a baby born at this time will require a stay in the special care unit but there hopefully will be no adverse outcomes."

"I see."

"Regarding the surgery, the plan is to do a Caesarean section delivery followed by debulking of the mass all in the one go – there is no point in doing two lots of surgery. Now there is quite a high chance that a total abdominal hysterectomy will have to

212

be carried out – that is the uterus and both ovaries and maybe the omentum too. Would you be okay with this or are you planning on any more children?"

"Oh, believe me, Doctor – I am done. You can whip the lot of it out for all I care."

"Well, you do know that you will experience earlier onset of the menopause?"

"Ah, the change of life – sure I might as well get it over with now than in a few years' time."

"Okay, good – now, unfortunately, unlike most C-section deliveries you will require a general anaesthetic so you won't be awake when your baby is born and Noel won't be able to be present either. There will also be quite a few teams, headed by myself, involved in the surgery – an obstetric team to deliver the baby, paediatrics, and then the surgical team to remove the mass."

"Sounds like there'll be no staff left in the hospital!"

"Now how are your pain levels today?"

"I'm okay."

"Well, tell the nurses if you need anything and try and rest as much as you can tonight because you have a tough few days ahead of you and you need to be as rested and relaxed as possible."

"Relax – in this place? Are you mad?"

I told Noel when he came in later. He breathed out slowly.

"So it's all systems go then?"

"Yeah." Even though it felt like I had been hanging around here for ages, it still felt as though it came on quite suddenly in the end.

"Are you all set for it – do you have everything you need?"

"Well, can you bring in the bag with the baby's stuff that I have in the spare room?"

"I'll bring it with me in the morning. Will I be allowed into the theatre?"

"No – he said you wouldn't be allowed in because I'll be out cold."

"Right, well, sure I'll be here anyway for the moral support." He reached for my hand on the bed and squeezed it.

"Thanks, love. I can't believe that by this time tomorrow the baby in here –" I pointed to my bump, "will be born!"

We chatted about the kids and the weather and then June came around and gently suggested that Noel should head on home because we had a long day ahead of us tomorrow. He leant over and kissed me goodbye and said he'd see me bright and early in the morning.

I didn't really sleep that night. I felt a mixture of nervous excitement because I had been waiting for this day to come for months now. Everything hinged on tomorrow's operation and the results of that. I was just glad that I was finally getting the keys to get away from this limbo state.

The next morning, with Noel by my side, June helped to move me onto a trolley. Noel gave me a kiss on the forehead and said he'd be waiting for me when I came around. Then they wheeled me down to theatre.

Even though Doctor O'Keeffe had warned me, I was still shocked by the size of the team waiting for me.

"All this for me? I feel very honoured."

"Are you okay?" Doctor O'Keeffe asked.

"Just a bit nervous, that's all, but sure I'll see you on the other side."

"Of course you will." And for the first time since I had been under his care he smiled at me.

The anaesthetist put the mask over my face then and chatted away to me so I relaxed and then he counted me out.

Chapter 37

I woke up in the recovery room and the first face I saw was Noel's. His face was blurry at first but then the edges around me sharpened as I began to focus. He was smiling down at me.

"You're awake!"

I smiled back up at him.

"Well done – we had a little girl!"

"A little girl – well, isn't that great!" My voice was crackly.

"Here, have a sip of water."

He held the glass to my lips.

"That's better. How is she, Noel?"

"She's a tiny little thing but she's doing really well. They're giving her some treatment at the moment to help with her breathing but they said she'll be fine. She just needs to get a bit bigger and stronger."

"Oh, thank God!" The relief coursed through me.

"How are you feeling?"

"Sore." My whole body felt bruised and battered. My skin was on fire.

"I'll go and get June. She said to call for her if you woke up."

He came back into the room with June following behind him.

"How are you doing, Eva? You are hooked up to a morphine drip. If you want to press this pump here every time you're in pain, it will help. Be aware it will send you as high a kite though."

"Thanks – I've always wanted to try morphine – it's the closest thing to heroin I'll get. Do you know how the surgery went?"

"Unfortunately you'll have to wait for Doctor O'Keeffe to find out about that – he should be around to see you soon."

"Can I go to see her?"

"The baby?"

I nodded.

"Not just yet, dear. Wait for Doctor O'Keeffe and then we'll bring you up. But, don't worry, I was just talking to the special care nurse and she assured me that she's doing really well."

Doctor O'Keeffe came around a while later. This was the bit that I was dreading. I knew by his face that it was serious before he even started to talk.

"How are you doing, Eva?"

"I've been better."

"Congratulations on your baby girl."

"Thank you."

"She's doing very well, I believe."

"She's a little fighter by all accounts."

"Well, I'm sure you want to know how the surgery went – we managed to debulk some of the mass but it wasn't as successful as I had hoped. Unfortunately we had to do a total abdominal hysterectomy. In the meantime I will send the biopsy to the lab to confirm whether or not it is malignant."

"Right, so it's a waiting game until then?" Noel asked, giving my hand a quick squeeze.

"Yes, I'm afraid so – hopefully we will know more soon. In the meantime try and get some rest. I know it's easier said than done but your body has been through a lot and an operation like that will take a lot out of you. You will be tender for a while too so just be careful getting out of bed not to put pressure on the wound."

That evening they brought me up to the neonatal intensive care unit in a wheelchair. I was pushed along the vinyl corridor with my drip trailing beside me. I was still woozy after the surgery. Noel was beside me.

I was shocked by all the beeping machines and wires everywhere, the clinical starkness of the room.

"Oh God!" I shrieked.

"It's okay – parents always get a fright when they come in here for the first time." The special care nurse came over to me. "It looks worse than it is. You have to remember that all these machines are helping your baby. She's over here."

I was pushed along behind her and I saw my beautiful baby girl. She had a pink hat on her head and was wearing a nappy which seemed to cover up most of her tiny body, but otherwise she was naked. The needles and tubes sticking out of her were frightening. She looked lost – a tiny baby inside a huge incubator.

"Look, Noel, look at how small her hands and feet are!" All my other children had been born at full term so I had never seen a baby so small before.

"She's small but perfect," the nurse said to me softly over my shoulder. "She's strong."

"What will we call her?" I turned to Noel.

"Well, I was thinking of this while I was waiting for you to come round. How about Aoife? It means beautiful."

"It's perfect for her. Can I touch her?" I asked the nurse.

"Of course – she would love to hold her mammy's hand."

I slotted my hand in through the holes of the incubator. She immediately curled her small fingers around my index finger like she knew who I was. I wrapped the rest of my palm around her small hand and held it in mine. I felt such a surge of love for her – it was like my heart swelled again just like it had with the others. I thought of all the heartache and worry over the last few months but I knew I had done the right thing.

Chapter 38

I tossed and turned all night long waiting for the time to come when I would know the biopsy results. I saw every hour on the clock. I wasn't sure what to expect but, from the sound of it, Doctor O'Keeffe wasn't confident it would be good news. I tried to stay positive but it was hard in the early morning darkness when everything seemed so bleak. I almost welcomed the lights being switched on at 6 a.m. and the sound of nurses bustling around getting ready to start a new day.

A lady came in pushing the breakfast trolley. She put the tray on the table at the end of my bed and pushed it up towards me. The smell of the scrambled egg was nauseating – even the sight of the melting butter on the toast made me want to vomit. I pushed the table away as best I could without stretching my stitches.

"Morning, Eva – are you not in form for your breakfast this morning?" June came in sunnily and stood beside me.

It was the same every morning – sometimes I might pick at a slice of bread or have a yoghurt, but for the last few mornings I couldn't face eating anything.

I shook my head.

"Do you want me to take it away for you?"

"If you wouldn't mind, thanks."

"Well, I know you're anxious to speak with Doctor O'Keeffe. He has just started his rounds so he should be with you soon."

"Oh thank God – the worrying and not knowing is a killer."

"I was talking to the nurse on duty in special care last night and she said Aoife had a good night and they hope she'll be breathing by herself soon."

"Oh that's good news. Thank you, sister." My heart surged with love for Aoife. I longed to be able to cuddle her properly, away from all the tubes and wires and this blasted hospital.

She left me alone then and no sooner had she pulled the curtain back along on its track when Doctor O'Keeffe pulled it back and stuck his head around. My heart started thumping at the sight of him.

"Good morning, Eva. How did you sleep last night?"

"Not great."

"Well, I hope you're taking all the pain relief available to you?"

I nodded.

"So . . . I have your results here." He tapped his folder. "Would you rather I waited until Noel gets in?"

"No! C'mon – spit it out. I'm going out of my mind with worry here."

"All right. I'm afraid, as feared, the lab results have confirmed that the growth is malignant. I'm sorry, Eva – I truly am. What we're dealing with here, is ovarian cancer. Our next step is to assess how far advanced it is and whether . . ."

I sank my head back on my pillow and closed my eyes. This was not what I wanted to hear. He talked to me some more about our next steps but I didn't hear what he was saying and I didn't even notice him go back out of the ward.

June came in soon after and fixed the sheets on the bed.

"How are you doing?"

"I just can't believe it, I can't take it in."

"I'm sorry it wasn't good news, Eva – it always comes as a shock to get news like that. Is Noel coming in soon?"

Noel had been trying to come in to visit during the day since Aoife was born.

"He'll be in in a while – Seán had a football final this morning so I wanted him to go to it – so at least one of his parents would be at the sidelines to cheer him on." I could hear the bitter edge in my own voice. I felt I had missed out on so much over the last few weeks.

"Well, that's good. Look, I know it's not easy but try to stay positive, Eva – treatments are very advanced nowadays. It's not like it used to be when the C-word meant a death sentence."

"I know," I said wearily.

"We're just going to take you down for your scan now, dear."

"Scan?"

"Didn't Doctor O'Keeffe tell you? He told me he did – he wants to check for metastases to see if the cancer is localised to the ovaries or if it has spread."

"Oh sorry, I just zoned out after he told me the biopsy results."

"Of course you did, love. You've had a lot to take in today. Once you have the results of the scan back Doctor O'Keeffe will have a better idea of what we are dealing with and he can plan your treatment accordingly."

I was glad I'd been alone when he told me – it gave me a chance to get my head around it before I saw Noel.

When he came in that afternoon the familiarity of my husband brought it all to the surface and the tears started instantly.

"What is it, Eva – is everything okay with Aoife?"

"Yes, don't worry, she's fine – she's doing great."

"Well, what is it then?"

"My biopsy results came back –"

"And?"

"I have cancer, Noel."

"No, Eva – please tell me this isn't happening. Oh Eva!" He broke down.

As he sat there, heaving in the chair beside me, it was unnerving.

"This whole thing is a nightmare – what did we ever do to deserve this?"

"I know, love, I know, but we just have to stay positive." I knew it was a platitude but I couldn't think of anything else to say. "Cancer isn't a death sentence any more. There are lots of treatments for it nowadays." I knew that I was copying what June had just said to me but I couldn't think of anything else to say to him.

That evening Doctor O'Keeffe came around to give me the scan results. He pulled the curtain around me again. I was really starting to despise its old-fashioned terracotta-and-yellow floral fabric. Noel was sitting beside me and he reached out for my hand and gave it a reassuring squeeze.

Doctor O'Keeffe nodded to me and then turned to Noel. "Good evening, Noel." He didn't sit down.

Noel mumbled hello.

"Okay, well. I haven't good news, I'm afraid . . . the scan has shown secondary metastases on your liver and lungs . . . what we are dealing with here is an advanced form of ovarian cancer. I would like to treat the remaining tumour – the part we couldn't get with the surgery – and metastases with further treatment asap, I'm afraid."

I was too stunned to speak. From my limited knowledge of the disease, I knew that once cancer had spread to other organs it wasn't good news. I had heard of people in Ballyrobin being diagnosed with cancer but when it had spread, that was it, it was curtains then.

"I would like to start chemotherapy treatment as soon as your body has had a chance to regain some strength after the surgery."

"And then what?"

"We will then see how well it has responded to the treatment before deciding on our next steps."

I looked at Noel, watching his whole face changing as it registered with him what the doctor was saying. It felt like they were words for someone else.

Doctor O'Keefe talked me through all of the side effects that I had heard about – nausea, exhaustion, susceptibility to infections, hair loss, loss of appetite – and I tried to make a joke of it, saying that the loss of appetite might be a good thing but they had both looked at me like I was daft so I had shut up pretty quickly again.

Long after Doctor O'Keeffe and his white coat had left, his words were still ringing in my ears. Noel and I sat in silence, ruminating over our own thoughts, and then one of us would speak and then we would go silent again.

We went up to visit Aoife, Noel pushing the wheelchair. I needed to be close to her.

The special care nurses said she was doing very well. She was breathing by herself now which was great for her prematurity but she was being fed through a tube until her sucking reflex developed some more. We watched her stretch out her little body, arching her tiny back and straightening her skinny arms above her head. I reached into her little world and gently stroked the soft skin on her hand and the downy skin of her arm. *Metastases, secondaries, chemo* – the words kept playing on a loop inside my head. I didn't understand most of what he had said, only that it definitely was cancer and it had spread. And judging by his reaction it wasn't looking good.

"You're strong, Eva – you will beat this," Noel whispered to me as we both stared in at our tiny baby daughter. "There is no way, after all you've done to get Aoife here safely, I'll let you be taken away from us – no way. You're like Aoife, you're a fighter."

"I hope you're right, Noel, I really do." The tears started up again.

He leant over me in the wheelchair and pulled my head in against his chest as if he could protect me there.

"Is everything okay here?" It was the special care nurse.

I pulled back from Noel's chest and wiped my eyes.

"Yes – sorry, we're going now."

Noel wheeled me back down to the ward and helped me back

onto the bed. Even that short activity had left me exhausted.

"We have to tell the kids," Noel said.

"But they already know."

"C'mon, Eva – they haven't got a clue how serious it all is. They need to be told. If things get . . . worse . . . well, it will come as an awful shock to them."

"Not yet, Noel – can we just wait and see how the chemo goes – there's no point in worrying them unnecessarily. They've been through a lot lately."

He sighed heavily. "All right, it's your decision," he said, putting his hands up in the air.

Noel brought the children and Mam in to see me the next day. They all wanted to see the baby and I felt awful telling them that they weren't allowed into the special care unit. So instead they sat on various chairs around the bed.

After a few minutes I could see the boredom starting to kick in again. Seán asked me when I was coming home and I said soon. I could see Noel's disapproving look from the corner of my eye. Kate sat there sullenly, with her Walkman on that she had got for Christmas last year. The music could be heard buzzing through the headphones so it must have been blaring. She had dark eye make-up on, thick-pencilled eyeliner and charcoal eye shadow – if I didn't know her and just saw her in the street, I would find her intimidating. The contrast was harsh against her blonde hair and pale skin but I said nothing. I asked Noel to bring them all down to the coffee shop for a bit – he knew that I wanted to talk to Mam on my own. I could see the kids were delighted. They were fed up of this place. I couldn't blame them – I was too.

"How are you feeling today, love?"

"Still sore and tender. I managed to walk a bit earlier on but I was knackered before I even got out of the room."

"Well, take it easy now, do you hear me?"

"I just want to get Aoife and myself out of this place."

"Well, you'll both be able to come home soon."

"I have cancer, Mam."

"Ah no, Eva, no!" She pressed her fingers into my hands. It hurt.

I nodded and then I couldn't help it, tears filled my eyes and started spilling down my face.

Her first reaction was to start praying and I didn't have the heart to tell her that it would take a lot more than prayers to cure me now.

I asked her to keep an eye on Kate. I knew she was a typical teenager feigning indifference but I also knew her well enough to know that she was finding this whole thing very hard.

I just needed to get well enough to be allowed home to get everything back on track again. Noel was doing a great job but he was being pulled in ten different directions between coming in to visit me, worrying about our new baby, keeping the three of them at home out of trouble during the summer holidays and then trying to run the farm so we could keep a roof over our heads.

Mam said another prayer before she left and blessed me with her rosary beads.

Chapter 39

The surgery had taken a lot out of me. I felt weaker than I had felt since the whole ordeal started. My body no longer had to support a baby, part of the tumour had been removed yet I felt at my lowest. I hadn't expected that. Doctor O'Keeffe told me that he wouldn't start the chemo until my blood counts had improved and I was a bit stronger. The time passed very slowly, the days were long as I waited in limbo until I could start my treatment to fight the disease.

I would go up and sit with Aoife and marvel at how much modern medicine can do for tiny babies. She was growing much stronger and I was allowed to hold her now and I would spend hours cuddling her in my arms. And I missed the kids desperately. It just felt like one hurdle after another. I worked hard at trying to get my body stronger. I would eat small amounts of food and sleep whenever I could – I didn't have much else to do anyway.

After I had started my first round of chemo, Doctor O'Keeffe said there was no point in keeping me in hospital any more. I was delighted to be allowed go home after weeks of being on St Brigid's ward. I would still be in and out of the hospital every day to see Aoife but she was nearly at a weight where they would let her come home with us soon. I willed her to keep growing strong. I just wanted to get some normality back into our lives. I felt if we could just get her home then everything would be so much better – no more driving to the hospital and back, nearly an hour each way, over bouncy bog roads.

I told Noel not to tell the kids that I was coming home because I wanted to surprise them. As soon as I got in the door though, I realised that things had changed drastically with Kate. She hadn't been in to see me in two weeks. Her heavy eye make-up was only the start of it. She walked into the kitchen with a nose ring and nearly had a heart attack when she saw me in the room.

"What are *you* doing here?" she asked.

"Well, thanks for the nice welcome home!" I said sarcastically. "What's that thing in your nose? I told you that you weren't allowed to get one of those."

"You can't just come home after weeks away and start giving me orders." She was angry and I knew she was taking it out on me.

"Oh yes, I can, Kate, I'm your mother. I may not have been around for the last few weeks but this is still my house and my rules apply."

"'*My house and my rules!*'" she mimicked.

I was only just home and I didn't want to ruin it by getting into a fight with her so I let it go.

Seán and Patrick came running into the room and over to me and gave me big hugs.

"Where's Baby Aoife?" Patrick asked.

"She's still in hospital but she should be home very soon. She's thriving now. She's even taking her feeds by mouth, would you believe!"

"You won't be going back there then, Mam, will you?" Patrick asked.

"No, love, that's it now."

Noel glared at me.

"How can you lie to them like that?" he said after the boys had gone off outside to play football.

226

"I didn't lie."

"You haven't told them the truth! For all you know you might very well need to go back in. It's not fair to only give them half the picture, Eva."

"Ah stop Noel, I'm only home – I don't want to fight with you. You never told me about Kate getting her nose pierced!"

"I know, I said I'd wait till you were home. She just came home with it last week – she never even bothered to ask."

"She has some cheek, that one."

"Now don't be getting yourself stressed out about Kate, it's not good for you. You heard what Doctor O'Keeffe said – you have to take it easy now."

We were allowed to take Aoife home a few weeks later. She was still so tiny – she wouldn't even have been due yet. We bundled her up for her first journey home. The cool autumn air had started to creep in. Leaves were falling from the trees, gathering in huge rusty piles begging to be jumped in. It was September so the kids were gone back to school and it was a relief to have order and routine back in our lives once again.

Kate and Aidan were still going strong. He would walk her home after school. She had managed to persuade her dad to let her go to a concert in Galway with him. I wasn't happy about it but she wasn't listening to me at the moment. It was like she was punishing me for my absence over recent weeks.

I continued going back to the hospital for my weekly chemo sessions. It was gruelling and exhausting and, even with the anti-nausea medication, Noel would have to pull over on the road sometimes to let me be sick into the ditch. My throat was raw from vomiting. It was tiring at the best of times having a newborn in the house. I knew that already because I'd had three of them, but doing it while going through chemotherapy was in a different league altogether. I would hear Aoife crying in the cot beside me at night and I wouldn't have the energy to get out of bed to see to her. Noel was great and he took over most of the night feeds and Mam came over every day to help me out while Noel was out in the fields. I didn't want to worry them but I wasn't feeling any better, I was still in a lot of pain and I was having trouble catching my breath – the littlest thing would leave me breathless as if I had run a race. I would have to go into the bed and lie down and when I would wake up again half the day would be gone. My hair had started falling out after the second session – great big clumps of it came away in my hand one morning as I was brushing my hair. It was frightening. I immediately stopped brushing because I was afraid that I was making it worse but, even if I didn't go near it, another bit would fall out. I'd find it on my shoulder or some on the floor. I would put my hand up and feel a huge bald patch on my scalp. I put on a headscarf and felt utterly ridiculous – it was like it spelled out 'cancer victim'. There was no way I would go out in public with it on me. When Kate had seen it she started to laugh and then I had laughed too.

"You should at least get a wig, Mam."

"Yeah, I think you're right, love."

Although I hadn't exactly told Kate I had cancer, she knew I was having chemo. I'm not sure whether she understood what it actually meant. I had warned her that I might start losing my hair. I never thought I'd say I was happy to lose my hair but it was a relief to laugh with my daughter again – it had broken the ice between us.

I was trying to stay positive about the whole ordeal. I was due to have my last session the following week and then it would be back for the moment of truth where Doctor O'Keeffe would do another scan to see if it had worked.

Chapter 40

"So what do I do now?"

Doctor O'Keeffe had just delivered more bad news. The blood tests and scans had both shown that the chemo hadn't worked like he had hoped and there wasn't much more they could do for me. The cancer was too widespread. Noel was sobbing like a baby in the chair beside me but I was too stunned to do anything except somehow on autopilot to reach across to find his hand. He grabbed onto it as if he was holding on for dear life. As if by holding onto me tightly, he might be able to stop me from leaving his world.

"I'm afraid we've reached the end of the road, Eva – there isn't any more we can do for you. I'm truly sorry."

I tried to digest what he was saying. "So that's it? This is the end?"

"I'm sorry, Eva, the prognosis isn't good."

"Please say you've got it wrong, please? This can't be happening?" Noel was saying.

"How long have I got?" It seemed as though someone else was asking these questions, not me.

"I would expect four to six weeks."

I felt as though I was winded. Four to six weeks!

"I see."

I didn't expect it to come that quickly. It was an awful thing to be told you had such a short time left. The shock felt as though it had sucked my breath away and I couldn't breathe. My first reaction was panic – panic for all the things that I still needed to do. Panic because I wouldn't be there to watch my children growing up, all their milestones and big occasions. Patrick would be making his confirmation next year. And Aoife wouldn't even remember me. I started hyperventilating and somewhere on the periphery I could hear Noel saying "No, this can't be happening. This isn't happening. Someone has made a mistake!" over and over again. And I wished he would stop. He was still squeezing the life out of my hand.

"How's your pain, Eva? Are you managing okay?" Doctor O'Keeffe asked me.

I nodded because I couldn't think of anything to say.

"Well, I'm sure you'd rather be at home at this time but if it gets worse I can refer you to a hospice for palliative care. Don't suffer unnecessarily, Eva – we can give you pain relief to help you through it."

"But that's it then – it'll be curtains for me, won't it?"

"Well, I don't like to be bleak but yes . . . usually the end of life isn't too far away at that stage."

"How will it happen?"

"Do you mean, what is the next stage?"

I nodded.

"Well, usually after the patient comes in for pain relief, they tend to sleep a lot more and gradually sleep most of the time and after that stage it is usually a matter of days. If it helps, they usually pass peacefully."

"But there must be something you can do – there has to be something?" Noel said. "Some new treatment or therapy or even a clinical trial drug? There must be nearly a cure for cancer at this stage. With all those degrees you have up on the wall there, there has to be something you can do!"

"I'm afraid not, Noel. While we have made great progress in fighting the disease in recent years, there is still so much that we don't know about it and in Eva's case it's too far advanced. I'm sorry."

"What about radiation treatment? You haven't tried that!" He banged his fist on the desk and I jumped in my chair.

"Unfortunately in Eva's case the cancer is so advanced that the levels of radiation required would be too much for her body to take," Doctor O'Keeffe said softly.

When I got out to the car park I had to run to be sick into a flowerbed. The shock and devastation started to hit me. We sat into the car but Noel didn't start the engine. We both just sat there staring straight ahead at the drops of rain running in rivulets down the windscreen in front of us.

I felt a sheer overwhelming sense of injustice and anger. This wasn't fair. I was a good person, wasn't I? I didn't deserve this – my family didn't deserve this!

"I'm not ready to die, Noel," I whispered. He leaned over across the gearstick and held me in his arms. "I feel so robbed. I'm being cheated out of my future – the kids' future. I won't get to help Kate over a broken heart or watch Patrick try on his secondary-school uniform for the first time. Or Seán when he scores a goal in the County Final. Or get open-mouthed kisses from Aoife and watch her take her shaky first steps . . . Or dab calamine lotion on red chicken-pox welts. Everything. I'm going to miss out on so much . . . And I'm scared of what lies ahead for me . . ."

"It's okay to be scared – I'm scared too, Eva. I want to hit out and shout at God or whoever is taking you away from me. It's not the way it was meant to be. We were meant to raise the kids and then kick back ourselves, maybe go to visit your sister in New York or go to see the Eiffel Tower like you always talked about."

"Oh God, Noel, how on earth are we going to tell the kids?"

On the drive home, I watched the trees, now bare, whizz by the window. The cycle of life continued – the leaves that had budded in spring, grown leafy and green through the summer and shed

231

their leaves in autumn, were now dead. Exactly like me except I had never had a chance to reach the winter of my life or even the autumn. We decided to tell the three of them together. We felt it would be better to do it united as a family and hopefully they could help each other through it.

"Your mam and I need to talk to you all," Noel said when they were all gathered around after dinner that evening.

Aoife was sleeping peacefully in her crib. She was such a placid child, God bless her. She slept and ate and you didn't hear a thing out of her in between.

"What is it?" Patrick asked.

"Well . . . we got some bad news today, I'm afraid."

"What?" Kate asked. I could hear the panic in her voice.

I took a deep breath and said, "I'm afraid I haven't got much longer to live."

"What?" they all asked in unison.

"But you can't – what's wrong with you? You seem fine!" Patrick said.

It was hard for them to see it. They saw me looking a bit thin and hair gone but otherwise going about as normal. They couldn't see through my body to where this cancer was eating me up on the inside.

"I'm afraid I have cancer and it has spread."

"I knew you shouldn't have had her!" said Kate.

"Who? Do you mean Aoife?"

"If you didn't have her none of this would have happened."

"But Aoife didn't cause me to get cancer!"

"No, but you could have started treatment earlier – I heard you and Dad talking about it – I'm not stupid, you know. You think you whisper these things and '*Oh, we won't tell the kids*' but we know everything going on. You're selfish." She was pointing her finger just inches from my face. "I heard Dad telling you that you had to take the treatment but you chose Aoife over the rest of us."

I could see the worried faces of Patrick and Seán looking at me in confusion, not really understanding what was going on, but wondering if what Kate was saying was true all the same.

"I didn't choose Aoife over anyone – I just wanted to give her the best chance. It was a horrible decision to have to make. I really didn't think it was cancer, Kate – I thought it was benign and that it would all be okay and any risk to Aoife was unnecessary – but I was wrong."

"Yeah, but even if you knew it was cancer, would you have taken the treatment when you were pregnant?"

I said nothing.

"Well, would you?" Her index finger moved even closer to my face and her eyes were wide with rage.

"Probably not, if I'm honest."

"See! You obviously don't give a damn about me or Patrick and Seán – Aoife has caused all of this. You're a selfish bitch!"

"Kate – do not speak to your mother like that!" Noel thundered.

"Or what? You heard what she said – she's not going to be around for much longer so it doesn't matter what I say to her any more." She stormed out of the room.

I could see Noel blazing, about to go after her.

"Leave her, Noel – she's just angry."

"Mammy, are you really dying?" Seán asked, tears welling up in his eyes.

"I'm sorry, love, I'm so sorry." I snuggled my son into my chest and breathed him in.

"But who will look after us?"

"Daddy will. And Granny will help out too."

"But I need my mammy."

I wiped my tears away before they fell into his hair.

"Patrick, are you okay, love? I know it's a lot to take in."

He hadn't said a word since Kate's outburst. Patrick was the serious one of the three. He was the thinker and he would internalise his feelings.

"When will it happen?" he asked.

"The doctor thinks in few weeks."

"But what about my confirmation?"

It was taking place in February, less than five months away.

"You're going to have a lovely day and your daddy will make

it extra special. And I'll be there watching over you. I'll make sure the sun is shining for you."

"Are you scared, Mam?" Seán asked me. He was fiddling with the gold cross on my neck.

"No. Sure what have I got to be scared of? Aren't I going to a better place where you can eat all the chocolate and sweets you want and you won't get fat and you can play outside all day long because it never rains."

He smiled at me, his innocent face looking up at mine in wonderment.

"Can you get Monster Munch there?"

"Absolutely, all the Monster Munch you can dream of."

I spent the next few days under a black cloud. I just couldn't stop crying, I would spend hours alone in my room because I didn't want anyone to see me upset and then I would feel so guilty for spending the last few days of my life stuck down in my bedroom alone instead of with the people that I loved and I would feel even worse then.

I would cradle Aoife and stare down at her delicate perfection but then I would hand her back to Mam or Noel again just as quick. If I was honest with myself I was afraid to get too close to her because I was going to be taken away from her soon. It was better that she formed a bond with the people who would be there to look after her when I was gone. I also hoped, maybe a bit selfishly, that it would make it easier on me too when the time came to say goodbye. So even though it killed me and went against all my natural maternal instincts to leave my newborn out of my arms, I would hand her over to someone else and pretend that I needed to go and do something. Mam would say something like "Would you just sit down and rest, for God's sake?" and put Aoife into my arms again but I began to get good with my excuses. I think Mam thought that I was angry with Aoife because, when it came down to it, I had essentially sacrificed my life for her, but that wasn't it at all. I still didn't regret my decision to forgo treatment but I felt angry that both of us couldn't live. That was cruel. It was hard to rationalise why I would be given a baby when I was going to be taken away from her before she even had a chance to know who I was. That just didn't make any sense to me.

Kate was avoiding me. She was gone from dawn until dusk, out with Aidan or her friends. If I did see her she would swerve past me to get out of the room. She was so angry and I wasn't sure what to do. I wasn't sure how to handle it and I didn't want to spend my last days fighting with her.

Noel was spending a lot of time out on the land. I knew it was too hard for him to be around me. This was how he coped and I had to let him do it but I felt so lonely and isolated. My heart broke whenever I looked at him and I felt guilty because he was going to be left on his own to raise four children and try and make a living off the farm. It was only when we were in bed at night that he would take me in his arms and we would talk about what would happen after I was gone. Afterwards he would fall asleep and I would lie awake into the early hours, my mind whirring in anger at the injustice of it all. I'd had so much energy and fight when the mass was first discovered back in that first scan but over the last few months, as well as growing rampantly throughout my body, it had eroded my spirit.

Word had obviously started filtering through the village that I wasn't well – neighbours and old school friends and people I would have known when Kate was in primary school – people I hadn't seen in years – had started calling over to visit me. There were new people every day. It forced me to put on a brave face because I knew they would be awkward and embarrassed if I got upset or let them know that it got me down. I would hold court and offer a plate of biscuits and I knew that they were wondering to themselves whether I was really terminally ill at all. If I appeared calm and accepting it was much easier for all of us.

The pain was getting worse. I now had difficulty getting up out of a chair or walking. Spasms would grip my abdomen like a vice. I knew it was only a matter of time before I would need to go into the hospice and then, well, I didn't want to think about what came next . . .

Chapter 41

I don't know at what stage I accepted what was happening to me but I no longer felt like there was a raging battle inside my head. I didn't want to waste another minute of the time I had left being sad and depressed. The fight was gone. But I was still frightened about what lay ahead for me – the fear of the unknown – what would it feel like to die? Would I be aware of it? Was there such a thing as life after death? I knew my mother would balk at that one. I tried to push the fears back out of my head as soon as they surfaced and instead I focused on enjoying the simple things. I was too exhausted to go anywhere so that ruled out doing things like making a last-ditch effort to see bits of the country that I had never seen before like the Giant's Causeway, but I was able to enjoy long chats reminiscing with friends or when Noel and I recalled funny things the kids did when they were small. Like the time Patrick had said he told us he was running away and when we looked inside his sports bag to see what supplies he had packed it was just full of his books.

My sister Anna came home from New York to see me. She said she wanted to see me now and not 'after'. The 'after what?', went unspoken between us. She stayed for a few days and then flew back again. That was a hard one – each of us knowing that we would never see each other again. We had hugged, too afraid to let go, until I had eventually told her to go on or she'd miss her flight.

I woke up one morning with a raging fever and I was writhing and moaning in the bed with pain. The tablets I had been given no longer seemed to be having the same effect. My whole body felt knotted with the cancer as its cells gradually took over whatever was left of my good ones. Doctor O'Keeffe had warned us that this might happen. With the chemo I was susceptible to all sorts of infections that an ordinary person would fight off. Noel phoned Doctor O'Keeffe to tell him and he had written a referral for the hospice. They were expecting me later on that day. I hadn't eaten much over the last few days. I didn't recognise myself when I looked in the mirror, I never thought I would use the word 'gaunt' to describe myself but that was how I looked. My clothes, which were once tight, now were falling off my body. Most days I just stayed in my pyjamas and dressing gown because I didn't have the energy to get dressed and I spent most of my time in bed anyway. Noel said I was like a bag of bones and was constantly at me to eat something but I couldn't stomach food. Still he would persist – he would bring me my breakfast on a tray before I got out of bed in the mornings and he would set a place for me at the dinner table in the evenings.

It was surreal wandering around my house for what I knew was the last time. I gave Aoife a kiss and a cuddle – I had told Noel that I didn't want her to be brought into the hospice to visit me. It was no place for a new baby and she was still so fragile. She smiled a gummy smile at me and hooked my baby finger inside the ball of her fist. I raised her fist towards my mouth and kissed each of her dimpled knuckles in turn. She was almost twelve weeks old now and was gurgling away, oblivious to all of the drama that she had been born into. She was such a good little baby – she was already sleeping through the night and she only cried to be fed or changed. Her eyes stared at me like she had been here before. It was as if she knew what was happening and she was playing her part in making it as easy as she could for me.

I couldn't believe it was going to be the last time I would get to hold her.

I didn't have a chance to see Kate before I left for the hospice. She had been staying in a friend's house ever since we broke the news to her. I had overheard Noel on the phone to her friend, asking her to have a word with Kate, that it was urgent, and to get her to come home and talk to me but she still never came. Noel had been in contact to make sure she was okay but she just didn't want to be around us, so we gave her space. I desperately hoped that she might come to visit me. I didn't want to leave on bad terms – I wanted her forgiveness.

Once in the hospice, I wasn't in any pain. They had given me medication to help bring down my temperature and hooked me up straight away to a morphine drip. The relief was almost instant. I knew it was my time. I felt calmer and more accepting of what was to come. I had heard it said that a certain serenity descends on a person as they reach that transition between this world and the next. I wondered if this was the start of mine.

I was starting to sleep a lot more, the morphine making me drowsy. Sometimes I would wake up and wonder where Noel and the boys had gone to and then Sister Rita, the nurse looking after me, would tell me that it was the middle of the night and that they had gone home hours ago.

I opened my eyes sometime a few days later to see the blurry face of our parish priest, Father Ball. He was sitting on the chair beside my bed, wearing his usual black slacks, black short-sleeved shirt and white collar. His bulbous red nose seemed to grow bigger every time I saw him. He was fond of the brandy by all accounts.

"Well, now that you're here, Father, I know I'm on my last legs."

"Well, we always should have hope because without hope we've nothing," he said.

"Ah come on, Father, even I know that my body has given up on me."

"Well, the Lord is watching over you at the moment and he will help you through it."

"Does he have morphine?" I started to laugh. "It's great stuff!"

He looked taken aback and wasn't sure how to respond. "I thought you might like me to hear a confession for you?"

I thought about Kate – she was the first thing that popped into my head.

"My eldest, Kate – I'm sure you know her – well, she's very angry with me at the moment. She won't come in to see me and the last time we saw each other ended in a blazing row so I guess if there's anything . . . I'd like to make peace with that . . ."

"The Lord is listening, Eva, and he knows. What about the funeral arrangements?"

"Well, I want to be buried in the family plot – definitely not cremated – that'd be too scary for me."

"And are there any hymns or prayers you would like?"

"I like that one – what's it called . . . 'Sing to the Mountains'?"

I watched as he made a note in his little flip-top notebook just like a Guard would do.

We sat in silence for a few minutes. I didn't have much to say to the man. I wasn't the most religious person in Ballyrobin. I mean, I made the effort to go to Mass whenever I could but I wasn't too put out if I had to miss it for whatever reason. I wasn't like some of the Holy Joes around the town who were almost bribing Father Ball just so they could do a reading or become a minister of the Eucharist yet again.

"Oh and if they could get someone to sing 'Pie Jesu' – that would be nice too. If it's not too much trouble . . ."

"Would you like to pray with me?"

"Sure it can't do any harm, now can it?"

He started off an 'Our Father' and I mumbled along with him, more for his sake than my own.

"Oh, Father Ball – I wasn't expecting to see you here!" Noel said as he came in with the boys a while later.

"Well, I was just leaving anyway, Noel." He stood up and took his coat off the back of the chair and put his arms into the sleeves.

"Well . . . em, goodbye, Eva, and remember the Lord who brought you into this world will be with you when you leave it."

I could see Patrick looking at me. I knew three-year-olds with more tact than Father Ball.

"And, Noel, remember your family in the church will help you through it."

"Thanks, Father," an embarrassed Noel mumbled.

"Mam, what was the priest saying?" Patrick asked as soon as he had left.

"Aragh, you know what priests are like – they're not happy unless they're spouting some religious mumbo-jumbo."

He smiled at me, freckles from the summer spent playing in the fields gracing his cheeks and the tip of his nose. He was going to grow into a handsome young man, I thought sadly.

"Here, I'm parched, will you two go down and buy me a bottle of water?"

"But sure haven't you a jug of it there beside you?" Noel gestured to the locker.

I winked at him and he knew then I wanted to talk to him alone. He rooted around in his pocket and pulled out a five-pound note. "You can get yourselves something nice with the change."

The boys ran out giddily with Seán trying to grab the money out of Patrick's hand. "Give it to me!"

"What was he doing in here?" Noel asked.

"I'd say Mam told him to come. What is it they say, Noel – the end is nigh?"

"Don't say that."

"Ah come on, Noel, I'm on the way out."

"It doesn't make it any easier though."

"You look tired." I noticed his face was more lined than I remembered.

"Do I?"

I nodded. "It's taking its toll on you."

"I'm grand."

"Well, make sure you look after yourself, do you hear me? I know you're busy looking after everyone else at the moment but if you were to get sick then we'd be really up the creek."

"Will you look who's talking? The words pot, kettle and black spring to mind."

I smiled at him. "Oh, would you get me some Vaseline? My lips are all cracked."

He opened the pot and, using his index finger, he gently applied the balm to my parched lips.

"That's better. Thanks. Look, Noel, I don't think you should bring the boys in to see me any more – I don't want them to remember me lying like this in a bed all tubed up." Something like this would stay with them forever. Plus I was starting to sleep a lot more and I knew they were bored hanging around. It wasn't fair on them – they were only children.

"I see . . ." He trailed off. "Are you sure that's what you want?"

"I think it's for the best. I don't want any goodbyes either, do you hear me?"

"What, you just want them to go out of here tonight and say nothing – no goodbye or anything?"

"I think it's for the best, Noel – I don't want them getting upset. It's best not to say anything to them."

"Does it not seem a bit . . . well . . . mean?"

"Noel, I haven't long left. I don't want my last few days to be full of tears and maudlin goodbyes."

"Okay, whatever you want." He put his hands up.

"How's Kate? Has she come back home yet?" It shredded my heart in two to know that the last words we spoke to each other were raging and wild and said nothing of the love I had in my heart for my firstborn child.

He shook his head. "She's been back a couple of times to get things – clothes and the like – but she's still sleeping in Sorcha's house."

"Does she mention anything about me?"

"Not really."

"So you mean no, then?"

He nodded.

"Will you ask her again to come into me – I want to see her before I –"

The unspoken word hung in the air between us.

"I said it to her again this morning but you know how stubborn she can be."

"Don't I know it . . . And how's Aoife doing?"

"Well, she's good, putting on lots of weight. Getting nice and chubby now."

"Ah good, God bless the little thing! What a start she has had . . . At least she's too young to understand any of it." My heart ached for my two daughters.

"It's a blessing all right."

"This morphine is great stuff, I tell you, Noel – and I can have as much as I want because it doesn't matter if I get addicted to the stuff now. That is the plus side of this death business."

"You have to look at the positives, I guess. You always were the more optimistic one of the two of us."

"Now I don't want you lolling around that house moping to yourself, do you hear me?"

"What do you mean?"

"After I'm gone, I want you to find someone new. Someone not quite as beautiful as me because I'd be jealous then but close enough – maybe someone with a bigger nose or frizzier hair."

"Ah stop it, Eva!"

"I'm serious, because the first thing I'm going to do when I kick the bucket is to go looking for John Lennon. We're going to have a right 'oul party."

He was smiling at me but I thought I saw tears in his eyes.

When Noel took the boys home later I gave them each a big hug. I took my time breathing in their scents when they hugged me. I didn't want to let them go. I forced back the tears that filled my eyes – I didn't want them to see me crying. It was hard to believe that this was the last time that I would ever get to hold them – the babies that I had brought roaring and screaming into this world.

"You'd better go on – you've school in the morning." I forced my voice to remain level.

"Night, Mam!" Patrick sang.

"Night, love."

"Night, Mam."

"Night, Seán."

Chapter 42

"Are you okay?"

It was Sister Rita coming around to check on me. I had actually grown quite fond of her over the last few days since I had been under her care. She was a neat little woman with soft grey hair peeping out from underneath her white habit. She still chose to wear the habit even though most nuns had given it up years earlier. Her white nurse's uniform was always pristine and starched and she always wore beige soft-soled loafers so you never heard her footsteps when she walked.

"I'm all right."

"Were they your boys that I saw earlier?"

"Yes," I said and her gentle manner caused the floodgates to open. "I don't want to die – I don't want to go!" I started to cry.

"It's natural to feel like that, Eva." She sat up on the side of the bed, pulled back the sheets and started to massage my feet.

"I'm going to miss out on so much . . ."

"Tell me who has gone before you?"

"What do you mean?"

"Well, have you lost a parent or someone else close to you?"

"My dad died when I was a teenager."

"Well, then, I'm sure he'll be waiting on you to guide you

through." Her gentle hands were kneading and plying the balls of my feet.

At a time when I just seemed to be aching all over, it felt heavenly.

"Can I ask you a question, Sister?"

"Of course, ask away."

"Do you really believe in all of that stuff?"

"How do you mean – the afterlife?"

"Yeah?"

"Yes, I do actually."

"But that tunnel of light business – don't you ever doubt it all sometimes?"

"I've been close to a lot of dying people – it's part and parcel of doing this job – but it's a privilege actually to be close to people at such an intimate moment of their life as they get ready to start the next part of their journey."

I looked at her like she was crackers.

"No, really it is, Eva – I've seen death up close, I've looked it in the eye and I know that when my time comes, I won't be afraid. There is a look – a peacefulness – on the face of the dying just before they leave us and a contentment that I have still never seen on the face of a living person. Of course we don't know what it is that makes them so calm as they leave this world but I like to think that they are being reunited with their loved ones that have gone before them."

"Kate won't come in to see me," I whispered.

"That's your daughter, right?"

"Yes."

"She's a teenager – she's going through a tough time and she's angry – she just doesn't know how to express it."

"I never got a chance to say goodbye to her."

"Well, why don't you write her a letter? Tell her everything that you would tell her if you saw her?"

"I suppose I could do that."

"I'll nip out and get you some paper from the office."

"Thanks." I began to plan what I might say as I waited for her to come back.

"Here," she said when she returned. She handed me an A4 leafpad and gave me a pen. "Sorry I've nothing fancier."

"Thanks, Sister."

"I'll leave you to it. I'll be around to check on you in a bit."

Even though I was exhausted, I sat on the bed under the lamp and concentrated hard on writing my letter and putting everything I wanted to say down on the sheet of paper in front of me. I made sure the words were just right and said exactly how I was feeling because it was my last gift to Kate.

Eventually I must have drifted off to sleep because I woke up to find my sheets were damp under me. I tried to speak but all that came out was a low moan. Sister Rita appeared back at the end of the bed again like some kind of white angel. She switched on the light and looked at me before putting her hand on my forehead. She went to fetch some water and a facecloth and sponged my face. The coolness of the damp facecloth was a welcome relief. She gave me some more medicine that she said would help bring down the fever.

Noel appeared sometime later, I remember it was either very early or very late for him – I didn't know which. I could hear him talking to me but I didn't have the energy to answer him so I closed my eyes and let them talk around me as I drifted in and out of sleep. I had vivid dreams of playing on hay bales with Anna as a child and picnics in the fields. I was twenty-three years old and performing on the stage in the Ballyrobin Amateur Dramatic Society's annual show. Then I would wake up and Noel would be telling me stories from when the kids were small. I liked hearing them again – his voice was comforting. He told me how much he loved me and that it was okay for me to go and that they would all be fine. I closed my eyes and listened to him but I wasn't able to respond. He was stroking my skin and his touch felt good. Then I was back sitting on the sand on Mulranny Strand with the sun warming my face. I watched as the kids jumped over the waves, Noel the biggest kid of the lot of them. I waved at them and they waved back at me, squealing in delight as the cool water washed over their skin. Gulls squawked on the warm air overhead. The waves were breaking in arcs on the sand in front of me and the water was rushing up towards me. I thought I was going to get wet so I got up and moved my towel back up the beach a bit further. I spread it out again and sat down and watched them all playing a while longer. A shivering Kate was now making her way back up the beach to me, the water running off her in drops. She left a trail of prints in the sand as she walked. I stood up and took a towel out of the bag. I held it out open until she reached me and I wrapped her close into its warmth.

28/10/1992
Dear Kate,

I am sleeping a lot more and soon I probably won't be in any fit state to write this for you. Kate, my darling girl – I'm so sorry that we never got to say goodbye properly. I know you're angry with me and you have every right to be. The problem is that we are so alike, you and I – you remind me so much of myself at that age – headstrong and impulsive.

Remember, Kate, that I love you – you were my firstborn, the one to amaze me with the wonderment of motherhood and how intensely we can love another person. It breaks my heart that I won't be around to watch you grow up, to guide you on your journey into adulthood and to watch you become a young woman. Or that I won't be there to listen as you swoon over a boyfriend or to help you through a broken heart.

I know your dad will do a great job in raising you all – believe me, there is no better father out there, which helps me be in peace as I go but I wanted to write this letter to you so you can turn to it whenever you're having a bad day – I might not be able to be there for you physically but I will be with you through it all and my words are here whenever you need them – I hope they'll be of comfort to you.

I hope one day, maybe when you have your own children, you will understand my decision and that it wasn't easy for me. Try to help your dad with the younger ones – the next few months will be difficult on you all but on the up-side you'll have no one banging your bedroom door with the Hoover when you're trying to sleep in on a Saturday morning!

You are my treasure. Always remember that you were put on this earth because you are special, so go and put your stamp on the world, my beautiful girl.

With love always,

Mam xx

Noel

1992

Chapter 43

As soon as I heard the shrill ring of the phone cutting through the night-time stillness of the house, I knew. I got out of bed and ran down the hall to pick it up before it woke the kids. I talked briefly to Sister Rita before hanging up. I rubbed the palms of my hands down over my face. This is it, I thought, this is actually it. I picked the handset up again to ring Josephine to come over and mind the kids.

And she knew it too. It was unspoken between us and if she found it hard to be left behind while I went to say goodbye to her youngest daughter then to her credit she never let on. She shooed me out the door and told me to drive safely and to ring her as soon as I could.

I turned the key in the ignition and the car started up. I cursed its loudness in the yard in case it would wake the kids. I pulled out onto the dark road and set off for the hospice. After a few minutes the red light for the petrol gauge lit up on the dashboard in front of me. *Damn it to hell – the one time that I was in a hurry!* God only knew where I would find a petrol station open at this hour of the night. I had no choice but to keep going and hope that it would last until I got there. I knew I was driving fast but Sister Rita had never rung me during the night before so I knew it must be serious. Somehow, I made it there, probably just on the fumes alone. I took a deep breath of the crisp night air in the car park to steady myself and then I went inside.

I met Sister Rita in the hallway outside Eva's room.

"After you left she developed a bad fever, Noel. Sometimes this happens before . . ." She spoke in hushed tones.

"Are you saying what I think you're saying?"

"I'm sorry –" She paused, taking a deep intake of breath. "I think it's time, Noel . . ."

I followed her into the room and when I saw Eva again, the same woman that I had seen only hours earlier, I couldn't believe how much she had deteriorated. She was lying on the bed, covered by a single white sheet and even though there was a chill in the air, beads of sweat glistened on her body. She was gone so thin and her skin was so translucent that you could almost see right through her like a ghost. Her lips were blue and her face was ashen. She didn't open her eyes when I came in. I sat down on the chair beside her and reached out for her hand. It was freezing. Every now and then she would writhe and moan in the bed and I would feel utterly helpless. I was so angry as I thought about how unfair it all was. If there was a God out there why would he allow someone to conceive a child if he was going to give them terminal cancer as well? What kind of a God would do that? She had managed to get Aoife here safely but at her own expense. I prayed for him to do something. For a miracle. He owed it to her. Although I wasn't in agreement with her decision not to take the surgery, I'd had to accept that it was what she wanted. But I don't think any of us had thought that this was the way it was going to end.

"Is there anything you can do for her?" I said, turning to Sister Rita when she came back in a while later.

She upped the dosage yet again to keep her comfortable and her whole body seemed to relax a bit more when the pain relief kicked in a few minutes later. I slumped back down on to the chair beside her bed. I still couldn't believe that we had come to this.

"You know, it might not seem like it but she can probably still

252

hear you – our hearing is always the last sense to go," Sister Rita said softly.

I nodded. I remembered hearing that somewhere before.

"Keep talking to her, Noel, so she knows that you are with her and that she is not alone. Tell her that you love her and that it is okay for her to go."

So I did as she said and kept talking to Eva, telling her that she was going to a better place where there would be no pain, even though I wasn't sure if I really believed it. I told her that it was okay to go, that she had nothing to worry about and I would look after everything here. But it wasn't okay – I didn't want her to go.

I loved Eva so much. Where some men talked about their nagging wives and spent their time longing to escape them, I hated every minute of being apart from her. From the moment I had first seen her on the stage when the Ballyrobin Amateur Dramatic Society were putting on a production of *My Fair Lady* and she was Eliza Doolittle, I had loved her. When I saw her delivering her feisty monologue I knew she was the one. She had the whole audience in the palm of her hand – her charisma had radiated off the stage. She loved acting and she was good at it too but, when Kate came along, it had slipped away and she didn't have the time to commit to it any more. She kept saying that she must go back to it but she never did. I should have made her go back, I thought sadly. I should have done everything possible to let her do what she loved doing.

I stayed like that all night on the uncomfortable plastic chair talking to her. I would remember funny things that had happened with the children and I would tell her. Her breathing was rapid and rattling and sometimes it would stop altogether and I would think this is it – this is the end – and my heart would start thumping in my chest but then she would start again. Sister Rita was in and out giving more medications to keep her comfortable.

When dawn broke I opened back the curtains to let some light into the room. A magnificent red ball of fire lit up the sky.

The sunlight glinted off the glass. It was going to be one of those autumnal days that Eva loved, cool, crisp and sunny. I looked back at her on the bed, her lips had turned up at the sides and a smile had crept over her face. It was like she knew that the sun was shining, I walked back over and sat down beside her again. I took her frail hand in mine and then she left this world.

I don't know how long I stayed there sobbing as I held her hand, which was already starting to go cold. Sister Rita came in then and went to give me a hug and I'm ashamed to say it now but I stood up and kicked the metal pedal bin in the corner. I just wanted to lash out at something.

I drove home barely able to see the road in front of me through my tears. The roads were empty at that time of the morning and I drove fast. The car hopped off the crests of the road surface. I remember thinking that if I crashed and died now too that it wouldn't be so bad but then I would think of our four children and I knew it was selfish of me.

I let myself into the kitchen quietly and Josephine stood up and walked towards me. We met and clung to each other with heaving sobs.

Telling the kids was one of the hardest things I have ever had to do. Josephine sat with me and she cuddled them all as they cried. Kate took it particularly badly. She sobbed until she was hyperventilating and I wondered if we should call Doctor O'Brien up to the house to sedate her. She eventually fell asleep from sheer exhaustion with Josephine stroking her face as she laid her head on her lap. My heart broke as I looked at my eldest, her hair was clinging to her damp face in ribbons.

I heard Aoife cry then. I had almost forgotten about her. I went over to her crib and picked her up. Her smile lit up the room and I thought how lucky she was to be spared all of this heartache. She was too young to understand and it was a blessing. She cooed at me like it was any other day and not the day the woman who had brought her into this world had just left it.

We had the funeral as she had wished and Father Ball did a lovely Mass and the choir sang the songs that Eva had wanted. Kate wouldn't go to the funeral so she stayed behind at home and Aidan came up to sit with her. For once I said nothing and let her do as she wished. It was hard enough on her without me being on her case. One of the neighbours had offered to take Aoife, which I was relieved about.

A long queue of people came to pay their respects and offer me their condolences in the church. All their faces seemed to blur together as I shook hand after hand. Rough, smooth, broad, narrow, they all merged into one. The smell of incense wafted through the air. My heart broke for the two boys – they looked so lost amongst the huge crowd of mourners. Their school had made a guard of honour for the coffin as it went into the church and I knew they felt self-conscious as hundreds of eyes bored into them as we walked past them all. Eva's sister Anna had come back from New York again – this time her whole family were in tow and I watched as the boys warily eyed up their American cousins with their strange accents, who they had only met once before.

When we went back to the house, I noticed that the neighbours had made trays of sandwiches and cakes and were serving up endless cups of tea to everyone. People were busying themselves in my house opening presses and drawers trying to locate things. Someone asked me where we kept the teabags and I got up to show them. It all seemed surreal. It didn't seem like this was my wife's funeral. Even though I had known she was dying, it still came as a shock in the end if that makes sense? I would be okay for a few minutes and I would drink the tea that was poured for me and talk to someone and then I would remember it all again. Someone told me that the meat factory was going to be closing after over fifty years in business and I remember thinking that I must tell Eva, but then I remembered I couldn't. And it hurt as bad every time I remembered. I just wanted her back – this wasn't what we had signed up for. We were meant to be raising our children together and then when they had flown the nest, it was time for us. That was the way it was supposed to be – not me watching as her coffin was lowered into the ground. The boys played with their friends, which I was grateful for – it was a distraction for them. Kate stayed down in her room with Aidan. I could hear her music blaring through the door but I let them at it.

Everyone cleared out that evening until there were only a few left behind doing the washing-up. The neighbour brought Aoife back home and said that she had never seen such a good-natured baby. Josephine took her into her arms and sat cradling her for the rest of the evening.

"She looks so like her mother at that age, Noel," Josephine said to me wistfully as she stared down at the sleeping baby in her arms.

I knew her heart must have been breaking. The natural order of life had reversed itself – she shouldn't be burying her daughter.

After a few days everyone was gone. Anna and her family had caught their flight back home – the neighbours had left us alone and stopped bringing dinners in the evenings. Josephine told me to send the kids back to school, that it would do them good to try and keep routine and some sort of normality in their lives. Kate had withdrawn into herself completely. She never mentioned her mother – it was as if she had never existed at all – and I wasn't strong enough to bring it up with her. I didn't trust myself to talk to her without falling to pieces.

I would go out into the fields and not want to go back and face the house because it felt so empty without Eva's presence. I hated those first few minutes when I would come in the door and acutely feel her absence. She could fill a room just by being in it. I always used to love coming home to her after a day on the farm and now I just felt lost in my own life and I didn't know what to do about it.

And I had so many questions about Aoife. Although Josephine came over every day to help out with her, once I was alone, I realised that I wasn't sure of so many things like how many bottles Aoife should be having? Or how was I supposed to know when she needed more? What age did you start them on food? And even then what do you give them? When she was cranky one day, I didn't know if she was sick, teething or if it was just a bad day. This was all stuff that Eva knew and I desperately missed her and although I had always helped Eva out when the kids were babies, it was always with Eva's instructions. It was only now that she was gone that I realised how on top of everything she had been. She just got on with things and everything ran smoothly in the house when she was around. Now the school uniforms weren't even washed, let alone ironed. The house was filthy. A layer of dust ran along the surfaces and the white enamel bathtub had a grey scum along the waterline. Josephine was great and tried to take over Eva's role in the household as best she could but she couldn't do everything. And it wasn't fair on her. She was nearly seventy. But I knew she wanted to do it. She needed to do it. She said it helped her to feel closer to Eva. She had decided to take Aoife to her house to give me a hand, at least take that pressure off me, but I still struggled to look after the other three as well as run the house and the farm.

"What will we do for lunch, Dad – there's no bread?" Patrick would stand looking into the empty fridge and I would root around for some money in my pocket and tell them to buy something in the town. I knew Eva would be turning in her grave at the thought of them buying their lunch in the chippers.

Josephine made our dinner in the evenings but she already had a full-time job in minding Aoife. And she had her own house to run as well. We were so tight financially too – I had let things slide on the farm a bit over the last few months with Eva being in hospital and everything, so now we had very little to live on.

And I was starting to drink. Not much by some people's standards but I was never a big drinker and I knew it was too much for me. Instead of coming home at lunchtime for a sandwich, I would go to Doyle's and have a pint. Sometimes I would go down after work too if Josephine was able to take care of the children. She didn't say anything at first but I could see her looking at me with her eyes narrowed or she would say "You're going down again" and it wouldn't be a question – it was a statement.

"I won't be long," I would offer, both embarrassed and disgusted with myself at the same time.

And all the time in the background were reminders that Christmas was coming and the sight of all that tinsel and those baubles everywhere just made it all the more painful. Eva had loved Christmas – it was her favourite time of the year. She would go to great efforts to make sure it was special for the kids – Santa letters were written well ahead of time and posted to the North Pole. Decorations were handmade. The tree was put up in the first weekend of December. We would all go to visit Santa and go for a bite to eat afterwards – it was a tradition now. The house would be full of the smell of mulled wine and mince pies and she would bake gingerbread men and decorate them with the kids. She had special Christmas plates and a tablecloth that got taken down just for the day and were put away again for the following year. The house would be stocked high with tins of sweets and biscuits so that we would be eating them for months afterwards.

Christmas Day was hard for everyone – her presence was sorely missed all day long. I had bought the wrong Nintendo game for Patrick and, although it wasn't said, we all knew that Eva wouldn't have made that mistake. I had bought Kate a make-up set full of colourful shades of pinks and blues – the woman in the chemist had assured me that she would love it. But her look told me that it wasn't what she had wanted at all. Josephine had cooked Christmas dinner for us and, although it was a fine meal, the table lacked its heart.

Aoife and Josephine had grown very close. Josephine always seemed to have her cradled in her arms. And when she did give her to me to hold, I always felt slightly awkward doing it. I would have the position or the angle wrong and Josephine would gently suggest that I try to sit her forward a bit more but she would cry and then Josephine would say "Oh, she must have wind". She always knew what to do with her and I had to admit that I would be lost without her.

Kate was my biggest problem. There wasn't a week that went by where she wasn't on detention for something after school. She got suspended for giving cheek to her history teacher. Then I had been called in because of her absenteeism. I was shocked because as far as I was aware she was going to school every morning but then I learned she had been spending the day sitting watching TV in Aidan's house while his parents were at work. I was at my wits' end with her. She wanted to leave school but there was no way I could let her go without doing her Leaving Cert. The thing was, she was bright and intelligent but she had lost all interest somewhere along the way and now she saw school as something to fight against. I knew Eva wouldn't have wanted her to leave before completing her education either though what she chose to do after that was up to her. So I held firm on it, no matter how much she acted up. She ignored Aoife completely. I knew she blamed her for the fate of her mother, but she was only a tiny baby and couldn't be held accountable for it all. Even Aidan, in fairness to him, would go over and look at her or tickle her under her chin at least. Kate still had so much anger inside her and I didn't know how to help her. God knows, I had anger too. This was where I needed Eva.

Chapter 44

The time went by somehow, although I don't really remember much about it now. I often wondered, if she'd had the surgery before the cancer had claimed her whole body, would she still be with us? But she was caught between a rock and a hard place – maybe Eva might still be with us but little Aoife may not have been – or maybe neither of them would be? Who knows how things might have turned out? And it was futile going over it all again – it still wouldn't change the outcome.

I felt her presence everywhere – a song would come on the radio that reminded me of her and the day of her Month's Mind there was a documentary on the TV about *My Fair Lady*. And call it a coincidence or whatever but the sun had shone brightly at Patrick's confirmation – just as she had promised.

I would go up to tidy her grave or just sit and talk to her. Sometimes I would bring Aoife with me because I knew Eva would want to see her. She had grown into a wobbly toddler with straight white-blonde hair. She was learning to talk and would walk around the place pointing to different things saying "Wat dis?" "Wat dis?" She was still staying with Josephine – it was a habit we had fallen into and neither one of us dared to address it. I knew she had grown very close to Aoife and I didn't want to be the one to disrupt it, especially when she was still grieving for Eva. Plus, if I'm entirely honest, with the farm and everything, I wouldn't have been able to cope with a small child – I was already struggling to look after the other three. The arrangement worked for us and I still saw Aoife every day – Josephine would bring her over to the house or I would call over there. She called me 'Dadda' – she knew who I was – she just didn't live with us. The boys were so good with her. They would patiently lead her by the hand, showing her the flowers in the garden, or read stories out loud to her. They loved their little sister.

Kate, on the other hand, didn't want to know the child. If Aoife was crying, Kate would ask someone to make her quiet. If Aoife waddled over to Kate with her doll or something, Kate would get up and walk out of the room.

The day I opened the bin to put a teabag into it and saw the pregnancy test sticking up from the top of the rubbish, my world stopped. In slow motion I took the stick out of the bin. It could only belong to Kate. I wasn't sure how to read it so I had a look around the rubbish for the instructions but they weren't with it. Did this mean that she was pregnant? Dear God, no. I was already in a delicate state but this would be the thing that would break me altogether. She was only sixteen – I knew that she and Aidan had been together for a while but they were too young to be having sex and *unprotected sex* at that.

I was waiting for her when she came in the door in her uniform – tie missing, the top button of her blouse opened, her tatty army-green canvas schoolbag destroyed with black permanent marker.

"Where were you?" I stood up and walked over to her.

"School – where do you think?"

"Don't use that tone with me! What's this?" I held up the stick for her to see.

"Where did you get that?" she said quickly.

"You didn't do a great job of hiding it in the bin!"

She wouldn't meet my eyes.

"Well, are you?"

"What?"

"Pregnant, Kate!" I was shouting now. "Are you pregnant?"

"No, Dad – I'm not, actually, if you must know."

The relief washed through me.

"Well, thank God for that!" I let out a long sigh, "What are you playing at, Kate? You're only sixteen – you have your whole life ahead of you – why would you want to ruin it all?"

"My life is already ruined."

"Kate, please, I know these last few years have been hard on you and I also know that you and Aidan are going to have sex no matter what I say but get yourself down to Doctor O'Brien and get the pill or whatever it is that girls take nowadays . . ." This was where I needed Eva.

"I already have."

"Well, that's something, I suppose," I mumbled. "Look, Kate, just be careful, yeah?"

From that point on something changed between us. We tolerated each other now. I had to respect the fact that my little girl was now grown up and having sex. I hated to think of it but I had to be realistic as well. I wished that Eva was here. She would have had 'the talk' with Kate – she would have done a far better job than I ever could. I knew I had to trust Kate to make the right decisions – I couldn't be there to police her all the time. But although she still asked constantly about leaving school, I held firm. That was the bargain – she did her Leaving Cert and I left her alone. We both knew as the Leaving Cert came closer that it was going to mark a change but I never thought she would just up and leave the day after she had finished her exams. She never said goodbye or told me she was going. All there was left was a note saying that she would call me in a few days' time and to tell her gran and Aidan that she was sorry.

That was it – that was how it happened. Just like that, my daughter was gone as well.

Kate

2012

Chapter 45

Ben had gone into the spare room after our argument. I lay there under the duvet reading the letter over and over again. The bedside lamp cast shadows around the room as I ran my fingers along the notepaper that was still slightly indented with the blue ballpoint words that she had written many years before. I traced my finger along the slope of her writing.

For the first time in twenty years, I allowed myself to cry. It was like a dam had been opened, years of pent-up hurt and anger flooded out of me and once I had started I just couldn't stop. The last time I had cried about Mam was the day that Dad had told me she was dead. The feeling of desolation and despair I felt that then, the physical pain of her loss, still haunts me now. I never let myself cry over her after that, I was too afraid of what might happen if I did. It was like my whole body had shut down emotionally after her death but now I lay there on the bed until my whole body was heaving with sobs. I couldn't believe that the letter was able to do this to me – that the whole thing still had an effect on me. And as for Dad, why was he only giving this to me now? What did he think he was doing all these years by holding onto it? I was trembling with rage and scared at just how easily the words in that letter could transplant me back to those awful days in Ballyrobin and open up those wounds again, just like it was yesterday. So many painful memories were recalled – the last time I had seen her alive and we had fought. The weeks where I knew she was dying but just couldn't get my head around it or face up to it. Dad asking me every day if I was going to go and see her in the hospital and that she was asking for me and me fobbing him off with my array of excuses. The terrible months afterwards when I just felt so lost and alone. And empty – that awful gnawing emptiness. How angry I was with her for not having the surgery to try and win her battle with cancer – how angry I *still* am. My fury at how selfish she was being. How I just wanted to be able to escape my own life. How everyone in the village whispered as I walked – "That's the girl whose mother died" or the auld biddies who said "Her mother would be turning in her grave now with the carry-on of that one". Or then there was the pity which was almost worse: "She's a wild one that one but, God love her, isn't she only after losing her mother?"

How I had resolutely made a pact with myself to get the hell out of Ballyrobin as soon as I could, no matter who I was leaving behind me.

Ben had stayed in the spare room that night and, when I got up the next morning, I saw that he had already left for school. My stride was fast and purposeful as I walked from the Tube. I heard my mobile ring and I fished it out of my bag. Dad's number flashed up and I knocked it to voicemail. He probably wanted to see if I got home okay and whether I had read the letter but I was so angry with him I couldn't talk to him.

I reached the gallery and pushed the door open.

"Hi there! So how did your weekend at home go?" Nat asked me as soon as I came in the door.

I walked over and plonked my bag onto the desk and hung my coat over the back of the chair.

"As expected, a complete and utter disaster. Ben's not talking to me. I knew it was a bad idea to go and then Dad gave me this when I was leaving."

I pulled the letter out of my bag and gave it to her. I waited for Nat's reaction as she finished reading it.

"Oh my God, Kate!" She gasped as she looked up at me. "How come you only got it now?"

"I'm not sure what Dad was thinking by not giving it to me for all this time."

"He was probably too scared that you'd rip it up or do something stupid with it."

"Well, he's probably right, I would have."

The letter sat on the desk between us.

"How do you feel about it?" She nodded at the piece of paper. Its stiff creases from years of being folded divided it in four.

"I don't know how to feel, to be honest – I'm angry at Dad for not giving it to me sooner and then when I read it, I'm angry at Mam all over again, y'know?"

Nat nodded sympathetically. We were interrupted by a customer coming into the gallery.

"I'll go," said Nat, getting up from the stool and walking across the floorboards. I folded the letter up again and slotted it back inside my bag. I watched Nat from behind as she went over to greet the woman. She still seemed so down since Will had left. I wished I could do something nice to cheer her up but, whether it was my baby brain or not, I just couldn't think of anything really special. I had mentioned it to Ben and he had suggested taking her away for a spa day or something, but that wasn't very original. I wanted to do something different that showed I had put a lot of thought into it so that she knew how much I valued her as a friend.

The rest of day went past slowly – we only had a handful of customers in. We sold half the amount of photos these days than we did a couple of years ago. Outside of our exhibitions, if it wasn't for tourists and middle-eastern collectors, there is no way we would survive on a day-to-day basis. Tabitha never mentioned the drop-off in business. Knowing the eccentric character that she was, she probably didn't notice. Once the business wasn't losing money she was happy to coast along because she was too busy enjoying life in her Tuscan villa.

"Kate, you wouldn't mind if I went to visit my mum for a few days, would you?" Nat said later on. "I've just checked and there are some cheap flights going at the minute."

"No of course not – that's a great idea. You could do with the break. Our own summer isn't up to much anyway." Nat's mum lived in Spain.

"Yeah, I just want to get away from everything for a while – chill by the pool and get some sun on my bones."

"That sounds like heaven. I'd nearly go with you except Tabitha would have a fit."

"Thanks Kate, I'll book the flights now then before the price goes up."

At six o'clock we set the alarm and turned the hanging window sign to 'closed'. I said bye to Nat and locked the door behind me.

Chapter 46

As I walked along to the Tube station that evening, my phone rang again. I took it out of my bag and saw it was Dad again so I let it ring out. When it finally stopped ringing I was convinced that I could hear footsteps echoing mine on the pavement behind me. Their sound carried on the cool evening air. I slowed down to try to hear better and the footsteps behind me slowed too. I turned around but there was no one there. I started to walk quicker and the footsteps did too. I came up near the park perimeter. I was just giving out to myself for being a pathetic scaredy cat when I felt an arm grab me around my neck from behind. I went to scream but nothing would come out. I tried to wriggle out but the grip tightened until I could barely breathe, so I stopped struggling. My heart was thudding in my chest. I could taste the bitter tang of the leather from his jacket in my mouth. He pulled my bag off my shoulder with his free arm before releasing me and running off.

Then I remembered the letter.

"*Wait!*" I screamed. I tried running after him but I couldn't with my big tummy. "*You can have the money and everything else in the bag!*" I cried breathlessly. "*There's a letter . . . I just need the letter. Come back . . . pleeeease!*" I was screaming after him but it was futile. He reached the end of the railings, rounded the corner and was gone out of my sight.

I felt my mouth water and I thought I might be sick. A man crossed the street and came over to me. He was dressed in baggy jeans and a hooded top pulled up over a baseball cap. His clothes were what Ben would jokingly refer to as *Boyz n the Hood* gear.

"You all right there?"

"He's taken my bag!" I gasped, pointing to nobody in the distance.

"He's well gone, love. Sick bruvver doing that to a pregnant lady and all!" he said in a thick London accent. "The name's Terry by the way – what's yours?"

"Kate."

Terry rang the police for me then straight away. I never even thought about them. My whole body was shaking from the shock. I felt wretched. This letter, despite my feelings about it, had just come into my life and now it had gone out of it again just as quick.

"Here," he said, handing me his phone after he had told the police what had happened and where we were. "Do you want to ring someone?"

I nodded, taking the phone from him, and with shaking hands I dialled Ben's number. He said he'd be there as quick as he could.

A police constable was on the scene within minutes. Terry had waited with me until he came and I thanked him profusely for helping me. From behind his jeans were desperately low and, as I watched him walking away, I found myself wondering how he kept them up.

The constable took a statement and said they'd let me know if there was any CCTV footage in the area – I knew to him it was just another snatch and grab and, in the grand scheme of his job, wasn't really worth the time or energy to spend investigating it but it was so much more than that to me. I told him that I didn't care about the bag but that there was a letter inside it that I needed to get back. I could see it in his eyes that he thought I was raving mad but he said that he'd try his best anyway.

Ben arrived on the scene soon after and came running up and put his arms around me.

"Are you okay? Are you sure you weren't hurt? I hope to God that they catch that bastard!"

"I'm fine – but the letter, Ben – the letter Dad gave me when we were going yesterday – it was from Mam. She wrote it for me before she died. I had it in my bag!"

"Oh no, Kate – fuck!"

I nodded. The shock soon subsided and the tears started. I was distraught. The policeman went on his way again, promising he'd call me if they found anything.

We went home and Ben made me a cup of sugary tea and then set about ringing the bank to cancel my cards while I sat on the sofa and cried.

"I can't believe I've lost her letter, Ben –"

"But it wasn't your fault –"

"I never should have brought it to work with me –"

"Okay, Kate, you've got to calm down. This isn't good for you or the baby."

"But it's all I had – the letter was all I had left!" I wailed. "I've lost her again, Ben . . . it has just come into my life and now it's gone again."

He wrapped me into his arms and stroked my hair, letting me cry it all out.

"I'm sorry for being such a bitch at the weekend," I whispered.

"What did she say in the letter?"

"The date on it was the day before she died – she basically was saying goodbye to me and how hard it had been for her to make the decision about whether or not to have the surgery."

"Wow." He was stunned. "But how come you're only getting it now?"

"I don't know – I'm so mad at Dad – he obviously had it for all these years and never gave it to me."

"Well, I'm sure he had a good reason."

I glared at him.

"Kate, I don't want to go through this all again. After the weekend we've just had, the last thing I want is to have another argument with you."

"I know you're still pissed off at me but you need to understand how hard all this is for me still."

"I'm trying, Kate, believe me I'm trying," he said wearily. "I know the letter is irreplaceable but it was given to you for a reason and look at what has come from it – you're finally opening up about your mum's death. You never really talk about her." His tone was softer now.

"Well, that's because it still hurts, Ben. A lot."

"Of course it does," he soothed. "I know I can't understand how hard this still is for you but I'm here, whenever you want to talk about it."

"How about never?"

He shook his head despairingly. "Why don't I run you a bath, huh? You've had a really shit day."

"That'd be lovely." I forced a smile onto my face. "Thanks, Ben."

Ben insisted on escorting me to work the next morning even though there were usually lots of people around in the morning rush-hour traffic so there wasn't much chance of anyone mugging me then. I was okay, though I was still a bit shaken up. When Nat, who happened to be coming along the street at the same time, saw Ben kissing me goodbye outside the gallery she knew that something was up. She was in shock when I told her what had happened.

"I'm so sorry, Kate, I should never have left you. It's all my fault!"

"But, Nat, I always walk to the Tube station on my own."

"But maybe they saw you locking up and followed you because they thought you had money?"

"Nah – I was just unlucky – he saw his opportunity and he took it."

"Well, that's it. I'm walking you to the Tube in the evenings from now on."

"You can't do that, Nat, you live in the opposite direction and you'd have to walk back again on your own."

"I'm not letting a pregnant woman walk up there on her own again."

"But what happens if someone attacks you then on the way back?"

"If someone attacked me they'd know about it. Now that's it – end of!"

I knew there was no point in arguing with her.

A few days later PC Black had rung me with an update to say that unfortunately they hadn't been able to find any CCTV footage in that area – if it had been a few metres further up the street, it would have been picked up but in the spot where I had been attacked, there was nothing.

"That's probably why he did there," he had said. "These guys do it for a living – they're professionals. They know exactly where and where not to do it. Unfortunately we're seeing a lot more of these types of attacks with the recession."

I was shocked that the muggers had the city mapped out and had pinpointed the best places to attack people. I just had to accept that it was gone. Well, I hoped karma would reach up and bite him on the arse one day.

Chapter 47

It was when I was alone in the gallery one morning while Nat was in Spain with her mum that I had an idea for something nice that I could do for her. I couldn't believe that I hadn't thought of it earlier. The more I thought about it, the more excited I became. I just hoped that my plan would work.

I logged on to the computer and went through Nat's files and found exactly what I was looking for. I felt a buzz of excitement flow through me. I really hoped that she wouldn't get mad at me. It was a bit risky and the last thing I wanted was for it to backfire. I made some phone calls to a few of our printing and framing suppliers but when I told them that I needed it for the end of the week, they had all balked at the tight timeframe. I had to beg them and they agreed that they'd do it this once as an exception seeing as the gallery put so much money their way every year. I rubbed my hands in glee. It was all starting to come together.

I told Ben what I was doing and while he agreed it was a great idea, he also said it was brave of me, which made me start to doubt whether I was doing the right thing. What if Nat hated it? Something like this was very personal and she might not even be comfortable with it. I was wondering if maybe I should just forget about the whole thing. The last thing I wanted to do was to upset her more. But I had already put the wheels in motion, so to speak, so I couldn't very well back out of it now.

I asked Ben to pop over to the gallery on his way home on Friday evening to give me a hand. My stomach was full of butterflies as I stood back and watched Ben hanging Nat's photos up on the gallery walls. Nat's subjects were always people. There was an old woman dressed decadently in furs, fingers heavy with jewellery, wearing a pair of slippers and pushing a shopping trolley with what looked like her belongings inside it. I remember Nat saying she had taken it on Kensington High Street. There was one of a bearded Jewish man with a kippah upon his head, deep in prayer. Another was one she had taken of a class of little girls with straw hats and ribbons in their pigtails from a local Montessori school crossing the street, following in an obedient line behind their teacher. There was one that she had taken of turbaned man manning a stall in Portobello Market. The photos looked amazing, they really and truly did. Her work should have been on these walls years before now. As we both stood back to admire them I felt goosebumps pop up along my skin. I just hoped Nat would feel the same way.

"I can't believe Nat took all of these!" Ben said again.

"I know. She's really good, isn't she?"

"She has a great eye. Why did she never exhibit them herself?"

"Oh, you know Nat, she wouldn't have the confidence – plus she doesn't see herself as a 'photographer' – more someone who likes taking pictures as a hobby."

"Well, she is every bit as good as these other people." He gestured around the room.

"Oh, I know, I keep on telling her that. But hopefully this will make her see it for herself."

I was a nervous wreck all weekend, thinking about how Nat was going to react. I couldn't sleep with worry. Ben had to keep

Caroline Finnerty

telling me to relax. I think he was afraid I'd send myself into premature labour.

The following Monday morning I went in to work half an hour earlier than usual just to make sure that I would be in before Nat. I was giddy with excitement as I looked at her photos displayed on the wall again. They looked great, there was no doubt about it. I just hoped Nat would think so too.

At five minutes to nine I watched her tie her bike on to the railings outside the window. She looked radiant and sun-kissed and it was clear that the break had done her the world of good.

"How was the holiday?" I asked as soon as she came in the door.

"Amazing! I just ate, slept and drank. The only exercise I did was to turn the pages of my book and lift my wineglass to my lips. It was exactly what I needed. And it was good to see Mum again too. Were you okay for the week on your own?"

"All good. As you see, the place didn't fall down without you. But I was lonely talking to these four walls every day."

"Aw, poor Kate!"

"I have a surprise for you." I bit down on my lip. I always did it whenever I got nervous.

"What is it?" she said warily. "You know I hate surprises!"

"How can anyone hate surprises? C'mon, it's upstairs."

She climbed the stairs after me until we both stood on the mezzanine floor.

"What's going on, Kate?" She looked at me in confusion. Then she moved closer to the walls and started looking at her photographs.

"Welcome to the exhibition of works by Natalie Anderson!"

I had tied a red ribbon around the central picture.

"But how did you . . ." She was speechless.

"Don't ask! Let's just say I pulled in a few favours!"

"But you can't just put my photos on the wall!"

"Don't worry, I've run them all past Tabitha first."

"Did you tell her they were mine?"

276

"Well, not exactly . . . I just said that you were a new photographer we were working with."

"Oh God, Kate, I'm going to kill you!"

"Well, she was very impressed actually. She said that if we keep finding talent like that she'll be a happy lady, so there! And here, there's just one more thing . . ." I handed her the invite that I'd had Charlie design and print.

"What's this?"

"Read it."

"But this says that I'm having an exhibition . . . starting next week." She was horrified.

"Yep."

"But I can't, Kate!"

"Why can't you? It's all arranged and we've already had loads of RSVPs."

"Oh my God, Kate, I can't believe you did all of this!"

"Well, someone had to. I've known you for so long and you've never had the guts or belief in yourself to do this. I knew that if I left it to you, you'd never do it."

She started to cry then. "Thank you, Kate – this is one of the nicest things that anyone has ever done for me."

Relief flowed through me. "You're welcome, you deserve it. You have such talent – I just know the exhibition is going to be a big success."

"I wish I had your faith . . ." She walked back over and started looking at her photos closely. "How did you even find them?"

"On the computer, of course, but there were so many to choose from – I could have done three exhibitions easily."

"Well, let's just see how this one goes first, yeah?"

"Are you excited?"

"Are you mad – I'm far too petrified to be excited! I still can't believe I'm having my own exhibition . . ."

After lunch a man came into the gallery. He was dressed in jeans and a jacket with a V-necked pullover underneath. I guessed he was probably in his mid-thirties. He was wearing thick-framed tortoiseshell glasses. I could tell he was a real arty type just from the way that he dressed.

"Check him out." I elbowed Nat.

She looked up from the computer. "Yeah, he's good-looking, I suppose," she said half-heartedly.

I guessed she still wasn't back in the game. I would test her from time to time but she had yet to get excited over a fine male specimen.

I climbed down off the stool and walked over to the guy.

"Hi there," I said. "If you need any help just shout."

"Thank you," he said.

He wandered around the ground floor for a while before climbing the stairs. I could see him up over the balcony. He came to a stop in front of one of Nat's photos. I knew which one it was – it was a simple black-and-white photo of a young woman sitting on a park bench. The woman's hands were clasped together on her lap while she stared off into space. She didn't seem to notice the pigeons that had gathered around at her feet. He stood fixated on the photo for a long time, way longer than usual. I went upstairs to him. I must say I was finding the stairs hard work these days. My hips, my knees, everything seemed to be aching constantly.

"Can I help you there?"

"That picture – who took it?" He pointed at the wall but didn't take his eyes off the photo.

"It's lovely, isn't it – hang on until I get the photographer herself and she can tell you all about it." I shouted down to Nat. "Nat, can you come up for a minute?"

She came up and joined us on the mezzanine.

"Nat, this gentleman was just wondering about this photo?"

"Where did you take it?" he asked her abruptly.

"I, um . . . just took it in the park over the road, one lunchtime. Why?" she said nervously.

"I'll take it."

We both looked at him.

"Em . . . okay . . . don't you want to know how much it is?" I said.

"It doesn't matter."

"Right – okay, I see. I'll take it downstairs and wrap it up for you."

There was something on edge about the man. He didn't seem to be on the same planet as us at all, whatever was going on inside his head.

We went back downstairs and over to the till. He picked up one of the fliers for Nat's exhibition off the counter and read it while I wrapped the photo in brown paper and tied it up with string. He paid over the money and then disappeared out of the gallery.

"That was a bit weird, wasn't it?" Nat said to me, coming up behind me at the till.

"Yeah, he seemed a bit . . . unhinged or something."

"I thought I was in trouble because I didn't ask the woman in the photo for her permission first. I'm still not sure of all of the correct protocols. God, I really hope this exhibition will be okay . . . I feel like I'm in over my head – you saw what I was like there and that was just one person!"

"Don't be worrying, it'll be grand."

Chapter 48

The day of Nat's exhibition came around quickly. I shooed Nat out the door at lunchtime to get her hair done.

"Go on – no one wants to come to an exhibition and look at your scarecrow hair. Sort it out."

"You cheeky mare!"

While she was gone I set about arranging the wineglasses on a table just inside the door. I had picked up fresh hydrangeas from the market earlier on and I distributed them in vases around the gallery. I lined up chairs along the mezzanine and set up the microphone as we always did for our exhibitions. I stood back and looked around the place. I had been working on exhibitions for a long time and couldn't believe that this one was finally Nat's.

"*Swit swoo* – check you out!" I said to her when she came back later that evening. Her thick auburn hair was blow-dried with a bouncy wave and she had changed into a black V-neck dress with a chunky red-beaded necklace and super-high platform heels. She looked stunning. I felt like a fat frump beside her. I had brought a change of clothes to work with me. It was another magnificent jersey ensemble but this time in a fuchsia colour. God, I couldn't wait to start wearing regular clothes again. And high heels. I'd had to discard my high heels weeks ago when I had started to feel like a sumo wrestler on stilts, standing on top of them. I missed my heels.

"So how are we looking?"

"All done, I think – I've the champagne chilling in the fridge. Let's have a glass."

I took out a bottle and popped the cork. I poured her a frothy glass and a thimbleful for myself.

"Thanks, Kate – I need this to help steady the nerves."

We clinked our glasses together.

"Here's to a successful exhibition and the start of a glittering photography career."

Nat gulped her glass back while I took a small sip from mine, wanting to make it last.

"Have you practised your speech yet?"

"Damn it – I knew that I was forgetting something!" She slammed her glass down on the counter so a small bit of the champagne sloshed over the side of the glass. She reached down to pick her bag off the floor and pulled out her notebook where she had been scribbling notes as they came to her over the last few days.

"Don't worry . . . as long as you thank me, that's all that matters . . ."

"You wish, Flynn!"

I heard my new phone vibrate on the desk beside me. I picked it up and when I saw it was Dad I switched it off and put it back down again. This was the second time that he had rung me today. Ben had given him my new number. He had tried calling me several times since my trip home but I hadn't answered any of the calls. I knew he probably wanted to explain to me his reasons for holding on to the letter for all these years but I didn't want to hear them.

A few people started to arrive into the gallery just after six. I went over to greet them. I offered them a glass of champagne and handed them a brochure for the exhibition. Nat looked really nervous. I could see her over the balcony, pacing nervously and fiddling with her necklace. She came back down the stairs.

"There's hardly anyone here!"

"Relax – people always arrive late to these things, you of all people know that."

"Yeah, I know. You're right." She took a deep breath.

Fifteen minutes later and Jensen's was full to capacity. I had sent the invitation around to our entire mailing list. It was always hard to know how many would actually turn up on the night but this was brilliant. A lot of our regulars knew Nat personally over the years and so they were delighted to come and show their support. Ben had come along with another teacher from the school who was also into photography. Lots of friends of Nat that I knew had turned out too. It was all going really well, except for the fact that I was running around like a mad-woman. Nat went upstairs to mingle with her guests and I was greeting all the newcomers downstairs and trying to keep everyone's glasses topped up.

After the guests had moved upstairs Nat made a lovely speech where she gave me a special thank-you. My hormones had lost the run of themselves these days and I had tears in my eyes. People were so impressed with Nat's photos and were coming up and asking her about them. It was the first time that many of her friends had actually seen her work. I was inundated with people asking questions and trying to red-sticker the ones that people wanted to buy. I was running up and down the stairs trying to take for the photos that had been sold. I couldn't keep up with all the people so Ben had to step in and wrap the photographs that were sold to free me up.

"Eh, isn't that the same guy from the other day?" I whispered to Nat as I put another red sticker onto a photo behind her.

She spun around and saw the man from last week, his eyes fixed on her photos so that there were only inches between his eyes and the photograph. "All he's short of doing is studying them under a magnifying glass!"

We observed him for a while before we were called away by

a journalist looking to get a photo with Nat and myself.

"That went really well, didn't it?" I said to Ben who had stayed on to help us clean up after we had closed the door behind the last guest. I had been so busy between greeting guests, selling pictures and telling people about the work that the evening had flown past and I couldn't believe it was nearly nine o'clock.

Nat came down the stairs with a tray of empty champagne glasses.

"Leave it, Nat – we can't have the artist cleaning up after their own exhibition!" Ben said. "I'll give Kate a hand here – you go on and meet your friends for a drink."

"Are you sure?" She looked at me.

"Go on – we're just going to clear up the glasses – we can sort the rest out in the morning."

"Oh my God, I'm literally buzzing. This has been one of the best nights of my life and it would never have happened without you." She wrung her hands. "Are you going to come?"

"Nah, I'm exhausted but thanks anyway. Have a great night. You deserve it."

She picked up her bag and walked towards the door.

"And take your time in the morning," I said. "I'll be fine for a few hours on my own."

She stopped at the doorframe and swung back around. "Kate?"

"Yeah?"

"Thank you, thank you so much." She grinned as she went out the door.

After Nat had gone, with only the two of us left behind, the usual stillness of the gallery was restored.

"Here, this is for you." Ben took a wrapped photograph out from under the desk and handed it to me.

"What's this?"

"Open it."

I opened the brown-paper wrapping and took out the

photograph. It was the one I had told Ben was my favourite. It was a sepia-toned photograph inside a brown wood frame, of a mother holding the hand of a toddler. Nat had taken it from behind as they walked ahead of her on the path. It was so simple but moving. I'd had tears in my eyes the first time I had seen it.

"Thank you!" I said, throwing my arms around his neck. "You remembered."

"Of course I did – I knew you liked it and I didn't want anyone else to buy it first so I put a red sticker on it and wrapped it up when you weren't looking. And you deserve it – you did so much for tonight." He raised his champagne glass. "To new beginnings!" he toasted.

"To new beginnings!" I clinked my tumbler of sparkling water against his glass.

"Look, the red light is blinking on the answering machine – do you want to check it before we go?" Ben said just as we were getting ready to go home.

"Nah, it'll be fine until tomorrow. C'mon, I'm exhausted."

Chapter 49

The next day in the gallery, I couldn't help smiling when I thought of how happy Nat had looked last night. I was dying to see her to hear how her night had gone after. I went into the kitchen and made myself a cup of tea. I came out and sat down at the desk. I switched on the computer and, while I was waiting for that to start up, I pressed the button on the answering machine to listen to the messages. Instantly Dad's hesitant voice filled the air

"Eh . . . Kate, it's me, Dad . . ." I was just about to press the delete button but there was something about his tone that made me listen to the rest of his message. "Look, I've been trying to get you all day on your mobile and I didn't want to leave a message for you in work like this . . . but eh . . . it's your gran – she's not well. She's been rushed to hospital. We think it might be a stroke. Give me a ring me when you get this, yeah?"

I picked up the phone on the desk straight away and tried phoning Dad back but his phone kept ringing out.

I rang Ben next. Luckily he wasn't yet in class so he hadn't switched off his phone. I told him what had happened, the words spilling out of me like I was watching the situation from afar. I couldn't think straight about what I needed to do to get back to Ireland and be with Gran.

"Right, Kate, get in a cab and I'll meet you back at home, okay?"

On autopilot I locked up the gallery and went out to flag a taxi.

When I got home and saw Ben, it all hit me and I fell apart. I tried Dad again but I only got his voicemail. I rang Patrick and Seán's phones too but neither answered. Ben did a quick search on his laptop to see which airport had the next scheduled flights. He reckoned Stansted was our best bet – there was a Ryanair flight to Dublin leaving soon. The flights to Knock, which would have been closer, had already departed for the day. He ran around and put a few things in a bag for the both of us then I followed him down the stairs and into the car. We drove to the airport in silence. My mind was whirring with worry. I felt so guilty when I thought back to the last time I was home in Gran's kitchen when I was mean to Aoife. Is that what had caused the stroke?

Occasionally Ben would reach across and rub my hand and tell me it was going to be okay. But I wasn't so sure.

Chapter 50

It took four sets of traffic lights, one overtaken bus, three loops of the multistorey car park, one queue at the wrong ticket desk, one queue at the right one, two tarry coffees, five cartons of UHT milk – and one embarrassing scene where I tearily begged a flight attendant to let me board without a doctor's letter before Ben and I were sitting on a flight bound for Dublin.

I prayed even though I'm not religious. I bargained with God. I would take the stairs instead of the escalator every day for the next month. Year. I would stop swearing. Whatever it took, I would do it. I would visit home more often, I would ring Dad weekly without fail, I would even try to make amends with Aoife. Whatever it took to keep Gran with us, I promised that I would do it.

As we descended into Dublin, my heart started up again. The man beside me had claimed our shared armrest so I sat with my elbow leaning on the left and my head resting against Ben's shoulder. I looked out the window as we made our descent into Dublin.

We caught a thermal stream coming down and the plane jolted before steadying again and then we were down on the ground. The sounds of the engines roared as we landed, the wing flaps popping up to slow us down.

As we hadn't checked on any baggage we were able to go straight through to security and then out to the Arrivals hall. I tried Dad again as soon as my phone picked up the Irish network but there was still no answer. The not knowing was horrendous. Horrible scenarios were spinning around inside my head.

"They're all probably at the hospital," Ben offered, giving my hand a reassuring squeeze. "They probably have to switch them off in case they interfere with any of the machines."

I nodded. I belatedly texted Nat to tell her what had happened because I knew she would be worried when she arrived at work to find the gallery closed.

Ben followed the signs for the car-hire desks and I followed behind him. We were given a Fiat Punto with an apologetic smile from the woman manning the desk and we set off.

As we drove along the M4 I continued my bargaining with God – I would be nicer and more patient with people. I wouldn't watch television for a whole year.

Finally Dad phoned me back. She was in intensive care but stable. They were still waiting to hear from the doctor.

It was nearly six o'clock in the evening by the time we pulled up in to the hospital car park. I felt my blood run cold when I thought about the last time that I had been here. I hated this place. Everything about it reminded me of Mam. The grey pebble-dashed walls, the hospital-perfect neat grass verges. The way people spoke in low hushed tones. The sterile smell. The orderly politeness of the other people you met there – the forced camaraderie because you were all in this together. Like everyone was trying to be on their best behaviour. The anxious relatives you met in the corridors as they waited on their loved one to come out of surgery or the lucky ones smiling as they came through the doors, ready for home.

"You okay?" Ben said, turning to me as he took the key out of the ignition and turned off the headlights.

"Yeah, I'll be fine. C'mon, let's go inside," I said sighing. I unbuckled my seatbelt and stepped out of the car. I walked up to the sliding doors and went up to the reception where they directed me to her room.

I met Dad, Patrick and Seán in the corridor outside. They were all standing around clasping polystyrene cups.

"Kate, Ben!" Dad exclaimed when he saw us. "You got here!"

I nodded hello at Patrick and Seán.

"How is she?" I asked.

"Well, she's come round and she knew who we were but we won't know the full extent of its effects until they assess her tomorrow. They said that if Aoife hadn't noticed the signs and acted so fast, things could have been very different."

"Where's Aoife?"

"She's sitting with Gran. We just came out here to get a cup of tea and stretch our legs for a few minutes."

"Can I go in?"

"Of course. We were just going back in ourselves."

I pushed open the door and we all filed quietly into the room.

I got a shock when I saw Gran lying on the bed looking so frail. She was sleeping. I watched her chest rise and fall in shallow beats. She seemed to have shrunk since last weekend. Her shoulders had narrowed and the blue hospital gown dwarfed her. Aoife was sitting up near her head, stroking her hand. She was pale and darkness shadowed her face.

"How's she doing?" I said to Aoife.

She turned to look at me and turned back towards Gran again. Her eyes were red-rimmed and she looked wretched.

"So you were able to come then?"

"I got here as fast as I could –"

She cut across me. "How many times did Dad have to ring you before you phoned him back?"

"Well, I –"

"Dad rang you yesterday evening, Kate – yesterday evening – and you only bothered to call him back today! And yet he still makes excuses for you 'Oh, Kate's very busy in London' or 'She has a lot on her mind with a baby on the way, y'know'. Gran could have been dead and you would have been oblivious to it because you're too far stuck in Kate Flynn world. Well, I'm sick of it – everyone pussyfooting around you like you're the bloody Queen of England returning home and we should all roll out the red carpet because *Kate Flynn* has decided to grace us with a visit!"

"That's enough now, Aoife. This is not the place." Dad stepped in. "This won't help your gran. You've had a rough day. I think you should go home and get a few hours' sleep – you're exhausted."

"Don't worry, I'm going." She stood up and kissed Gran gently on the forehead before storming out of the room.

"I'll go after her," Seán said. He bumped into a nurse on his way out the door.

"What's going on in here?" The nurse looked at him and then to the rest of us for an explanation.

We all avoided eye contact with her.

"You can be heard out in the corridor!"

We stared down at the floor.

"Well, whatever it is, it certainly isn't doing Josephine any good – it's very important that she gets her rest. I think she has had enough visitors for today."

I instantly felt guilty.

"Sorry – we'll go now and leave her in peace," Dad said.

The nurse nodded. "Visiting time tomorrow is between twelve and two."

"Right so. Look, sorry again about that." Dad said getting up from the chair and putting on his coat. "It's been a long day – I think we're all a bit tired."

She nodded.

We got outside the door.

"We should all head on home and get some rest, yeah? There's nothing more we can do here," Dad said.

We walked down the corridors until we were back at reception. We went back through the sliding doors and out into the cold evening air. We stood chatting for a few minutes under the amber glow of the car park lights before we said our goodbyes.

"We'll see you back at the house," Dad said.

We followed Dad's car back to Ballyrobin. We went across back roads that I wasn't too sure of. I would definitely have got us lost.

It took almost an hour before we turned in our gate. We followed Dad into the kitchen where he automatically turned on the kettle. He had left the radio on in the kitchen as usual – he never bothered to turn it off when he was going out.

I felt my stomach rumble and then I remembered that I hadn't eaten anything all day.

"Do you want a cuppa?"

"No, thanks," Ben said.

"No, thanks, Dad, not for me. I might just grab a slice of toast if that's okay?"

"Of course it is. There's bread in the press. Sorry I haven't anything organised for dinner with everything going on."

"Don't worry about it, toast is fine."

"So how was the flight?" Dad asked as I pushed two slices of bread down into the toaster.

"It was fine – a bit bouncy on the way down though."

"Well, you were lucky to get on a flight with such short notice."

I went to the fridge and took out the butter.

"She's going to be okay, isn't she, Dad?"

"Well, they said, we got her to the hospital in time so hopefully she'll be alright but she is nearly ninety, Kate, and this will take a lot out of her. Luckily Aoife was there with her and noticed something was wrong – if she had been on her own, well, I don't even want to think what might have happened."

I felt a shiver run through me at the thought.

The toaster popped and I took out the bread and started to butter it. I offered Ben a slice but he declined. He had eaten a sandwich on the plane but I hadn't been able to.

"I didn't have a chance to make up the bed for you with everything going on."

"Don't worry about that, sure I'm just glad to have a bed to fall into. I'll get fresh sheets in the hot press."

"Well, try and get some sleep, you've had a long day."

We said goodnight and then Ben helped me to make the bed.

The weight of my body sank into the soft mattress. I lay there and stared at the shadowy ceiling. Even though my bones were aching with tiredness, my head was buzzing. The day just started to hit me and I felt wired. I tossed and turned but sleep wasn't coming. I heard Ben snore softly beside me. Eventually, knowing there was no chance of me sleeping, I gave up and got out of bed. I threw on a jumper over my pyjamas and went along to the kitchen.

I was surprised to see light filtering out from under the doorway. I opened it and saw Dad sitting at the table with his head in his hands. At first I thought he was asleep but then he raised his head up to look at me.

"Ah, Kate! Can you not sleep?"

I shook my head.

"Me neither. What a day, eh? It's only starting to hit me now."

I pulled out a chair and sat opposite him at the table.

"Do you reckon Aoife was all right after?"

"I rang Seán a while ago and he said she's fine. She went straight to bed when she got home."

"Does she normally flip the lid like that?"

"Honestly? No. I've never seen her lose her temper like that before. She's just tired and the stress of the last twenty-four hours is taking its toll on her."

"She's right though."

"How do you mean?"

"Well, I did avoid your calls. Only that you left that message at the gallery, I wouldn't be here . . ."

He looked across at me.

"To be honest, I was so mad at you for not giving me the

letter after Mam died like you were supposed to."

"I figured as much. So you read it then?"

I nodded. "Why did it take you so long to give it to me?"

"I don't know. I suppose I just never really thought the time was right."

"Well, what about the time when you were supposed to give it to me? After Mam died?"

"I'm sorry, Kate – but you were so angry, I was afraid it would make everything worse or you'd tear it up or something!"

"Things couldn't have been much worse than they were, Dad!"

"I know, Kate, I know," he sighed. "There just never seemed to be a good time. I've been waiting for years to give it to you. After she died, I was afraid you would destroy it without opening it or do something you would regret with it. Then you left home and, well, I suppose it just didn't happen. And then the years went by and I didn't want to drag it all up again for you, especially when you seemed to be making a new life for yourself over in London. But I thought . . . well . . . now that you're in the family way yourself that the time was right."

"Well, it was mine – it was meant for me. You should have given it to me when you were supposed to."

"I know, Kate, I'm sorry, love. I really am. Do you think if I had given it to you earlier, it would have helped?"

"Probably not if I'm honest. It still wouldn't have changed what she did."

"Your feelings haven't mellowed to her at all after all these years, have they?"

"Well, have *yours*?"

"Staying angry with her about her decision won't change anything, Kate."

"So you've forgiven her then?"

"I can see you're still angry – Lord above, so am I, but it won't change anything now. She made her decision. She did what she thought at the time was best and we can't undo that now, can we?"

"I guess so. I have something to tell you, Dad."

"Oh – what is it?"

"Well, I was mugged a few days ago –"

"You were not! Are you okay? You weren't hurt, were you?"

"Sure can't you see yourself that I'm fine? But the letter – it was in my bag. It's gone, Dad. The police have been checking for CCTV or something in the area but there's nothing."

"Sure it wasn't your fault."

"But I feel like I've let you and Mam down – you'd only just given it to me."

"You haven't let me down at all. It was your letter – your mother wrote it for you."

"I've tried to write down the bits of it that I remember but it isn't the same – it's not her voice."

"Look, you know what your mother was like – she wasn't one for the sentimental stuff."

"She was great, you know . . . she had a real wry sense of humour."

"She did, love."

"Do you miss her, Dad?"

"Every day. Every single day when I come in the door I always think how empty the house feels without her – even after twenty years."

"Me too. It was so unfair, wasn't it?"

He nodded. "I still get angry about it all, to be honest, Kate, and when I feel it coming on me I take off into the fields and it helps to calm me down again. This sounds silly but when the wind is swirling around my ears it's like I can hear her voice wrapped up inside it telling me to cop myself on and to stop being a bleddy eejit!"

"That's exactly what she would say!" I said, laughing. "What was it like at the time, Dad – was she scared?"

"Well, I suppose she was – it's only natural. Although she didn't let on . . . she was a desperate woman for putting on a brave face. When they first found the mass, she was sure it would all be grand – she never thought for a minute that she was in any danger. And you have to remember it was nearly twenty years ago and things weren't as advanced then as they are now. But after Aoife was born and we knew things weren't looking good for her . . . then, I think, yes . . . she was a bit frightened by what lay ahead. And angry too. I said so many Novenas and had asked Father Ball to mention her in his Masses but they all went unheard. I think the way she saw it was that it was her job to get Aoife here safely and then she would start her treatment and get better for all of us . . ." He let out a heavy sigh. "But it didn't work out that way . . ."

"I regret so much not talking to her during her last few weeks."

"I know you do and, don't worry, she knows it too – that's why she wrote the letter for you. She didn't write one for any of the others, by the way. You were a teenager – she knew that it was hard on you. But you know your mother thought the world of you, don't you, Kate?"

I smiled at him. "We were very close in our own way – I know we fought a lot but I always think that if she had lived longer and I had outgrown my awful teenage years and stopped being such a bitch then we would have been best friends."

"Your mother knew you were just being a headstrong teenager."

"If it were now things might be different," I said.

"Who knows?" Dad said. "But I'm sure medicine has moved on a lot from those days. God, it was a horrible thing, that chemo – it killed everything in her body – the bad stuff and the good stuff with it. Thank God nowadays it's a lot more targeted. Your mother would be so ill after her sessions but she put a brave face on it."

"I remember it."

"Do you?"

I nodded. "I wish I didn't but I can remember those days coming home and she was like a ghost blending with the white sheets on the bed. She would try to force herself to smile but I could see it in her eyes. The sickness. *The fear*. So then I just used to leave her alone. I didn't want her to think that she had to put on a brave face for me."

"It was hard on the three of you – probably more so for you. You were that bit older, you were at that awkward stage between girl and woman and you needed your mother, not some auld farmer who didn't have a clue."

"Ah Dad, you did well!" I laughed and placed my hand over his on the table.

"Not initially I didn't – sure I went to pieces. I was never around – I was always out on the land – or if I could get Josephine up to the house to mind you at night I was down in the pub sculling pints and just making myself feel worse. If it wasn't for Josephine, well . . . I don't know what would have happened. She was busy with Aoife and trying to keep an eye on the rest of ye. She was nearly seventy as that stage and she was grieving for her daughter but she never once complained. The whole place would have fallen apart if it wasn't for her. She was very good to us – I'll never forget that."

"I've always wondered how come you never took Aoife back to live with you?"

"I've thought about it myself from time to time but I suppose it just never happened, Kate. I don't know why . . . I think your granny had grown very attached to her . . . she had just lost her daughter and now she had this newborn baby that reminded her so much of her own daughter as a baby . . . so I think having Aoife helped her to grieve. And it suited me as well because I was so buried under my own grief that I could barely manage the three of ye and run the house and the farm. So it was an unspoken thing that just went on. Then as the years went by, it was just the way it was. I know to most people it's an odd arrangement but it worked for us. Aoife always knew that I was her dad and that Patrick and Seán were her brothers and that you were her big sister living in London. I saw her every day and we would all eat our dinner together in the evenings – but at the end of the day your granny raised her and that's where her home will always be."

"I hated her, you know – I couldn't look at her without blame."

"It wasn't her fault, Kate – she was only a helpless baby that didn't know a thing about the world she had been born into."

"I know that, Dad – logically, I know that, but I resented her because the way I saw it was that Mam chose her over the rest of us."

"Your mother had a horrible decision to make and she didn't see that she was choosing Aoife over the rest of you because in her heart she truly believed she'd recover after the surgery. She didn't choose Aoife over you or your brothers, Kate – you know that, don't you, love?"

"I guess it must have been an awful decision to have to make . . ."

"Yeah, it wasn't very nice and we fought a lot about it at the time and your mother and me never fought but I wanted her to have the surgery but she wouldn't do it. She could be very stubborn when she wanted to be."

I smiled. "Ben says the same thing about me."

"Well, you didn't lick it off the ground!" He grinned at me.

"Was Gran really pissed off with me after my last visit home?"

"No, you know your gran – she loves you no matter what you do, you know that. She knows that it's still hard on you."

That was another thing. Because I'd been her only granddaughter I had always been Gran's favourite. My Auntie Anna who lived in New York had had two boys and Gran had only met them a few times in her life. But then when Aoife arrived, it seemed that Gran always had her in her arms. Suddenly, I felt pushed aside. Although I know it was probably only in my head that that had happened.

We both fell quiet then. The condensation from the milk carton had pooled on the table between us.

"Dad?"

"Yes?"

"I think I'd like to go and see Aoife in the morning."

"Well now, Kate," he was hesitant, "I don't think that's a good idea, do you? I don't think any of us want a repeat of what happened at the hospital."

"Don't worry, Dad, neither do I. I just want to talk to her. Properly."

I could see him raise his eyebrows and he studied my face for a minute.

"Okay – we'll go over there in the morning." He sat back in his chair and swallowed back the last mouthful in his mug.

Chapter 51

The next morning I gently woke Ben and told him where I was going.

"Do you want me to come with you?"

I shook my head. "No, you sleep on – I won't be long."

Dad drove us over to Gran's house. It was only across the fields as the crow flies but it was still damp and drizzly out so neither of us fancied walking. I followed him into the kitchen where the TV was on. It was showing a rerun of some eighties quiz show. The presenter was a skinny guy in a faded brown suit. I thought I recognised him from when I was a child.

Aoife came into the kitchen with a white towel wrapped around her head. She looked startled when she saw Dad and me in the kitchen too.

"Aoife, you look much better!" Dad said. "That sleep did you the world of good."

She nodded. "Well, I'm nearly ready and then I just want to gather up a few things for her before we go. Can you drive me in?"

"Of course I'll drive you but the nurse won't let us in until twelve. They're strict about visitors. They don't want us to tire her out."

"Oh, right. I see." She sounded disappointed as she sat down on a chair.

"While I'm here, I'm going to have a look at that door handle that your gran was giving out about last week." It was obvious that he was making an excuse to leave us on our own.

Aoife nodded. "Yeah, she's afraid that if she goes into the bathroom that she might never come out again."

Dad went down to the bathroom and it was just the two of us left on our own together then. I tried to think back. I didn't think I'd ever been on my own with her before. Even when she was a baby I had always managed to somehow avoid it. She unwrapped the towel from her hair and put it over her shoulders.

To look at us, you could tell that we were sisters. Our appearances were similar, although unlike me, her childhood white-blonde hair had never darkened and she didn't have an expensive highlight habit to maintain. She didn't even have any frown lines – at eighteen I'd had a few wrinkles, probably from all the smoking and drinking that I used to do. But even though we were sisters, we were effectively strangers – I didn't know anything about her.

There was an awkward silence and I wasn't sure what exactly I was going to say to her. I pulled out a chair from the table and sat down opposite her.

"Looks like you were right earlier – I was avoiding Dad's phone calls," I said eventually.

"Well, I'm sick of everyone making excuses for you, Kate. Gran was in Intensive Care and you were too busy swanning around London to care."

"That's not true – as soon as I heard what had happened I came here as quick as I could."

"But why would you ignore Dad's calls? Why would you do that? All he does is say how great you are!"

I squirmed in my seat. "The reason I was ignoring Dad was because the last time I was back Dad gave me a letter."

Aoife's clear blue eyes opened wide. "What was in it?"

"It was a letter that Mam wrote for me the night before she died. It was her way of saying goodbye – you see, we had fought for weeks before she died and I refused to go and see her in hospital. I regret it so much now – believe me if I could turn back the clock I would . . . but Dad never gave it to me until I was home the last time."

"But why would he do that?"

"I don't know, he said he wasn't sure how I'd react. He was afraid I'd tear it up or something. He's right though, I probably would have."

"Well, then, maybe he was right to hold on to it. You know, you think you were the only one affected by it all. Myself, Patrick and Seán lost our mother too – Gran lost her daughter, Dad lost his wife. We all lost her, Kate, not just you!"

"Yeah, but you didn't know her."

It was probably the worst thing I could ever have said to her.

"Do you not think I wish I had?" Her eyes blazed and her voice climbed higher. "Do you know how hard it is to grow up not being able to remember your own mother?"

"But you didn't have to watch her die!"

"I know that and it must have been an awful time for you all but will you stop feeling sorry for yourself! You're lucky you can remember her. I would give anything to even just have one memory of her."

I had never thought of it like that before. I had always just assumed that she was the fortunate one because she couldn't remember any of it. Because she was too young to experience the pain.

"Look, Kate, this isn't a Top Trumps competition about who misses Mam more."

"You're right, Aoife," I sighed. "You're right. Look, this isn't an excuse for my behaviour. But this whole thing – well, I still find it very hard, to be honest. That's why I never come home to visit. I find it too upsetting and I get all uptight and end up rubbing everyone up the wrong way – but it's because I'm nervous."

"I know."

"You do?"

"Yeah, I was talking to Gran after you went back."

"I think I owe you an apology. I'm sorry about the last time I was home," I blurted out. "I really am – I was rude, arrogant and out of order. I'm sorry for blaming you for all these years. I suppose I never tried looking at it from your point of view before."

"It's okay – sometimes I blame myself too."

"You do?"

"Well, sometimes." She took a deep breath. "At times, y'know, like when it's her anniversary or at Christmas and I know that everyone is missing her and finding it tough going . . . well, I feel a bit left out at times like that because I have no memories of her, I can't join in and reminisce about her." She lowered her voice. "And sometimes I wonder if secretly they are thinking that it's all my fault . . ."

"They don't think that!"

"How do you know? You do, so why shouldn't they?"

"I don't, Aoife – not really. I just wanted someone to blame and you were the easiest person. You couldn't even fight back. Sure no one knows – even if she had taken treatment earlier she still might not have made it."

"Maybe. And we'll never know now, will we?"

I shook my head. "It's not fair – life isn't fair. I spent so many years being angry about it all but I had a big chat with Dad last night and I can now see that I'm only wasting my energy – it won't bring her back."

"What was she like, Kate? Sometimes Dad or Gran will mention her in passing but I've always been afraid to ask too much about her in case they get upset."

"You would have loved her – she was a great mother. She had this great big smile – she was one of those people who smiled with her eyes. She had wild curly blonde hair and she was forever trying to tame it. I used to think she was the most beautiful woman in the world. She had to put on her mascara every morning, even if we weren't going anywhere – she said she felt naked without it. I would stand beside her at the mirror and she would hand it to me then and I would put it on too. I'm sure

I must have looked a fright going to school as a five-year-old with mascara on me but she never said anything – just how I looked so pretty."

"You're so lucky to have memories of her. I only have the photos that Dad gave me. Sometimes I try to imagine the woman in the photos talking or doing stuff but it doesn't work." She smiled sadly. "I don't really feel that you and Patrick and Seán are my sister and brothers. I feel removed from it all and I'm afraid to show emotion in case I'm accused of being fake. It's like you're all wondering how I could understand what you're all going through because I didn't know her."

"No one thinks that – Patrick and Seán think the world of you, and Dad and Gran too – if I'm honest the reason I was such a bitch to you last weekend was because I was jealous of you and how much they all think of you. If anyone is an outsider, it's me! They all know you and love you – you belong in this family."

"Thanks, Kate – it means a lot to hear you say that."

"Look, Aoife, I know we don't really know each other very well and I take full responsibility for that – I never really gave you any time – but I was fourteen when Mam died and, even though I knew she was sick, I never thought that she would *die* so it came as a huge shock to me when she passed away. Sometimes I still can't believe that she is actually gone, y'know . . ."

"I can only imagine."

"I was angry for a long time – very angry. I still am, to be honest. But . . . well . . . maybe it's time for me to let it go." I sighed. "I have to accept that that was the decision she made at the time and we'll never know what way things might have been if she had chosen to get the surgery. I know there's years of old ground and it can't all be changed overnight but if you'll let me . . . then maybe we could get to know each other properly?"

"I'd like that," she smiled at me.

Chapter 52

By the time Aoife and I had finished talking, it was time to go back in to visit Gran.

I had a quick shower to freshen up back at Dad's but the lack of sleep from thinking about it all meant I felt like I was dead on my feet. I nodded off in the car as Ben drove us back to the hospital. Dad and Aoife were travelling together. I felt as though I had literally closed my eyes when Ben was gently shaking my shoulder to tell me we had arrived.

"C'mon, love, I know you want to go and see your gran."

We met a nurse coming out from her room.

"How was she overnight?" Dad asked.

"She's doing okay. I have to warn you though that her speech has been quite badly affected – try not to be alarmed when you try to talk to her. Although sometimes speech and language difficulties can rectify themselves in stroke victims, so try not to worry just yet." She lowered her voice. "It also looks as though she might have some paralysis in her right arm."

"Oh no!" Aoife's voice broke and she dissolved into tears.

"Come here, love," Dad said, wrapping Aoife into a hug.

"You need to be aware that because of her age and after an incident like this, there is a possibility that she won't regain her full functionality and she may need full-time care."

Aoife shrieked in horror.

Dad rubbed Aoife's shoulder brusquely.

"As in a nursing home?" Dad said.

The nurse nodded. "I'm sorry."

"I see." He exhaled heavily.

We went inside and sat down on the various chairs around Gran's bed. She was sleeping.

"There's no way I can let her go into a nursing home, Dad," Aoife said as she dabbed at her eyes with a tissue.

"Don't worry, love, we won't let that happen. We'll look after whatever care she needs between us all."

Aoife nodded. "She'd hate it – I couldn't do it to her."

"And we can look at getting a home help too," Dad said, "Y'know, maybe for a couple of hours a week? We'll work it out anyway."

I looked at the swirly pattern on the grey vinyl floor, feeling even guiltier if that was possible. I knew that no matter what care options they decided on for Gran, I wasn't going to be a part of it.

Patrick and Seán came in a while later. They were visibly upset when Dad relayed what the nurse had told us.

Gran struggled to talk when she woke and what the nurse had warned us about soon became obvious. Her speech was difficult to understand. Her muscles were too weak to articulate what she wanted to say. I tried hard not to let my sadness at hearing her voice sound like that show in my face. I looked over at Aoife who had tears in her eyes. We sat chatting amongst ourselves and Gran fell in and out of sleep.

"Make sure you don't tire her out now," the nurse warned, coming back into the room.

"We'll head on shortly," Dad said.

Outside in the car park I said goodbye to Patrick and Seán before getting into our car.

"I hate seeing her like that, Ben." My voice broke and gave way to tears.

"I know, love, I know it's horrible seeing her looking so feeble – but you heard what the nurse said – it's still early days. She might still make a recovery."

"But she's nearly ninety, Ben!"

"I'm sorry, Kate – I wish there was something that I could say or do to make it better." He reached across for my hand.

I turned my head and looked out the window, where crumbling stone walls and knobbly fields zipped by outside and prayed that Gran would be okay.

When we got to the house Dad started to put on dinner for all of us. Aoife was there. She was helping to peel potatoes and carrots so I took a knife out of the drawer and started to chop them.

"Are you on your holidays now?" I asked.

"No, I still have one more exam left."

"Ah right, well, nearly there now."

She nodded.

"What are you planning on doing for the rest of the summer?"

"Well, Seán said that Acton's are looking for someone to do a bit of filing and other admin work so I might try and get a job there. The girls in college are all going off to Boston on their J1's but I couldn't leave Gran after all that has happened."

We both fell silent then but there was a closeness in just peeling and chopping together – something we would never have done before.

Patrick brought Luisa and their children over. They seemed to have warmed to me a bit more. We all squashed in around the table, keeping our elbows tucked in neatly to make room for everyone, and helped ourselves to the food that Dad had served up for us. We chatted about the recession and Dad was giving out about politicians that never seemed to change. "Different face, same arrogance," he said. We didn't talk about Gran. Her presence was missed and it was like we were all too sad to speak about her. We sat watching TV for the rest of the evening.

Ben booked flights home for the following day. He was able to get one from Knock, which was a lot closer than driving back to Dublin. I hated walking out on Gran when she was like this but Dad told me I had to go, he was nervous of me being so heavily pregnant. And Ben had to go back to school. But I felt guilty all the same knowing that when Gran came home from hospital, the reality of the situation meant that Dad and Aoife were going to have to be her carers.

I woke up early the next morning. I couldn't sleep in at all lately, which I thought was ironic because every second person kept advising me to sleep now while I still could. They meant well but, my God, it wasn't like I could store up the sleep to tide me over when the baby was born and giving us sleepless nights. I think this early-rising lark was the body's way of preparing me for the lack of sleep that lay ahead.

Eventually, I decided to get up. I tiptoed past Dad's bedroom door so that I wouldn't wake him. I went out to the kitchen. Aoife had stayed over last night too but she must have been sleeping in. I flicked the switch on the kettle and waited for it to boil for what seemed like ages. I popped a teabag into a cup. While I was waiting I looked out across the fields. The grass was silvery with dew. It looked like it was going to be a nice day – the sun was out and it was one of those days that lifted you up and made you feel all was well with the world and you would forgive the weather gods for the poor summer that we'd had up to now.

I opened the back door and let the kitchen fill with fresh morning air. Walking over to the dresser, I picked up the family photo of my Confirmation off the dresser. I was wearing the hickest matching jacket and dress in an orange floral fabric – I will never forget how much I had hated that outfit. Mam and I had rowed for weeks beforehand because I did not want to wear a dress. You never would have guessed though with the smiles that we all had plastered onto our faces. Mam stood behind me with her arm on my shoulder – her candy-pink lipstick looked so dated now but she still looked good. I did a quick calculation and guessed that it was probably taken shortly before she had found out that she was expecting Aoife and then had the tumour.

There was something I needed to do before I went back to London. The last time I was home I still wasn't ready to do it but now, as I found myself alone in the empty kitchen, I knew that I had to. I went back down to the bedroom. I would be lying to you if I said that I wasn't nervous – my heart was racing in my chest.

I scribbled a quick note for Ben and threw on a pair of jeans and a jumper and set off.

The roads were quiet at that time of the morning as I walked along. At least I didn't have to worry about bumping into anyone. I noticed more this time – things I had missed the last time. It was still raining though. I walked through the square, crossed the bridge and finally I reached the graveyard. The iron gate groaned as I pushed it back and let myself in. The last time I had been here was for my other granny, Dad's mother's funeral. I knew Mam was probably buried nearby. Overhead oak trees shaded the path beneath it and the lower branches wafted gently on the breeze. I walked along the path, cracked from the roots trying to push up underneath it. I had watched a documentary once where the roots of a tree had grown so large that they caused all four walls of a house to separate.

I finally came upon her headstone. I was glad to see it was neat and well kept. Flowers were planted and I could see someone had weeded it recently when I looked at some of the other graves whose plants were overgrown by weeds. Seeing her name there etched in gold paint on the cold granite slab made it very real. There it was written in front of me.

I began to speak to my mother. The words, although whispered, came out loud in the quiet graveyard.

"I'm sorry I lost your letter. I tried my best to get it back. I really did. I'm so glad you wrote it for me, Mam. It meant a lot to have that little piece of you. And I'm sorry I was such a bitch before you died – I regret it so much. If I could take back those words, believe me I would." My bump was starting to weigh me down so I lowered myself on to the edge of the kerbing. "I miss you, Mam. Every day. Even the Hoover banging off the bottom of the door on a Saturday morning – I'd let you do it every day for the rest of my life, if it would bring you back."

I looked around at the other headstones, each with their own story and loved ones left behind. The cycle of life, it was the one thing guaranteed, but human nature was a funny thing because even though we knew it had to happen sometime, we still found it so hard to accept when someone belonging to us passed over to the other side.

"I wish you could be here to meet Ben – and Baby Pip. Can you believe I'm having a baby, Mam? Sometimes it scares the life out of me that I'm going to be entirely responsible for a little person and that they're going to call me 'Mammy'. To be honest, I'm a bit scared, Mam – a lot scared actually, so please stay close to me, yeah?"

I stayed like that for a while, listening to the birdsong on the cool morning air. It was such a peaceful place. I now understood why people liked to visit graveyards. I always thought, whenever I had heard someone saying that before, that they were loopers, but there was something soothing about being here and for some reason I definitely felt closer to her.

When I went back to the house everyone was up eating breakfast.

"Kate, where were you?" Ben said.

"I just went for a walk to get some fresh air – it's a beautiful morning out there."

"Well, pull up a chair – get some breakfast into you, love," Dad said.

I sat down at the table and helped myself to the fry that Dad had cooked.

We headed into the hospital then. It was hard saying goodbye to Gran. I leant in to hug her and I could feel her trying to hug me back as best she could but it was obvious she wasn't able to. The good news was that they said she'd be able to come home soon.

We had a few hours to spare before we drove to Knock to catch our flight. I chatted with Dad and Aoife and we pored over old photo albums together and recalled long-forgotten anecdotes from my childhood. I felt at ease in their company. It was such a relief, after years of tension, to finally just relax together. I could see Aoife was enjoying hearing more about the mother she never had the chance to know. I noticed that she and I had some of the same mannerisms – she would scrunch up her nose when she smiled broadly and she had the same habit of wrapping her hair around her index finger and rolling it onto the middle finger and back and forth again too. I invited her over to stay with Ben and myself for a weekend to do some shopping or maybe even to catch a show. It was a big step in our relationship. I hoped we were ready for a whole weekend with each other but she said she might and I really hoped that she would.

They made me promise to bring the baby back to see them when she was born and I knew that I would – it wasn't just an empty promise. I had decided that I was going to be a regular face in the house now and Pip would know where her mother came from.

"Dad?" I said with a lump in my throat as we said goodbye.

"Yes?"

"I love you." And for once I didn't cringe as I said it.

Chapter 53

I was exhausted when I sat down onto our sofa that night. The emotional rollercoaster of the last few days was after catching up with me. Seeing Gran like that, then talking things through with Dad and then Aoife had taken its toll. Twenty years of emotions had been thrashed through in one weekend. Although I was glad to finally have talked to Dad and Aoife properly, it had been difficult dredging it all up again.

Ben plonked down beside me so the sofa gave a little poof under his weight.

"I'm proud of you Kate, you know that?"

"Thanks Ben . . . look, I think I owe you an apology for how I've acted over the last few weeks."

"Don't worry about that now – I'm sorry for not really getting how hard all this still is for you. Your mum sounds like she was a lovely woman."

"She was, Ben – I loved her so much. I know I might not show it, but I miss her every day. Every single day. There is not a day that goes by where I don't wish that I could talk to her just once more. Even just for five minutes."

"Oh Kate, of course you do, love. But why didn't you talk to me about her before?" He hugged me close against his broad frame so I could smell the fabric softener on his T-shirt.

"And especially now that I'm pregnant – that's when you really need your mum to ask her all those questions, y'know, about her own pregnancies or how her labours were. And then when the baby is born I'm sure I'll have millions more to ask her."

"Well, you know my mum thinks the world of you and she would be delighted if you ever needed her help or to ask her something."

"I know that, Ben, and don't get me wrong – your mum is great – but it's not the same as having your own mum there, is it?"

"No, I suppose not."

"Do you think she knows that I was hurting and that I just didn't know how to express how scared I was?" I regretted so much not seeing her before she died and that our last words were words full of anger. It was something I could never make up for. I could never take those words back.

"Of course she does – I bet she's watching you right now with a big smile on her face."

"She was so much fun as a mother. She always spoke her mind. I remember one time in school when my teacher in third class, Mrs Maloney, sent a note home in my journal because I hadn't learnt my nine times tables off by heart. I thought Mam was going to go through me for a shortcut but she came into the classroom behind me the next day and told her off, saying that in all honesty weren't there more important things in life than nine times tables and sure couldn't I always use a calculator if I ever found myself in the unfortunate situation of having to multiply something by nine when I got older! You should have seen the look on Mrs Maloney's face. It was priceless."

Ben started to laugh then. "Your mum sounds like a right old character. I'm glad the pupils I teach don't have parents like that!"

"You would have loved her, Ben – she didn't suffer fools gladly," I said wistfully.

"This is the first time you've let me in, you know," he said.

"What do you mean?"

"Let me right in close, let me get to know the real you."

"But you've known me for seven years!" I said, drying my eyes with a tissue.

"Yeah, but only up to a point. There was always this . . . I don't know . . . wall or something around you that I couldn't get past. You were always so guarded with your emotions."

"Jesus, Ben – a wall – you're not half dramatic, are you? I never knew you had such depth!" I picked up one of the cushions off the sofa and playfully hit him over the head with it.

I rang Dad on my way to work the next morning. He said Gran had done well overnight and they were hoping she would be allowed home later that day. She would be going to stay with Dad, and Aoife was going to move in with them too. I hoped the arrangement worked out for them because it would be really hard to see Gran going into a nursing home. I told him I'd ring him later to see how she was.

As I walked along the street, I felt so much lighter. I can't explain it but I felt a huge weight had been lifted off me. All the years that I had been running away and I was now finally ready to step up and face it. I didn't care when people wouldn't make room for me to get on the Tube – I just let it go and waited for the next one. Or when the escalators were out of order yet again so that I had to climb a mountain of stairs to get out of the Tube station it didn't make me mad like it usually would. Although I hadn't realised it, those years of being angry and carrying all that guilt around had taken their toll on me.

Nat was in first when I reached the gallery. I told her about Gran and about Dad and Aoife.

"I'm so proud of you, Kate – I know it can't have been easy dealing with everything you've gone through over the last few days." She handed me a cup of coffee.

She was slowly coming back down to earth from her exhibition. Cards sat on top of the counter, thanking her for a

wonderful evening. She had been overwhelmed by the feedback
to her work and she was buoyed up and encouraged to go out
and take more photos. I was delighted to see that the old Nat
was slowly returning.

We decided to tackle the dusting – we tried to do it once a
week – one of us would do downstairs and the other would do
the mezzanine although sometimes it must be admitted that
neither of us could be bothered. But today I didn't mind doing
it. As I ran the cloth over the tops of the frames, up along the
banister, across the desk and the computer screen, I was able to
switch off and get my head around everything that had
happened over the last few days.

I suggested to Nat that we should go to Portobello Market the
following Saturday. I thought it was something that she might
enjoy – she used to love going there for a browse. It had been
ages since we'd been – we used to be regulars, scouting around
the stalls and then grabbing something to eat afterwards. She
agreed, so the following Saturday afternoon we took the Tube
down to Notting Hill Gate. The street was already thronged
when we got there – it had got really popular over the last few
years with tourists. Since it had featured in the film *Notting Hill*
they would come in their droves, photographing themselves in
front of the pastel-coloured buildings or standing beneath the
Portobello Road street signs as the fed-up locals walked around
them impatiently. We browsed through some of the antique
stalls, which I loved. Old trunks and suitcases stacked on top of
each other stood beside a stand of leather rugby balls and cricket
bats. There were tables full of cloth-covered books with their old
inked inscriptions from loved ones. Other stalls displayed
antique china sets and silverware.

I always said that if Ben and I ever managed to afford to buy
a house, I would come here and fill my house full of stuff from
this market.

"Remind me never to come here again on a Saturday," I said

as a wall of people pushed me to the left as we walked along.

We stood and listened to a girl sing in French and play an accordion before strolling along until we came to the food stalls. The smell of fresh cheeses and baked goods filled the air. Nat was sampling the foods on offer from the different stalls and taking photos. At least she had started taking photos again, which was a good sign. Another man was shouting, "*Peaches three for a parnd, three for a parnd!*" from behind his table of fresh fruit. We sampled some delicious baklava from another stall.

"Hello, darling. It's a sunny one today, innit?"

The sticky sweetness was delicious so I bought a few to take home with me.

We continued on to the clothing stalls. Fashion students displayed their designs, trying desperately to stand out from the rest of the stalls and to make a name for themselves.

Soon we were at the cheaper end of the market. These were the tacky stalls selling plastic toys from China and offering 2 for 1 deals on washing powders.

"Kate, isn't that your bag?" Nat said suddenly.

She was pointing at a stall claiming to sell 'vintage' handbags. There were lots of stalls here claiming to sell vintage clothing, some of it was genuine, some not so.

I swung around from the rail that I had been thumbing through on a nearby stall. My eye was immediately drawn to the bright yellow of my satchel, which was sitting on the table amongst all the other bags. I would know it anywhere. I ran over towards it.

"That bag – where did you get it?" I asked the Asian guy manning the table.

He shrugged his shoulders at me. I wasn't sure if he understood me.

"I think it's mine." I went to lift it up but his hand moved across my arm to block me.

"No try – you must buy."

"How much?" I said quickly.

"Twenty pounds."

I rooted in my purse but I only had a ten-pound note.

"Here, I have money," Nat said taking another ten-pound note from her pocket and putting it with mine to give to the stallholder. "I can't believe you've got to pay to get your own bloody bag back!"

He handed me the bag then. I took it from him and examined it – it was slightly scuffed on one of the corners, exactly like my one had been. It was definitely mine. We stood to the side of the stall, out of the way of people.

My heart started beating wildly. Nervously, I opened up the bag. There was a small zipped pocket inside the bag, disguised against the turquoise lining. That was where I had last put the letter. I begged Mam, if she was listening, to let the letter be still inside it. With trepidation, I pulled back the zip and saw the white envelope was still there. I carefully took the letter out of it and unfolded it. I held her letter in my two hands, studying her familiar words once more. I felt tears come into my eyes. *Oh thank you, thank you, thank you!*

Nat and I both started jumping up and down. People in the market started to look at us but I didn't care, I was so elated. It felt as though I was somehow closer to her by touching the paper that she had once touched too. It was like a little part of her was still living.

"She's looking down on you, Kate," Nat said.

And she was right – I could definitely feel her presence around me right then. It was like what Dad said – there was a sense of her whispering in the breeze around me.

Chapter 54

A few weeks later, Gran and Aoife were settling well into Dad's house. They had a routine worked out and Seán, Patrick and Luisa took turns to help out. The health board had approved a home help for a few hours each day too. Gran's speech, although still affected, was starting to improve but the power in her right arm never recovered. Aoife had installed Skype on Dad's computer and I called them on it after work every evening. They were all delighted when I told them that I had found the letter and we laughed together that I had to buy back my own handbag.

The bell tinkled and I looked up to see the man who had been acting strangely at Nat's exhibition come in through the door again. He shook the rain off his umbrella before folding it down. He nodded in acknowledgement to us before heading upstairs. He was starting to make me nervous.

"Oh my God, what is he doing here again?" Nat said.

"I'm starting to think that he has a screw loose. What do you think he wants?" I whispered as I observed him over the balcony.

"I don't know but he's really freaking me out!" she hissed.

He came back down the stairs a while later and walked over towards me. Nat was in the storeroom out the back, looking for a frame. I felt myself tense up.

"Does she have any more?" He opened his satchel and took

out the photo of the woman on the bench that he had bought a few weeks ago.

"Yes, there's some more of her work upstairs," I said, confused. He was after spending the best part of thirty minutes staring at it all.

"No, I mean more photos of *this* woman."

"Okay, well, I'll just go and check with the photographer." This was such a strange request. He was really creeping me out. I left him standing there and went out the back to Nat. She was bent over, pulling out frames and examining them.

"Nat, strange one for you – that man wants to know if you have any more photos of this woman?"

"The woman? What, is he stalking her or something? I'll have to check through the shots from that day."

She followed me back out to the front.

"If you just want to hang on for a minute, I'll check through the other photos from that day," she said to him.

"Thank you," he said.

He stood at the desk while Nat clicked through files on the computer. She brought him around behind her, to show him what she had. "I just have a few more of the same shot, I'm afraid." In one the woman's eyes were closed, caught mid-blink. "Sorry, that's all I have."

"Can you check what date they were taken on?"

"Okay . . . em . . . hang on a sec and I'll see . . ." She clicked on the photos. "March third last. Look, do you know her or something?"

"She's my sister."

"Oh, I see. Well, I hope she likes the photo." I could hear the nervousness in Nat's voice.

"She died last month."

We both stopped what we were doing and looked up at him.

Nat's hands flew towards her mouth. "Oh God, I'm so sorry – I'm so, so sorry. I had no idea."

"You weren't to know." I could hear the emotion in his voice, which threatened to break at any moment.

"Well, you are most welcome to have any of these other shots, if you'd like, although they're all pretty much the same, I'm afraid."

"Thanks. It's the way you've shot her – she looks so beautiful, so pensive. She was a painter and she would often go to the park and sit there lost in her own world. Hours could pass her by and she wouldn't feel it. Look at it . . ." He held the photo back for us to see. "She doesn't even notice the birds around her feet." He started to laugh then. "Even as a child her head was always stuck up in the clouds. You've captured everything that I loved about her in that photo."

"How did she die?" Nat asked softly.

"A car accident on the M25. There was a pile-up in bad fog." He lowered his voice. "She didn't stand a chance."

"I am truly sorry," said Nat.

"She was only twenty-nine. The family, well . . . we've all taken it pretty badly actually."

"I can only imagine."

"That's why, when I came in here and saw this picture, I just felt it was a sign, y'know, that she's okay wherever she is out there . . ."

I of all people could relate to everything he was saying and I felt awful for misjudging him as some psychopathic weirdo when really he was just lost under a mountain of grief, trying to make sense of a needless tragedy like I had done for so long.

"Sorry, I never asked your names?"

"I'm Nat and this is Kate."

"Well, it's lovely to meet you," he said, shaking our hands. "I'm Richard."

"Nice to meet you," I said, shaking his hand. "And I'm so sorry about your sister."

"Thanks, Kate." He turned to Nat. "Your work is really good, Nat, by the way – you're very talented. I'm so grateful you took this picture – you will never know how much this means to me and my family."

"I'm just glad it might give you all some small comfort."

The next day a bouquet of sunflowers arrived for Nat with a note to say thank you. His name and number were scribbled on the bottom of the card. Nat called him to thank him and they chatted away easily on the phone. It turned out he had his own graphic-design business just up the street. They decided to meet for a coffee and I listened as they made arrangements.

"What?" Nat said at my smile when she had hung up the phone.

"I said nothing!" I put my hands up in mock defence.

"Yeah, well, it's just a coffee."

As I looked around the gallery walls that afternoon I couldn't believe that it was almost time for me to finish up work. I was starting my maternity leave the following week and although I was counting down the days, it would still be weird not coming to work every day. But I wouldn't miss standing on the Tube during rush-hour while people pretended not to notice that I was heavily pregnant so that they wouldn't have to offer me their seat. And I wouldn't miss traipsing up and down the gallery stairs any more either. I was going to miss Nat of course but I knew that we would see each other all the time anyway. We had found a temp to replace me, a young photography graduate who was looking to get some experience, so it had worked out well.

I had another hospital appointment at four o'clock so I kissed Nat goodbye before I left and walked on to meet Ben.

"I don't think I have ever seen you look more beautiful," Ben said as I came up towards him.

I reached up and gave him a kiss on the lips.

"Well, I must have looked really awful before I was pregnant then!"

"No, you really are radiant."

"Oh here we go, the usual tell the pregnant woman she's 'glowing' because you can't think of anything else to say to her!"

"I never said 'glowing' – that'd be pushing it now."

I punched him playfully on the arm and we strolled along with my arm looped through his.

We reached the hospital and climbed the steps to the antenatal unit. We sat in the waiting room waiting to be called in for our appointment. Finally I heard my name and we went into the darkened room, which was unnaturally warm from all the humming equipment. The sonographer performed a quick scan but the baby was too big to see all in one and now we could only get a view of different body parts: a leg, the top of the head or a foot.

"Okay, now look away if you don't want to know the sex."

I looked towards the door but Ben was still looking at the screen.

"Ben!" I said.

He dutifully turned away. "It's killing me, Kate! Don't worry, I couldn't see anything anyway."

"All looks good, guys – your baby certainly seems very happy in there. You're having a textbook pregnancy."

It was like getting a gold star for getting all my spellings right in the weekly spelling test but it always put a smile on my face to hear that Pip was happy. I know it sounds ridiculous but I often wondered if she was lonely in there – Ben laughed at me when I told him this. "Not everyone is like you, Kate," he would say. "Some people don't mind being on their own. Pip is happy growing away and doing his or her own thing until he or she is ready to come out into the big bad world."

"It's definitely a girl," I said when we were outside of the room.

"Oooh, you're very confident, Kate!"

"I'm telling you Ben – I just know she is."

"Well, I take your girl and raise you a boy."

"Well, we'll see soon enough," I said confidently.

"Well?" I said when Nat came back in the door a few days later after meeting Richard.

"It went well – we talked and talked. I could have stayed there for hours."

"Why didn't you?"

"Well, I couldn't leave you fronting the gallery all day on your own."

"Of course you could have. Did he talk about his sister?"

"A little bit but it's still quite raw – we have a lot of things in common actually."

"Like what?"

"Well, *The Catcher in the Rye* is his favourite book too, we both love live gigs – and photography of course."

I couldn't help but think how suited they would be together.

"Are you going to see him again?"

She smiled. "Stop it, Kate! I'm not looking for anything right now and neither is he – he has just lost his sister."

"Yeah, I suppose." But there was a smile on her face all the same. Slowly my friend was returning.

Chapter 55

I strolled down the street on the crisp autumn morning. The sun was low in the sky and I had to put my sunglasses on to stop the glare. I was wearing my woollen winter coat and a scarlet beret but I could no longer close the coat across my huge bump. It was only September but it was a chilly morning that served to remind us that winter was on its way. I was on my way to yet another hospital check-up. I was now five days overdue and the hospital had me in every few days to keep an eye on Pip. This time Ben wasn't able to come with me because there was an important staff meeting in the school that morning.

I had arranged to meet Nat in the deli close to Jensen's first. She was going to nip out of work for half an hour to meet me. I went in and ordered a coffee.

"Oh, you're not still here, are you, love?" The woman who had been telling me from twenty-weeks that I was 'nearly there now' looked at me pityingly.

I gritted my teeth. I took my coffee and sat down at a table to wait for Nat to arrive. She came in soon after and I was glad to see that she had put a little weight back on. After Will had left her, she had almost stopped eating and I had been worried about her but she looked a bit healthier today. She was wearing a huge green patterned scarf over a grey woollen dress with tan leather riding boots. She ordered a coffee and sat down opposite me and we chatted away.

"So how's my replacement?"

"She's nice but she's no Kate Flynn."

I'm ashamed to say that this made me feel good. "She has big shoes to fill."

"She does."

"So have you seen Richard since?" I tried to sound nonchalant.

"Well, we went to the Tate Modern last Saturday."

"Fancy!"

"Yeah, I got some great snaps there."

"I suppose it helps that he's easy on the eye."

"He is, isn't he?" she said, smiling at me.

I was relieved that she seemed to be in good form and her SLR was back around her neck wherever she went. We chatted some more before hugging goodbye and then I headed on to the hospital.

"Your baby is very happy in there," they said to me yet again after they had done a scan to check fluid levels.

I sighed. They had said the same thing to me last week and I had hoped it would have budged by now.

"Why don't you go for a big long walk – sometimes that helps to kick-start things?"

I knew the midwife meant well but I had tried everything. I had never walked more in my life. I was exhausted – I felt I had done my part of the deal. I had carried this baby to term but it was like the goalposts had been moved out on me. As the days went on and the more overdue I became, it felt like an eternity. I was too big to go anywhere and I couldn't go too far anyway in case labour started. I did not want to be out in public when my water went and make a scene. Ben had his phone glued to him just in case and he would ring me every hour on the hour to ask if there was "any news yet". "No," I would reply testily. All the well-meaning calls and texts from friends, my family and Ben's family were beginning to get on my nerves. Even Gran was on my case when I talked to her on Skype in the evenings. I knew they were just excited but I wanted this baby out as much as any of them and if one more person suggested some other 'guaranteed' way to kick-start labour, I might just punch them.

Deflated, I came out the door of the hospital and just walked. I kept on going, feeling dozens of pitying eyes watching every step that I took. That made it all the worse. I was starting to feel very sorry for myself. I passed by the steps of St Paul's and came up to a little park gate nestled amongst all the offices. I was tired so I decided to go in and sit down in there for a while. Although tall buildings loomed overhead, once inside the gate it was like a tranquil oasis. The noise of the city instantly quietened, replaced instead with birdsong ringing clear on the air. That is another one of the things that I love about London: whenever you need a break from the madness – you are never too far from a park. You can escape the hustle and bustle in seconds, making you forget you were in the thick of one of the world's busiest cities. I walked around by the small fountain with its giant goldfish. A grey squirrel ran out in front of my path and scooted up into a nearby tree.

I noticed some people standing under a wooden awning so I walked over to have a look. The wall underneath the canopy was covered in small ceramic plaques, all with blue-and-green fonts on cream backgrounds. One by one, I started to read them.

HENRY JAMES BRISTOW AGED EIGHT – AT WALTHAMSTOW ON DECEMBER 30 1890 – SAVED HIS LITTLE SISTER'S LIFE BY TEARING OFF HER FLAMING CLOTHES BUT CAUGHT FIRE HIMSELF AND DIED OF BURNS AND SHOCK.

FREDERICK ALFRED CROFT, INSPECTOR, AGED 31, WHO IN 1878 ATTEMPTED TO SAVE A LUNATIC WOMAN FROM SUICIDE AT WOOLWICH ARSENAL STATION BUT WAS HIMSELF RUN OVER BY THE TRAIN.

Another was more recently erected:

LEIGH PITT, REPROGRAPHIC OPERATOR, AGED 30, SAVED A DROWNING BOY FROM THE CANAL AT THAMESMEAD, BUT SADLY WAS UNABLE TO SAVE HIMSELF, JUNE 7 2007.

Entranced, I kept reading one after the other: people who had drowned saving others from canals or the Thames, people who had sacrificed their own lives to save people from burning buildings and train wreck.

I read the information post. It was a memorial to heroic self-sacrifice and all the plaques were erected in memory of someone who had died while heroically trying to save the lives of others.

Plaque after plaque told another heartbreaking story, each with an ending just as sad. Tears came into my eyes. All were courageous people who had put another person's life before their own, just like Mam had.

I took a seat on a nearby bench and put my hands across my bump and felt Pip stretching out a leg or an arm, I wasn't sure which. I tried to imagine how I would feel if I was told that I had cancer while I was pregnant with Pip – how would I feel having to make the same decisions as her, knowing that my baby's fate was in my hands? And at a time when surgical methods wouldn't have been as advanced and specific as they are today? Maybe I had been too harsh on her, too quick to judge her without really trying to see it from her point of view? Maybe it wasn't as black and white as I was used to thinking and she wasn't being selfish, just trying to do what she thought was her best in unfortunate circumstances.

I wondered if she had led me here.

I told Ben about it all when he came in from school.

"Yeah, I remember learning about that place in school . . . what's it called . . . Postman's Park, isn't it?"

"Why is it called that?"

"The General Post Office used to be nearby and the postmen would sit out there on their lunch-breaks. God, I'm wrecked." He sat wearily down on the sofa.

"*Eh*, in case you've forgotten, you're not carrying another human around in your stomach."

"That baby is going to need an eviction order – do you hear that, Pip?" He bent down and spoke to my bump. "We're serving notice that you have to vacate your home – there are people out here waiting to meet you."

"She's not listening."

"Or he."

"It's a she."

"Well, he or she takes after their mother – already showing signs of stubbornness."

"Oi, less of that, cheeky!" Then I sighed. "When is she going to come out, Ben?"

"When she is good and ready."

"But I feel like I've been waiting for forever to meet her."

"Look, she'll be here in a matter of days and then you won't remember any of this."

"I'm not so sure. Oh God, Ben, what if I'm a rubbish mum?" And tears that I don't know where they came from started up. My hormones had gone into overdrive over the last few days.

"You're going to be great, I just know you are."

"But I don't know any nursery rhymes or fairytales."

"What's that got to do with anything?"

"I don't know – but I don't even remember the words to 'Twinkle, Twinkle, Little Star' or how *The Three Little Pigs* ends!" I wailed. "I'm going to be useless. I need Mam. I miss her."

"Kate, you're just starting to get nervous, it's only natural. It's a big step becoming a parent."

"I just don't know if I'm going to be any good at the motherhood lark."

"You're going to be just fine, Kate. I know you will. The fact that you're even worrying about it shows that you will be." Ben put his arms around me. "And you've got me too – we'll get through it all together and, besides, I know the ending to *The Three Little Pigs*."

"You do?"

"Yeah, the pigs get the wolf in the end."

"They do? Well, good for them. I like a happy ending."

Baby Pip entered the world exactly eight days late and I instantly forgave her for her late arrival. When the midwives in the hospital told me it was a girl, I said, "I know." Ben and I were overawed by how perfect she was. He was a natural with her and helped the midwives give her her first bath and I knew they had already formed a bond. It was surreal to see him cradling her on his chest while I sat back on the bed taking the scene in.

"Happy birthday, baby girl," he whispered to her. "You have a perfect blank canvas on which to paint." And I thought that I might just burst with love looking at the two of them.

Chapter 56

I rang home to tell Dad that she had arrived. When I told him that we would like to call her Eva, he had cried down the phone. He put Gran on the phone and her speech, although still not as clear as it once was, had improved a lot. He passed me to Aoife then and we had an emotional phone call too. It was nice to have my family back in my life again, especially to share something like this.

Ben's mum had driven up to see us the day after I came home from hospital. She was so excited and I watched her as she held her first grandchild with tears in her eyes. Geoff didn't come. No one mentioned it though. It wasn't a big surprise but I knew that Ben was disappointed, as was Edwina. I think they both thought that the arrival of Eva, as the start of the next generation of the Chamberlain family, would have been the catalyst to thaw the frost between them.

Although we were managing surprisingly well, Edwina was going to stay for a few days to give us a hand. I was glad to have her there in case I had questions to ask – questions that you might normally ask your own mother.

Ben's sister Laura took the train down from Manchester a few days later.

"Congratulations, you guys!" She hugged us and then Edwina. "So where is my new niece?" she asked giddily.

I brought her over to the Moses basket where Eva was sound

asleep. That was one thing – she slept a lot. I knew it was a good complaint to have but sometimes I would hover beside her crib just to make sure that she was still breathing. She was lying back with her hands clenched in little fists at either side of her head.

"Oh my God – she is just so beautiful!" There were tears in her eyes. "You guys are so lucky."

"Thanks, Laura."

"So when does she wake up so I can get a hold?"

"I'll be due to feed her soon."

"Are you breastfeeding, Kate?"

"Yep, it's like Cravendale Dairies here."

We sat down on the sofa and Ben made the coffee for everyone. Eva started to stir then and Laura rushed over to her.

"Can I pick her up?" she asked me excitedly.

"Of course you can."

"Come here, little one." She delicately lifted Eva out from her basket and sat back onto the sofa with her in her arms. "Oh, she is just divine! I'm Auntie Laura. Yes, I am. And I'm going to spoil you rotten and let you do all the things that your mummy and daddy won't let you do, isn't that right, little lady?"

"Don't worry, we'll get our own back when you have kids of your own," I said.

"I want one of these!" She was stroking Eva's silky hair.

"Well, you'll have to get Tim Templeton on the case then."

Laura looked thoughtful at this. "By the way, why isn't Dad here?"

No one answered her.

"Would anyone like another coffee?" Ben asked.

"Go on, I'll have another cup," Laura said. "That muck they serve on the train really shouldn't be allowed to be called coffee under the fair trade descriptions act. I must complain – I think I'd have a pretty strong case."

Ben got up, walked over to the kitchen and flicked the switch on the kettle. He took down four clean mugs and opened the fridge to take out the milk again.

"Damn! We're almost out of milk!" he called from the

kitchen. "I'll just run down to the shop."

We were lucky there was a corner shop just up the street from us. It sold one of everything, whatever you needed – you were guaranteed to find it in the shop and if they didn't have it on the shelf, they definitely would have it in the stock room out the back.

"So Dad is still being pig-headed I take it then?" Laura asked me as soon as Ben was gone out the door. "I thought Ben was going to have a fit when I asked where he was. When is he going to stop giving him a hard time about being a teacher?"

"I ask myself the same question every day," Edwina sighed resignedly.

"I think Ben's a little disappointed that under the circumstances he couldn't just let it go and come and meet his granddaughter," I said.

"Well, Geoff Chamberlain is a very thick man," Edwina said. "He will not just swallow his pride and apologise to Ben."

"I can't believe what a cantankerous old fool he is being! Well, it's his loss – if he wants to miss out on this gorgeous little pudding then so be it." Laura was cradling Eva up against her shoulder.

Motherhood was insane – I actually missed her already. I was jealous of Laura holding her in her arms and I wanted her back in mine again.

"But I know it kills him that he still hasn't seen his first grandchild," Edwina said.

"Do you think?" I asked.

"He's not completely made of stone, you know. I know he wants to meet Eva – I can see that he is thrilled to be a grandfather – he just doesn't show it in the conventional way."

"He is such a dinosaur," Laura said angrily. "Well, his stubbornness is going to be the ruination of him – he's going to miss out on all of this if he doesn't learn to move on and let bygones be bygones."

"I've tried talking to him but he just won't listen to me. I'm wasting my breath at this stage."

Ben returned a few minutes later with a litre of milk and we all quickly changed the subject again.

Chapter 57

After Edwina and Laura had gone home we were left on our own as a family. We were settling well into parenthood but no one could have prepared us for how we would feel about her. She literally was the best thing to ever happen to either of us. Everyone tells you before you have a baby how amazing and special it is but I don't think you can really understand it until your bundle arrives and then . . . well, it is the best bloody feeling in the world. I could spend hours just staring at her and snuggling her neck, the feeling of the silkiness of her skin under my fingertips. I could plant a thousand kisses on her head every day for the rest of her life and it still wouldn't be enough – I would always want to give her another one.

I would often ask Ben what was it we did before Eva arrived. We must have spent so much time just doing nothing and not appreciating the free time when we had it because now there was always something to be done. I would get up to put on a load of washing and then get distracted by ten other jobs that needed to be done along the way. As soon as we brought her home from hospital it became obvious that our flat was way too small. It was already cramped before when it was just the two of us and now there wasn't the space for all of us, let alone the amount of stuff that came with Eva. Plus the washing was a nightmare. I had a clotheshorse stuffed into our bedroom and every radiator in the place was taken over with tiny babygros and vests. We needed somewhere with a small garden where we could hang out laundry and where Eva could play when she got a bit bigger. We had started house hunting but, although the property market had supposedly taken a nosedive, prices were still far beyond our reach. At this rate, we would have to move out to the countryside but, as we both worked in central London, we didn't fancy long commutes. Especially with Eva – we didn't want to have to leave her for long days in childcare. Plus, as Ben had pointed out, what we might save on the cost of the house, we would be spending on train fares in the long run. So we kept on living as frugally as we could and saving every penny we could manage to put away.

Nat was great with Eva. She would take her off out for a walk and let me go back to bed for an hour or she would call over and cook dinner for Ben and me. She had given me a framed picture she had taken of me staring down at Eva as she slept in my arms. I hadn't even seen her taking it but she had somehow managed to capture exactly my feelings for this wondrous little person. I knew it would always be one of my most treasured possessions. She was doing well and was slowly coming round to the Nat that I knew. Things were going well between her and Richard – they were taking it very slowly and getting to know each other properly. The romantic in me loved the fact that her photo had brought them together and that his sister, although no longer still with us, had led them to one another. They came into each other's lives when they were both at a low ebb and needed someone. For me it was another sign that our loved ones who had gone before us were definitely somewhere out there watching over us.

We were just clearing up after dinner one evening when Ben's phone rang. He answered it and I knew by his tone that he was uncomfortable talking to whoever it was. He was giving yes and no answers before he got up from the sofa and went out of the room and finished the rest of the conversation out in the hall.

"Who was that?" I said when he came back in.

"Dad."

"What did he want?" I lowered the volume on the TV with the remote.

"He says that he's in the area and he wants to stop by and see Eva."

"Well, I hope you told him where to go?"

"Eh no, not quite . . ."

"What do you mean?"

"He's on his way over here now."

"Dear God, no." I wasn't in the mood for a confrontation or his snide and cutting remarks.

I'm sure he'd have plenty to say about our flat and the area that we lived in. He had never come to visit us before. I hopped up and started tidying up, picking my breast pump off the side of the sofa and stuffing it into a press in the kitchen, gathering up muslins belonging to Eva, folding newspapers and fluffing cushions. I hated the way Ben's father had this effect on me.

The buzzer went a few minutes later. Ben went out to let him in.

A few moments later he followed Ben into the living room. He was dressed in a long navy woollen overcoat and had a yellow-and-grey striped scarf wound around his neck several times. He was wearing a suit underneath so he was obviously in London on business. He was carrying a bunch of lilies.

"Kate," he said, giving me a kiss on the cheek.

"Geoff."

He handed me the flowers. I took them from him. I noticed that the petals were starting to brown at the tips. He'd obviously picked them up hurriedly.

"Thanks."

"My car – it will be all right out there, won't it?"

"Well, we've never had any trouble in the four years we've been living here," I said tersely.

"Yes . . . I suppose it will be okay."

But I knew he was still nervous about it.

"Would you like to see Eva?"

"Please." He was being very polite now that he was on our patch.

Ben led him over to the Moses basket. He peered in over the top and put a hand in to touch her little hand.

"I'd forgotten how small they are. It's been a long time since I've seen a newborn."

"Well, we think she's got really big in the last *two weeks*," I said, emphasising the 'two weeks'.

"She is very beautiful – just like her mother."

"Thanks," I mumbled, embarrassed by the unexpected compliment.

"I'm sure everyone is telling you to enjoy her – it goes by all too quickly," he said wistfully.

I looked at Ben – he seemed to be as shocked as I was by the uncharacteristic emotion in his father's voice.

Ben excused himself to make the coffee.

"So were you working down this way today then?" I asked, making conversation.

"Yes, I was in the Supreme Court all day – the Blanchford extradition case – you've probably seen it on the news?"

I hadn't. I barely had time to go to the loo these days let alone keep abreast of London's legal scene. We lapsed into awkward silence then until Ben came back. I was relieved. I had nothing to say to the man and I was still so angry after the last time.

"How's school, Ben?"

"Great."

"That's good."

I was waiting for the belittling remark but it didn't come.

"And I presume you'll be off for a few months, Kate?"

"Yes, I don't know how I'll ever be able to leave her though to go back." I looked towards the wicker basket.

If he thought of making a comment about being able to afford to stay at home if Ben had pursued a career in law, he didn't. He kept his mouth shut even though it probably killed him. I could imagine the words all piling up and crashing against his clenched teeth as they came up his throat.

We chitchatted awkwardly for a while longer before Geoff said that he had better start making tracks back to Surrey before Edwina sent a search party out for him. I stood up straight away as soon as he went to leave. I was eager to have him gone and have the atmosphere returned back to normal again. I wasn't into Feng Shui or any of that kind of hocus-pocus stuff but I was pretty sure that if there was such a thing, then Geoff's visit had knocked it completely off balance. We kissed goodbye and Ben saw him out into the hall.

Eva was just starting to stir, her tiny mouth making little sucking motions, so I took her up to feed her. I could hear Ben and Geoff talking in the hallway.

"Look, before I go . . ." Geoff cleared his throat nosily in a way that made me want to get sick, "I think I owe you an apology – my behaviour on your last trip home was out of order. Your mother is still very angry with me . . . and rightly so."

"It's okay," I could hear Ben mumbling.

"I can see you're clearly very happy and why wouldn't you be? Don't you have a beautiful girlfriend and a darling baby daughter? To be honest, Ben, I've probably always been a bit jealous of your courage to go and follow your dreams."

"But why would you be jealous of me?"

"Well, believe it or not, I always wanted to play rugby – I was good at it too. Who knows, maybe if I had committed to it, I could have gone all the way . . . but it didn't go down too well arriving into a courtroom with a black eye or bandaged hand so my father said that I had to give it up altogether. I was upset at the time but he had my best interests at heart, I suppose . . ."

"I never knew that."

"That's life, son."

"Well, thank you, Dad . . . it really means a lot to hear you say that."

"Well, I'm sorry it has taken me this long to say it. Don't make the same mistakes I did, Ben – if anything good is to come out of this, learn from my mistakes. Be there to enjoy your children when they are small – it goes by in the blink of an eye. I was always working when you and Laura were little and I wish I had kicked back a little more – the world wouldn't have ended if I had taken a half-day to watch you in the school play or gone to your school sports day. Let little Eva do whatever makes her happy." Then he laughed. "And, of course, if she wants to follow in the family tradition of law then I will welcome her with open arms!"

Ben chuckled. "Well, we'll just have to wait and see . . ."

There was a small pause. "Look, I don't want to speak out of turn and please tell me if I am, but well . . . I can't help but notice how tight for space you are here."

"We manage," Ben said tersely.

I felt myself tense up again. I really hoped Geoff wasn't just about to undo his apology with another below-the-belt dig at Ben.

"Of course you do. You mother said that you and Kate are saving to buy your own place. I promise I'm not trying to stick my nose into your affairs but as you know I have a rather large property portfolio around the city and most of it is mortgage-free at this stage. I can talk to my agent and see if any of the leases are due to expire soon. You wouldn't have to pay any rent and it would help you save faster to buy your own place. If you like . . . I mean there's no pressure . . . I know I can never undo the past but it would be my way of attempting to make a proper go of it this time for little Eva's sake."

I was stunned.

"Well, thanks, Dad, I'll talk to Kate."

They said goodbye then and I heard Ben shut the front door.

"Wow!" I said when he came back in. "Did I just hear what I think I heard?"

"The man apologised, he actually apologised. I'm glad you heard it too or no one would ever believe me. Did you hear him offer us one of his houses too?"

I nodded.

"What do you think?"

"Well, if he's offering then why not? It makes sense. I mean, we're cramped here and it would mean we're not wasting any more money on rent."

"Okay, well, I'll talk to him and see what he has."

"Do you reckon Laura had a word with him?"

"Maybe. But I think becoming a grandfather has made him see what really matters."

"Well, I'm glad, Ben, I'm really glad for both you and for Eva."

Ben lifted Eva out of my arms. "Do you hear that, little one? You're only two weeks old and you have already managed to thaw your old grandfather's heart! You see, you already have the men in your life wrapped around your little finger!"

Two Months Later

"Have you packed the nappies?"

"Uh-huh."

"And the baby wipes?"

"Yes."

"I need them back here a minute," I said. "She's done a right messy one."

I stood looking around Eva's nursery, which we had just finished decorating. We had moved into a three-bedroom house with a little garden in Hampstead, belonging to Geoff, just two weeks before. We didn't know ourselves with the extra space and we were still so central to everything. We had set about decorating Eva's nursery first. Ben had ripped up the old carpet and sanded down the floorboards. We painted the walls a lovely biscuit colour and Ben had stencilled a clown print all along the top border of the room. A polished mahogany cot stood in the centre of the room with a mobile of colourful circus animals hanging above it. I was really happy with how it had turned out.

I changed Eva again and bundled her into her snowsuit before handing her to Ben. He strapped her into her car seat while I ran around checking and double-checking that we hadn't forgotten anything. *Nappies, wipes, clothes, cream, cloths . . .*

"Come on, we don't want to be late," Ben pressed.

"Right, okay," I sighed. It still amazed me how long it took to leave the house with Eva in tow. "I think that's everything. Oh crap, did you put the buggy in – it's in the utility room?"

"Don't worry, it's in the boot."

"Right," I said, "we'd better go." I grabbed my down jacket off the coat-stand and put my arms into it. I wrapped my lambswool scarf double around my neck.

We went outside and Ben clicked Eva's car seat into the back and I got into the front seat. It was a cold November morning and I could see my breath on the air in front of me. Ben had had to de-ice the windscreen and the puddles were covered with a lid of ice begging to be jumped on. He started the car and we set off.

We hit the rush-hour gridlock and, as we sat there, my eyes kept checking the clock in case we were going to be late. Finally, the traffic moved on and we reached the airport. We parked the car and hurried in to the Arrivals hall to wait for them.

"Can you see them?" I asked Ben as I scanned the crowd of people. He was taller than me so had the advantage when it came to things like this.

"No sign of them yet anyway – they're probably stuck in baggage reclaim – you know how slow it can be."

"Yeah, you're probably right," I said nervously.

"Kate – just relax. It's all going to be fine." He put his arm around my shoulder. He had Eva in her sling and her little head was cuddled in against his chest as she dozed. It was at times like this when I looked at the two of them together, the two people that I loved most in the whole world, that I felt my heart surge with happiness. I leant over and kissed her downy hair. I would lay my life on the line for her.

Finally I spotted them coming through the crowd, wheeling their cases behind them.

"Dad, Aoife, over here!"

They were coming to meet Baby Eva for the first time. Gran was going to stay with Patrick and Luisa for the weekend. They picked us out amongst the sea of faces and waved. I ran over towards them, ready to start this new chapter with my family.

Look at you there, doing great – you're a natural at it, Kate. You've taken to motherhood like a duck to water. I knew you would though. Yourself and Ben are doing a great job. Sure you don't need me at all – I would only be in your way. You got a good one there, Kate, let me tell you – she's a dream baby. And, my goodness, she's a little beauty, isn't she? She looks just like you at that age. Oh, and I love the name! Enjoy those newborn cuddles, there is nothing quite like them. They don't be long growing up and, before you know it, you'll have a head-banging two-year-old on your hands. I'm glad you've made up with your dad and you're working on getting to know Aoife too – you don't know how happy this makes me. You of all people know that sometimes life can be unfair, Kate, but you've picked yourself up and I'm so proud of the way you've turned out and the woman that you've grown into today.

THE END

Acknowledgements

Firstly, a big thank-you to the team in Poolbeg who really do an amazing job in such difficult times. You are all so good at what you do. I am honoured to call you my publishers. Paula Campbell, you are a one-woman wonder. And the brilliant Sarah and Ailbhe – it is a pleasure to work with you. Thanks also to Gaye Shortland whose skill was really tested on this book – thank you for helping me to see the wood from the trees, and your enthusiasm and encouragement are always so helpful.

Writing this book definitely has not been a solo effort. There are some people who deserve huge thanks for making it happen:

My husband Simon for his support and for keeping the ship afloat so that I can do this. For all that you do for us every day, I am very grateful. My love, always.

My beautiful daughter Lila who amazes me every day, making me so proud to be her mother, and of course for all the 'zzzzzxcggggggggggxxxjjjjjjjjjjj' that she added to this manuscript along the way.

My twins Tom and Bea who were so small when I started writing this story. Thank you both for being such good babies and for taking turns to keep my knees warm while I write.

Mam and Dad for all that you did for me growing up and still do for me now, especially since I've had my own children. Thank you for your unwavering belief in me, Mam. I know I told you I'd dedicate a book to you one day but I never really believed that it would happen. You were the one who kept me going when the self-doubt was creeping in, so this is for you.

My family, Niall and Nita and Dee-Dee who gave me a place to stay for 'research' purposes. And to Tom Finnerty for answering my questions about primary school – love you all.

My other family – Mary and Neil, Abbie, Enda, Lucy, Eoin, Sophie and Andrew – thank you for your support, especially Mary and Neil who really go above and beyond the usual grandparenting duties.

Dr Gráinne Flannelly and Joan Cuthbertson of the National Maternity Hospital, Holles Street, who helped me with my research for this story even though they are under huge time pressure. I do appreciate how busy you are, so thank you for taking the time to answer my questions. Any errors or inaccuracies in the story are wholly mine.

The very talented Laoise Casey for enthusiastically sharing her love of London and for first telling me about Postman's Park. She also makes me salivate on a daily basis with her blog www.cuisinegenie.ie. She has a sticky-toffee-pudding recipe to die for – you should have a look but don't blame me when you eat the whole thing in one sitting.

Rebecca, for always being there.

Margaret Scott for understanding what it's like and keeping me sane with coffee and cake.

And lastly, there is not a day that goes by where I don't thank my lucky stars for the privilege of being able to do this. I really appreciate how fortunate I am to be able to thank people in print. So a big thank-you to the booksellers, librarians, bookbloggers and most especially the readers who pick up this book. Thank you all so much. With much love, Caroline xx

Now that you're hooked why not try
In a Moment
also available?
Here's a sneak preview of the prologue
and chapters one and two.

In a Moment

CAROLINE FINNERTY

Prologue

She felt her knees buckle beneath her and she reached out to grab onto the post of the staircase. She used it to guide herself downwards so that she was sitting on the bottom step. Just as she thought she might be starting to heal, taking tentative steps forward, this had come and knocked her off balance again. She wasn't expecting it – it was like a below-the-belt punch coming at her, leaving her reeling in its wake. She needed to see his face, as if somehow by looking at him it would confirm that he had been a real person. She ran upstairs and into her bedroom. Pulling out the drawer of her bedside table, she reached for his photo.

Chapter 1

Winter, 2010

The lift doors separated and Adam White stepped out into the bright reception of Parker & Associates. As he walked across the high-glaze cream travertine tiles he was almost overpowered by the scent emanating from the two extravagant conical vases standing on either side of the reception desk. They were brimming with fresh metre-high arrangements of snapdragons, burnt-orange birds of paradise and fuchsia-toned orchids. The area was minimally furnished with only a simple Scandinavian-style bench, which was more for show than functionality.

Parker & Associates was a young firm of business analysts located just off the Grand Canal on the south side of Dublin City. Their ultra-modern headquarters took over the entire top floor of the building and consisted of floor-to-ceiling glazed offices surrounding a central roof garden. Depending on which end of the office you went to, the view extended all the way up to Howth Head on the north side of the city or down to Killiney Hill on the south side.

By the time Adam had grabbed himself a coffee, sat at his desk and switched on his PC, his rising in the small hours of the morning seemed like eons ago. He rubbed his eyes for the umpteenth time. He felt fuzzy with tiredness, he found it hard even to think straight, his reactions were slow and his whole body felt heavy as if he was lugging two huge suitcases on either side of him whenever he walked. As he tried to concentrate on a spreadsheet on the screen in front of him, the rows seemed to merge together.

Although it was eight thirty, it was very early by Parker's standards and the office was still largely empty. On any given day the majority of people wouldn't arrive in until nine at the earliest but normally on Friday people didn't show their faces until much later after the ritual of Thursday-night drinks. Fridays were a write-off as far as work was concerned; it was generally accepted that you did only the bare minimum to get by and then spent Monday to Thursday making up for it. The company prided itself on its 'relaxed and casual' culture. The open-plan office was decorated with leafy, tropical foliage and beanbags were interspersed randomly to help soften the corporate feel. Croissants and pastries were delivered fresh from the local bakery every morning and there were always baskets scattered arbitrarily around the place, brimming with sweets and chocolate. Employees were also welcome to help themselves to the fully stocked fridge which was laden with ice-cream and soft drinks. It was lamented by all who worked there that once you joined Parker & Associates, there was no avoiding gaining the 'Parker-stone'.

A while later Adam's colleagues started arriving in. He greeted them and watched as one by one they dropped their bags at their desks before heading straight to the staff room for a pecan-nut pie, the only pastry deemed suitable for the hangover of Fridays.

Emma made her way with slow footsteps down the grey vinyled corridor. As she walked, she couldn't help but think what a contagious shade of grey it was; it wasn't the soft dove-grey of a cashmere sweater or the inky grey of a storm cloud before it burst – it was that awful shade of grey that sucked the life out of you just from merely looking at it. As she rounded the corner, she could hear the high-pitched screeches coming from behind the canteen door. Well, 'canteen' was probably stretching it – it was a room barely six metres square. The floor was covered with worn lino and it was sparsely furnished with a Formica table, six red shiny plastic-backed chairs, a cork noticeboard and a dire fridge where, no matter how many group emails were sent warning users to discard their foods after their best-before date, no one ever seemed to lay claim to the mouldy ham.

You could almost tell the day of the week it was by the roars that filtered out into the corridor. Fridays were full of raucous laughter; Mondays were a more sombre, almost silent affair.

Emma pushed open the door and glanced around at the usual posse of girls sitting at the table scattered with takeaway sandwich-wrappers and foil crisp-bags. The roars from two seconds earlier disappeared almost like someone had twisted a volume-switch on the whole room. Nothing new there, she thought to herself. She was used to having this effect on people recently. The stench from some rice-and-ham dish that Dan from IT was reheating in the microwave almost made her gag.

"Hiya, Emma. Busy?" Helen the receptionist chimed, in an overly cheery voice.

"Y'know yourself, kept going."

Helen nodded. "Tell me about it."

What would you know about being busy unless it's trying to stick your gel nail back on and answer the phone at the same time?

"That won't keep you going!" Helen nodded to the teabag that Emma was taking out of the jar above the microwave.

"I'm not hungry just now, I'll grab something later."

Emma knew her tone sounded defensive, but she felt self-conscious in front of the group about her lack of lunch – but she just couldn't stomach anything right now. She turned away from Helen and her cronies and as soon as the kettle had boiled she busied herself by pouring boiling water onto her teabag.

Helen turned back around to her gang and proceeded to moan about how her bridesmaid had put on weight since the last dress fitting and that now she would have to get the dress altered for her. Her audience tutted in sympathy and agreed that her friend had some cheek to gain a few pounds. One of them even added that if she were a real friend she would *at least* offer to do the cabbage-soup diet to fit back into the dress. Emma wasn't included in the conversation, nor did she want to be.

Emma worked on the creative team for A1 Adverts but A1 Adverts was not your typical glamorous advertising agency residing in beautiful glazed offices with a sea view and bountiful budgets. Rather A1 specialised in bright and zingy 'can't get it out of your head' type adverts for their clients. A1's specialty was the discount market; they didn't do the high-end adverts that won awards. How she would love to work on campaigns such as those! A1's customers were discount furniture stores, tile shops, budget airlines and basically anyone in the business of discount retailing in Ireland. All their adverts were the same: flashing bubble-text on a neon-coloured background and always backed with shouty voices. In fairness to A1 Adverts, it was a model that worked; they were cheaper than their competitors and they were tailored to that end of the market. But it was a long, long way from the glossy editorials with their subtle imaging that she had spent so much time analysing in college. Emma was a 'campaign developer' – in other words, she had to come up with new ideas for their clients' adverts.

She went back, sat at her desk and sighed wearily as she scrolled down to the next red-flagged email from her overflowing inbox. No matter how hard she tried, she never seemed to be able to get on top of the work that was piling up around her. At the moment she was working on a pitch for a company called Sofa World which had asked Dublin's top advertising agencies to come up with a tag line for their Christmas campaign. Oh, she was a long way from Chanel adverts starring Keira Knightley! It was very late for launching a Christmas campaign. A1 suspected Sofa World had rejected other advertisers' efforts before turning to them at the last minute.

Moments later, Emma's boss Maureen Hanley popped her

head around the screen of her cubicle. Her frizzy hair was tied back with a scrunchy in a manner that made Emma wonder if the woman even possessed a hairbrush.

"Hi, Emma – can you come in for a chat in five?"

Emma felt herself redden as if Maureen could read her mind about what she had just been thinking. "Sure."

"Don't worry, it's nothing major," Maureen added, obviously noticing Emma's red face.

Emma hated her high colouring; it always betrayed her innermost feelings. At the drop of a hat her cheeks would go red for almost any reason: embarrassment, frustration, alcohol, spicy food, and God forbid she should try to tell a lie. Emma just had to accept it was part and parcel of the raw deal of having fair skin.

She watched as Maureen walked back to her office in her black pencil-leg trousers that didn't quite meet her court shoes and revealed her white cotton socks. On top she wore a brown tweed blazer buttoned entirely up to the top so that it was puckered across her large bust; she'd had that blazer ever since Emma had started working there seven years ago and Emma imagined she had probably had it at least seven years before that. Maureen was a harmless enough sort of woman – well, as much as a boss can be harmless. She had never married; she'd been too busy sacrificing her life for A1 Adverts. The woman lived and breathed A1, so Emma suspected that the only reason she wanted a meeting was probably because she wanted her to jump up and down about the chance to pitch to Sofa World. But Emma would not be doing any jumping.

Five minutes later Emma grabbed her A4 refill pad so she could scribble down any ideas that would be thrown at her and walked back down the life-sucking, grey-vinyled corridor towards Maureen's office. She knocked on her door and let herself in. Maureen looked up from her computer, almost in confusion.

Don't tell me she doesn't remember asking me to come in five minutes ago?

"Oh yes, of course, Emma – come in and sit down." She let out a heavy sigh as she set about clearing bundles of paper and mugs with coffee stains running down the sides off the messy desk in front of her.

Emma did as she was told and sat opposite her.

Emma cut to the chase. "Did you see the email from Sofa World?"

"What?" Maureen was distracted. "Oh yes, I saw that. You might draft something up and send it on and we can sit down then and have a look, yes?"

Emma was taken aback. What did Maureen want her for if not that?

"Well, Emma . . ." Maureen paused.

Well, Maureen. Emma felt she should say something but Maureen's tone told her it wasn't her place to speak.

"Well . . . God, Emma I'm not sure how to broach this . . ." She breathed in deeply through her nostrils, so that they flared slightly. "Well, it's just I've noticed you've been putting in a lot of hours here lately. Some of the times on your emails have me worried – eleven p.m., midnight – there was even one at two a.m. last week! Now don't get me wrong, I'm all too happy for people to show their commitment to A1 Adverts but well . . ." She hesitated. "Just with everything going on, I'm a bit worried about you, that's all." She was starting to get flustered. "What I'm trying to say is – and I'm not doing a very good job of it – I know you're a good worker, I've never had a problem with your work. I just want you to make sure you're looking after yourself? That's all."

Emma was stunned; she wasn't used to such public displays of concern from Maureen. She instantly felt the heat creep into her cheeks. *I don't want to talk about this.*

"I'm okay, Maureen," she said coolly so that Maureen would know it wasn't a discussion she wished to get into.

"Well, that's good then," Maureen added nervously. "It's just, you're not long back and well . . . well, I think you should ease yourself in a bit, that's all."

Emma shifted in her seat and the discomfort between the two was palpable.

Caroline Finnerty

"Okay, so you'll send me on your proposal for Sofa World then?" Maureen said in an obvious decision to change the subject.

"I'll have something for you by Monday afternoon," Emma replied curtly.

"Great, so."

"Right, if that's all?"

Maureen gestured to the door, indicating Emma was free to go. Emma stood up to leave. She wanted to get the hell out of there. She wasn't a person who liked discussing her feelings at the best of times, least of all with her boss.

She went back and sat at her desk and the more she thought about the conversation she'd just had, the more she felt rage building inside her. Why were people so nosy, always trying to push it with her to see if they could be the one to make her crack and fall apart into a mess? It was nobody's business what time she worked until. If she was skiving off, they'd be on her back – she couldn't win! She was used to Helen and the rest of them pushing her buttons, trying their best to see if they could be the one to elicit a reaction. But Maureen? She had expected more from her boss. They had always had a perfectly healthy standoffish relationship, so what the hell was Maureen doing trying to change the playing field?

Jesus, what had got into the woman? Surely she was too old for the menopause?

352

Chapter 2

Come three o'clock and as the hangovers began to ease, Parker's entire workforce were already planning where they would head later on that night and at five to five they began to pack up to leave.

Adam was just heading for the lift when Ronan from Accounts joined him.

"Are you coming for one?"

"Nah, I should probably be heading home." Adam was hesitant. Not that it would make any difference, he thought bitterly to himself. She barely spoke to him anyway.

"C'mon for one!"

"I'd better not – maybe next time, yeah?"

"Are you sure?"

"Yeah."

"No worries."

They took the lift down.

"See you Monday, so," said Ronan.

"Have a good one!"

Ronan joined some of the others and Adam stood watching as they walked over to McCormack's bar, carefree and untroubled. How he wished he could join them – he would rather be going anywhere else but home.

He took his bike from the shelter and headed for Rathmines. He pedalled slowly and allowed the cool evening air to fill his lungs, feeling his chest rise in fullness before falling again. He felt his thigh muscles work hard as he pedalled up the steep incline before turning left over Harold's Cross Bridge. His cycle to and from work was the only time of day he had with his thoughts to himself. It was his time when he got to think about everything that had happened and try and make sense of it all. It was still so fresh. He only had to look at himself to see angry reminders criss-crossing his skin. Usually when he cycled he racked his head trying to remember the exact sequence of events but his brain would only allow him to go so far.

When he reached their house, he pushed open the wrought-iron gate and wheeled his bike up the path. He could see the lights were all off downstairs. He fumbled with his keys in the lock for a few moments before he was finally able to get into his house. Today's post sat waiting for him on the mat inside the door. He stooped to pick it up. The envelopes told him it was nothing more interesting than bills, junk mail and a bank statement. He placed them unopened on the hall table. He shouted out to see if Emma was home but no voice answered his call. He hardly knew why he did that as he knew she wouldn't answer anyway. He went into the kitchen and took a cool beer out of the fridge. He pulled off the metal top and gulped it back.

Emma's head hadn't been up to much for the rest of the day. She'd tried her best to think of some winning tag lines for the Sofa World campaign but she didn't have much luck.

The office began to empty out after four with everyone heading off to various parts of the country for the weekend and by seven she was alone in the open-plan office. She preferred it that way; she could concentrate better without the constant drone of voices. She tried putting some words onto her notepad but nothing was coming. Eventually, after nine, she admitted defeat and knew that stupid tag lines for springy sofas would be swimming around in her head all weekend long.

In keeping with their low-cost strategy, A1's offices were located on Rosses Street, in a dingy part of Dublin City, which was long overdue rejuvenation. It was a notorious area for muggers, so she made her way hurriedly down towards the quays. She watched as hordes of teenagers, hen and stag parties, already bladdered, made their way towards the city's current hot-spots, gearing themselves up for a heavy night of drinking.

She didn't want to go home just yet so she decided to keep walking and headed down towards Dawson Street. The narrow paths were crowded with gangs of smokers standing outside so she turned onto a cobble-locked side-street where crowds were sitting along the outdoor terraces under café-bar awnings, protected from the cold evening air by patio heaters. By immersing herself amongst these people, she didn't feel so alone.

She wandered aimlessly for a while until she felt her stomach growl and she suddenly realised she was hungry. After skipping lunch, she had forgotten to eat anything for the rest of the day. She looked at her watch and it was nearly eleven o'clock so she hailed a taxi and headed home to Rathmines. She climbed into the back, stated her destination and sank into the leatherette upholstery. She sat listening to the constant buzzing and conversation over and back on the radio between the base station and the different drivers. The driver made half-hearted chit-chat with her – well, he talked and she made occasional sounds of agreement, which seemed to be enough for him to keep rambling on. By the time they turned onto Rathmines Road, she could feel her stomach begin twisting into its familiar knot and, as the car pulled up outside her home, Emma felt her heart lurch. She took her time to locate her money in her wallet before paying him and slamming the door shut.

At least the lights were off.

With trepidation and slow steps she walked up the driveway to her home. No matter how hard she tried and how successfully she carried it off at work, once she was on her own doorstep, she couldn't push the reality of her life out of her head any more.

Interview with
Caroline Finnerty

1. Where did the idea for *The Last Goodbye* come from?

The idea came from a story a friend told me one day about a woman she knew that was confronted with the same dilemma facing Eva. The lady was pregnant and learned she had an aggressive form of cancer. She refused to take the treatment offered and unfortunately neither she nor her baby survived. This story really affected me when I heard it – it got me thinking about how a person can be in one way be so selfless for their unborn baby that they put their own health second but it also left me wondering if she had taken treatment, would she and her unborn child both have lived?

Around the same time I read about Sheila Hodgers, the County Louth woman who was refused cancer treatment during her pregnancy in 1982 because her practitioners claimed it would harm the foetus. She was left without treatment or even pain relief until she delivered her baby two months premature in March 1983. Sadly her baby didn't survive and she died two days later.

Although different to the storyline in *The Last Goodbye* because the character Eva was not denied treatment, in fact she was encouraged to take it, I wanted to explore the idea of a pregnant woman being a vehicle for her unborn baby, which essentially Eva is, although it is by her own choice.

2. How did you research the storyline?

The main difficulty I had was that Eva's story is set in 1992 and most information on the internet was relevant to the present day so I had to ensure that the storyline reflected treatments available at that time. Therefore I read medical journals both primary literature and reviews that were published in the early 1990's so that my research was as accurate as possible. I have a Masters degree in Biology so I would have a general understanding of medical terminology, which definitely helped.

When I had a basic level of research carried out, I devised a medical questionnaire and I contacted Dr. Grainne Flannelly of the National Maternity Hospital in Holles Street who very kindly answered my questions. I hope I have reflected medical treatments as accurately as possible but any errors or deviations from correct practice are my fault.

I think it's important to point out that recent studies have shown chemotherapy to be safe for the foetus after the first trimester, which is welcome development for any woman who is faced with this awful dilemma.

3. Do you have a favourite character?

I have to say I have a soft spot for Kate, the main protagonist. She has spent her life running away from her problems and I'm sure the reader will find her quite frustrating as a person to begin with. I know I personally just wanted to shake her at times but by the end of the book I think she has grown and developed as person.

4. What scene was the most difficult/interesting to write?

I found Eva's last scene, where the she is dying in hospital and she finally opens up about her fears of dying with Sister Rita emotional to write. For the first time, the reader gets to see Eva without her usual brave face and jokey manner. Also later that

357

night when Noel is at her bedside and she is reminiscing back on a day that the family had at the beach in happier times, being a mother myself, I found that scene hard to write.

5. The character of Eva tends to bury her head in the sand rather than face up to her problems, was that an intentional character trait?

It was intentional. I think Eva is an eternal optimist, she has an 'ah sure it will all be grand' mentality and doesn't like to dwell too long on her problems. I think she really believed that it would all be okay, she didn't see her decision as heroic or as a form of self-sacrifice. She believed that once she delivered her baby, then she would take her treatment and get better too and that is why she made the decision that she did.

I'm sure the reader will notice that Kate seems to have inherited her mother's inability to face up to her problems, which is why she spent so many years of her life unable to confront her past. I deliberately wanted them both to have this trait to help to show their similar personalities.

6. Your first novel *In a Moment,* and *The Last Goodbye* both have a 'what would you do?' moral dilemma at their heart, why is that?

I think there are lots of situations in life where there are no easy answers. As a fiction writer I have the benefit of being able to explore both sides of a dilemma. Sometimes when I am writing, I ask myself 'what would I do in that situation?' but then when I think about it from the other point of view, I can often empathise with that viewpoint too.

In Eva's case if she had taken the treatment offered to her she may have survived but would Aoife? In my first novel, *In a Moment*, the character Jean struggles with a decision, which goes against all her maternal loyalties to her son Paul.

I suppose there are situations in life for which there are no easy answers, we just have to make the best decision we can at that time. Sometimes we get it right, sometimes we get it wrong.

7. Have you always wanted to be a writer?

I was always bookish as a child and have memories of ripping pages out of copybooks, drawing pictures on one side of the paper and writing stories on the other. Then when I was finished I would staple them all together into a book. In school I loved nothing more than mulling over an essay topic that the teacher gave us for homework or writing arguments for debates. I've always found it easier to say something on paper than express it verbally so I suppose my love of writing has always been there but I just didn't recognise it in myself. I always thought writing books was something that 'other people' did. It wasn't until my mid twenties that it occurred to me that I too could write a book so I decided to give it a go. After a few false starts, I had the idea for *In a Moment*, after my first child was born and I knew I had to write it.

8. Tell us a bit about your writing process – do you like to plot much before starting a novel or do you prefer to dive straight in?

I fall into the latter camp. I have tried plotting my novels chapter by chapter in the past – I think it would be much easier to sit down at the laptop every day if I knew what I had to write about for that day, but it just doesn't work for me. I find I only really get to know my characters when I start writing them, that's when they take me off and teach me things that I never knew about them.

When I have an idea for a story I will let it sift around in my head for a while and flesh out the characters a bit before I will start writing. I usually start with a rough outline of the themes of the novel, the general story and some key scenes. Sometimes I will know the ending but not always. It's a bit of a scarier way to do things because it's like setting off on a journey with a map but it means I get to take the scenic route and see new things and visit different places along the way.

9. Who are your favourite authors and why?

As a teenager I would devour Deirdre Purcell and Maeve Binchy novels. I also love Marian Keyes and Ciara Geraghty who are both fantastically talented Irish authors. I also enjoy reading JoJo Moyes, Maggie O'Farrell for emotional sagas and David Nicholl for humour.

10. Tell us a bit about your next book – have you started writing it yet?

I am nearly halfway through it. The main protagonist, Conor Fahy has just lost the love of his life, his long term partner Leni who died tragically when she was knocked off her bike a few months previously and Conor is struggling to cope with everyday life.

Jack White is eight years old. He likes Ben 10, Giant Jawbreaker sweets and reading books. He likes his Dad - when he doesn't shout. He doesn't like the bad monsters that are eating up his mammy inside her tummy.

It is the story which explores the unlikely friendship between a boy and a man who come into each other's lives when they both are in need of a friend.

≋ WARD RIVER PRESS
titles now available and Autumn 2014

Ruby's Tuesday **by Gillian Binchy**
now available

Sing Me to Sleep **by Helen Moorhouse**
now available

Into the Night Sky **by Caroline Finnerty**
coming Autumn.

The House Where it Happened **by Martina Devlin**
coming Autumn.

Levi's Gift **by Jennifer Burke**
coming Autumn.

If you enjoyed this book from
Poolbeg why not visit our website:

www.poolbeg.com

and get another book delivered straight
to your home or to a friend's home.

All books despatched within 24 hours.

POOLBEG

Why not join our mailing list
at www.poolbeg.com and get some fantastic
offers, competitions, author interviews
and much more?

 Follow us on **twitter**

@PoolbegBooks

 Find us on: **facebook**.